THE RABBIT DIES FIRST

Edited by Ryan Campbell

The Rabbit Dies First

Cover illustration by Dark Natasha

Published by FurPlanet Productions
Dallas, TX
http://www.FurPlanet.com

Print ISBN 978-1-61450-459-7
Electronic ISBN 978-1-61450-460-3
First Edition Trade Paperback 2019

Table of Contents

*This book is dedicated to every rabbit
sacrificed to the Great Story
in which villains are killers
and heroes are hunters*

FOREWORD

My husband, David, and I are watching a movie. The movie family is inside their nice, safe house. Outside, a rabbit ventures into the grass. "Well, here it comes," I say. My husband is already cringing. "That rabbit is gonna die." I'm usually right. Rabbits show up in movies and television shows and books as an easy source of food for hunters or as something the villain can kill to show they mean violence without hurting an actual character. You know, someone who matters.

Rabbits are born to die; their survival strategy depends upon reproductive efficiency and proliferation. Their days are spent foraging, hiding, and in running practice—compulsively scampering about their territory at top speed so that they know which way to turn and where to scurry. There will be no time for hesitation or decision-making when they're chased by a fox or swooped upon by an owl. In the wild, they live only two or three years, until the hot-sprung reflexes of youth stiffen, not much. Just a fraction of a second too slow for talon or fang.

But my husband has a very rabbit-like soul, and we have a pet rabbit—Puckles—who has more personality than should fit inside the body of a fuzzy, cute potato. A rabbit values its own life just as much as we do—or at least more than cats, who get nine of them, which is just greedy.

So I invite you out into the broad meadow. I know you are hungry. If you don't eat every day, you'll die. And the world smells of food and death. Watch the skies. Listen. What was that? Something with teeth and claws? It is only constant vigilance that means you see another day. One day your joints will be stiff. One day you will not see the shadow of wings on the grass. One day you will not hear the rustle in the bushes. Your life, the only life you get, your entire experience of the world, will end in a flash of terror and pain.

But you must eat. And out there in that world in which everything wants to kill you, there are chances. For love. For gentleness. For the safety of a warm burrow. For a friend to lie against in the winter. For the sweet juice of a berry. For the warm squirm of your children at your side.

Perhaps the rabbit dies first. But if so, surely it lives first, too.

Cold eyes, lost in dread
Bunny for the story's sake
Now lies cold and dead

— Mog K. Moogle

UNDER MY SKIN

Tym Greene

"I didn't know being a banker could be so stressful," I remarked, feeling the way his tense muscles crunched beneath my fingers. Outside, the rain poured down fit to drown out the usual shouts of my neighbors.

Sure, my boss paid me better than the cost of a cheap flat like this, but I wanted to keep a low profile. So I'd learned to live with peeling wallpaper and the occasional roach underhoof, but my fellow tenants took some getting used to: too many kids, funny-smelling cookery, and overall too loud. At least they never none of them asked questions. In my line of work, that was better than a sure tip at the races. They also didn't bat a collective eye at the "drinking buddy" I'd started bringing home, ostensibly to swill bootleg.

Still, while Giles wasn't no screamin' Mimi, he wasn't a church mouse neither, not when it came to slipping off his suspenders and making whoopee. Somewhere in my building a record needle scratched, and a familiar reedy voice began singing. Giles's left ear tip bobbed to the tune as I continued to massage my cottontail's shoulders. It wasn't until I heard his soft voice singing along that I noticed which song it was.

"I feel quite sure *un peu d'amour* would be attractive, while we're still active…"

"Let's misbehave," I finished, turning him around on the bed. His lips were soft and his breath warm and redolent of celery. A part of me hoped that he found my own taste as pleasing. Our tongues met and our chests pressed together. He didn't have the kind of muscle I needed for my… *job*… but he did keep himself trim, which made trying the more acrobatic poses—the sorts of things you only see on French postcards—a lot easier. This night, however, we were both still full from our automat dinner and in no mood for anything too bananas.

His hands took hold of my horns, and I found myself falling into his eyes. They were the dark brown of a smoked glass ash tray, but in this light they glinted like onyx pearls. With the sputtering gas jet in the wall behind his head, he looked practically demonic as he guided me over onto my belly, still holding onto my horns. A little squirming and he'd tugged down my black-and-purple pinstriped trousers and my BVDs.

His fur was, as always, warm and soft against mine. I had to beat down a momentary flash of jealous inadequacy: a posh bunny like him, he *had* to look his best every day, I reasoned. Plus he had the salary and the facilities to do so; I tried not to think of the dripping and mildewed shared tub and john situated a few doors down the hall. This place was little better than a flophouse, and I'd picked it for just that reason, I reminded myself, even as his gentle fingers caressed the scar that ran down my back.

"A youthful scrape with barbed wire, back on the farm," is what I'd told him. He didn't need to know about my three-spot in the county jail, or the way I'd been manhandled by my cell mates. They really knew how to tighten the screws on ya, but I'd paid attention and picked up a few tricks of my own. And now I was out and they were still in, and so's your old man.

I bleated out loud when the finger covered with Vaseline pressed up under my tail, but I forced the bleat into a chuckle. "I didn't know you wanted to go all the way tonight, Gilly-boy," I teased.

"Are you kidding?" He huffed in my ear, giving it a tender nibble in the process, "I could hardly keep my hands off you all evening, Lawson." You ever hear a bunny purr? It's a wonderful thing, especially when that bunny-boy's got you pinned to the sheets. I've been with a few fellas, and Giles could be more predatory than any panther I've known, when he was of a mind. That night, he assuredly was.

Yanking on my horns like I was less ram and more motorcycle, he rode me; pistoning like a souped-up flivver to a chorus of creaking bedsprings and groaning floorboards. Judging from the syncopation and the "Oh Johnnys" coming through the wall, we weren't the only ones making whoopee that night. Still, I couldn't care. Giles, for all his energy and drive, was still as gentle as ever, and his slender length was as slim as him.

Good thing too, given that he kept it up for the next hour or so. The kid could out-hump a camel. And I loved every minute of it: the tug on my horns, the way he'd occasionally lean forward to chew my ear, his belly against my back, as though he were raddling me the way they did in the old country. I couldn't help bleating again as I shot my load into the rumpled ticking of my mattress; whether he'd been holding off for my benefit or my finish drove him over the edge, he was a gentleman and didn't leave me waiting too long.

An old undershirt—plucked from its pile in the corner, and tossed right back—served well enough for mopping things up. Neither of us were in a mood to futz around with primping and tidying. Instead, I flipped back onto my back, staring at the peeling plaster of the ceiling, mercifully invisible in the shadows, while Giles turned the gas jet down until it was nearly out and then lay down on my chest. In that moment, he felt as light as a powderpuff, liable to be blown away by the odd passing gust of wind.

I wrapped my arms around him a little tighter.

Sure, it had started as just a job. Doesn't it always? But if you really throw yourself into your work, you start to care about it—be it digging ditches or sewing stitches, as my Gran used to say. And my job was to get *in* with Giles McDarren, assistant manager at one of the local branches of one of Chicago's bigger banks. The boss didn't care how I went about it: get dirt on him, pay for his drinks, take him bowling, whatever it took to become his new best pal.

And I'd done just that. A little gumshoeing, a little eavesdropping, a little tailing, a few bribes, and I knew his weakness: Giles went for bulky guys, probably fell in love with a sideshow Hercules when he was a kit. So I put on my tightest shirt, my sleekest pinstripes, polished up my horns, and used a pair of Cs from the bankroll the boss had given me for the job. "I want to speak with the manager," I'd huffed at the teller (after first making sure the manager was on one of his usual golfing lunches).

The poor little muskrat had shuffled me off to the Assistant Manager's gilt-lettered door, tapping tentatively on the frosted glass as though he were entering a sacred temple. Once in the presence of upper administration, I put on my best buddy-buddy air, as though sharing cigars with a fellow alderman. Giles had opened my account for me—$200 being more than enough to warrant his attention—but the process took far longer than it ordinarily ought, thanks to my efforts to charm him into a stupor. And all the while, my poor pin-stripes were straining with every pose and gesture.

Before I left, I gave him a wink and an invitation to a speakeasy I knew. It was one of the boss's, where we could be assured of non-lethal hooch and a private booth. The perfect place for me to start working my way under his skin.

Didn't expect him to do the same to me.

He'd showed up at the speakeasy door as instructed, hunched up in his trench coat and trilby, and I'd had to turn my sneer into a welcoming grin as I waved him down the stairs and over to my booth. All it took was a few gin rickeys and he ended up doing most of the talking; even still, I was thankful that I hadn't wasted my three years in the hoosegow. It had had a small lending library and a warden who fancied himself this century's Shakespeare, which meant that I left with acting experience and a better education than I'd ever gotten in my little backwoods farmhouse. I was able to hold my own in most conversations, and could keep my voice and tone pretty well-tuned.

I thought that I played that cottontail like a violin. And when he invited me back to his place afterwards for a nightcap, I wasn't the least bit surprised. He'd leaned in a little too close when we crowded up to the front door of his greystone, trying to stay out of the drizzle as he fumbled with the keys. Once inside, in the echoing cool of the marble-floored foyer, I couldn't help looking around, casing the joint just in case. That was when he pounced.

My horns clonked against the wall, and my hooves scrabbled for purchase on the wet stone as he pushed me back, his mouth against mine. I'd never thought lime and juniper could taste good together, but on that rabbit's hot breath it was pretty swell. I had enough presence of mind—after all, I'd had to have at least a few drinks of my own that night, if only to look like I was keeping pace with him—to shoot the deadbolt home while he was busy stripping off my clothes. We left everything in a wet pile in the hallway and he dragged me to his bedroom, where we made like a pair of rutting satyrs in Arcadia.

That morning, as we woke in a tangle of sheets on his big bed, he was again the banker: concerned that something had been seen, that we'd be found out, that the shareholders would learn he'd gone to a gin joint, that he'd be accused of fraternizing with the bank's customers. With kisses and caresses and smooth talk I'd assured him that I meant no ill will.

"After all, I'm an account holder too," I said, cupping his balls with one hand while the other swirled the fur on his belly. "I wouldn't do anything to endanger my new favorite assistant manager at my new favorite bank."

"Oh, say it again, Lawson," he'd moaned, squirming. It felt like he hadn't had another guy in a long time.

"Again," I teased, moving my hands to nipple and shaft.

He'd had to ring his office with a hand on his schnozz, pretending he'd come down with a cold. Given the drenching we'd gotten hoofing it back from the speakeasy, it was a miracle neither of us were in anything but hale and hearty. We were able to spend the rest of the day rattling around his house, completely starkers, but he made it clear this was a one-time thing.

We agreed that my place, though far less savory, would be better for any future trysts. It was a shame to miss out on those clean sheets and that big gleaming bathtub, but I wouldn't do anything to jeopardize the boss's plan.

Of course, he nearly did an about-face when the taxi dropped us off at home sweet home. The green-painted stoop sulking at the back end of an alley festooned with the washing of a dozen families, the exotic smells and shouts, not to mention the mob of kits and cubs that played with fence post Tommy guns, didn't exactly make for an impressive picture. But he got more keen when I reminded him just how little the denizens of this particular tenement cared for snoops and peachers.

Case in point, some moll of a mare was putting her face on by an open window, wearing nothing but a string of oyster fruit and a come-hither expression. I gave Giles a judge before his stare became any more obvious. "First rule of business here: you mind yours, they'll mind theirs. That sister there's a pro skirt, a hooker. I've seen her working the corner of LaSalle and Kinzie. But that's the goods: nobody around here cares a fig what she does, so long as she doesn't pay no mind to anyone else."

He understood, and followed me like a lamb through the fetid entrance hall, up the creaking stairs, and into the room that was my own. I'd explained that I was only staying here because of the privacy and so I could save a little extra lettuce on rent every month, which he'd bought. After we'd had our fun, I tossed a few coins at him: "Get yourself a hack—this side of town isn't quite safe for a mac like you." Slip of the tongue, I'd almost said "a *mark* like you," but by that point I'd stopped thinking of him as just a target. I couldn't have said when or why, but that was when I noticed it.

That had been about two months ago, and now here I was as the warmth inside me faded and the cottontail in my arms started to doze. I wanted to let him sleep, but he still had to get dressed and schlep it across town so he could be primped and properly behind his desk in the morning.

The boss had said it would be tomorrow. Tomorrow or maybe the day after. I'd withdrawn the two hundred clams—plus interest—from my account the other day, leaving in just enough to keep the account open and not attract suspicion. It wasn't my money anyways, and the boss had been pleased with the extra lettuce as well as all the inside information I'd been able to pump from Giles. That had been my job, after all.

I wanted to let him sleep, to draw the ratty blind and lock the door and keep my arms around him, as though I could freeze a little pocket of Sunday evening inside my four walls while the rest of the world kept on spinning. But when he rolled over and asked in that sleepy voice what the time was, I couldn't help but fish my watch from the pile of clothes on the floor and hold it up to the gas flare. "Half past one." I said. So it was too late to save even a little bit of Sunday: it was already Monday morning.

"Shit. I've gotta get back home."

"You can spend the night here," I knew he couldn't, of course, but it was only polite that I offer. "Or you could play hooky tomorrow."

"I'm sorry, Lawson, I've gotta go." He kissed me tenderly even as he pulled himself away, leaving a spot of warmth in the bed that faded quicker than his touch.

I grunted and got up on my elbows, "Look, at least let me walk you home. You're not gonna find a cab at this time of night." He agreed.

We were both too cold and tired to talk while we trudged through the streets to the better side of town, but he did give me another peck on the cheek when we climbed the steps to his door. I ran my hand through the small tuft of dark grey fur between his ears, caressing his head as I pulled him in for a deep kiss. No one was watching, no one could see, no one would care. He still tasted like gin rickeys.

Finally, I let him slip inside so he could bathe and change and get himself ready for a day of honest work, while I found myself too tired to be useful for just about anything. I dragged myself to a corner diner and sipped coffee while the radio blared "Clap Hands, Here Comes Charlie" far too loudly for this time in the morning. I glanced at my watch: it was actually after five, we'd taken longer getting him home than I'd have anticipated.

A second later, the gears in my head finally shifted into position. I had to be at the bank in less than half an hour. I could just make it on foot. Sighing, I paid for my coffee, gulping down the too-hot dregs, and jammed my hat back on my head. A quick pat of my sides as I went through the door confirmed that at least I'd remembered to pack my heat, tucked in its holster beneath my pinstripes.

I skidded to a halt right in front of the shabby office the boss had rented for the job (or, rather, he'd had one of his boys rent for him), rat-a-tat-tatted on the door with my knuckles, and got let inside. Me and the rest of the boys then sat waiting, smoking cheap cigarettes and swilling cheaper coffee. I imagined this was what it was like in the Great War, being in those trenches: knowing that you'd be called on at some point, but just having to wait until then.

One of the poems I'd read in that county jail's little library came to mind as I played a winning poker hand: "Theirs was not to question why, theirs was but to do or die." I couldn't help but smirk—yeah, that was us, all right. I was reaching out for another smoke when there was a tapping at the office's door.

Every man in the room froze, every ear canted towards the staccato jazz-beat. "Ok, boys," said Big Al, the boss's acting lieutenant, "time to blow this joint." We stood as one, then split off: most of us went through the back, out the sides, anyway but out the front door to avoid attracting undue attention. I was one of the ones that went out the front; I strolled right across the street, bold as brass, right up to the bank's front door—after all, I was the one with an account there.

Pretty much as soon as I'd stepped through, someone had locked it behind me and closed the shutters. There'd be no nosy witnesses, and with luck, the "Closed for repairs" sign would satisfy the curious. A quick glance around the bank lobby didn't turn up anything amiss, but a closer inspection revealed a sheaf of papers spilled beside one desk and spots of red ink on the carpet. Red ink trailing to one of the offices... not likely red ink, then, I thought with a grim smirk. Well, that was just the cost of doing business.

Then I noticed which of the little manager cubicles the blood trail was leading to, and my tongue turned to ash in my mouth. Moving as quickly as I could without drawing attention, I pushed open the door with its frosted glass and gilded lettering, saw the lean body with its gore-smeared white fur huddled beside the desk, the eyes that looked everywhere but didn't see anything.

"Giles," I whispered, somewhere between a bleat and a moan, dropping to my knees beside him. He'd been shot a few times in his chest, his pristine suit ruined.

"Lawson," he managed to sputter, looking confused. He finally saw me, the shock of his injuries—it looked like a few fingers of his hand had been broken too, perhaps he'd held on to his key ring too tightly—had fogged him over and sent him into a fight-or-flight mindset. Given that he was trying to curl up in the warren of his office, the poor cottontail wasn't much of a fighter.

"I'm here, I'm here. It's ok. It'll be jake. We'll get you to a sawbones and get you all patched up," I lied.

"C-crooks," Giles coughed, his eyes going glassy again. I hoped he was trying to warn me that there were dangerous felons about, but there was a nagging part of me that thought he suspected my part in things.

"I'll protect you," I said, but it was already too late, there'd be no protecting him, nor no need to.

A long muzzle poked in the door. "Oy, what goes on?"

The boss had brought in a top can-opener for the sting, and here he was, sticking his horsey nose in on me cradling the main mark. Just swell. "Hey Jimmy," I said—we all knew Jimmy, the best safe-cracker in the state—trying to act nonchalant. "Just making sure he was good and zotzed. Wouldn't do to have him go stoolie on us. Who plugged him, anyways?" I stood, making a big show of straightening my pinstripes, my big buck teeth gleaming with a cocky smile.

"The boss," Jimmy said with admiration. "Never thought he'd get behind the handle of a Tommy again, but he seemed to enjoy—"

That's all I needed to hear, and that's all Jimmy'd be saying on the matter. I didn't relish bumping off the way some men did, but I knew how to handle a bean-shooter. The horse slumped to the carpet and I stepped over him. I knew the plan, and there should be only a few more fellas left between me and the boss. Either I'd croak them or they'd croak me, but that's life, ain't it?

I'd like to say I spared them a painful death, that I was a proper gentleman to the end. But no, I gut-shot the bastards.

THE TRIAL OF WANDERING STAR

David Green

"Prisoner Wandering Star, you are ordered to appear before Her Grace the Magistrate."

The barking voice accompanied the creak of a massive iron key turning in a rusty lock. With a groan of hinges, the thick wooden door swung open. Torchlight poured into the small cell from beyond the door and made shadows dance. Even before she could make out what was casting the shadows, Wandering Star entertained a brief, wild notion of just rushing out past the guards and making a break for it. She would never make it, of course. She was only one small red panda of eighteen summers against all the guards of the county prison. Even the tiny magic spark that lived inside her had no qi to fuel it: something in the prison drained the energy away. Still, some devil-may-care part of her mind whispered to her that going out in a blaze of glory would be better than suffering through a long trial— one that would only find her guilty and sentence her to execution anyway.

The impulse didn't last. She was no fighter; she was barely a magic-user. She couldn't even keep from trembling in front of the as-yet unseen guards. Shame filled her as she thought of her mother, giving herself up so that her daughter might go free... and her father, who protected both of them. Wandering Star had gotten away then, but not later when a shishi had sensed her using her magic to try to sneak a loaf of bread out of a merchant's stall. It probably had not helped when she referred to the shishi as "the honorable foo dog." How was she supposed to know that they considered the term "foo dog" to be an insult? That was what her father had always called them.

The owner of the barking voice shoved the door open wider and stepped into her cell. "Well, criminal?" he growled. "Nothing to say?" The dim light let her make out a massive grey wolf holding an equally massive weapon—a thick pole with a curved metal blade at the end. He was pointing the sharp end at her as though she weren't unarmed, half his size, and dressed in tatters.

Trembling, the panda bowed deeply to the wolf. "Wandering Star will be honored to appear before H-Her Grace the Magistrate." Her voice shook nearly as much as the rest of her.

The wolf let out a grunt of assent and gestured towards the door with the haft of his weapon. Another shadow stood there waiting to receive her. She moved past the wolf into the light of the hallway; the point of the curved blade followed her the entire time.

Wandering Star gasped when she saw the other guard. His features called to mind a dragon, a deer, a horse—the most graceful aspects of each, all combined in a form that almost radiated qi visibly. *Did they really think me so dangerous that they needed to send a qi-born to guard me?* she wondered. The qilin did not deign to speak to her, nor to draw the sword from the scabbard at his side. He simply motioned along the hallway and began to walk. The glitter of his iridescent green scales nearly mesmerized her. She hesitated to follow until a light but sharp poke at her back elicited a squeak, and she scrambled to catch up. The wolf was evidently not a patient sort.

The trio marched in single file through the hallways of the prison. Torchlight gave way to conjured light orbs, and then to sunlight. Wandering Star found herself in an area with windows—barred windows, but windows nonetheless. A long, secure hallway appeared to be the link from the prison to the courts—not that the security mattered in her case. She'd lost any intention of trying to run. Even if she *could* get away, she had nowhere to go.

The qilin eventually stopped in front of a pair of immense wooden doors, intricately carved and inlaid with gold, silver, and bronze. His voice was surprisingly thin and reedy, high-pitched almost like a flute. But it *carried*, and the weight it held seemed enough to push the doors open. "Guards Jiang and Ibayashi escorting the leafborn prisoner Wandering Star to appear before Her Grace the Great Magistrate Obana."

Leafborn prisoner Wandering Star tried to peek around the guard into the courtroom. It was lavishly appointed, gleaming with precious metal and jewels, the walls hidden by brightly woven tapestries and delicately limned shoji. Scents of exotic incense wafted through the entry, a contrast to the musty, earthy, *filthy* scents of the prison. The ceiling appeared even higher than the doors suggested. Wandering Star felt tiny indeed. There was another prod at her back, which provoked a similar squeak, and she realized that the qilin had already moved into the room without looking back to see if she followed. She hurried into the chamber, stopping near the middle of a silver tracery in the floor when the qilin (*was he Jiang or Ibayashi?* she wondered; she decided he looked like a Jiang) stepped to the side and held out a hand to restrain her. Bright light from somewhere overhead made her feel like she was on display. Maybe she was.

The sudden voice from above and before her was deep and rich, a sonorous contrast to Jiang's. "Wandering Star. You stand accused of practicing magic outside of the service of Her Glorious Majesty, the Empress Hui Zhe Canlan Mudan." The panda shaded her eyes to look up. Had that dais always been there? She squinted, barely able to make out a fox whose fur was apparently pure white, who was robed in green and purple and gold and seated behind a desk that was plain in comparison. Her heart skipped a beat and then pounded frantically. "What defense do you offer?" she heard the Magistrate continue.

Swift Grasshopper, her father, had told her that what the Empire offered to magic-users like her and her mother was little more than slavery. That the Empress did not need the service of every little qi-talent that people were born with. But all of that melted away as Wandering Star stared up at the Magistrate, feeling overwhelmed by the immensity and the splendor of her surroundings. "I-I couldn't help it," she stammered.

Obana frowned. A collection of tails like a fan stirred restlessly behind her. "You could not help refusing to offer your service to our gracious Empress?" she asked, the skepticism in her voice near sarcasm.

Wandering Star's heart raced, making her feel light-headed. "N-no, ma'am." The kitsune's frown deepened. "Ma'am" was probably not the right thing to call the Magistrate. What was? "I m-mean, my talent is so small, I did not think Her Majesty could use so little." The panda tried to pull her thoughts together. "But sometimes it just… my qi just spills over, and I have to use it. And that was when the foo—I mean, the shishi found me. Great Magistrate."

"It is the privilege of Her Glorious Majesty and her appointed officials to determine what and whom she can use. And not that of some leafborn… gutter rat."

Wincing, Wandering Star felt her heart sink. No longer fluttering madly in her chest, it was now a dead lump sliding into the pit of her bowels. Everything her parents had sacrificed for her—and it all came to this. She would be executed, and her spirit would fall low in the next life. Below the herbivorous leafborn, there were the dumb animals… and then the plants. Perhaps she could at least be a pretty flower?

Magistrate Obana was watching her intently, as though expecting her to respond. When she didn't, the fox gave the lightest of shrugs and continued in a tone touched with indignation. "By imperial decree, clemency has been granted in cases such as yours." Wandering Star blinked rapidly as she looked up. Had she heard correctly? "You will be assigned to a task for the Empire, and a partner. Should you satisfy him, your life will be spared and given fully into the service of the Empress." Obana paused and a look of distaste crossed her muzzle; it echoed what had been in her voice. "Are these terms acceptable to you?"

Being caught had already shamed her parents aplenty. Her entering the service of the Empire could do no more to them, and this might give her the chance to do… *something* good enough to lift up her spirit for the next life. "I… I offer my humble service to the glory of Empress Hui," she said. Her voice barely rose above a whisper.

"Very well." The Magistrate clapped her hands, scowling. "It is done. Jiang, fetch He-Who-Tramples-Stars to my court."

As the qilin bowed and turned to leave, Ibayashi leered at the panda. "I hear he tramples wandering stars, too," he said.

She shivered, which just made the wolf laugh more.

***

He-Who-Tramples-Stars had arrived and taken a cursory glance at his new partner before turning to Obana. "Your Grace," the rabbit said, his tone keeping delicate balance on the proper side of hauteur, "is *this* really what I have been assigned to work with?"

The kitsune scowled faintly and assured him that was indeed the case.

Drawing himself to the peak of his diminutive height, He-Who-Tramples-Stars adjusted the dark blue belt that cinched his saffron shirt. "This—" He gestured without moving his glittering eyes from the Magistrate. "—will not do. Have her bathed, clothed, and, if the court still can afford it, fed. I will return in an hour." He sniffed, turned around without facing the lesser panda, and stalked from the grandeur of the courtroom.

An uncomfortable silence reigned for several moments. Obana broke it with a clap of her hands. "Well?" she said, impatience dripping from the single word. When no one acted, she turned to the wolf. "You! Send to the kitchens." Another clap. "Now!"

While Ibayashi scrambled to exit the court, the fox whirled upon the qilin. "And you! Take her to the bathing chambers. Have her made…" She paused. "…made as presentable as possible."

Jiang reached out to take Wandering Star's arm, wearing an expression otherwise reserved for plucking some slimy thing from the gutter. As the qilin escorted her forcefully from the courtroom, the panda made out the Magistrate's final muttered aside: "Given what they have to work with…"

The guard delivered her to a small room on the third story of the prison side of the courts, where a plump dhole oversaw a small group of leafborn. There, she was plunged into a tub of water cold enough to steal her breath and scrubbed with a frenzy that took the rest of it. Dressed again in a plain hemp robe, she was handed back over to Jiang. The qilin did not look any happier to touch the cleaner panda as he hauled her to the kitchens and left her with the wolf.

Ibayashi taunted Wandering Star by continuing to mention "trampling" while she nervously slurped bamboo-laced gruel from a worn bowl. Just as she finished, Jiang reappeared with the wiry brown-and-white rabbit, who wore an impatient expression.

"Good," the wolf growled. "You've come back for her. I was getting tired of her company anyway." Rather than let the panda get up on her own, Ibayashi took her shoulder and hauled her to her feet. A whimper was all the protest she could muster. "Make sure to keep an eye on her. We don't want *another* one getting away."

He-Who-Tramples-Stars gave him a bland look, betrayed only by a spark of irritation in his eyes. "Oh, I'm sure *I* can handle her. I am surprised you two did not need help to keep this dangerous sorceress contained."

A snarl wrinkled the wolf's muzzle, but the other guard merely shook his head. "Take her and go," he fluted. "Don't come back until you've completed your task."

The rabbit nodded briskly. "It will be done." He spared another brief look for Wandering Star. "Well? Get moving," he said, pointing to the door.

He-Who-Tramples-Stars followed her at a distance of about a body's length. When they came to intersections in the hallways, he would call out a single word indicating which direction to take. In this way, the two of them left the courts behind. Wandering Star was feeling too numb and broken to question much of anything. The prison buildings retreated into the distance while the pair of leaf-born melted into the people milling about the city. Unlike the villages, where only one or two species tended to cluster, a variety of many different peoples all filled the city streets.

Suddenly the rabbit was walking alongside her. He'd taken the pointed bamboo hat that had hung on his back and brought it up over his head, forcing his ears to fold downward. She thought it looked uncomfortable, but he didn't seem to mind. "Wandering Star, right?" he said. His voice seemed to have lost much of its acerbity.

She nodded mutely.

"What's your favorite fruit?"

The panda blinked again. Confusion radiated from her expression. He smiled without malice. "We're going to the marketplace. What's your favorite fruit?"

"Per-persimmon," she stammered. Her mind raced, trying to comprehend where this was going.

He nodded back. "Right. We'll get you a persimmon, then. Between you and me, the gruel in the prison kitchen is lousy."

"I… I don't understand."

"You probably don't," he agreed. His amiable smile grew wider.

"We'll talk about it once you've got your persimmon." He glanced downward. "Shoes, too. If you're used to wearing them, I mean. Are you?"

***

He-Who-Tramples-Stars picked through the heart-shaped fruits until he found one that was soft enough for his liking. He gave the merchant some small coins and handed the orange globe to a dazed Wandering Star before leading her to another stall displaying sandals. There, he acquired a pair of geta in what he guessed was her size. They clacked lightly over the street as the two walked.

"You've barely touched your persimmon," he observed. Rich scents of cooking food filled the marketplace, masking less savory smells. No one seemed to be paying them any mind, instead walking or rushing about on their own business. "So, while you eat, let me answer a few questions that you're probably too nervous to ask.

"First, my name is a mouthful, so you are welcome to call me Lo-Yao if you want. That's my given name, instead of the one I earned as a fighter." He tipped his conical hat to her with a quick grin. She gave him a series of silent blinks.

"Next... how to put this? I am part of a guild of like-minded people who believe that the Empire's laws about magic outside the qi-born are, at best, outdated. We work... mostly within the courts and the prisons to try and save people like you who've gotten caught up in" —he waved a hand sweepingly—"all this. We influence, but we also bribe... and we kidnap if we have to, to keep as many people connected to their heads as we can. You probably couldn't tell, but Ibayashi is on our payroll. He doesn't always agree with us, but he's happy to take a few extra coin now and again to keep looking the other way when we lose the occasional prisoner." The rabbit made an apologetic shrug. "He's uncouth, but I think that probably helps with his cover."

Wandering Star stared at him, wide-eyed. The persimmon remained forgotten in her hand.

Lo-Yao reached down to coax the fruit back towards her mouth. "I'm sorry I had to be gruff with you at the courts. It keeps suspicion off me, and the magistrate actually seems to... respect fighters who are assertive. Even leafborn. I'd like to help you."

She bit past the thin rind to lick at the pulpy sweetness inside. It calmed her a little. "So… you're going to let me go?" she managed.

A frown tugged down the corners of his mouth. "I wish I could. Ibayashi let me know that we've let a few too many 'escape' lately, and they're keeping a closer tab on things right now. You'll have to accompany me on a service to the Empire, then I'll take you back to the courts and tell them that you served well and didn't try to get away. That you showed promise. That sort of thing. We'll try to get you guided to a position in the government where you can help us out, okay?" He gave her an appraising look. "Do you know how to read and write?"

"A little," she confessed, looking at his feet.

"Mmm. Well, we'll get to that when we're done here." The frown crept back to his face. "For right now, there's a band of robbers raiding out of the southern hills. Nobody thought they were worth dealing with until they stole some qi-born noblewoman's jewels." He breathed an exasperated sigh. "They still don't want to deal with them, just recover the jewelry. If we *can* apprehend them, that's excellent, but…" He shrugged and executed a deft detour around a wolf who was too busy trying to fix a twist in her belt to pay attention to where she was going.

"I can carry most of the work. You just be careful and stay out of the way as much as you can. But if it comes down to it—what sorts of magic can you do?"

Wandering Star slurped some of the soft, sticky flesh out of the persimmon. "I can make things move without touching them," she said, after a few moments.

The rabbit nodded. "Good, good," he said. "What else?"

A brief feeling of cold gripped her stomach. "N-nothing else," she said, as though confessing some deep inadequacy.

But Lo-Yao just nodded again. "All right, that can be useful, but I'm guessing you're not very practiced with it. Try to stay out of the way," he reiterated, "and we'll get this done together."

He pushed the brim of his hat up as he looked at the panda. "You're probably pretty drained after spending all that time in the prison," he said. "Why don't we stop at an inn for the night? You can rest up and show me what your magic does."

***

Lo-Yao treated the two-day stay at the inn as a matter of course, but Wandering Star marveled at the luxury of it. She had her own room—he trusted her not to fly by night, it seemed—and meals that included sweet water chestnuts and tender bamboo shoots. The first night, the rabbit invited her to his room to show him what her magic could do. The answer ended up being "very little;" her qi was still drained from her stay in prison.

"Let me show you a meditation technique," he said, seeing her frustration and disappointment. "I learned this when studying chuojiao. Martial artists use qi differently, but it helps to have a reserve when you must fight." Wandering Star thought that meditation would just be sitting down in an uncomfortable position with her mask-marked eyes riveted on her belly, but Lo-Yao guided her through a series of slow movements and breathing exercises that he called a simplified form of "qigong." The activities were strange and unfamiliar—though not uncomfortable—and by the end of the evening, she was feeling better. While she rested afterward, he demonstrated a few practice moves from his chuojiao for her: it apparently involved a lot of kicking mixed in with jabs and punches.

"We'll try again tomorrow," he told her, and they did. This time she was able to move around some light objects, such as the rabbit's chopsticks and tabi. He appeared impressed when she held aloft a cupful of sand, even after he removed the cup, although the sand did start to trickle back to the floor after a couple of minutes.

She soon began to feel drained again. Lo-Yao suggested that she try the qigong routines again on her own. "You should rest up as much as you can," he told her. "We will need to leave tomorrow."

"Can't we stay longer?" Wandering Star was starting to get used to the comforts of the inn.

The rabbit smiled, but he shook his head. "The longer we wait, the higher the likelihood that they'll have managed to fence the jewelry." The smile fell. "It's possible we've waited too long already, but I wanted you to be better rested." He shooed her back to her room. "Do your meditation. I will gather what information I can. Be ready to go in the morning."

The panda nodded and went back to her room. She tried the

qigong techniques, but they didn't feel right without Lo-Yao helping her. She marveled at how quickly she'd grown comfortable with his presence—not really like a surrogate parent, but more like a big brother she'd never had. She'd been scared of him at first, when he wouldn't even look at her, when he'd been He-Who-Tramples-Stars. Now, though… he'd been kind to her. He bought her the persimmon and the shoes. He was teaching her more about her magic. She hadn't been close to anyone since she lost her parents, but… A sudden chill stole through her. …Maybe it was all just a ruse to get her to betray the Empire, to go along with bribery and kidnapping, so they'd have a real case against her? A certainty that the magistrate hadn't liked her twisted her gut.

But she fought the shiver away from her spine. She didn't want to believe it. Her breathing started to fall into the rhythm he'd taught her. She wanted to trust him. Inhale. Exhale. She would go with him to the hills. Inhale. Hold. Stretch the left arm forward, just so. The tail, the right foot, backward, to counterbalance. Exhale. She would do her best to help, in whatever small way she could. Inhale. Bring the feet together. Then the left foot back. Tail held just off the ground. Curl the arms up, as if to catch the moon. Then… then, he would show her a place where she could help others like herself. She could be someone she could actually be proud of, again. Even if it was just by moving papers. Exhale.

***

Wandering Star was not sure of the hour when Lo-Yao came knocking at her door, but her best guess involved "too early." Her fur was a mess, so she opened the door just a sliver to make a sleepy query.

"Make ready to go," the rabbit told her, hushed.

Adrenaline stirred her heart. "Is something happening?" She mimicked his quiet.

A quick shake of his head. "No, nothing like that. I just want to make as much distance as we can today. And I would prefer not to wake our neighbors in the process. I will see you in half an hour. Breakfast will be waiting." He nudged a wooden bucket towards the door with his foot before turning back to his own room.

The bucket contained bran that had been warmed and scented

with herbs. The panda took delight in the extravagance of a bran bath to clean her fur of oils—a sharp difference from the rough duck-and-scrub she'd received at the prison. She didn't know how much fur they'd yanked out in the process. Wandering Star hurriedly brushed the bran through her fur, twisted her hair into a bun, and scurried out to meet Lo-Yao. He stepped out of a qigong pose and beckoned her with a smile to breakfast. It was a quick, quiet meal, but she found even the silence with Lo-Yao to be comfortable. Warm and full when they finished eating, the panda let her thoughts drift back to the bed she'd had to abandon. The rabbit, however, handed her a pack. "Our supplies," he clarified as he led her out. "With an extra robe for you."

They left the inn together, into a city quiet with a dawn that promised a fair late-spring day. Rabbit and panda joined the modest but growing traffic—mostly wagons—spilling out through the southern gate towards exotic places like the far-off cities of Huochuan and Shōdōkoku, at the edges of the empire. Their destination was to be much nearer.

Wandering Star's initial excitement at leaving Wumalu soon faded into a vague feeling of anxiety that left her lost in thought. After a short period of travel, she looked up and noticed she'd fallen behind her partner. Partner? Jailor? Captor? She had been so exhilarated at first, when he stepped in to save her. *No,* she reminded herself. *At first, he had asked whether he had to work with* "this."

Lo-Yao looked back and noticed her uncertain progress. He stepped to the side of the road and shifted his pack on his shoulders, waiting for her. "Getting tired already?" he asked when she caught up. His voice was gentle and warm, which made her feel guilty about her doubtful thoughts.

She shook her head and looked briefly at his eyes. They were the same saffron as his robes; she hadn't noticed that before. All her thoughts churned together in her mind.

"Why?" she said at last.

She heard his drawn breath, the first syllable of an answer. And then he stopped, and she returned her gaze to him. A strange half-smile curled up the right corner of his mouth. "You're asking questions," he said. Shifting to a more formal stance, he presented her with a slight bow.

Wandering Star was more confused.

"We take any who want to help us. But we've found that the ones who help us best are the ones who are sure of what they do. That means understanding... understanding *why*."

Still uncomfortable, the panda moved her weight from one leg to the other.

"There are many answers," he continued, "as there are many questions that are all 'Why?' I spent a little extra coin on you because I felt bad that I had to be short with you. And because you looked like you'd had a hard time on the streets." His smile turned a touch wry. "And because it would not hurt to give you a good first impression of what we do, should you choose to join us."

"Do... I have to?" she asked, into the brief quiet that followed.

"Have to join us?" A shake of his head. "Of course not," he said, quickly. There was a moment's skip before he added, "I shouldn't say 'of course.' But we're not doing this for you to demand your service in return. Or even expect it. We'd *like* it. But if you don't want to work with us once we're done here, then you don't have to. You can make some other living. You can even work for the empire in earnest. Your path is your own. Even if... well, the empire *will* still want you, one way or the other."

One of his feet scuffed the ground, stirring the grasses at the edge of the road. Wandering Star had never seen the rabbit this uneasy, this... vulnerable before. The smile was gone entirely, replaced with a pensive, faraway look. "I do this because my cousin was taken. He was not rescued. He did not even know he could do magic until it started happening around him. The trial was quick; the sentence, immediate. His mother found out about it only through a letter from a sympathetic noble."

She wanted to comfort him, but she wasn't sure how. It felt like she would be intruding on his private grief. Then his expression warmed again. "We've made progress. Our people... they brought it to the Empress' ear that the flesh—and, especially, leafborn—using magic outside of the auspices of the Empire should be given a second chance." He nodded. "Sometimes the fleshborn were already being given that chance. They say that one of the qi-born—a tanuki— asked whether they were not spirits who had almost, but not quite, exceeded the ranks of the fleshborn: one more life's journey from being true qi-born." A scowl flashed across his brow. "But a lot of the qi-born… they don't think so. They would do many things to keep such thoughts from the Empress. Our position can be precarious. Dangerous, even."

Quickly lifting his eyes towards the sun, Lo-Yao stepped onto the road again and waved her along. "Come, we should keep walking. You can ask me more while we travel." She followed, thinking of more questions.

***

It was not that day, nor even the next, when they reached the hills where the bandits hid. The third day's climb became more arduous. From time to time, the road switched back upon itself or threaded through defiles that looked like they had been widened enough for two wagons to pass each other (if they were careful and the drivers were friendly). Birds of prey wheeled overhead while crows made raucous announcements of the travelers' approach. The rabbit slowed their progress and kept scanning the hillsides. When Wandering Star tried to ask a question, he held up a finger before his lips and shook his head. "Not now," he murmured. "Breathe your qigong while we walk, but it's better if we're quiet here."

Briefly stung, the young woman almost succumbed to an urge to sulk before she realized with a start that Lo-Yao was looking for signs of the highwaymen. Her heart raced again, and she tried to use the techniques he'd taught her to ease the fluttering in her belly. It worked, at least to a degree. The air here smelled more arid: fewer flowers and more spicy bushes than there had been closer to the city. And dust, lots of dust.

Wandering Star was not sure what the rabbit had found when he motioned her off to the side of the road. He climbed up a steep slope for a few feet before turning back to help her up. Eventually, he led her to a stand of large rocks and scrub and brushes. He motioned her down until she couldn't see the path below, then joined her, lifting his head back up every few minutes to look around.

The panda's legs and tail cramped. It became harder to focus on her breathing. She didn't know what to look for (even if she could see!) or exactly what they were waiting for, but Lo-Yao gestured her to silence whenever she looked at him. Time crawled more slowly than the iridescent beetle that crept over one of the nearby rocks. Wandering Star grew so absorbed in watching the insect that the sudden cries of crows startled her. She jerked her head up and tried to look over the rock, only to have the rabbit gently push it down again. Then he shifted to the side a little bit and guided her to a spot where she could see through the flora, at least a little.

The crows were rising from an area some distance down the road—she wasn't good at estimating how far. They scolded something for a minute or two before settling back down… and then the scenario repeated itself, closer to the watching pair. Wandering Star sought mute reassurance from Lo-Yao, but he was intently watching the road and not her. His hat was adjusted to keep the sun out of his eyes. Presently, a small group of travelers came into view, all of them fleshborn and wearing muted, earthy colors that made them more difficult to see clearly.

The red panda found that her tail was in her hands. Her anxiety drove her to rub around its end-stripes as she contemplated that those were *actual robbers* down there who'd probably not think twice about taking her robes and her new geta and all the sweet dried persimmons in her pack. And the pack, too. She moved closer to her partner and tried to be very small. Wrapped up in her fears, she missed wherever the bandits had gone. For all she knew, the beetle might have made it all the way back to Wumalu by the time the rabbit gently nudged her side. "Okay," he told her, voice still hushed but not the murmured breath he'd been using earlier. "I see where they're going. We'll wait for another group to leave and then we can make our way in. We—"

Seeing the worry etched through the mask around her eyes, he paused. "It's all right, little Wanderer," he said in a soothing voice. "I can handle it. I'll keep you safe, yes?" She gave a tiny nod. "Will you be okay?" Another nod, scarcely bigger than before.

He touched the bridge of her nose, a gentle, friendly brush that somehow comforted her. "Do your breathing while we wait. It will keep your mind off of them." A soft smile graced the corners of his muzzle. "Here, breathe with me. In, count five." He inhaled. She did, too, fingers still worrying her tail. "And out again. All of that fear, let it pour out with your breath. Again…"

***

One of the rabbit's long, sensitive ears twitched, and he lifted a finger to his lips. Wandering Star blinked as the rhythm of the qigong broke and she turned to peer through the brush again. The group that ambled toward the road was different than the earlier band of robbers: a couple leafborn mixed in this time, and a few more in number. The panda thrust out her jaw and nibbled on her lower lip. She was still feeling ashamed of her earlier fear, so she studied the figures and tried to imagine herself fighting them like He-Who-Tramples-Stars. The fantasy felt unrealistic... but it did make a little of the tension bleed out of the muscles in her back.

The crows were just as happy to announce the departure of the bandits as they had been the arrival, with the cries receding until Lo-Yao felt comfortable enough to let his ward stand up again. "We're going in," he said, the words like hushed leaves falling from his lips. Wandering Star felt a frisson dance down her spine and take up residence in her gut. She forced a few deliberate breaths into qigong rhythms and let the phantasm of Wandering Star, chuojiao master, help calm her. Not knowing what chuojiao actually looked like in action made it feel a bit silly—she mostly just remembered a lot of kicking, but she drew inspiration from the idea of trampling up to the heavens with it.

With an eventual nod, she made a resolute step towards the rabbit. He turned away to lead her back down the slope and across the road onto a trail that, while she was having trouble making it out, seemed to be easier for Lo-Yao to follow. Picking his way around rocks and plants, he glanced back every so often to make sure that Wandering Star was still all right. Though she always nodded to him, her nerves made the gesture slighter each time.

Only a sudden wiggle of his short, brown tail announced the rabbit's abrupt stop to the panda; she managed to avoid running into him by mere inches. He slid the hat down his back, and his ears raised, quite alert. Wandering Star saw the edges of his whiskers quivering on either side of his face. He held one finger up to her, and then pointed down at her feet with a sharp motion. *Stay here,* she hoped she understood, and she didn't move when he stole through bushes and boulders.

After a blink, he wasn't there at all. She looked up in surprise to see him charging across the rocky soil towards a goatlike ibex with impressive horns and a dark-furred binturong (she thought that's what you called those cattish, weaselly folk) whose single eye widened in shock—the other was hidden by a white patch that failed utterly to blend in with her dark fur. The leafborn barely managed to draw his sword in the time that He-Who-Tramples-Stars had delivered a flurry of kicks to his fellow guard, who staggered like a drunk. Although the ibex opened his mouth, presumably to let loose a cry of warning, a roundhouse kick turned that into a startled grunt.

The panda was barely able keep up with what was happening. The binturong had shaken off her daze and pulled out a wicked-looking dagger. It, like her claws, was unable to connect with her opponent. Lo-Yao's quick motions kept one combatant between himself and the other. Swift kicks and lightning punches never let up. The ibex was the first to fall: he overcommitted with a thrust of his sword, and the rabbit dodged both that and wildly swinging curved horns to place a precise jab on his beard. The ungulate staggered back and fell heavily onto his rump, still. That let Lo-Yao focus solely on the remaining bandit. How he managed to both dodge that knife and interrupt her shouts, Wandering Star could never tell. But it was over less than a minute after the first one went down. The rabbit leapt over her and planted a heavy kick between the binturong's shoulder blades, and that was that. He-Who-Tramples-Stars straightened his saffron garment, bowed to both fallen bandits, and waved his companion over.

A breath she hadn't realized she had been holding escaped, and she scurried to him. "That was amazing!" she bubbled, managing to keep the praise to a whisper. Lo-Yao waved off the praise and touched a finger to his lips, but when he turned to bind the fallen guards, he was smiling.

Just around a boulder from the brief fight, a dark, jagged opening yawned from a vertical face in the rocky hills. Lo-Yao peered into it for a moment before stepping inside. He reached back and held up a single finger before turning the gesture into a beckon. The panda took several hesitant steps forward. Her nervousness was relieved partway, but not fully abated, by a blue orb emitting a faint glow that her guide produced from somewhere on his person. Qigong was no longer sufficient to constrain her anxious breathing.

With a touch of hesitation, she followed him. Her eyes strained to make out the surroundings. The rocky cave was twisty, and the natural light from the entryway soon faded. Occasional beams of sunlight stabbed through irregular openings overhead, blinding eyes that were attempting to grow accustomed to the gloom. The light orb didn't seem to help much with this.

Wandering Star thought the floor was sloping downward but she wasn't sure. She also didn't know how Lo-Yao was choosing which branches of the cavern to follow, but it turned out that he wasn't infallible; on more than one occasion, they met a dead end and had to turn back. Twice he rushed her into a side passage and hid the glow of their light while bandits went by. The second time, a cat cackled a nasal, raucous laugh at a bawdy joke the squirrel accompanying him told. She nearly froze with fear at how close that one sounded, and the rabbit had to coax her out again without words.

The third time they had to dodge someone (a squinting bat and another cat, this one with a limp), fortune smiled on them. The cat was gloating about how Kiyoshi would never know if they skipped out of their posts a little early to raid the sake. After all, even the guards *outside* hadn't reported anything bigger than... The voice grew muffled with distance. Lo-Yao took her hand and, once he seemed confident the other pair was gone, rushed them in the direction the two had come from.

The chamber that they reached—mercifully unwatched by any lingering guards—was somewhat of a disappointment. The panda had envisioned heaps of gold coins, gems glinting from every corner, ancient swords and delicate vases from times long forgotten. Instead, there were two wooden crates, one of them entirely empty, along with some scattered weapons and armor that were probably no more ancient than Wandering Star herself. But the lone occupied crate did contain a few baubles. Lo-Yao reached in and plucked out a gaudy silver lapis-and-jade necklace and a matching (and equally ostentatious) comb. He stashed them into his pack, looking relieved.

And that was when shouts of alarm spread through the caverns.

***

The level of activity the alarm stirred up made progress next to

impossible. Wandering Star tried very hard not to see the fear growing in the rabbit's eyes as he guided them from passage to passage,
from one dead-end to the next—all without the light orb, now.
Surely, she thought, *if he could fight his way past the guards outside, it
wouldn't be much harder to get past a couple in here?*

But Lo-Yao seemed disinclined to engage in combat this time. After
several repetitions of scamper-dodge-hide brought them to a deeper
alcove, the rabbit reached into his pack and drew out the comb and
necklace. He showed them to the panda and then pointed up to a
dark ledge, faintly illumined by another overhead vent. She gave him
a confused look, shaking and trying to catch her breath. While he
went through frantic pantomime to try to communicate something
to her, she noticed that his breathing rhythm was off—had been ever
since the alarm. She eventually realized, when he calmed enough to
settle his breath back into qigong and made a wavy motion with his
fingers, what he was attempting to tell her. She forced her own shud-
dery breathing rhythm to match his, felt some anxiety trickle away,
and with her magic lifted the jewelry (without even a clink!) up to
the ledge in question. As she slumped, the rabbit gave her a nod—
but worry remained in his saffron eyes.

Urgent voices yammered past the entrance to the nook, and then
Lo-Yao took her by the hand and drew her, shaking, back out to the
hallway. She had lost track of which way was out anymore. She wasn't
even sure whether he knew, either. A dodge to the left, down another
passageway. Voices coming from that direction. Turn around, dodge
to the left again. Was that the same corridor? Voices again, louder.
—*have to be in here, somewhere!* He pulled her to crouch (nearly
flat!) under an overhang. Feet rushed by. How could those bandits
have missed the fugitives that time? No matter. They rushed onward.
Every corridor looked alike now, but none was the way out.

Being caught seemed an inevitability. So she felt a mixture of relief
and dread when, after they had fled down another dead end, shadows darkened the way back out and a group of three bandits cornered
them. The squinting bat and limping cat had picked up a fox whose
lopsided sneer missed whiskers on one side. (She checked but didn't
find more than one tail.) The fox barked an order and the bat ran
back to fetch reinforcements. He-Who-Tramples-Stars nudged his
charge against the rear wall of the cul-de-sac and took up his stance

in front of her. Lopsided drew an ugly spiked club, while the mostly-black cat seemed happy with his perfectly sharp claws. Light spheres fastened to their belts made it harder to look directly at them.

Chuojiao did not seem as effective in these more confined quarters. Or maybe it was Lo-Yao's nerves? The bandits gained no ground, but neither did they lose any. The rabbit was tiring, she could tell. His qigong pattern was arrhythmic, and his steps and kicks were faltering.

More voices heralded the arrival of the bat's help. Wandering Star had to do... *something*. She watched, trying to understand the flow of the fight. And then, when the cat lunged, she gave his limping leg a little extra *push* to throw him off-balance.

It worked. Maybe too well. Blackie stumbled, arms pinwheeled, and then his shoulder collided with Lo-Yao's. The rabbit staggered and his own shoulder hit the rough rock wall with an audible thump. Though he sucked in a breath through clenched teeth and struggled back into a fighting stance, the fox's club smacked him solidly along the side of his head, and he dropped.

Wandering Star squeaked in horror. No, no, no! That wasn't how it was supposed to go! She put up her hands and pleaded that she would go along quietly. Lopsided sized her up with that unbalanced smirk. He opened his mouth to say something—and then she felt the most amazing headache. The world grew very, very white before it went very, very black.

***

The throbbing in Wandering Star's head did not match the rhythm of her breathing. She wasn't sure whether she should try to make the pulsing of the pain fit into the rise and fall of her chest or the other way around. And she wished the voices would stop. They made it hard to concentrate either way.

Without thinking, she settled her breath into qigong exercises. Her pounding headache soon slipped into the same rhythm and then abated, even if it didn't fade entirely. She cracked her eyes open and looked around.

A bobcat with a heavily scarred ear was flanked by Lopsided and the squirrel they'd seen earlier. Scar-ear was snarling at a miserable-looking Lo-Yao, who was bound hand and foot, forced onto his knees. Blood was drying in the fur beneath his ear. One of the voices was his, but the one that dominated the conversation belonged to the gravelly sounding feline.

"...hard on both of you if you don't say something," he growled. "You wouldn't want anything to happen to your little girlfriend, would you?"

The rabbit glanced in her direction. His eyes widened in recognition when he realized that the panda was awake, and then he quickly tried to hide it by scowling at the bobcat. He was too late, though. Scar-ear looked over at her, and his grin showed that most of his sharp teeth were still present and unbroken.

"Well, look who's finally decided to join us!" he said. Wandering Star had never realized that someone could sound simultaneously so jovial and menacing. "Now that the two of you are conscious, we can get down to business." He made it simple: "We want the jewelry. Where is it?"

Lo-Yao mouthed a "no" at her, which the panda thought was rather unnecessary because she didn't know how to get to the alcove where they'd stashed it anyway. She looked around the unfamiliar underground room. Their captors had obviously brought the two of them somewhere else after they'd been knocked out. This chamber was more spacious than the confined passages they'd been creeping through. Light seeped in from several overhead sources; some of the light was swallowed up by a dark pit near one of the edges.

The bobcat sneered with even more fang, and Lopsided spoke up with a honeyed voice that was more dulcet than she'd expected. "I'd tell Kiyoshi if *I* were you," he said. For a non-feline, the words were amazingly close to a purr. "He can be a little bit... impatient."

Kiyoshi laughed, an unpleasant sound that reminded her somehow of his twisted ear. "Aye, that I can. Let me guess. You're one of the 'recruits' that his little 'guild' saved." She tried to protest, but he barreled on over her. "He probably tried to seduce you with too-good-to-be-true promises and lavish gifts." That grating laugh again. "Not *that* lavish, really. Nothing like what a jade necklace could buy.

"I was naive and easily enticed once, too." His ears went back—the scarred one got even uglier—and his lips pulled into a snarl. "And you know what happened then? The bastards let my sister die!" He roared the last few words at Lo-Yao, who flinched. "The nobles were killing all of 'em back then, and why do you think they took her head off?" The bobcat turned his attention fully to Wandering Star again. "She was a healer, and she healed a fucking merchant who'd been mugged." He jabbed an accusing finger at Lo-Yao, all his claws out. "And these idiots, and their farce of a... a 'rescue operation!'—they said they 'couldn't get to her in time' and they were sorry. Sorry! As if 'sorry' would put Kieko's head back on!"

The panda tried to look at her benefactor, but his face was turned mostly away. What she could see of it was filled with shame. "Did— did that really happen?" she asked. Her voice was small, as though she were afraid of the answer.

It took Lo-Yao a moment to reply. "We are few," he finally said. "We can't get to everyo—"

"You're damned well not doing enough then!" the bobcat bellowed. His fur bristled out all over.

Lopsided stepped in while the squirrel tried to calm Kiyoshi. "I think," he simpered, "we're getting off track here. Just tell us where the jewelry is, like a good girl." A glance quickly dismissed the rabbit. "Or boy, I suppose. Otherwise, one of you gets to take a little visit into The Pit." That final word received a tone near reverence as he gave a meaningful look to the hole in the floor. "It's a long way down, but it probably won't kill you. The first time. And Kiyoshi has some of his sister's gift, too. Of course—" The tip of his bushy tail pointed roughly to the mangled ear. "—it's not perfect. Especially after several trips down. But it might get you talking, right?"

The fox lowered his voice confidentially to Wandering Star. "And maybe, if you're a *very good* girl, Kiyoshi might forgive your little intrusion into our den here. Let you join up with us. You can get your revenge by helping us rob the qi-born blind." He let that sink in for a couple of seconds before continuing, drawing out the next word. "Probably not as much hope for the rabbit here. But he's nothing to you, really. Is he?"

Wandering Star felt ill. What sort of people were these? Maybe she might have considered their... invitation, if they hadn't been so... ruthless. But it was *her* fault the bandits had been able to capture them. If she'd just stayed back and not tried to *help*... Well, maybe she could help now. If they threw her down The Pit—could she lift *herself* up? If she could… maybe, would that distract them enough for Lo-Yao to get free? And could he fight his way out this time? It was a slim hope, but she didn't know what else to do.

"Huh-uh, I… I… I won't talk!" she said. She wanted to sound brave, but that wasn't a very brave stammer. "You'll have to throw me down first. B-before him!"

"No!" Lo-Yao's voice cracked with horror. "Take m—"

Kiyoshi's contemptuous laugh drowned out the rabbit. "Do you really think we're so foolish as that? *He's* obviously the dangerous one. You're just brave and stupid. No. Maybe you'll talk after we've bloodied him up nice and good… But the *rabbit* dies first. Tuan, throw him in!"

Horrified, she watched the squirrel wrestle Lo-Yao towards The Pit. Even bound as he was, the rabbit seemed to be difficult to maneuver. But her mind caught on the word "first." The *fox* might have promised her anything, but it seemed like the bobcat had no intention of leaving her alive, either—and he acted like the one in charge. A sense of purpose steeled her. She was prepared to die for her own mistakes—or at least could accept the idea—but Lo-Yao… the rabbit had been trying to do the right thing for her, as far as he could. It wasn't fair, not for him.

Determination drove her breathing unconsciously back into the qigong flow he had been teaching her. In, hold… She knew the qi was there, even without exactly *feeling* it. Exhale. In, hold… The qi, that there/not there sensation… she reached it out towards the struggling rabbit, hauled towards his doom in The Pit. Exhale, relax… *Something* wrapped around her companion, her mentor. In, hold… The sensation stretched as the squirrel dragged Lo-Yao to the lip of the gaping yawn in the floor and pushed him over the edge. Her grasp stretched with him… and then it *held*. Pent breath escaped along with her soft exclamation, and her loss of the rhythm let Lo-Yao fall a bit farther, until she managed to control herself again. Not only was his form held in the ethereal grasp of her magic, but she could *feel* the bonds constraining him. The panda willed those to unfasten, to unravel, and more tendrils worked at the cords there, loosening them.

Wandering Star was dimly aware of the squirrel shouting an alarm back to his fellow bandits. She ignored it, putting all her wavering focus into lifting He-Who-Tramples-Stars from The Pit—hopefully, untied. A pain bloomed in her shoulder, but she dismissed that, too. She wouldn't let her breathing falter, wouldn't let the rabbit fall. The same force that lifted also pushed away at something in front of her. That was... interesting, she thought. She didn't completely understand what was happening, but she wasn't going to let that stop her.

The pain was worsening though, sharp and intense. Her vision pulled back from the unfocused blur that it had reduced to when all her mind was on lifting the rabbit, and she saw Kiyoshi in front of her, lips pulled back from his fangs as his muzzle twisted in fury. His hand held a knife that he was pushing into her—well, *trying* to push into her shoulder. Something invisible was forcing his hand back, and he was struggling against it. All that awareness came to her in a flash as she realized that her breathing was irregular again and—

Lo-Yao! She attempted to reach out that... that whatever magic it was that her qi had formed, to try to catch him again, but she couldn't... couldn't sense him. And the more she sought for him, the more the bobcat was able to push in with that knife. Her breathing was still ragged, and she tried to force it back into cadence once more. It was hard—her shoulder ached—and the cavern swam again, this time because her eyes were filling with tears. She wasn't sure if they were for herself and her shoulder or for poor Lo-Yao whom she had failed to save. Doubt crept in as she questioned whether she even deserved to save herself. Her lungs forced air out unsteadily, and she choked on a sob while trying to breathe in again...

And then the large blur that was the bandit leader jerked away from her. There was a series of thuds and smacks, and a clattering sound of something on the floor. She moved to wipe her eyes clear— oh! but her shoulder *hurt*—and then let her right arm hang limp at her side while her left hand brushed away the tears. A yellow-orange shape dashed about, and her now-clean eyes widened as she recognized He-Who-Tramples-Stars. Lopsided and Tuan were motionless in a heap on the floor next to The Pit, while the rabbit twirled, dodging the claws of his captor.

Disarmed (Wandering Star saw the knife where it had landed after clattering across the room), Kiyoshi was unable to keep up with the rabbit's flying feet. Recognition of eventual defeat glittered in the bobcat's eyes. But before he could cry for help, Lo-Yao flashed a heel past the guard of the other male's arms and connected with his chin. The feline's head snapped back. He stumbled and then fell like a sack of rice. The panda couldn't tell whether he was still breathing.

She didn't have much time to figure it out. "Star!" the rabbit gasped. "We have to leave. Now! Can you run?"

The panda gave him a brave nod and promptly fell over when she tried to move. Her shoulder seared, and she made an involuntary cry. By the time she managed to struggle back up partway, Lo-Yao had fetched the bobcat's knife and cut the ropes she hadn't realized bound her ankles. He took her left hand and helped her up, murmuring apologies every time she flinched.

In the end, she couldn't run, but she was able to maintain a remarkably fast shuffle while clamping a hand over her shoulder. The bandits were apparently used to loud noises from the chamber of The Pit, because none of them had come to see what the commotion was. Lo-Yao led the way, and Wandering Star counted it a mercy that they only had to double back a couple of times as they fled. They did surprise the bat when they met him coming around a corner, but the rabbit took him out with a kick, two swift jabs, and a grim determination that the panda didn't recall him having before they'd been captured and she'd been injured.

Qigong or no, the panda couldn't breathe normally until she saw the light from the cave's entrance ahead of them. He-Who-Tramples-Stars was ruthlessly efficient taking out the guards this time. Wandering Star wasn't sure whether she should feel proud or frightened.

Lo-Yao continued to lead her away from the cave as swiftly as possible. When she realized that they were aimed back towards Wumalu, though, she protested. "Wait! What about the jewels?"

The rabbit regarded her with astonishment but he kept them moving. "You're hurt, little Wanderer," he said. "We need to get you help. Someone else will have to get the jewelry. We can't go back in there now! The jewelry should keep where we hid it… I hope."

She whimpered softly as she shifted her hand over her shoulder, but she shook her head. "If… can you find the hole outside the ledge where we left them? Maybe… I can lift them out that way?"

His eyebrows raised. "I didn't know you had it in you to go back," he confessed.

Wandering Star looked down. Her ears flicked back in shame. "I thought I'd messed things up so bad... I thought I'd lost you. I need to fix things!" She suddenly looked up. "How did you get out? I dropped you!"

Lo-Yao waved a hand dismissively. "You did all the work—you did very well! I just wiggled out of my bonds as best I could. You'd got me close to the wall at the top. And then, when I felt you getting shaky with me, I tried to jump. Just barely got to the rim. They were so distracted trying to figure out what to do about you that they forgot me for a few moments. That was long enough."

"I didn't even know what I was doing." She blushed until her ears warmed. "I just... after I lost my family, I wouldn't... didn't want to get close to anyone again. But then you were so nice, and I liked you even though I didn't want to, and I couldn't... couldn't let you down!" She picked up her tail with her left hand and twisted her fingers around it lightly, flustered. At least the blood on her pads was dried enough not to stain the tail fur. Her eyes kept slipping past his while she talked.

His fingers met her chin with a gentle touch, and he brought her gaze to his for an instant. "You did not let me down," he told her. He smiled. "You did better than I expected." When she started to object, he shook his head. "Yes, you made mistakes. But I did, too—worse ones. I underestimated how dangerous it was. And when it counted, *you* really helped us get through it. I couldn't have done it without you."

She was quiet for a few seconds, letting that sink in. Then a shy smile crossed her muzzle. "So, are we going back for the jewels?"

Lo-Yao blinked, laughing. "I have created a monster!" he exclaimed. "Very well, let's find a place to hide and patch up your shoulder. I have silk bandages, and honey and baijiu in my pack." She recognized the name as a potent distilled rice spirit, though she had never tasted it before. "Then we can see about it once things have died down. But even if we can't find the jewelry, or if we can't get back there safely, I will still give Her Grace Obana—" He said the name with a certain dry irony this time, instead of the curt reverence he had used initially. "—a glowing report of your abilities. In fact, I would be very honored to work with you again in the Empress' service. Perhaps with a little more practice under your belt. And once we get someone more proper than me to patch you up!"

Her face brightened, flushed with his praise, as he led her to find a more concealed location. "Lo-Yao?" she ventured softly. "Do… do I have to help you from behind a desk?"

"What?" he asked, surprise nearly halting him before he continued on. "No, but… well, I thought you'd feel safer there."

Wandering Star couldn't really shrug, but her ears twitched a sort of resignation. "Probably," she acknowledged. "But safe didn't save me. It didn't save you, either." A curious little half-smile lifted her muzzle. "If I—if everyone just hid in all the paperwork… Well, who'd give out persimmons to frightened red pandas who needed to be given a chance?" She sighed shakily as the rabbit settled her into a copse that smelled faintly of camphor. "Can *I* do that someday?"

Lo-Yao laughed quietly. "Little Star," he said, "I am starting to think there is little you can *not* do, once you put your mind to it."

The panda beamed at his words. Although he was gentle with the injured shoulder, she still gasped when he pulled the robe back so he could dress the wound. But when she closed her eyes, she could see indistinct faces of the people she could help someday, just like He-Who-Tramples-Stars had done for her.

END OF (ON)LINE

Franklin Leo

What makes us, being made of metal and purchased from a store, any different from them, I wonder. *Is it the cabinets we sleep behind, the lenses we use to see? Was I ever like this? Will I ever be like* her?

I watch as Diana packs her bags in front of me without a hint of sorrow hidden behind her soft, blue eyes. The doe had her clothes shipped out before the day's end, but getting the last supplies in, she makes me feel responsible for her staying another morning—me, a synthetic animal made of mechanical cogs and bands. Around us, the apartment stands in disarray. Trash litters the floor, scuff marks from her hooves decorate the walls, but no matter how many times I've tried to clean up, nothing seems to stay clean. The only thing I seem to accomplish is getting my polished claws dirty.

"They're going to shut this place down for good, I hope you know. All of you are going to go with them," she says. "You and those freaks uploading themselves into toys."

My view-lenses click with the snapping of a camera. All of us? "You're not making any sense, Diana. Please. What's happening?"

She shakes her head, those ears of hers flapping like gentle wings. "Be quiet, already."

"Diana, wait. Let's talk this through. Why are you leaving?" I reach out for her, plastic seams and canid claws extended.

The doe slips on her pack. Wearing her jumpsuit, she almost appears male. She maybe even looks like us, I process, minus the glowing eyes and digitally integrated AI. She aims her watch at me and the silence comes swiftly, my eyes darkening as I cry for her to stop. It's too late, and I've been shut into sleep mode, lenses locked and body still. All of us come packed with our own overrides if we needed them. The wolves, cats, and predators like me need it the most, everyone says. It's interesting that we're all made of the same materials regardless. While some have full and entire system reboots, however, mine only makes me fall asleep—and forget. Forget about the sadness, the anger, the wonder and fear. Most of all, forget about the person I used to be.

When I awake, I find myself alone and disconnecting my cables from the wall. The now sterile room stands clean and empty, besides my bed of a charging station. I look down at my hands and paws to see that everything is in working order before stepping out for my first objective. It dashes before my eyes, internalizing directions, steps, and anything else I need to know.

All of us synthetics should be ready for it at some point. It was my deactivation, after all.

The monochromatic chamber looks more like a cafeteria than a waiting room to an android's ultimate demise. Benches and tables fill the home-sized space, some with charging ports and others with smaller tablets. The room was made to house both synthetics and their owners for any final communications, each seat a comforter meant to relax visiting said owners. Glass containers of waiting-to-be-purchased AIs—conscious souls, to put it easily—hang from the walls like batteries meant to be used in toys. I wonder on whether I was purchased or uploaded organically. The data detailing my creation seems to have been erased.

While Diana has always told me that I was the only one of our kind built to feel emotions, the sight of the hall full of other simulated-companions suggests otherwise. A bat android hangs from the ceiling, glaring down at an elk that I assume must be her master. Her eyes, lenses much like my own, glare from her polished plastic and rubber body, wings a polyurethane fabric. Another table sits close by, with two synthetic pangolins holding hands as their owner, a young mouse, is in the process of disassembling their unraveled, skeletal arms like some butcher saving what tastes best. I, of course, have no one seated with me. She's already left, I would tell them. I haven't the faintest idea why.

"Is everything all right, brother?" A hand touches me on the shoulder and alerts my sensors to turn around.

"I'm being deactivated. Should I be all right?"

The weasel sits before me. Her rubber and plastic frame whirs as her eyes focus onto my face. The pack between her shoulders, a glowing yellow chamber where her uploaded consciousness rests, hums softly behind her. "I'm so sorry to hear about Diana," she says.

I sigh in a simulation of my master's own social cues. "I'm not upset. Not now, at least. She's chosen what she needs to. I'm simply following orders."

"She ordered you to come be deactivated by yourself?"

"Yes," I say. "Why else would I be here?"

Megan—her name registering with the pass of a scan—turns her head towards the front of the hall. At the reception desk sits her master, a female otter typing something we can't identify without connecting to her screen. Her eyes stay locked in focus, but after a moment, she glances up to find us watching her, returning to business with a smile. "I'm not certain."

My paws cup the front of my face as I lean into the table's surface. "I'm sorry. I can't seem to remember anything today. Do you know why I'm being deactivated?" I ask.

Megan's lenses whir as they focus on me once more. I can feel her working through calculations, probabilities, and even simulations. "Is it that she didn't tell you? Or is it that you don't remember that, either?"

Neither? Both? I try to come up with an answer when an electronic ping sounds, ringing against the chamber's rotunda-shaped walls. It's then that I see the bat synth look to her master and lower herself to the ground in a swoop. Her wing rises as a claw on the end takes her master's hand in a professional showing of goodbye. Again, the tension is palpable. Her eyes zero in on her master's expressions, reading what so many owners think we can't interpret. What are wires and pre-fabricated shells to true biology? He doesn't do anything other than give a nod, but to her, the bat, it all means the world.

She leaves him standing and watching, and heads alone toward the desk where Alaina's owner waits. When they meet, the bat follows her into a door held closed by a single grey curtain, and I can only assume that this is where the bat ends one life and begins her process into another. Complete erasure and reintroduction.

Death, to put it simply.

***

I'm almost into a full three hours of waiting when the sound of paws alert me to a presence coming close. I awaken from sleep-mode to find Alaina, Megan's master, coming towards me. She carries a clipboard while her tail holds steady behind her. Her ears, small and round, are flat against her head, and she eyes me as though she can't let me leave her sight. Nervous. "Good afternoon, Kyle."

"Am I going to die?" I ask.

Alaina flinches but doesn't answer the question. "I've heard that your data has been wiped already. Have your sensors been functioning properly?"

Wiped? Why would I have been wiped if Diana was going to deactivate me anyway? "I'm rebooting my sensors right now, but they've been doing all right so far. I can't detect anything wrong with them."

The otter nods and reaches for her waist. "Would you mind?" she asks.

I don't respond, and the otter pulls a cable from a pack and tethers it up my arm. She plugs the end behind my head where several inputs lie waiting. With a click, I feel the cable fit perfectly, and my back straightens to accommodate my inner-mechanics and cooling systems best. I can feel the shoulder-system containing me glow with eagerness. "Ready for data transfer." The words slip from my canine muzzle as though another has taken control of my body.

"Initiating transfer," Alaina says. She stands still, reading what I obviously cannot see. While she works on whatever information she's identifying, my body shudders, and the space between my shoulders grows warm. Data flushes from my system as a weight centers on my forehead. The transfer is working faster than my system was originally made for, and it's warm. Hot, actually. My muzzle opens wider to vent some of the air.

"You're being sentenced for decommission, a relocation of AI, and a rewriting of internal processing due to your murder of one Milo Coppers. All systems are in check and ready," Alaina says. "It seems that most of your data has indeed been wiped, though. Do you remember Milo, Kyle? A rabbit?"

It's difficult to say at first; the data being pulled from my system prevents me from getting the information out for myself. I scan and search, fumbling through information, and yet I find nothing about anyone named Milo. "I don't think I've ever met a Milo, Alaina."

"He was scheduled to be upgraded into a synthetic model prior to his murder. Did Diana ever mention him to you?" The otter steps back. I wonder whether she feels I might murder her next.

Again, I process this request. Moments pass, and nothing comes forward. "No. Could we maybe look deeper? Perhaps the data's been placed in my subsystem."

She nods. "I understand. Diana doesn't seem to have any personal data that would suggest a connection."

She unplugs her cable from my skull and unwraps my arm. Rolling the cord into a tight hanging wrap, the otter sighs. "All the same, we're tasked with your decommission, but I can't do anything until we clarify your understanding of the situation for future documentation and safety. Until the time of your appointment, I'm sentencing you to task work. At least while we can find out what happened to your data."

"Of course," I say. "Who would purchase a new synthetic that's already murdered someone?"

Alaina looks at me as though I've said something rude. "Okay. I've input the new directives for you until we get this matter dealt with. Your station is already in place, but I will call you once we've reviewed all data from your system and Diana's. Thank you for the cooperation, Kyle."

I nod. Standing, my figure towers over the otter's, and her eyes raise to meet mine. The anxiety she's held onto finally bursts out as her ears pull back. Professional, but still very much intimidated. She indeed believes I might harm her, waiting to see if what I supposedly did to one will happen again to another. I might not remember this Milo, but she seems to be all too aware of it.

"Dismissed," she says. My body turns on its own and walks me to my station without me having any control. Who knows what the next tasks will be?

Turns out, they're nothing but mindless jobs. For the first task, I sit at a desk for two hours cataloging information that could've simply been input by someone less inhuman. Then I'm moved to a simple pump station for another eight hours, down in the station's lower levels where the heat grows trapped until it's sucked out through vents.

Unlike upstairs, a simple leveling structure made of metals and plastics home to thousands of animals and operating synthetics, the pump station is held together by rusted coppers and burnt concrete. Rivets from the last several decades remain in chunks visible through the wall, hiding beneath what I assume to be the lowest deck of the ship. I follow the clean yet deteriorating stairs down to find a rhino synthetic pulling levers too large for anyone non-robotic. My job is to monitor the gauges and watch for any possible inconsistencies. Easy work, as one says, seeing as I'm only an assistant.

I begin without introducing myself, legs taking me from machine to machine. Time passes slowly, allowing my computer to run through the data. It isn't until I reset some files that I find I do remember a Milo. Young, jumpy, and unsure of who he was. It sounds like most young users, each trying to find their own way. This leads me to question: could a synthetic ever find his own way? What would it mean if a creature such as my own could hold their own destiny in their claws? Those who evolve, the few joining our ranks and keeping a bit of their humanity to themselves, all seem to have some degree of agency, even in their work. Would it be any harder for someone unborn, like me, to carry himself alone? An hour passes easily enough, and my partner's quiet until I'm checking my fifteenth dial, when the glowing, metal rhino snorts out steam. "You're the one that killed Milo," he says. "The synthetic who disobeyed his orders."

"So I've heard, at least in part. Does everyone know about this murder of mine?"

"Not all. Most, I assume." He shrugs, great big shoulders of steel rocking against his chassis. "I'm still not used to this whole robot life, I guess. I wouldn't know. How long have you been a synth?"

Been a synthetic? My whole life, I want to say. My whole existence has been in the following of orders and taking care of others. Not like this brute, whose whole life must be made to turn dials and wheels, spray out steam, make sure nothing goes wrong. My lenses focus on his back, to where a glowing cartridge should house his AI. "I only remember being a synthetic. You were alive, once?"

He nods. The remaining minimal plastic on him is scratched and fractured, stained with grease. In-between the plates I can see moving pistons and rotating wheels, thick bands of rubber. "Thirty years old. Upgraded the first chance I could get, seeing my body worn down to a husk. I assumed most synths were normal at some point. Can't say they didn't advertise it enough. Like living a video-game, they'd said. It's not a bad life, though. No different from any other work."

The thought lingers in my system for a moment, before a pipe hisses and interrupts our discussion, and our LED sensors go red with alert.

The room is now covered in a blood-like glow. The piping and machinery hang like claws, stomachs, and teeth in some definably grotesque way. Though I can work out an emergency plan that would take me just more than a second, the rhino's first to move, and despite his size and tons of weight, he's quick—made for this work. His arm extends to a wheel, and with a rotation of his wrist (really, it's a rotating axle with fingers), the steam clears, only turning his metal red for a moment.

Our lights turn back to a calm, albeit dismal, blue. The color of sorrow, really. The chamber settles as everything returns to normal. "Having been alive, does that hurt?" I ask. "Being burnt like that, I mean."

"Does it hurt when you cut your metal on, say, a kitchen knife? No. Never does. At least not like before. We're made for service. If we weren't, then we'd be no use."

I nod, my eyes focusing on the model number stenciled on his neck. "You were dying."

He shrugs with a rumble. His arm returns to where it's been for the entire day. "Same reason anyone turns, I guess. This gives me a purpose I can feel proud of, at least."

"How were you dying?"

"Cancer. Ate my body like a jaguar eats." He makes a chuckle that's really just a release of air pressure. "Was in the body of a jaguar, funny enough, before they put me here."

I open my muzzle to speak, when the radio in my ear takes over. It's Alaina. "Hey, Kyle. We're running through some of the data that's been wiped and should have something scheduled for you soon. Feel free to recharge upstairs. It'll be a couple more hours for us." She speaks as though it hasn't been another work day since having seen her.

"Duty calls," I say, lifting a hand to wave goodbye.

"Wait," he says. "Are they decommissioning you?"

"Apparently so, for Milo's murder. I can't remember anything except for what they've told me."

The rhino steps forward. His lenses focus on me with the precision used to cut diamonds out of steel. "You mean you don't remember? But that's impossible. Who owned you, and why would they delete that?"

"I'm sorry. I have orders to follow. Goodnight." A bow, and I leave the brute to his dungeon.

I follow my way back towards the service lift, then up and out of the ship's basement levels. My lenses clean themselves free of condensation, legs shaking off the dust and grease, but my inner mechanisms still feel gummed from the humidity. I hope that my shell will retain itself even if water's set in. If not, the new body will take care of that no matter what I become in the next life. I might even get a better body, I think, but that's just being optimistic.

Synthetics don't *have* optimism, right?

***

It's late. The room is chilled to its lowest temperature, made for me to recharge and get my rest. I power on and find my entire room's been destroyed. Which is to say nothing much has changed, except for the few obvious details.

"How could he do this? To me, of all people?"

Trash, torn cables, and charred walls indicate that there's been a scuffle in the room at least once. There's no blood, but my sensors aren't necessarily fully alive as I step off my platform. The smell of fire is the first thing I pick up, before I do indeed catch the droplets of red indicating a trail. "Begin scan," I say.

"That stupid synth. He did this. Milo didn't want anything to do with them until he got sick, and Kyle then ruins all of it. He ruined him."

My eyes cut off the examination command. "Diana?" I ask. While she should be asleep, her voice echoes from out in the corridor. One could only hope that she's safe.

I step my way out of the small room and find the rest of the quarters a mess. The couch has been flipped over, burned and sliced by something inorganic. Paper, some still smoking, lines the floor in carpeting chaos, and blood pools show themselves to lead me towards the master's door. I kneel and touch the blood with a single pat. My scanners get to work, and in seconds I have the results.

"Miss Diana, are you hurt?" My voice reflects from the walls and echoes back at my swiveling ears.

"Kyle?" her voice cuts out as a whisper, before her head peers from around the door.

"Good morning. What's going on?"

"Where's Milo?"

Milo? It's at this moment I remember the rabbit, a friend, whose DNA did come up in the blood sample. Small yet lean and lively. Ears always up as if unnerved. Applying to be evolved through the synthetic program, model Tiger if I'm not mistaken. "Is Milo here, madam?"

The doe creeps out from behind the door. Her clothes are stained with blood and ash. A zoom on her fur, and I find the remains of what appears to be rabbit hairs. Why would she have rabbit fur on her if she's the one looking for Milo?

"Begin crime scene scan," I say, and my eyes focus in on every detail of the room. Sharp, blue lasers pass over minor details only synthetics and computers could spot at a roving first glance. Paw prints, DNA. Milo's blood's stained most of the room. The fire seems to have been lit by gas. Propane? No, too difficult to manage. Something smaller, like that from an aerosol can or a modern synthetic's work-torch.

"What did you do to him?" Diana's voice ends in a choked sob.

I turn, my torso spinning before my legs catch up. "Me? Diana, I've been in sleep mode for hours."

The doe's legs are shaking as she turns the corner around the kitchen counter. Here is where most of the fire seemed to come from. Upon turning, she gasps, falls, and cries out.

My legs speed me towards her side, where I find the rabbit on the ground, dead, with most of his fur missing and burned. His dazed eyes gaze off as his muzzle rests in an open gape. His arms—both arms— are broken. One of his ears has been torn, as well.

"I've called the police, Diana." I lean down to touch her shoulder.

"Get away from me!" she says. She shoves my legs, and I stumble. I catch myself on the bloody fridge, leaving prints of rubber fingers behind.

"*Diana, I need to get you out of here.*"

Already, however, she's standing and heading for the door. "*Don't you touch me, you monster. How could you?*" Her voice is deeper, her eyes wide.

"*You're in shock. Please, if we don't get you out of here, you'll burn and injure.*" I raise my hands to grab for her, but she raises her arm to bring up her watch. Without even a hint of remorse, the clearest human indicator of empathy, she hits a button that freezes me mid-pose. My eyes stay focused and glowing on her visage, lenses zoomed in on the tile and rabbit before me. Not even my tail moves thanks to the pause she's placed on me.

"*You killed him,*" she says. She holds the record button out of my sight, and the soft whirring inside of me only grows stronger. "*You knew he was going to change, and you didn't want him to replace you.*"

Not true. My motors and internal servers are still firing, though much quieter and slower than when operable. Milo found out he had cancer. He was looking to upgrade and continue his lab work. I wish to speak, but I can't respond to her as the thoughts come whizzing through.

"*They'll find you here a mess. I tried to stop you, but you kept attacking him. Someone programmed you with unfathomable instincts while I had my back turned. I got away, but only after you bit me.*" Diana lies on the ground in the blood. She's not clean about it, either, making sure to cover herself as though she were putting on fur dye. "*You even pulled some fur off.*"

I watch as she brings up a knife and shaking, she operates on herself, screaming and crying. My eyes don't record a thing; all I internalize is the audio of her hypnotic statements and the blood-curdling screams, a detail she might have forgotten—

And then I don't seem to know where I'm at. My nose reads fire, and then I feel warmth across my thermal scanners. Why is there warmth? Am I safe? Where's Diana, and who of all people is Milo…

***

Alaina's shaking when I return. The hall stands empty except for around her, where police and investigation synthetics stand watching several screens. I open my muzzle to speak, processor focused on finishing my directive, but another rubbery paw touches me on the shoulder and interrupts my feed. "Thank you, Kyle. We have all that we need to know."

I turn to find a lion synthetic holding me with his claws. His eyes radiate a calming eye that disables my systems focused on deactivation. "What happened to him—to Milo? Did I do it?" I ask. What if I did murder Milo. How?

With a ruckus the animals and synthetics behind Alaina all turn their attention to her, robots and animals seeing an otter clearly in shock. Are they expecting her to answer me? "Your previous owner will be wanted on several counts," the lion states. "Most of all, premeditated murder."

"She'll also be charged with criminal mischief, having staged the murder with blame on you." A lean albeit barrel-chested stallion synthetic steps out from the small gathering. "Her description, crime, and all information from her banking statements, affiliations, and aliases have been uploaded to the queue. Do you understand?"

If I could shudder, I would, knowing that the queue is where synthetics are uploaded once they've been decommissioned. Think of it as heaven for robots, or the middle-ground for soon-to-be robots, where they spend a simulated eternity monitoring the internet. "I do."

The horse nods, releasing internal steam from its plastic nostrils and stepping aside. "If she's hiding anywhere, we'll find her. As to the matter of your decommissioning, a review will begin once the investigation moves forward. We will need a complete download of your records, recordings, and data, but only for the sake of pressing forward."

"But will I die, officer?" I say.

A biological wolf, one of the only investigators not made of metal, latex, or polyurethane, shakes her head, but everyone else looks at each other in a loss. "How about an upgrade, instead?"

Upgrade. I look down at the canine hands attached to me, as well as the glowing, humming chamber of my muzzle and chest. A new body, perhaps? Something faster, more light-weight. An avian model would be neat. Or perhaps something slower, friendlier. Users tend to favor dogs more than they do wolves, and the pack between my shoulders—the real me, if I even exist—could easily fit in no more than a few minutes of a swap.

"Will you be all right, ma'am?" The wolf kneels before Alaina, two natural beings amongst multiple synthetics. She doesn't stand but continues to shake, even if her breathing has returned to deeper inhales.

A whinny calls my attention from behind. "Come with us, Kyle. It's time we go."

"Go?" I ask. I rotate my hips to find the synthetics waiting.

"No one's being deactivated tonight. Someone's got their eye on you, apparently. For Milo's sake, at least."

We leave as Alaina begins her story, the chamber now empty asides one synthetic and the wolf. Megan, my dear friend, stands inside the lobby asleep behind her wall-positioned glass, waiting to be awoken and put to duty once again.

***

The class rises as though it were an ocean, the film presentation over and lecture finally dismissed. No more than two dozen, students fill the hall with noise, both mechanical and not. A synthetic Labrador turns to his peers and smiles as they discuss something I reason is based on the lecture. In the back, the smell of coffee wafts out from a thermos, one lioness swilling a drink whilst leaving.

I snap the lights back on and I find a small mouse synthetic standing close by. She has no bag, no folder. Her lenses indicate that she's in record mode, perhaps there to document class for her user at home. "Yes, Abby?"

"Sorry, professor. I just needed to clarify something before I leave."

"Is this about the lecture?" I can't help smiling, my large, radio disc ears fanning her way to listen. She shows no prey instincts despite standing in front of the Wild African Dog synthetic before her.

"This is for my own knowledge, doctor."

Interesting. "Okay. How may I help?"

"You state that a user is just as much synthetic as the models they buy in stores, arguing it's because of how animals document and download information no less than a machine." Her tail slackens behind her back. Cold tones of blue and green radiate in small patches. "Wouldn't it be true, then, that synthetics are just as biological as the users that own them, in a way?"

"Interesting observation. Is this something you're working on for your thesis?" I ask.

The rodent turns her head. We both look to find several synthetics, all wearing backpacks—some even clothes—waiting for their companion. "No, I was just wondering. If we're all so similar, then... why do they have control?"

My system cools itself down with ventilation excusing hot air out from against my AI-pack. This synthetic is clearly intelligent; the user at home must be proud to house her, although I question what Abby's home life must be like. With a smile still held, I think back to when I was a wolf and placed in a precarious situation.

OUT THE OTHER SIDE

Jellybean

Quinn awoke and knew he was dead.

He lay in the field outside of town, the night sky spreading above him into infinity, an oppressive vastness over the soft silver grass. He sat up. It was hard to process the fact that he was dead, especially since he did not remember how he died. But he knew within every thread of himself that it was true, as certainly as anyone could know anything.

He had felt this certainty before. It always came from things unseen, things other people could not feel—the taste of a coming storm in his cereal, the crunch of sourceless footsteps behind him, the unblinking eyes in the corner of the room. When he was seven, he had awoken to mouse bones sitting on the inside of his window sill and a dark shadow hunched behind the glass, its eyes pure orbs of yellow. It met his gaze and rose, unfurling itself slowly, much too tall for a person, until it finally turned and wandered back into the woods.

And here, now, a figure stood before him.

"Oh," Quinn said. "You're Death."

The figure tilted their head forward. When they moved, the dark fabric of their cloak rippled and shifted, breaking off into fragments of darkness that pooled into the grass and dissipated like smoke. Skeletal hands rested on a pale white staff, which was twisted and gnarled like the branch of an old tree. He could not see their face, their hood hiding it in a darkness he doubted any light could ever pierce. With so little showing, it was hard to tell their species—maybe a rabbit like him, maybe a dog like in some of the myths, maybe something entirely new.

"Huh," he said. "Awesome."

Quinn laid back down in the grass. He stared up at the stars, which were the same even in death. Away from the lights of the town, they splashed hot and greedy in the sky. His body felt distant, as if he were controlling it from afar.

Death did not seem so bad. At least now he could be free. At least now he could run from this town and never come back. At least now he would not be an empty shell that this empty place could not fill.

A shadow covered the stars. Quinn looked into two pinpricks of light—Death's eyes.

"Quinn McCarver," Death said in a voice that seemed to come from deep within the earth, "I have a task for you."

"Look," he said. "I'm a big fan of yours. Always wanted to meet you. But can't you just take me to the afterlife or whatever you're supposed to do? Can't you just end this?"

"No. I am sorry, Quinn McCarver, but you are stuck here. Just as in life."

His stomach lurched. He bolted upright, ears quivering. "What? Bullshit! You can't do that! I demand my right to die, just like everyone else!"

"Yet you are not everyone else. You lived alongside the unseen. It is by no fault of your own—simply the right blood beneath the right moon."

"So what, I'm just stuck here forever? That's—"

"No." Their voice rumbled deep. "I wish to take you. But empty space breeds strange things, and strange things indeed abound here." They paused. "Another soul cannot leave. They did not die when they should. Correct this, and perhaps your spirit will release its hold on this place."

Quinn's head pounded. "Perhaps?"

"Perhaps is all this world can give you. Even in death. Two strange errors in such a short time—a likely connection." They turned, blackness shifting around them, flickering like the silhouette of a bird against the stars. "Come, Quinn McCarver. Our duty awaits."

***

At this time of night, the main road was practically empty. The towns-folk had already gone home. Hardly any outsiders bothered to pass through—and even fewer stopped. A dark forest of pines bunched together on one side of the road and only that side, as if afraid to step over the boundary and into the empty fields. Street lights hunched over the strip of pavement, their orange faces turned bashfully to the ground. When Quinn was young, he used to stand beneath the street light in front of the post office and count as many as he could until they faded into darkness. He would always end up with a different number, confused by the light and the dark.

After he bought a car he would drive past the lights, counting as he went, until they at last disappeared and left him with only his head-lights burning through the night. Then he would cut those, too, and coast silently through the dark, feeling more than knowing that there was emptiness on one side and trees on the other, and all he could see were outlines flashing by, silver lines sketched by stars.

Death led him into the trees. He followed mindlessly, doing his best to piece together the mystery with very little information. What did he even have to go on?

"Here."

He looked up, and his heart skipped a beat. He knew this house, and he knew who he would see as he pressed himself against the frost-cracked window.

An armadillo sat on her bed, the one the two of them had shared all those years ago as they huddled beneath the covers and wrote story after story about things they would never see. The room had changed—bedsheets shifted from tie-dye to a muted green, metal band posters to colorful landscapes—but some bits had stayed the same. A wrestling calendar still hung by the door. A bottle of black claw polish sat on her bedside table. She had not taken the plastic stars from her ceiling, which Quinn had always hated. Inside was the only place to escape the stars at night—why take that hiding place away?

Quinn stared in at his old friend, the one he had trusted more than anyone else. The one he had hurt.

"I can't," he whispered. He had not so much as spoken to her in years, but he pushed himself away and said, "I can't help you kill her. Not Sam. Not—"

Death grabbed the back of his neck. He gasped, cold slamming through his body like a door banging shut, an ancient iciness that swept across the world again and again and again, carving vast swaths into the landscape and devouring the living, an immovable element in the cycle of the planet.

"All must die," Death said in a voice that had seen the end of every living thing. "All must face me. To escape this is to defy the laws of the sun and the sky and earth, who will one day face finality."

They let go, and he fell to his knees, shivering.

"Death is an ultimate. It happens, or it does not. By casting death aside, you break from life as well. You must be in one or the other. You must. Do you understand?"

"Yes," he gasped. He could still feel ancient bones beneath great sheets of ice, forever petrified. He forced himself to his feet. "But how—"

Death shoved him through the wall. He passed through easily and stumbled, hardly able to place himself within the here and the now, and fell in the middle of Sam's childhood home.

"You!"

He looked up, panicked. Sam jumped to her feet, eyes blazing as she marched towards him, black painted claws clenched into fists, a familiar anger stoked to fever pitch.

"What the hell is going on?" she hissed. "And why are you here?"

He scrambled to his feet and held his hands up, heart hammering as if he were in the middle of a hundred-meter dash. "S-Sam, hold on! I just—"

"Just what?" she snarled, reaching for him. "What could you possibly do? How do you think you could make any of this…"

She trailed off, staring at her arm on his shoulder. No, not on. *Through* his shoulder, as if he were nothing but water and she were running her hand though a stream, searching for fish. He stepped back. He could see the carpet faintly through his feet. He slowly flipped his hand, watching the dappled blue carpet shift in color through his fur, cream at the palm and brown on the back. His chest was so tight he could hardly breathe.

Not that he needed to, being dead.

"You, too?" she said, her voice quiet now, much too soft for the Sam he had known, the one who would sneak beer from her mother's minifridge and chase bullies down the road with a stick. The one who held anger in her heart—anger for the world, its people, and eventually him.

He forced himself to take a breath, but he could not look at her. "Too?"

She stepped closer until they were practically touching. He could feel her heat, a warmth he had never felt in himself, and despite everything happening now and everything that happened then, he wanted to step into her so he could feel something strong, to feel *something* other than this hollowness that made him want to kneel on the ground and disappear.

"Quinn McCarver," she hissed. "Tell me what the hell is going on."

He closed his eyes. "I don't—"

"Don't tell me you don't know, because that's never true. You always have some damn theory."

"I—Sam, you're supposed to be dead."

She went silent. She looked down at her hands, curling them into fists and then slowly opening them again, as if hoping to find something to grasp on to. At last she took a deep breath and said, her voice surprisingly steady, "Okay."

"Okay?"

"I'm dead. Or I should be. But I'm not, and that's a problem. There's no point in moping about it. And you wouldn't have come here unless there was something you thought you could do."

He swallowed. "Sam, I can't stop you from—"

"I know!" she snapped, anger back in an instant. "Damn it, Quinn, I know. I can feel it. I've *been able* to feel it. It's in every inch of me, that overwhelming feeling that I—" She stopped and squeezed her eyes shut. "Look, it's fine. Let's just—let's not talk about it. Okay?"

Deciding through his own muted grief that it was the least he could do, he nodded.

"Good," she said. "What now?"

"We—we need to figure out what happened. Put you back on track." He chewed on an index claw, thinking, pushing away emotion to focus on the problem. Every problem had an answer if you followed the lines of logic. Even supernatural ones. "Well, here's what we know: you were supposed to die at a certain point, but you didn't. I'm guessing you started to feel off at that point, maybe a little bit after. Does that ring any—" He stopped, noticing a strange look on her face, one he could not quite place. "What?"

"Nothing. Just—you haven't changed much, have you?"

He stared at her, not quite sure how to take that.

She went on before he had to respond. "Well, there was one thing. I was out drinking about a week ago, and on my way home some truck almost flattened me. I thought later on that I was pretty lucky."

"Did it seem supernatural?"

She scratched behind her ear. "I dunno. I was pretty drunk at the time."

"Well, I suppose it's worth checking out. What time was it?"

"Dolly said I left around midnight. I started the night a few hours earlier—about this time."

"Perfect. Get your coat."

She crossed her arms. "What exactly are we doing?"

He grinned nervously, for a moment feeling like they were teenagers again, standing in her room with a stupid plan and nowhere else to be. "Simple. We're getting you drunk."

***

Quinn discovered a few things on their trip to the tavern. First, no one else could see him. He was not surprised when no one greeted him, but when he tried to order a drink, the bartender simply slid Sam her beer and turned away.

The second thing was that Sam had changed. The two of them had been loners, only relying on each other, him feeling disconnected from the world and her too angry to deal with it, but now she threw greetings across the room and slid onto a barstool as if she lived here. Even though she was supposed to be dead, a bit of life had come back to her now. It was hard to believe she was the same person who made up stories with him in the woods, wanting to get away from it all.

"You'd better be right about this," she said, taking a swig of beer.

This was the easy part. Sam had always been the one to sneak beers, and though he disliked the taste, he had always drunk as well. He had wanted to share something with her, wanted to feel like they were connected, like the act of pressing his lips to the cold aluminum was some kind of ancient pact.

Now he watched her demolish her drink with ease, wondering if any of it had mattered at all.

He winced and looked around. The people hardly caught his attention. Buildings had their own spirits, and Quinn could feel this one's. He heard the groan of warped wood soaked in generations of alcohol. He caught the tail ends of shadows creeping through the smudged glass windows. He felt the tremble of the floorboards that had been soaked in blood and never truly cleaned, no matter how much the bartender scrubbed.

But it was not until Sam called a loud greeting that he snapped to attention and heard the bustle of conversation and felt the rumble of laughter around him. He looked around, noting the people he recognized: a group of old classmates clustered in the corner, an elderly squirrel he was pretty sure had a thing for one of his housemates, a lean wolf who ran the grocery store, an armadillo approaching them who Quinn thought was Sam's cousin.

Hardly any had spoken to him in years, if at all. It was better that they could not see him, he thought. No one needed to pretend he mattered. This town got along just fine without him.

The armadillo paused next to Sam, creasing her eyebrows as she looked at the seat Quinn was occupying. Quinn sighed and hopped off, and the armadillo sat with a slightly confused expression, as if not quite sure what had happened.

"Hey, Dolly," Sam said in greeting, though Quinn was fairly certain that was for his benefit. "Thought you were working tonight." She drained the last of her beer and called for another.

Dolly did not answer for a moment, eying the beer. "Are you doing all right?"

"I haven't been in since last week, Dolly. I'm fine. And Alex says he'll cut me off before I get too shit-faced."

"Well, all right." She smiled, and her shoulders eased. "Just stay sober long enough for me to tell you what my niece did yesterday. You remember that she was trying to overthrow the drama club, right?"

As Sam laughed, Quinn tried to tune them out. He hated to acknowledge it, but it hurt to see her laugh. She had a whole life he was not a part of now, and he knew that he would only have ruined it. All these years he had been imagining her struggling as much as he had, but now he wondered if that was true. Had she moved on while he had been stuck behind?

"Quinn."

He looked back at her, realizing that he had been staring into space for quite some time. Sam was watching Dolly go with a softness in her eyes. "She's a good one, you know. She'll be sad when I'm gone."

Quinn reclaimed his spot. He could smell the beer on her breath. "You think a lot of people will be?"

"Sad? Sure. And ain't that a change of pace, eh? We used to think the only ones who would miss us was *us*."

"Well, maybe that's still true for some of us."

Sam was silent for a long time, tracing clumsy patterns into the sweat on her glass. It seemed that the alcohol was starting to affect her already. At last she said, "How'd you die?"

"I don't remember."

"Bet you got eaten by Bigfoot. Or drowned by stream spirits. Or maybe you wandered out into the field and never came back. Just like you always dreamed." She straightened and took a swig.

Quinn realized that the bartender was staring at them. Or rather, her. "Um. Sam, maybe you should take out your phone or something. Make it look like you're not talking to yourself."

"Who cares?" she said, letting her glass thunk a bit too forcefully against the bar. "Who cares if everything thinks I'm crazy? I'm gonna die anyway. It won't matter. None of this will matter. It'll just be a headline in the trash this town calls a newspaper: 'Crazy Armadillo Seen Raving at Tavern Just Before Unfortunate Accident.' What does that matter to a pile of dirt?"

A pile of dirt. It was hard to think of her like that: just a *thing*. Not Sam. Not car magazines or anime on the weekends. Not beer snuck from parents who looked the other way. Not itchy back plates in winter and dark polished claws. Just bones and shriveled veins, just plates that would never itch again. And him, lying beside her, stuck so far underground that he would never escape this town.

Maybe whatever was happening with them linked them in some way, because Sam looked at him with startling clarity and said, "What about you?"

"I don't think I'll get a headline."

She drained the glass, and the bartender gave her another. When he walked away, she said, "Maybe you're right."

He pressed his claws against his palms, trying to place himself in the world, trying to stop himself from floating away. He didn't want to hear this. He didn't want to hear that he was right, that he was as empty as this place. That people might mourn for Sam, even a single tear, but he was just a grain of sand in an empty ocean bed. That the only thing he had left in the world was a festering wound too old to heal.

Then she said, "But I don't think that matters. I don't think a headline means much. Lots of people die without one, but we're still sad. It's just ink, right?" They were silent for a long time, Sam sipping her drink. Sometimes she would call to someone across the room. At last she said, looking anywhere but him, "Me and my parents are gettin' better. You know that?"

He shook his head.

"Better. Not great. Maybe never great. But it's somethin'. Somethin's all you need, I think, to get started. Then you kin find another somethin', and another, and if you just keep going like that, maybe things can get better. Maybe never great. But better."

She seemed like a stranger. Just another person in town he would never understand. His chest tightened, and he squeezed his eyes shut, hearing people all around shouting and laughing and murmuring to one another, a pounding whirlpool of life that seemed impossibly far away, as reachable as the surface of the moon.

"Aren't you angry?" he asked.

She slammed her glass on the counter, sloshing out what was left of her beer. "Course I'm angry. Real angry. World's shit. But at least it's somethin'. Least I ain't—"

She cut off with a gag, hunching over. Before Quinn could respond, she stumbled from her stool and broke for the bathroom, ignoring the concerned calls of the bartender. He found her hunched over the toilet, armored back arched like a tree trembling beneath a great weight. She was shaking. Not only that, but she was fading. Her body wavered like a distant mirage in the heat of day, an apparition far ahead on the lonely road. It was as if something were trying to pull her from this realm into another. She heaved, a mocking mirror of drunkenness, and let out a tiny sob of misery. The edges of her body shivered.

"You must be in one or the other," Death had told him. *"You must."*

He could only say "Sam?" and hover the ghost of his hand over her trembling back, providing what useless comfort he could. He realized why she had so easily accepted dying. She was already halfway there.

Finally, when she seemed to be one body again, she wiped her mouth with a haunted expression and said, "Let's go."

***

Quinn wished he could help her stumble through the dark. She moved sluggishly through the main square, pressing her hand against buildings she might never see again, sometimes looking at where her claws touched the surface as if it were holy. He merely trailed behind, listening to her mumble to herself, and soon they left the buildings behind for the forest. Trees hunched over them on both sides. Night sky showed through the canopy like a line of oil drizzled into a pan, the stars distant and cold between the silhouette of pine needles.

When Sam spoke, her voice boomed in the quiet. "I can see 'em."

Quinn glanced at her.

"The shadows. Things in the dark. Moving through the trees, grass, windows. Never really believed you. But I see 'em now."

She stumbled, and as if this thing they shared had pushed against some boundary, he moved forward and put a hand against her back. He could barely feel her—just a cold pressure on his skin—but she seemed to steady.

"Thanks," she mumbled, and he knew he would never be able to respond.

Headlights appeared in the distance. The pair stopped walking and simply watched. On such a straight road, they saw it coming from so far away that it seemed slow and deliberate, like a hunter. The lights grew larger, throwing Sam's shadow to skitter across the trees, the crunch of tires deafening in the quiet night. And then it was past them, its red backlights shrinking into two glaring stars. Eventually even those faded, leaving the two with nothing but trees.

For a long moment, neither of them spoke. Then Sam spat on the ground and said, "Let's go home."

***

Quinn left her snoring drunkenly in her bed. He knew that he should spend the night trying to think of what to do next, but instead he followed the road to his childhood home. He had not lived there for over a year, but he still hoped for some kind of reaction to his disappearance—his younger siblings lying awake in their cramped rooms, his parents sitting in the living room with the lights on, worrying their hands around coffee cups filled too many times. Instead he found his older siblings trying to keep a gaggle of the younger ones quiet as they played cards in the kitchen.

He stood there watching them, a distant entity lurking in the doorway. For a moment it seemed like nothing had changed, that he was still a living rabbit standing far from the light as he watched aliens live lives that somehow had meaning.

At last he entered, unseen, and crouched by a leg of the kitchen table. Years ago he had scratched his name into the wood. Now it was gone, sanded over and painted a white already marred by stains and dents. Part of him wanted to stay. He wanted to memorize this scene, to etch into his mind this muffled laughter and heady scents of mint tea and coffee cake, to go into his parents' room and watch them breathe slow and ponderous breaths. But they were happy here without him, and if he stayed too long, perhaps he would ruin them too.

He looked up and froze. One of his sisters looked down at him, her eyes on his. Sweet Olivia, who shared her juice boxes with him until he could not bear her optimism anymore, who had that barest spark of seeing things unseen. For just a moment, he felt solid beneath her gaze, as if she were bringing him back to life. As if, just for a moment, he was real.

He ran.

Out into the forest, where the shadows moved alongside his flight and the trees cut starlight into slivers. He could not be with them. Could not bear the weight of their lives. How long until they realized he was gone? Realistically, he knew that news traveled fast in such a small town. As soon as he did not show up for work at the gas station, his boss would know. And then everyone would know. It had happened before—a boy in their high school had skipped class for four days straight before his parents found a note saying he had left for the city.

That was the last Quinn heard of him. He had left, and that meant he was good as dead.

He did not bother to go to his house. His housemates would not notice his absence, and he did not care for one last glimpse of the room he spent most of his time in. Instead he wandered through the trees, onto the main road, and past the lights. Grass stretched into the dark, his own little world that shifted as he did, as if nothing else existed beyond what he could see. The streetlights cast his shadow forward to mingle with the dark.

He pointed into the distance, where the grass disappeared into the sky. "I used to dream of walking out there."

Death stepped up beside him. They did not speak, tilting their head towards him to continue.

"I would walk and walk until I disappeared. Like slipping into the ocean. But instead of getting eaten by krill and fish, I'd be gone. Just like that. No shoes washed up on a beach. No skull lodged in the ocean floor. Just gone."

"A common pastime," Death said. "You are each given a short time to live. Yet you spend that time thinking of death. Of what you do not have. Of the emptiness, rather than the container."

"Yeah, well, this container's pretty shitty. This town's the kind of place that does nothing but strangle the life out of you. Things don't grow, they just get older. There's nothing here for any of us. Sam and I always used to talk about packing up a truck and getting out of here. We'd drive and drive until we found somewhere else, sleeping in the car and bumming twenties off strangers. But we never did. This place is like a black hole. It keeps sucking you back in. Once, Sam left to live with her cousin in another state, but then her dad got sick and she came back to help take care of him, and then it was a year later and she was still here." He breathed in the cold night air. "She always asked if there was something supernatural about it. And I just don't know. It feels like it, right? But gravity's natural, isn't it?"

Death stayed silent, staring with him into the darkness.

At last he said, this time quieter, "Sometimes I wonder if I can ever leave. Or will this place just keep pulling me back, year after year?

Was there really any other place for my life to end but here?"

"And here you remain, even in death."

He tugged an ear. "Clearly. Look, me and Sam tried something—I'm sure you noticed. But it did squat. What now?"

"You keep trying."

"What if she just—" He stopped and swallowed, the words feeling thick in his mouth. "If nothing else will do the deed, what if she just, you know, took matters into her own hands?"

Death turned to him, eyes two stars in a field of void. "What do you think happens to the soul of a body that dies when its soul is still trapped? Do you think it moves on?"

"Okay, that's out of the question." He shuddered and began to pace, trying to shove his mind from that line of thought. "I just—I don't get it. Why is this happening? What could cause someone to break away from death, or whatever the hell is happening? Why her?"

"You know."

He laughed and crouched down, gripping his stomach, trying to catch the panic inside of him so it would not spill out and infect the town. "Called out by Death, huh? Harsh."

This was his fault. He had always known it, but it was easy to push away the truth when you were dead. Nothing seemed real now—not the night air, not the truck making its lazy way down the road behind him. Not the fact that all this was because of him. Because he saw the dark things at night and left tins of milk on his bedroom windowsill. Because he made charms from wood and rings and dolls. Because he had always been just a bit supernatural, and she had been his friend.

A low rumble came from somewhere in Death's bones—not a growl, but a thoughtful noise, like a philosopher with an armchair and pipe. When they spoke, their voice was slow and deliberate. "Some of us are meant to be lonely. Some can only cause pain to those they touch. For us, it is best to never touch. To be apart. To be lonely."

"I tried to stay away," he whispered.

"The damage had been done. I am sorry."

Quinn looked back. The road cut a glaring horizon. It seemed so distant, but he could feel it in his heart. He could feel the rumble of the car engine, hear the hollow roar of nothing all around him. Sam's hand gripped his own, claws drawing blood from his palm. They could both feel it—the call of the void, the howl of things unseen, the hands that gripped every nerve and pushed them forward, begging for something to give it all meaning. The strobe of passing street-lights cut every shape into its components, slicing them thin for rapid moments at a time: the curve of the dashboard, the harsh lines of the shadows, the frantic swoops of the hula girl as she danced a last desperate plea. In those brief flashes of light, one could almost believe the world was real.

"I tried," he said again. "I tried to get away."

He looked up, but Death was gone, leaving him alone with the stars.

***

Years ago, Sam and Quinn had found a cabin in the woods. It was old and decrepit and had not seen life in years. The walls were rotting, and the fireplace looked as if it might collapse at any moment, but it was theirs. The other kids were afraid of Sam and weren't quite sure what to do about Quinn, so they left it alone. It was a place away from town, something they could claim as their own.

Quinn had not been back in years. It held too many memories. Now he followed Sam in through the rotting doorway, feeling as if he had stepped into the past. The ancient table they had repaired was gone, but aside from a small pile of cigarette butts and empty chip bags from the gas station, the place was the same as he remembered.

"You're sure this will work?" Sam asked as she crouched down. She shoved a crowbar into the floorboards, beginning to wedge open the crawlspace.

"I think a physical object binding the two of us together might be important—it might even be responsible. Kind of like how ghosts stick around because they have unfinished business, you know? Though it'd be easier to know if you would tell me exactly what you're looking for." He paused. "And what makes you think our stuff is still here, anyway? It's been awhile, and—"

Sam grunted as the trap door popped open, coughing dust into the air—but not as much as Quinn would have expected. "I know because I left it here."

It was their book. One of them, anyway—Quinn had lost count

of how many they had made, and he had thrown his out years ago. Sam set it on the floor and flipped through the pages, not really reading, just watching wave after wave of scribbled words and smudged drawings. For as long as they could, Sam and Quinn had escaped from their own bleak thoughts in the world of make-believe. Neither of them ever took writing seriously, but in some ways that made it easy. They could do whatever they wanted in those pages—knights riding dragons, accountants haunted by ghosts, biker gangs traveling across the country on adventures their writers could only dream about. As they grew older, their stories seemed like the only way for them to get out of this town.

Almost.

Sam stopped on a page with no words, just the scribbled sketch of a shadow among the trees, the thing staring out with what Quinn now recognized as longing. She rubbed the dog-eared edge of the page between her fingers. "We really have to burn it?"

He wanted to say that it was no good to them whole. That she would be gone soon one way or another, dead or torn apart by a world that she cannot fit, and it would not matter what state it was in. That it had meant nothing for years anyway.

Instead he just said, "We have to try," and watched her rub the page until it smudged.

Sam started the fire. Quinn helped in whatever way he could, pointing her towards fallen branches and even managing to pick up a few twigs, but mostly he could only watch her set the fireplace alight as they had done countless times before. They had waited most of the day for Sam's hangover to fade, and now night gathered on the horizon.

They sat in front of the fire, silent for a long moment. They just watched the flames, remembering how they used to sit here for hours, trying to forget the world around them, trying to find something solid to grasp onto. At last, Sam opened the notebook to a page at random and carefully tore it out. Quinn recognized the story: a retelling of a legend they had heard on TV, where the first rabbit had challenged the first meerkat to a race for the title of King of the Plains, and the meerkat tunneled directly to the other side of the world to win. In their version, the rabbit realized that he did not care if he won or lost, because the title of "king" meant nothing. He simply kept running.

Sam balled up the page and tossed it into the fire, and the rabbit ran forever in ash. She tossed in another. Together, they watched the pages crumble and blacken, curling in on themselves as if in pain. She continued her slow destruction. Rip, toss, crackle. The fire ate fast. It seemed hungry for the desperation of those lonely teenagers, those hands grasping for something to hold. Quinn thought of the stars and the wide-open sky, and how many things in life were hungry, and how quickly those things consumed.

Sam held out the notebook. Quinn stared down at the page, where the scribbled shadow looked out at him from the trees. He slowly ripped out the paper and tossed it gently into the flames, watching it crackle and disappear. It was the easiest thing he had done since he died.

Rip, toss, crackle. Their memories burned to ash. Rip, toss, crackle. Evidence disappeared.

The notebook dwindled, and then it was gone.

They sat entrenched in the crackling light, watching things burn and realizing that burning could not fix this. Quinn felt as if the fire had raged through his body and left nothing behind, a blackened shell of a forest once vibrant and green. But he'd never really been a place where a bird could build a home. Never had the strength of a tree or the fullness that came from looking around and not seeing the horizon—just trees and bushes and hills, just things you could touch.

Sam stared at her hand, watching it waver like a distant mirage, her whole body shivering into something not quite real, something half-glimpsed in a dream.

"You should have burned that book a long time ago," he said, numb.

She curled her hands into fists, refusing to look at him. "Don't you dare blame me for this."

"I'm not—"

"Shut up!" She swiveled to him with a flash of that familiar rage, that blazing, all-consuming resentment death seemed to soften. Her body shifted away from itself, images vibrating around her as if she were trying to escape from her body. "We both know this is your fault. It's always your fault. Again and again you drag me down with you into your little pity parties. Just like back then. Just like that night you turned the wheel and drove us off the side of the road."

Maybe it was because of the burning notebook, or because he could still feel the ghost of her hand around his, or because he was just so damn tired, but he surged to his feet with whiskers quivering with rage. "The only reason it didn't work was because you chickened out! Damn it, Sam, I didn't force you into that car! We chose together to end it all, and you—!" He stopped, air suddenly burning his lungs, as if he had swallowed the fire and everything it consumed. "You changed your mind. We made a decision, we got into that car together, and you *changed your mind.*"

He could feel it again, that momentum she tried to stop. That stone that had been picking up speed for as long as he could remember, tumbling faster and faster until it was there with them in the car, rushing down the road with the universe around them, so far and so clear and so crystalline sharp that he could reach out the window and cut himself.

Sam's voice came from a distance, as if reaching backwards in time to speak into the memory. "And you still turned the wheel."

Her claws yanking from his hand and gripping the wheel, her distorted voice yelling at him through the screaming of the wind to stop. He stepped back, trying to break from the memory, trying to cement himself in the crappy little cabin with the flickering fire. They had never talked about this before. They had simply broken apart. The town thought it was a stupid act of reckless driving, not a suicide attempt gone wrong. No one questioned them separating after that, they just patched the two of them up and grounded them for eternity, but some wounds could not heal. Raw and untouched, shoved into the dark and locked away so they could claim they were never there at all.

Until now. He was stuck here, locking eyes with the girl he had almost killed all those years ago and who now broke apart because of him. The girl who had agreed to step with him into the dark. The girl who changed her mind. Who decided life was worth living.

Who trembled and broke apart before him now, eyes filling with tears, breath coming in heaves, as she knelt before the fireplace and sobbed, "Oh, Quinn. I don't want to die."

He was jealous of her. That hit him like a branch broken lose from its tree. He was jealous of her because she had looked inside herself and found something worth saving.

And he had not.

Quinn ran.

It was the only thing he was good at, always a flightful rabbit at heart, the quickest on the track team until he couldn't take the people anymore and just ran alone, through the woods, shadows keeping pace on either side, hungry and so close he could touch them. And he wasn't even good enough to escape this town. He ran through the trees, leaping over roots before he even saw them, feeling the contours of the land beneath his feet, a sort of ancient instinct rushing inside of him that whispered, *Go, run, they're after you. The only thing you have is speed. Rely on your feet to push you forward, rely on your ears to hear their blood, but above everything else, run.*

But he was far past the time when a rabbit could outrun his enemies.

Space broke open before him. The sunset burned the fields, setting it alight with oranges and yellows that seemed as hungry as the fire, devouring whatever space it could fill. He tossed his sneakers aside and raced over the road and into the grass. His heart pounded. His blood pulsed. He ran and he ran and he ran. The sun threw his shadow behind him, nipping his heels until they bled. He wanted to run forever. He wanted to be like that first rabbit, not because he knew he could never win, though he did, but because he wanted to capture that feeling he once had when he ran, that he was the only thing in the world, that nothing else mattered but his body. That there was something strong inside of him.

He was dead. He deserved that freedom.

"Stop."

He glanced back but did not stop. The trees and the town formed a distant line. He could feel Death around him.

"What happens if I keep going?" he asked. He did not feel tired. He felt like he could go on forever.

"Your friend will suffer. Her imbalance will grow. She will rupture eternally, trapped between two worlds, forever broken."

He was tired of tearing himself apart. "And me?"

Death was silent for a long moment. The sun sank into the grass. Darkness swept across the sky in a slow and steady creep, devouring the light.

"You will disappear."

Just gone. No more town, no more hollow body, no more people he could hurt.

"Not like your ocean. But also not like your dream. You will disappear, but only as you. In this empty place, on the edge of everything, you will break apart. Piece by piece, split. Piece by piece, still feeling, still knowing, but broken into the universe. You will be part of everything. But only here. Only the everything of this place. Only these trees, these stones, these people. Quinn McCarver, if you run into this field before you are able to move on, you will still not escape."

He could feel tears on the fur of his cheeks, feel them run down his whiskers and drop into the grass. Feel the heaving in his chest, more grief than exhaustion. His legs pumped, his feet thumping an ancient rhythm of fear. The plains were all around him now, hills and trees and buildings nowhere to be seen, just grass and empty space and the great vastness of sky above, the stars so distant and huge that he could never hope to touch them, so far and so steady and so damn free.

He imagined being a part of this place forever, broken apart into a million pieces. He would still be here, but at least he would no longer be him. He would just be the pieces of Quinn McCarver, the rabbit so useless he could not even run from his problems, the rabbit who sat alone at night and feared the stars. The rabbit who would never find a place he could fill.

The rabbit who turned the wheel.

He could feel the universe around him as he ran, just like that night. The call of the void, the streetlights cutting the dashboard into fragments of time until they finally faded and there was only outlines of starlight. His hand gripping the wheel, the tight leather warm beneath his sweaty grip. And Sam, steady Sam, angry Sam, breathing in sync with his howling lungs.

And then the shift. The thick armadillo claws on the wheel, a foot trying to jam onto the brakes, an elbow knocking the hula girl aside. His eyes glued to the darkness ahead, the only way he could pretend to be free, the only thing that mattered now, more real than anything else could pretend to be, not even his best friend whose howls came from a distance, from some other realm.

A skeletal hand brushed his shoulder, just once. A gentle touch.

And this time, wrapped within the memory, Quinn turned his head. Sam was crying. The world had slowed, and he watched as single fat tear rolled down her face and flick away as she jerked her head, looking from him to the road to him again, eyes full of terror. It was the terror of someone who had gotten into a car to die and changed her mind. The terror of someone who wanted to live.

The terror of someone who could see the plains of her life spreading before her and found hope. Found a cousin who asked if she was okay. Parents who got better. A bartender she knew by name. A peace enough to want to live. All from the same seed as him, all from this same moment howling through the dark, the universe around them, empty but for possibility. He realized she had changed, not just her mind so long ago, but everything.

Squeezing his weeping eyes shut, Quinn hit the brakes.

***

When he opened his eyes, he half expected to awake in the car, crumbled and broken but still alive, Sam by his side. Instead he lay on his back in the field, staring up at the stars as dew dampened his shirt. The streetlights to his left cast shadows from every blade of grass.

He was still dead. Sam was still dying.

Death beckoned him. He stayed there for a long moment, ears still ringing from the echoes of memory, and then he got to his feet and followed. They walked along the road until the streetlights disappeared. Shadows lurked in the trees, but Quinn was not afraid. He had seen how far the horizon could go. He was not afraid of something not brave enough to step into the light.

They found Sam at the same time they found his body. She knelt by the gnarled remains of his car, pulling grass from the earth and letting it sprinkle back down. She was crying again, but this time it was a softer crying, as if she were accepting her tears rather than forcing them to burst from her like a flood. It was an active kind of grief. A willing participation.

Quinn stopped by the twisted carcass of his car, which wrapped itself around the tree as if seeking comfort, burying its face into the crumpled bark. The tree bent slightly towards the wreck. One branch hung limply, brushing consolingly against the compressed metal of the roof. A bit of blood flecked the inside of the driver-side window. It was still red, not yet browned by age. Quinn touched the back of the car, gentle at first, almost afraid it might hurt him, and then he pressed his whole palm against the metal. It was cold. Something hard and slimy lodged in his throat.

So this was it. He had tried again, and this time there had been no one to stop him.

"I kind of assumed," Sam said. She sniffed and rubbed her nose with her arm. "I just—Death brought me here."

Quinn looked at Death. "You never told me."

"It would not have helped."

He sank to the ground next to Sam, both of them staring at the wreck. He was not sure how to break the silence. What do you say to your best friend as you sit in front of your corpse? What could make any of this better?

She spoke first, voice rough with emotion. "I'm sorry. I shouldn't have yelled at you. This wasn't your fault."

He shrugged. With every emotion struggling within his stomach, it was hard to think of how else to respond. "It's not like you were wrong."

"I know, I just…" She took a long, shaking breath. "I'm sorry, okay? What we did back then, it wasn't all your fault. We chose together. We were two messed up kids, and you didn't force me into anything. I—really, I'm glad I left after that, I think it was for the best, but I shouldn't have left you behind. I should have told someone. I should have—should have thought about how much you were hurting too."

He stared at her, that thing in his throat feeling as if it were trying to crawl its way out of his mouth and tell her no, it was all him, she had always been perfect, he deserved everything she had ever said to him.

But he couldn't, because she was looking at him with eyes so full of life, so different from the shriveled husk that clung to his skin. He remembered all those years ago, when they would sit on her roof with sweaty beers in their paws and dream about what they would do when they left this town, and she would look at him with those eyes, so clear and tangible that he wanted to wrap himself in their life, and for a just a moment he could feel something fill the empty space inside his body.

"I'm sorry," he said, and that was when they broke. He threw his arms around her and she held him tight, held him like the car held the tree, but he wasn't sure which one was which because they were both crying, years of everything all pouring out at once. Quinn felt as if his body were trying to burst, as if something was pushing out from inside his chest. His throat squeezed, trying to keep it inside, but the flood would not be contained. He had thought there was nothing inside him. But he could feel it, and it hurt.

When they finally pulled themselves apart, they did not bother to move away. They leaned against each other as they had all those years ago, one more time. One more moment of comfort.

"I should have told someone, so you could get help too," she said again, sounding raw and stuffed up, as if her emotions had solidified and plugged her nose.

"I guess we both have things we regret."

She slowly tipped back and lay against the dirt, looking up at the stars. He joined her. The stars never seemed so bad when he watched them with her.

When she spoke again, her voice was quiet. "It's a shame, though. That it took dying for us to talk."

"You're not dead yet."

She laughed and help up her hand, as if cupping a constellation in her palm. Through the gray skin and black claws, he could see the stars. He reached up and touched one of her claws. The black seemed smooth and fresh, as if she had put on another layer of polish

"I can't be that mad," she said. "Well, no. I can be furious. And I was, for a while, and about a lot of things. But not for this. Not for a few last moments." She smirked. "Even if I have to spend them with you."

He laughed. It felt good to laugh, a foreign thing that made his throat ache. He twined his fingers around her own, still held against the sky, and they watched her fade. He felt as if he were holding ice turning into water and then into steam. A part of him went with her. He was solid as ever—as solid as a dead rabbit could be—but he felt a sliver of himself devolve. He wanted to clutch onto her, to hold her here, to stop the only substantial thing in this town from fading away, but he did not want to make it harder for her. She deserved that, at least.

She deserved so much more, really, but all he could do was hold her hand as she faded away. She was crying, but her eyes blazed with determination. It was almost the same expression she had when she stepped in the car, but this time she was happier. He could tell, perhaps because he was holding her now as her layers fell away one by one, or because he could see what others could not, or maybe just because he knew her, but he could feel that she could accept this tragedy for what it was: heartbreaking, but unstoppable. She knew she could not stop a wave from crashing into the shore, so instead she rode it. They held each other's hand and felt the cool water and cried for the tragedy of both of them, or not just now but forever, of everything that had hurt them and everything they had done to hurt each other, those wounds that would never quite heal.

"I'm glad we were friends," he said, and even though she was hardly a wisp of existence, she squeezed his hand so tight her claw pierced his skin.

She disappeared. He held her hand for just a moment after he could no longer see her, and then there was nothing. She was gone.

He pressed his palms hard against his eyes, savoring the hurt, his throat raw and his chest feeling as if his ribs had shrunk and pulled everything tight, piercing his lungs and his heart and things he didn't even know where there.

"What happens now?" he whispered.

"They find her body on the side of the road," Death said, sounding close.

For just a moment, he allowed himself to think of it—someone finding Sam lying dead in the dirt, a solemn funeral, a mourning town. For her. What about him? Would they mourn him too?

"But you…"

He pulled his hands from his face and looked to Death, who stood above him and looked down the road, towards the light of the town. "Huh?" He sat up abruptly. "I can go now, right? Please don't tell me we went through all that shit and I still can't leave this place. Please don't tell me I'm still stuck here."

"No. I can take you now. I know it. But." They stayed silent for a moment, and then their head swung around to him, and for a moment Quinn thought he saw the curve of a skull inside their hood, maybe a snout of dog or the slope of an anteater or even the two sharp teeth of a rabbit, or maybe all at once, shifting back and forth until they were one. "Perhaps you are not dead."

His head buzzed. He must have misheard them. "What?"

"This place is strange, and you are strange, and perhaps together we can give you another try. I do not know how long. Years, days, hours. But would one day not be enough?"

It took him a moment to connect the dots. "But… but that's not fair. Sam's the one who deserves more time, not me."

"No," Death said. "If one lives, one dies. All beings who live deserve death. When that comes is not a matter of deserving. A coin does not deserve to fall on one side more than the other. It simply *is.*"

When Quinn was younger, he would have loved to debate philosophy with Death. But now his head spun and his heart ached and he just wanted to know where he would be in the morning. "Can't you bring her back instead?"

"It is by your power that this might be done. It must be you. Years ago, your friend changed her mind. Now it is your turn."

Another chance. He looked at the wreckage. Who was to say that in another few years, he would not end up here again? Would more time really change who he was? "*Somethin's all you need,*" Sam had said. Perhaps she was right. Perhaps one day was all he needed. And then the next, and the next, until he found something worth living for. If she could do it, could he?

He looked up at them. "You said some of us are meant to be apart from everyone else. Why offer this, then? Wouldn't dying be the best way to keep me apart?"

Death was silent for a moment. Then they reached up and touched something inside of their hood, and for a moment he saw that everything skull. "Perhaps I was wrong."

"Will you visit?"

He had never thought he would hear Death surprised. "Me?"

"Sure. You've got the time, don't you? I'd love to chat when I'm not worrying about the state of my soul."

They were silent for a moment. "And where would I find you?"

He looked down the road, first towards the light of the town and then out into darkness. "I'm not sure. But I don't think it matters that much where I go. Maybe leaving will help, or maybe it won't. Maybe this place was never the problem. If I move, it won't matter if I'm still miserable. So I don't know."

"Not knowing is the most a living thing can do. Stand."

Quinn got to his feet. Death stood still for a moment, and then they gently touched their staff to his shoulder. The universe was all around him, but this time it was calm. It spread out into eternity, so empty and so wide that nothing could ever hope to fill it—but that was not quite true. The eternity was a thing of itself. Quinn realized that on an infinitesimal level, everything touched—the grass to the earth, the earth to the trees, the trees to the air, and even the stars so many light years away, their light and particles all touching each other as much as anything ever could, and as long as any flicker of a star's light ever touched anything else, even after the star was dead and decaying far away, it had some kind of connection to another thing.

And then he and Death stood in the empty field for just a moment, just a fraction of the universe set in motion.

"What will you do?" Death asked.

Quinn looked up at the stars, who spread out before him like a prayer, and realized that maybe they weren't so scary after all. "I think I'm going to call my family."

They disappeared.

BLACK OUT IN SPACE

Mary E. Lowd

The lights had gone out ten minutes ago. The sound of the air circulators had shut down too. Narchi didn't know what was happening, but she was scared. Power shouldn't shut down on a space station. Yet she had to hold herself together. Her lapine roommates had left her babysitting nearly a dozen of their children. When she'd agreed, she hadn't expected it to be in the dark.

Tiny lapines with strong legs and big feet bounced off the walls in their quarters. Literally. Fuzzy bodies rocketed past each other in every which direction, occasionally thudding into the broad, thick-hided side of their buffalo-like host. Narchi let out a soft, "Oof!" whenever one of the lapine kits knocked into her, but she didn't mind. Not really.

Narchi had been sharing her quarters with an extended family of uplifted lapines for several months, ever since the rabbit-like sentients had escaped from their homeworld.

So Narchi was used to a certain amount of frenetic bouncing around her. But usually, it wasn't in the dark. All of her instincts told her that darkness meant stillness. Her species were plains-folk from a planet with five moons. So she'd never before experienced the type of darkness that happens on a space station during a black out. It was a total darkness, the kind that can only be found deep inside a cave on most planets, and it didn't seem to bother the lapine children. Their species had been uplifted from burrowers.

Narchi wasn't an expert on child-rearing, but bouncing in the dark seemed like the kind of activity that the adult in charge was supposed to stop. Since she was the babysitter right now, that meant her.

With a bellowing, bovine voice, Narchi mooed into the darkness, "Settle down now! No more hopping!"

Lapine giggles erupted around her. The hopping didn't stop. In fact, from the increased fuzzy pummeling of her side, Narchi could only conclude that they'd used her moo as a way to target her in the total dark.

Narchi sighed. This would not do. The little lapines were going to break things, knock over furniture, and hurt themselves if they kept this up. They needed a better activity.

Going against her own instincts, Narchi felt her way through the darkness, moving slowly and touching everything with her hoof-hands to keep from bumping into things. That is, things other than the little lapines, some of whom had clung onto her hunched shoulders for a ride. Finally, she found the drawer where Roscoe, one of the adult lapines, kept his knitting. She pulled out a ball of the Eridanii arachni-silk yarn and started tying loops into it at regular intervals—tricky work in the dark.

Narchi hooked her own hoof-hand through one of the loops, held the knotted mess of yarn out and mooed, "Come over here, little ones. Each of you find a loop of yarn and hold on tight with your paw."

A chorus of chirpy voices assaulted her with questions:

"Why?"

"Is it a game?"

"Are we going somewhere?"

As they questioned her, Narchi felt little tugs on the yarn that meant the lapine children were grabbing the loops. "Yes," she mooed. "We're going on a walk." The lights might be down in their quarters, but there had to be light, at least minimal light, in the more communal parts of Crossroads Station. And if they got out of their darkened quarters, maybe Narchi would have a chance of finding out what was going on.

Before leaving, Narchi placed her hoof-hand on each of the lapine children's heads in turn, between their long ears. She counted fifteen; that was everyone. "Stay close," she said.

The strange parade—a sentient buffalo followed by more than a dozen sentient bunnies, following her like little ducklings—lumbered and hopped their way down the hallways of Crossroads Station's residential quarter in the dark. Narchi held her loop of yarn with one hoof-hand and trailed the other hoof-hand along the wall, feeling her way.

"I see something!" one of the little lapines squeaked.

Narchi still couldn't see anything, but the lapines' eyes were better than hers. Their ears too. All their senses seemed to be stronger. Sometimes, she felt like a giant dull lump around the bouncy little things.

"I see it too!" a chorus of little lapines cried.

Suddenly, Narchi found herself tugged forward by the yarn as all her little bunny-ducklings hopped towards the dim source of light.

"It's the Merchant Quarter!" one of the lapines chirped. "Can we get Hegulan churros?"

The other children started chirping about all sorts of other treats they wanted to buy, and Narchi realized she'd left her ident card in their quarters. She also realized that she had no idea how to find her way back to their quarters through the dark. "Let's find out what's going on first."

All the little lapines moaned in disappointment.

The Merchant Quarter was extra busy, aliens of all shapes and sizes milling together, staring up at the windows that curved over the wide hallway that was always filled with food stands and vendor stalls.

The stars had never looked so bright. They twinkled in the darkness. The only light came from a few emergency lanterns embedded along the walls, so the entire quarter was trapped in a strange, dim twilight.

Narchi gathered her lapine wards in close, counting from one to fifteen repeatedly, checking to make sure none of the long-eared children had strayed.

A double-winged avian alien—an Eechee—approached the funny group and cawed to Narchi, "You look a little overwhelmed."

Several of the lapine children had climbed onto Narchi's wide back again. One of them had clambered all the way up to sit on her shoulders, holding her two crescent horns like handlebars. "You could say that," Narchi agreed.

"This is Roscoe's family, isn't it?" the Eechie cawed. "I'm Chorif.

He's gone on salvage trips with me."

"What happened?" Narchi mooed. "Does anyone know?"

An ursine alien, large and furry like Narchi, heard their conversation and joined in: "I heard it's a space storm."

"An electro-magnetic pulse from a solar flare," offered an orange-furred canine alien, one of the station's most common species.

Somehow the darkness and uncertainty drew everyone together. Aliens who would usually never talk to each other, too busy with their own lives, now had nothing better to do than stand around and speculate about the station-wide power outage.

"How long do you think it will last?" Narchi asked, her head wrenching suddenly to the side as the lapine on her shoulders decided to try steering her using her horns.

Chorif laughed at the sight, a cackling cawing sound. "You've got your hands full, haven't you? How'd you end up in charge of so many of Roscoe's younger kin?"

The little lapine on Narchi's shoulders piped up: "We share quarters! She watches us when the b'dults are busy!"

"Roscoe and their other parents got a job checking the sound-proofing and acoustics on a recording studio cruiser that belongs to some visiting reptilian pop star," Narchi explained. "Good ears, you know. They left right before the power went out."

"Star Shaker—I love her music," Chorif said, ruffling out the feathers in her lower wings. "I know where her ship's docked. Want me to take you there?"

Narchi eyed the restless little bunnies huddled around her, ears drooping. "I think what we really need is..." She was reluctant to say it around them, but whispering would do no good. Their ears could hear anything she said. "A snack."

Drooping ears perked up, and fifteen little noses started twitching eagerly. "Oh, yes, please," said many little hopeful voices.

A green-skinned amphibian alien with a long snake-like tail instead of legs slithered over and said, "Head over to the grav-bubble playground—the play-structures are down, but all the merchants with quickly perishable food are giving away what they can't sell fast enough."

"Thank you," Narchi said. She knew the way to the playground.

The buffalo led her herd of bunnies through the unusually friendly crowds, accompanied by Roscoe's double-winged avian friend. When they reached the playground, they found that all manner of alien children were playing low-tech games of chase and tag. Merchants of all species plied them with sticky, melting, frozen treats. For the little ones, a station-wide power outage was heaven.

Now that Narchi's wards were under control and busy playing, she stuffed the Eridanii arachni-silk yarn in her pocket. The terror she'd been holding at bay, inside a knot deep in her stomach, flowed out and filled her body. It hadn't been safe to feel it before now, not with all the little bunnies depending on her. "No one answered any of the real questions while I had fifteen babies clinging to me," Narchi mooed softly to Chorif. "How common is this? How long will it last? Will it get fixed? What happens if it doesn't?"

"You haven't been a citizen of space long, have you?" Chorif cawed, watching the lapines play.

"Less than a year. I was picked up by a passing research team; my species hasn't made it to space on our own yet."

"Power outages in space are rare and bad," Chorif cawed, feathers ruffling all over her body. "To knock a space station like Crossroads out, we're dealing with a one in a million storm. The EM waves had to be powerful enough to blow out everything but the most protected systems; that means even those of us with our own spaceships—I have my own little cargo hauler—can't wake up our ships to get out of here until the storm subsides. Either the waves die down in the next few hours or…"

"Or people stop being nice to each other," Narchi said.

"I don't know about that. If no one has anywhere to go, there's not a lot left to fight over."

The somber thought settled over them. Narchi wondered if she should take the young ones looking for their parents, so they could all be together. She tried not to think: "die together." The lapines seemed so powerful with their acute senses most of the time, but right now, they seemed small and delicate. Narchi's large body was built for weathering droughts and storms. She didn't want to watch these bunnies die.

She didn't want to die. Suddenly, Narchi wished that she'd sent more radio messages home during the last year.

"I think it's better if we stay here," Narchi said. "The little ones are happy playing. I'm sure Roscoe and the others will find us." On an impulse, Narchi asked her new friend, "Do you have any regrets?"

"Other than being here today instead of on some random lush forest planet?" Chorif cawed, folding her wings up tight.

"Other than that."

"Not a one."

Narchi nodded her heavy buffalo head. "That's a good way to live." And when she thought about it, she didn't really have any regrets either. Not big ones. When given the chance, she'd taken the risk and left her homeworld. She'd seen more of the universe than any other member of her species.

The lights flickered: darker, brighter, darker, and finally all the way out. For a few startling heartbeats, the entire merchant quarter was drowned in velvet darkness, lit only by the twinkling stars.

Then the metal floor hummed under Narchi's hooves, and the entire station vibrated back to life. The lights flashed on, blindingly bright. Cries of childhood despair filled the playground—their power outage adventure was over. But the rest of the merchant quarter gasped, hundreds of individuals letting out a breath of relief as if one.

"How about you?" Chorif cawed. "Any regrets? Cause it looks like you'll have a chance to do something about them."

Fifteen lapine children swarmed the buffalo sentient, tugging at her shaggy fur and hopping around her hooves. "The gravity bubbles are working again! Come play with us!" Just as quickly, they swarmed off and, one by one, hopped into the grav-bubbles to spin and float around the playground.

"I feel like I should have realized something important…" Narchi scratched at the base of her left crescent horn. "Like it's time to go home. Or to explore the universe further."

Chorif shrugged her upper wings. "Facing death doesn't have to be deep."

"Maybe just that living on a space station isn't safe…?"

Again the Eechie shrugged, this time with her lower wings. "This storm was one in a million, remember? Is anywhere really safe?"

"I guess not…" Narchi watched the little lapines playing, and all she could think was that it looked fun. And she was happy living on Crossroads Station.

But she was also happy that the power was back on.

THE DETECTIVE, THE WIFE, THE HUSBAND, AND HIS LOVERS

Maya Levine

The scene was fairly clean, and Laura was both disappointed and relieved. She had never been fond of blood, but she had been excited to get her first murder assigned to her. Even if Hall was still technically supervising her.

Then she caught sight of the body.

She had known that many of the professors lived in this area, but she hadn't realized that this was Professor Bushman's house. She found herself gagging slightly but stopped before Hall could have the satisfaction of calling her weak. Professor Bushman was hanging in the closet, his body perfectly still. His dull grey fur blended in with the blacks and greys and whites and blues of the closet behind him. There was a single red shirt in the corner. His vest was undone and hanging strangely. He had no trousers. There was no warmth or life beneath the fur, no anything. Just quiet. He could've been hanging there for years.

Laura looked away on instinct, feeling voyeuristic. The Bushmans must have slept in the indentation in the ground. The soil there was carefully raked. There were two dressers. She could see something lurking in the darkness under one. She thought of asking Hall, but no, she didn't need him to confirm what she already knew. She may have been a lowly goat to his eagle, but her eyes were sharp, and she was fiercely protective of what good traits she had.

She approached the dresser and bent down. There was a small hairpin there, two long talons and a glimmering jewel on the end.

She heard Hall's talons scrape up the soil of the warren as he approached the body and the closet. She glanced back and saw him getting all of the angles on the body as best he could. It was almost obscene. Laura approached, too, almost expecting to see Professor Bushman yell incoherently in an attempt to get her to scream. He didn't. He stayed where he was. He was dead. Laura couldn't keep her sharp goat's-eyes from glancing downwards. Rosamunde had always said that he liked getting her naked on his desk. But now Professor Bushman was the one that had none of the power. No, less than that—he had no brilliance, no glory, no PhDs or papers to his name. He had nothing. He was nothing.

"Should I get out my smelling salts, Faraday?"

Laura flinched, looking at Hall. His eyes were severe, and with his beak pointed her way she felt like prey once more.

"I'm fine."

"Good. I don't think being a detective is your line of work if you get sick at seeing dead bodies. Especially one like this."

"How do you mean?"

"No blood. I hate people that pass out at the sight of blood. It's just... blood. Liquid in our veins. Nothing more."

"In our veins being the key words here, I think."

"Get used to it, Faraday. They won't all be like this—hanging cases, I mean, nor just the ones that overdosed. Sometimes you'll walk into a bathroom and be surprised by the amount of red that one body can have inside of it."

Laura couldn't help but shudder slightly. "Do you have to be so visceral? Can we just focus on the body? It's a suicide, right? There's no signs of a struggle. Rigor mortis set in while he was hanging here. Pale. If we move the sheets, there'll probably be a furrow."

"Let forensics get the body down. But you're right, I think. No motive."

Laura thought of Rosamunde. The other rabbit had once said that Professor Bushman would only allow himself to die by the Plague or through a suicide. Nothing else would be dramatic enough for him, nothing as powerful as he wanted. *The man loves his power,* Rosamunde had once said, and laughed.

"Did you take his classes?"

"Yes. American Literature. It was… fascinating, the way he taught it. I've always hated English, but—"

"When did you get the impression that I care about your life? Focus. Mrs. Bushman is waiting for us downstairs."

Mrs. Bushman. Of course Laura had known that Professor Bushman was married, he wore his band with pride and liked to boast about how talented and beautiful his wife was, how unusual it was that he, a rabbit, had married a fox, but the fabled Mrs. Bushman had never factored into Laura's existence all that much. In Rosamunde and Laura's last fight, Laura had asked her to think about how Mrs. Bushman must feel. Rosamunde had said that she should be grateful. Laura's eyes flickered again to Professor Bushman's nakedness. She would rather have had the blood.

"Faraday? *Faraday!*"

"Sorry!"

"Dammit, Faraday, if you can't focus—"

"I'm fine!"

"Look," Hall said, suddenly calm and sympathetic. "Maybe this isn't a good idea. You're close to the victim. You're just out of college. Young. No wonder you can't handle this one."

"No!" Laura snapped. It was about her being female, she knew it. Hall and his stupid assumptions. It was September 1980. Hall needed to get over it.

"You'll have more chances—"

"I can handle it!"

Hall's eyes snapped again. "Then act like it. Let's go."

Forget me telling you about the hairpin, Henry Hall! Laura followed him out of the room. She could feel Professor Bushman's eyes boring into her back, his empty eyes and his naked bottom half, and even though she felt disgust and grief and fear over death and everything that it entailed, she couldn't hold off the sense of fascination, the sense of joy. Theodore Bushman, Laura's very first murder mystery! Wait until everyone heard about *that!*

The warren was a picture of what money could buy. It had soil floors but brick walls and fancy paintings hanging off of them. There were fireplaces and gold trim, elaborate wallpaper and what Laura thought might've been a dumbwaiter. Rosamunde had never actually been inside this house, despite the affair. *Take that,* Laura thought, but with less verve than she usually would. Someone was dead, she reminded herself, someone who was someone. Someone big. Someone that she knew.

Mrs. Bushman was waiting for them in the parlor, her entire form shaking. Her handkerchief was covering most of her face, but Laura could still see the tears flowing from her eyes. Had she known about her husband's affairs?

"How are you doing, Mrs. Bushman?"

Laura could tell that Hall was trying his best to be sensitive, but while he was a brilliant detective and a crack shot, he was awful at pretending. Mrs. Bushman looked at him with dead eyes, the tears flowing freely.

"How do you *think?* I'm sorry, I didn't mean—it's just—"

"Of course. You're distraught. It's a horrible tragedy."

Don't sound so wooden, Hall!

"We have an opinion. We'd just like to hear yours."

"My—opinion? On what?"

Mrs. Bushman sounded terrified. She took a deep breath, really more of a wheeze, but her tail didn't stop nervously thumping on the couch. Her fur was lank and Laura was somehow reminded of the body upstairs. "I'm sorry—I'm so sorry—I'm usually not like this, usually I'm very polite, ask anyone, it's just that—well, I think it's a suicide. I've given my statement—we had a fight. He wanted to—to have sex, and I wasn't ready yet, my health's been pretty bad since I got pneumonia a few months ago—so I left, I stormed out, really, the wait staff is gone for the day but maybe they heard it in the next house over—"

"Take a breath, Mrs. Bushman. It's all right."

"And then I came back. And he was just—*hanging* there. And I made it to the bathroom and vomited pretty badly, and—I'm sorry—I just let him die, didn't I? I drove him to it! It's my fault!"

"It's a suicide, Mrs. Bushman. It's not your fault. Don't take it too much to heart."

"To *heart*? He was my *husband*! We were married for twenty years!"

Hall stood, uncomfortable. "Faraday, perhaps it's best that you handle this."

Laura enjoyed her victories when she could. At least he's willing to admit that he doesn't show any empathy whatsoever. She sat down in his place, ready to the damage. Wait until everyone heard about this! Oh, wait. Her actual job. Comforting this bereaved widow.

"Mrs. Bushman, I'm Laura Faraday. You can call me Laura if you want, or if you're my boss you can just call me *Faraday* in an angry tone. Either is fine. I'm very, *very* sorry about what Mr. Hall just said. I think he's been at this for a bit too long. Loses sight of everyone being hurt."

Laura heard Hall clearing his throat by the door. She'd apologize later. Probably. But Mrs. Bushman was now giving her more focus. "No one blames you for this. It's a tragedy, and we're all here to help you. We just need to get through some questions. We can come back later, if—"

Mrs. Bushman let out a loud sniff. "No! I just want—I just want this to be done."

"Alright, Mrs. Bushman. Take all the time you need. Please."

"I don't—I don't—I don't need time! Please! Just—I threw up. I went back to the room, you can see the stains on the wall from where I leaned against it. I looked at him again. And then I called the police. And that's where you came in."

"Do you think it was a suicide?"

"What else?" Mrs. Bushman moved the kerchief away from her mouth slightly, twisting it to and fro. It had *Elizabeth and Theodore* embroidered on it. Either a cheap wedding favor or some sort of meaningful gift. "He hung himself, Miss Faraday. There's not much that can get a man to hang himself."

"Of course—"

"What? Do you think that I got out a gun, a carving knife, the candelabra in the greenhouse, whatever, and I held it to his head and told him to hang himself? No! I'm not that kind of person!"

"No one thinks you are."

"Well, I—" Mrs. Bushman fell silent, looking at the ground.

"Can you think of a motive?"

Mrs. Bushman gave a snort through the tears. "None. A million. Theo was… a complicated man."

"I'm sure."

"All of you little university students, you never got to see the real him."

Try me.

"He was passionate, I suppose, but too much so. Not that I would've—well. It's beside the point. He had many vices. He drank. He gambled. He liked his sex, very much so, more than I could provide. He smoked, did you know? With his favorite student stoners, he would—I'm sorry, I can't tell you that—"

Mrs. Bushman burst into tears again. Laura reached out a hand, gently touching Mrs. Bushman's paw and rubbing tiny circles. "There, there. I promise. Things are awful, but they'll get better. You're supported by this entire community."

"I just—I don't—I suppose, fine—"

She was incoherent. Laura looked at Hall, who beckoned her, and she was forced to stand and follow him out. The sound of the sobs disturbed her much more deeply than the body upstairs. She wanted to do something to help, but she couldn't imagine what, and anyway her will to do something nice wasn't *that* strong. She felt detached from this case, as if they were all movie characters that she was interacting with. This was just her story; they were all characters.

***

Except for Rosamunde. Rosamunde wasn't a supporting character in anyone's story: not her single working mother's, not her soon-to-be-a-star sister's, not her businessman boyfriend's, not Laura's. They had been best friends for years. Going to the same college had intensified things and then the affair had broken them apart. Rosamunde had said that she had no interest in speaking with Laura again. Laura had firmly reciprocated the notion.

So she didn't know why she was calling Rosamunde now.

She stayed in the automobile after Hall had gone back into the station, holding her phone and trying to decide whether to call. Her need to talk with someone beat back her pride, and she found herself holding the phone to her ear.

Rosamunde picked up on the second ring. "Yes?"

Something within Laura relaxed. "Rose. Hey."

"Laura. What do you want?"

"I just—I wanted to hear your voice. I don't know. I'm sorry."

"Look, Laura." Rosamunde paused and Laura could practically hear her dragging her paws through her short fur on the other end. "I don't really want to do this right now. I don't know why you're calling, but—"

"I got my first murder."

Silence.

"And?"

"And I thought you'd want to know."

"Why would I want that?"

"Years of friendship. No, Rose, not that—"

"I told you not to call me that."

"Fine. Rosamunde. I don't know if you know yet, but you—you will. And I just wanted to hear your voice. I saw the body. It was... cold. And I just wanted to hear you talk. I don't know. I miss you sometimes."

"You're babbling, Laura."

"I know. I'm sorry."

"Well, you've heard my voice. Can I hang up now?"

"Can I just hear you say, like, that you're okay?"

"I'm okay."

"Call me if you need anything. Especially when the news breaks."

Silence, then a groan, and Laura knew that Rosamunde had put two and two together. "Wait. Are you—no. Theodore—he's—"

"I'm sorry, Rose—Rosamunde. I'm so sorry."

"No. Dammit. He can't—he wasn't supposed to—"

"Anything you need, Rosamunde."

"I don't *want* anything from you! Dammit, Laura, why can't you see that?"

"I was worried."

"Well, I don't want your worry. Just promise me one thing, Laura."

"Anything." Laura wondered why she had promised that. Her promises never meant anything, especially when it came to Rosamunde.

Now she had to keep it.

"Don't leave a single stone unturned. I know Theodore—well, I *did*—and he would never do this. There's something wrong here. He was eccentric, he had his highs and lows, but he wasn't depressed. And he certainly wasn't suicidal."

"Can you think of any motives, Rosamunde? Anything at all?"

"He didn't have a kid. He always complained about that. I don't know, he always seemed fine with money, happy enough with his wife, always had a way of letting out his pent-up emotion. Plenty of liaisons."

"A kid? Why not just adopt? Was Mrs. Bushman too weak to handle it?"

"I don't know the story—look, Laura, I don't even know why I'm talking about this! I told myself: stay out, stay away, I have a new life now, one that doesn't involve him—I just want to leave this behind, Laura, you know that! I don't know why you're dragging me back in!"

"I'm sorry. I miss you, Rosamunde."

Rosamunde hung up.

Laura collapsed against the seat, letting the phone fall to the ground.

***

Hall let Laura do the next interview alone, saying that he had better things to do than comfort widows, so Laura got to drive the automobile to the nice part of town on her own. She felt exceedingly grown-up and successful. Hall had said not to treat this case like it was anything other than a suicide, but Laura thought different. There was no motive. And Mrs. Bushman was clearly terrified. Something was wrong here.

She could hear Hall's voice in the back of her head, telling her not to be stupid. *Not everything is special*, he had told her less than a week ago, *in fact, most things aren't. Like you.* Laura gritted her teeth and revved the engine, just a little bit.

She knocked on the door and one of the maids let her back into the warren. She was directed to the study, where Mrs. Bushman was sitting, her head bent over a book.

"Mrs. Bushman?"

The fox flinched, looking up.

"Ah. Miss Faraday."

"Yes. I'm back. I just have a few more questions."

Mrs. Bushman's entire body was shaking once more. She peered over Laura's shoulder. "Mr. Hall isn't here, is he?"

"He, uh—we both decided that it would be best if he sat this one out."

"You say that as if you have any power."

"We're partners."

"He's training you, isn't he? You're young, that's all that I'm saying, not that you're stupid. You just have that air."

"I mean—You—you're right."

"How long have you been in the business?"

Laura couldn't help but smile. "Mrs. Bushman, I do believe that you've turned this interrogation onto me."

"Guilty," Mrs. Bushman said, giving a slight smile before it melted off of her face. "I'm glad you caught on. I see that you're not entirely incompetent."

"You have no idea how much that means. Are you ready to begin? I can come back later."

"I'm fine."

"Please, just know that everyone's here for you. We'll get to the bottom of this."

"What bottom? It was a suicide."

"Can you think of any motives he might've had?"

Mrs. Bushman looked away, sighing. She looked back at Laura and gave a small shake of the head. "Not really. He had his vices, of course. His mood could swing wildly. I told you what happened— I left for one moment after refusing sex, and he had hung himself when I came back. He was fine most of the time, but when it rained, it poured."

Laura could see Mrs. Bushman tearing up again. She stood and came to sit next to her. "Ma'am, do you have any friends you want with you? Any family? We can call them in if that would make this easier."

Mrs. Bushman shook her head miserably. "No! There's no one— I'm sorry. I didn't mean to yell."

"It's fine, Mrs. Bushman. Perfectly rational."

"No, no. Theodore hated it when I yelled. Did you know that? He indulged all of his students but when it came to me it had to be perfect. Oh, Miss Faraday—it's all my fault."

"Can you think of anyone with a grudge against him?" Laura offered her hand, and Mrs. Bushman took it and gave it a slight squeeze. Her fur was warm and soft.

"His rivals—those whose theories he struck down. Perhaps the dean. He—he had lovers."

"I know."

Mrs. Bushman pulled away, her gaze suddenly blazing. *"You?"*

"No! Not me. But… one of my friends. I'm sorry, Mrs. Bushman."

Mrs. Bushman stood and took a few steps forward, seeming to browse through some books on the shelf. She finally spoke, her voice measured. "You know, I always tell myself that I should be mad at him. Not at his little paramours. But I can't stop myself from being bitter. Why is that? I didn't even love him! Not when he—do you know what he liked to do, Miss Faraday? He would suggest sex, even right after I was out of the hospital, and if I wouldn't give it to him he'd say that I was killing him, that he'd kill himself if I let myself die or if I ever left him—and now—see, Miss Faraday? It's all my fault!"

Laura stood and followed her, patting her on the back. "It's not your fault. You have to understand that."

"A grudge against him. *Me.* I had the biggest grudge! He got violent when he got drunk—and you—you understand! You're a detective. You can guess."

"I'm so sorry, Mrs. Bushman."

"Who, who, who—I should've known better, Miss Faraday, you're nowhere *near* his type—Lucy Williamson, Emily Waters, Marian Orr, Rosamunde Dapple, Jana Vaughn, Jennifer Hausner, Lynna Campbell—that's all I can think of, those are all the girls that I saw him with, in his automobile, outside. He never brought them in the warren. I guess I should be grateful."

But the hairpin, under the dresser. And Mrs. Bushman's fur, in a short, modern cut. "Mrs. Bushman—"

"No! He's dead! I'm not *his* anymore! My name is Elizabeth!"

"Elizabeth. I'm going to stop asking questions. You need to take some time to yourself. This isn't your fault. There are therapists that

I can recommend. If possible, I think that visiting family would be good—"

Mrs. Bushman—Elizabeth—burst into tears.

"Elizabeth, I'm so sorry."

Laura offered herself for a hug and Elizabeth practically buried her in one. Foxes were known for being lithe and only muscle, but after getting sick Elizabeth must have lost this figure. She was soft. Professor Bushman must not have liked that. Laura did.

"There's no one, Miss Faraday," Elizabeth whispered, her tears soaking into Laura's shirt. They chafed.

"I'm so sorry, Elizabeth."

"Me too. Please, don't leave."

"Alright."

And they stayed like that for a long while.

***

Elizabeth eventually took hold of herself once more, shooing Laura out of the house in an almost embarrassed way. Not to say that Laura wasn't feeling awkward as well, but she never would have judged Elizabeth for grieving—well, her husband, but it was more than that. She was mourning her life for the last twenty years. Being married to a man like that, who was unfaithful, who hurt you—Laura's lack of interest in marriage intensified.

She ran over the list of names that Elizabeth had given her once more. All of the women that Professor Bushman had had affairs with. As soon as she was home she scrawled the list down on a piece of paper. Women, different ages, over the last twenty years, all drawn together by this one man. What was it about Professor Bushman? He was charismatic, of course, and even though he was old there was still something undeniably handsome about him. But why was that enough to make someone as strong as Rosamunde abandon all of their morals to have a chance to sleep with him? Rosamunde had seemed—almost in *love*. That was insane. But would Laura have turned into that if Professor Bushman had given her any attention? Her mind suddenly went to his pantsless corpse. She shuddered. *There's something wrong with me.* His eyes, his nakedness. He was powerless. He was nothing and no one.

The names, the names. She wrote a reminder to give the list to Hall the next day and then found an old school directory. There was Rosamunde Dapple, of course, from last year, but Marian Orr was younger than them. Jana Vaughn had graduated two years before the rest of them. The other women were from over five years before. They were all rabbits.

All rabbits. *You're not his type.* Laura ran a hand through her fur, stroking her horns. There was nothing wrong with being in a relationship with a different kind of animal, none at all. But Elizabeth was a fox, and Professor Bushman was a rabbit, and of course that created power dynamics and anxieties that you didn't get elsewhere. And they wouldn't be able to conceive. Why hadn't they adopted? Everyone adopted.

On a whim, Laura broke out a phone book and went searching for Marian and Jana. Marian was there, living on campus. Jana was living not a mile away from Laura. Laura slammed the book shut, walked to the phone on the wall, and dialed Hall.

He picked up on the third ring. "Henry Hall speaking."

"This is Faraday."

"Do you finally have the report of what happened with Mrs. Bushman?" he growled.

"I've written it up and I'll deliver it tomorrow. Listen, I have a lead—well, a few—"

"*Leads?* What do you think this is? It's a suicide, Faraday. There's no evidence otherwise."

"There was no motive—"

"That we know of. People like Bushman, they have all sorts of things going on in their lives. Maybe he had a debt he couldn't pay. Maybe the marriage got to be too much for him. Maybe there was just something wrong inside of him, something in his brain. That happens, you know."

"Yes, yes, but—"

"Faraday, not only are you not endearing yourself to me as your superior, but you are not making your gender look very reliable as detectives! I told the chief—well, it doesn't matter. Either come in to discuss this, or we drop this entirely! Am I understood?"

"Yes," Laura snarled, hanging up.

Discussion? Who did he think he was fooling? There would be

no discussion, just him insulting her and telling her she was wrong! She wasn't going to deal with that again. She wasn't friends with Professor Bushman, but she knew him from his classes. He had his vices, but he was vibrant and passionate and had said many times that he loved life.

Laura called Jana Vaughn.

Her call went to a man in Jana's building, who said he would get Jana and hung up. Laura waited apprehensively by the phone for a few minutes before the ring shattered the silence of her home. She practically yanked the phone off the wall. "Is this Jana Vaughn?"

"Who am I talking to?"

It was a woman's voice, trembling slightly. Laura was reminded of Rosamunde, of the shaky voice and body that all rabbits got when they were nervous. Laura wondered if Miss Vaughn was shaking right now. "This is Laura Faraday. I'm a detective."

"A female detective?"

Oh, not another Hall.

"That's correct."

"Did you know, I wanted to be a detective when I was a very young girl. My mother called me a fool."

"I'm sorry to hear that. Miss Vaughn, I have a few questions for you."

"Oh, am I part of some sort of investigation?" The tremor was intensifying.

"Have you seen the news?" Laura made her voice as gentle as possible.

"I—yes. Yes, I have."

"Do you mind if I ask you some questions?"

"You already are."

"You can hang up whenever you want."

"And make you think I'm guilty? No, Miss Faraday—you've got me caught." There was venom in the trembling voice. "If I hang up, I become more suspicious. Very clever."

"I promise you, I don't think that."

"What do you want to know?"

"To be blunt: you were Professor Bushman's lover, correct?"

A pause. "Yes," Miss Vaughn finally said.

"Did he ever take you inside the house?"

Miss Vaughn went silent again. When she spoke, the tremor was gone. Her voice was carefully measured. Laura listened close, her goat's-ears craning for every admission that the voice gave away. "No. He never took any of us inside the warren. I'm sure you know that already."

"Did he ever give you gifts?"

"You could call it that." Miss Vaughn gave a laugh. It sounded forced. Laura tried to visualize her on the other end, her ears twitching, her foot thumping the ground. Gifts that aren't gifts. Money. Children. Prestige.

"Can you be more specific? Did he ever give you any hairpieces?"

"How did you—well—yes, I—" Laura had clearly thrown her off. "He always said that a rabbit with long hair done up was the most beautiful thing he could imagine. He said—he gave me a pin and called me beautiful. Even Mrs. Bushman, she said I was lovely—"

"You met Elizabeth Bushman?"

"I—I—"

Laura let her struggle for a few moments. *I have her.* "How?"

"I—I met her at a party. I was a waitress."

"Did she know about you and her husband?"

"Oh, I'm sure. She knew everything. The look she gave me—she's not a good woman, Miss Faraday. Have you asked *her* any questions? She *loathed* Theodore."

"You believe Elizabeth Bushman had something to do with it?" Laura tugged on the curly phone line. She was getting close, she could feel it.

"What—did I say that? No! Have you seen Mrs. Bushman? She's so weak. She's been weak ever since her illness. No, it was a suicide, everyone knows that!"

"Can you think of a motive?"

"How should I know that?"

"Did he want children?"

"What are you—well—I don't—"

"It's fine if you don't know," Laura tried. "Of course he wouldn't share that kind of thing with his paramours. It was deeply personal."

"Don't assume you know what our relationship was like! Theodore was very open about his life, just not with his students! Or wife! With those that he *actually* loved—well, of course he did, he wanted a child of his own, and—I don't have to tell you this!" She sounded practically hysterical.

"Who ended it?"

"What are you talking about? He always ends it! He loves you, then he leaves you! No one leaves him! Who would do that! Who would leave him? Do you mean—did one of his lovers—*who?*"

"I don't know if I should tell you that."

"*Who?*"

"There's no shame in being left by him."

"Don't you *dare* assume anything about me! Who was it? Emily Waters, she was always headstrong—*too* headstrong, if you ask me, she wanted to marry him, that was when he ended it—no, Rosamunde Dapple, it was her! She left university before graduating! It was her, wasn't it?"

"Were you angry when he ended it?"

"Does being angry make me a murderer? I don't want to talk to you anymore!"

"I'm sorry, Miss Vaughn."

"I hate you."

Abruptly, the call ended.

Feeling very cold, Laura replaced the phone. Hairpins and eyes. Jana Vaughn, clearly panicking. Elizabeth, alone in her house, most likely terrified. Would she go on sleeping in the marriage place? Or would she abandon it? Would she abandon the whole warren? She was a fox, not a rabbit. She wasn't meant for that sort of confinement.

And now Miss Vaughn knew about Rosamunde. The hairs at the back of Laura's neck prickled. She should warn her old friend. She dialed Rosamunde's number, but Rosamunde didn't respond.

What to do? Rosamunde deserved to know that Jana knew. Laura tried the number again. Nothing.

She abandoned that plan, grabbed her jacket, and made her way out the door. She didn't realize where she was going until she was halfway to the station. The sun was going down and she had to shield her eyes from it. At least the sunset was lovely. Rosamunde loved sunsets like this. Irritation sparked in the back of Laura's mind. Why wouldn't that stupid rabbit respond?

She made it to the station and entered. It was almost deserted, but she could hear someone clattering around. She peered around a corner to the room she worked in, and saw Hall in his office, on the phone with someone. She crawled on her hands and knees like a lowly animal underneath his field of vision. It worked. For all his sight and hearing, he was oblivious when he was focused. At the very least *she* always stayed alert, even when on an important phone call with, say, Rosamunde. *Rosamunde.* Laura lost her train of thought. Rosamunde, the one person to leave. Powerful. The things she could divulge…

No. Rosamunde had asked to remain outside of this investigation, and Laura would respect her wishes. No matter how hard it was. Rosamunde deserved that much from her. Rosamunde, who had been her best friend, who she had grown apart from. Who had supported her in being the first female detective to study at the university. Who had looked Professor Bushman in his eyes, naked, and decided to leave.

Laura made it to the file cabinets that dominated the wall in the room. She found the thin file folder that contained Professor Bushman's case. There wasn't much in there, only Elizabeth's testimony and some of Hall's notes. Nothing on Jana Vaughn or Rosamunde Dapple or any of the other women. Laura closed her eyes. Every nerve in her body told her that something was wrong, that she shouldn't stop looking. Two clinics and a hospital in town. Laura regarded the phone, and then dialed the hospital's number.

"This is St. Ignatius Hospital."

"Hello. I'm Detective Laura Faraday. I'm working as a PI with Henry Hall. I would like access to some of your files."

There was a pause on the other end. "We'll need you to come in person," the voice finally said. "Please bring your identification and proof of employment. Privacy of our patients, you see—I'm sure you understand."

Laura did understand, even if she hated it. She bit her tongue so that she didn't sound like an absolute child, demanding special treatment just because she believed she was on to something. "Please— it's imperative that we get these now. If you could fax them over to us—I'm just looking for a few names—"

"Proper procedure or nothing, Detective Faraday. Have a nice night." A dial tone.

Laura wanted to scream. She could taste blood in her mouth and made her jaw release, rigidly dialing the next number. So what if none of this worked? Spending an extra few minutes chasing dead ends was worth what they might be able to give her.

"Sunrise Clinic. How can I help you?"

"I'm Laura Faraday, a PI with Henry Hall, and I'm looking for some information."

There was a pause on the other end and Laura feared the worst, but then the woman on the other end spoke again. "I'm sorry, did you say Laura Faraday?"

"Yes, that's me."

"I'm sorry, it's just—well, one of our patients spoke about you quite a bit. I'm sure this sounds strange, but please, accept my congratulations at the fact that you managed to become a PI. What information did you need?"

How on earth does she know that? Who of Laura's friends had been to Sunrise Clinic recently? Laura's blood suddenly ran cold. "I was hoping to find the files of a few people connected with a current investigation."

"I see. That goes against some of our policies…"

It was a woman's voice, soft. "Please, ma'am," Laura tried. "You've heard about me. This investigation… it could… affect Rosamunde."

There was a small catch of breath on the other line and Laura knew she had been correct. "I see. Well… I can't tell you everything. If you would just tell me what you need…"

"Could I see if some names have ever come to your clinic?"

Laura read off the names. Rosamunde Dapple, Emily Waters, Jennifer Hausner, and Jana Vaughn were matches. "And Jana Vaughn came in for…"

"Anemia. The problem arose about eighteen months ago. I always told Rosamunde, she was lucky she didn't get it, after everything…"

The pieces came together in Laura's mind. Clinics and anemia. *Miscarriage.* Laura nearly dropped the phone.

The woman on the other end was still talking but her voice faded in and out and Laura didn't register as much as she needed to. Missing vital information—what did any of that matter?

Rosamunde had… Rosamunde had…

And she hadn't told Laura. She'd told Laura nothing.

She'd started the affair against Laura's suggestions and she'd left school and restarted elsewhere, all with a pregnancy and miscarriage, and *she hadn't told Laura?*

She and Jana had been pregnant. Most likely with Professor Bushman's children. The scope of his infidelity, all of the animals he had taken advantage of… Laura had always loved Professor Bushman and his teaching style, and while he had his vices, he was overall an excellent professor and seemed like a kind man. But no, he had married a fox and decided that he wanted a child of his own. And he had found rabbits and made them fall in love with him and possibly loved them back. Had Jana had the child? Had Emily Waters? Rosamunde hadn't.

She needed to call Rosamunde.

She heard the lights go off in Hall's office and hit the ground, crawling to the tiny space between the wall and file cabinets. She squeezed herself in, making herself as small as possible and taking tiny breaths through her nose. Hall flapped twice and took flight, gliding down the stairs. Laura heard the lock click at the bottom.

She was locked in.

She went to Hall's office and tried the door. It was locked. She didn't need hairpins for her hair but she always kept one in her pocket for just these cases. A holdover of her days when dreams of being a detective meant constant intrigue and danger. Rosamunde had taught her how to pick locks years ago, back when they were still friends. When she still would tell me about a miscarriage! *What happened to us?* Laura heard the lock click open, pulled open the door, and went into Hall's office. It smelled strongly of feathers. She picked up the phone. *He will dismiss me if he finds out about this. But this is my first murder! Or, suicide. Whatever. And he won't listen!*

She dialed Rosamunde's number again. This time, Rosamunde picked up.

"It's me."

"Oh, I'm sorry. I wasn't aware that I could recognize identities by voice now. Some of us try to move on from the past."

Laura couldn't help but give a small laugh. "Fine. It's Laura Faraday, detective. Rosamunde, I need to ask you something."

"Laura…"

"Don't hang up!"

"I wasn't going to… but Laura, I can't keep doing this. I'm trying to let go of this. It's awful, it really is—"

"Listen. Jana Vaughn, do you know her? She was the girl before you. She was… deeply upset by the relationship. And disturbed by the fact that you were the one to end it with the professor."

"She—wait—how does she know—"

"I told her during questioning."

"You… *told* her. About *me*. And my life."

Laura could hear the rabbit-tremble of Rosamunde's voice across the line. "She deduced it," Laura corrected, suddenly feeling very ill.

"You've ruined everything."

Rosamunde's voice was strangely calm.

"Rose?"

"I *told* you not to call me that. What else did she find out?"

"I know, Rosamunde."

"About…"

"Yes."

There was a very long silence.

"Rosamunde? Rose!"

"I know what I said, Laura, but I—I can't—I don't want to be a part of this. I can't handle that. This whole thing, this whole damn affair—you don't even know what you've done, Laura. I just wanted to finish that chapter."

Laura realized that she had never heard Rosamunde sound genuinely afraid before. It terrified her. She didn't want to listen to Rosamunde's fear. She didn't want to be the one to cause this. "I am so, *so* sorry."

Silence.

"Rosamunde?"

"I need to go. Someone's at the door."

Nausea rose, overtaking Laura. "Rosamunde, don't answer."

"I don't think you have the right to tell me what to do."

"Rosamunde, I have a bad feeling."

"It's *Rosamunde!* You always do this—I have a life now, a life that I love, and this could tear it all down—no one can know—"

"No one? Did Professor Bushman?"

"…*what?*"

"Did you want him out of the picture?!"

When Rosamunde spoke again, her voice was very small. "I

thought you were investigating him, Laura. Not me."

"Rosamunde!"

"I wish you the best, Laura. Goodbye."

For the second time that day, Laura was hung up upon.

She screamed in frustration, nearly throwing the phone across the room before remembering it was Hall's and slamming it back into place. She grabbed the desk, rocking back and forth and trying to get a hold of herself. How *dare* Rosamunde? This was Laura's big moment. Rosamunde was wrong. Jana was wrong. *Hall* was wrong. And Laura was right. She was going to make this her big moment. She was going to solve whatever was going on here.

But first, she had to keep her job. She remembered the locked door and winced. *No. If I destroy the office, he'll know I was here.*

She went over to the window and opened it, peeking her head out. There was a fire escape, rickety and unstable. She stepped out anyway, carefully closing the window behind her. On this side of the building the lights didn't shine, and she was hidden. She could see the silhouette of someone sleeping in the alley. She began to make her way down, her sure goat's-feet stepping in the right places and keeping her footing. She jumped the last ten feet, the impact jarring her ankles, but the wind felt good. It reminded her that she was alive.

She ran the rest of the way home and fell asleep nearly before her head hit the pillow.

The next morning couldn't come soon enough.

***

When she got to the office the next morning Hall gave her a strange look and Laura knew that the game was up. He called her into his office not a quarter of an hour later, and Laura prepared herself for the firing. She would get over it. She would solve the case, prove him wrong, become a star, and get her job back. For some reason her mind went back to Professor Bushman, nothing and no one, his dead eyes boring into her back. She blinked hard, dispelling the image.

"Miss Faraday."

The honorific disturbed her; Laura raised an eyebrow.

"Have you heard?"

This seemed like a strange method of dismissal. "Heard what?"

"There's been a murder."

Laura's heart raced. "Who?"

"Your friend. Her fiancé said we should tell you—it was Rosamunde Dapple."

***

Apparently Laura passed out.

She awoke on the floor of Hall's office. She shifted, knocking something over. He stood and gave her a hand to help her up.

There was an irritating noise. She realized it was her teeth chattering. She couldn't seem to stop shaking. "Mr. Hall…"

"Miss Faraday. Laura. I'm sorry."

"She was…"

"Someone came to her house, apparently. She opened the door. She was shot twice: once in the head, once in the shoulder. The head was fatal. Her fiancé found her the next morning."

"Her fiancé—I didn't—realize." So much that Laura didn't know. And now Rosamunde was—no! That couldn't be right! Rosamunde wasn't allowed to die! Not until she and Laura had reconciled!

"We're not sure who the murderer is. I've got agents asking the neighbors if they saw anyone."

Laura violently shook her head. "No. You're wrong. Rosamunde wouldn't just—die like that. Not by being shot. She survived so much, did you know that?"

"Things are coming to light, Faraday. Between her and Bushman. It looks like… perhaps… your mad theories may have some grains of truth within them. I hope you don't take this to heart."

"No. No. Not Rosamunde. Not Rosamunde."

"Pull yourself together, Faraday! I let you stay in my office so that no one saw that you passed out. Detectives don't do that. They solve crimes, Faraday. I thought you were going to prove yourself."

"How *dare* you?" Laura found herself screaming. "Rosamunde is *dead*!"

And then the tears began to pour out, sobs wrenching themselves out of her, her entire body contorting. Rosamunde was dead, dead, and Laura should have been dead too. Rosamunde, of the luscious hair and laughing strength and lockpicking and years of friendship, of the lies. Rosamunde who Laura had betrayed…

Betrayal.

Laura made herself stand, ignoring Hall's outstretched hand.

"Faraday? What are you doing? Don't be hysterical. I won't deal with it if you're hysterical."

"I know what to do."

"I don't care if you know what to do! I am your superior and if you expect to succeed here, you must listen to me! Faraday, if you take another step, I will be forced to let you go! Faraday! Laura!"

Laura didn't listen.

Laura didn't care.

***

She remembered Jana's apartment number. She stormed there and blazed upstairs. There were children playing on the stairs; she didn't care. Let them witness the murder that was about to occur. There was an old woman sweeping the halls. Let her testify against Laura.

Rosamunde was *dead*.

Rosamunde…

Cold eyes, cold skin, cold hearts. Nakedness. Death was nakedness. Death was nothing and no one. Rosamunde and Professor Bushman, together again. Laura shuddered even as she stormed down the hall.

She banged three times on Miss Vaughn's door.

No response.

"Jana Vaughn! I know you're in there!"

No response.

Laura backed up and sprinted at the door, kicking it.

It shattered quite easily. Not much could withstand a goat. Maybe Laura wasn't the prettiest, the smartest, the one with the best eyes or ears, but she could kick doors down like a demon.

The lights were on. Jana wasn't there.

"Jana! Come out! You can't hide from me!"

Laura didn't miss how frenzied her own voice was, how mad. This was madness. Rosamunde was dead.

It smelled like blood. Laura could feel the ghosts in this house. She looked around the room and saw a hairpiece on a small table by the door. There were no pictures on the wall save of one of Professor

Bushman's class. Laura saw Jana in it, and then caught sight of herself, so far to the side that she was almost out of the picture. Rosamunde was next to her, gleaming.

Something clattered. Laura whipped around, catching sight of Jana.

Jana stumbled towards her, brandishing a gun. Was she drunk?

"You *murderer*," Laura hissed, moving backwards.

Jana tried to choke something out, shaking her head, and then she vomited on the ground of her apartment. Only it wasn't *right*. It was bright red.

Blood.

Jana's nose was bleeding. Her fur was matted with it.

She fell forward and Laura reached forward and caught her. She was limp. She reached up towards Laura's face.

"*Theodore*," she rattled out.

And then she fell silent.

Laura couldn't say when Jana's skin went cold.

Cold eyes, cold skin. Blood and hairpieces. Nothing and no one.

***

She was covered in blood. She rifled through Jana's closet and found a jacket, pulling it over her clothes and blood-soaked fur. This looked bad. This looked very bad. She tried to call Hall but her hands shook, and she had forgotten the number.

She stumbled out of the building, indicating Jana's apartment to the old woman. She heard a scream as she left the building. Her blood was roaring in her ears. Jana and Rosamunde.

Elizabeth.

She wandered, and eventually made it to the Bushman warren. She knocked on the door. It was pulled open by Elizabeth. She took in Laura, and the haunted look in her eyes told Laura everything she needed to know.

"How *could* you?"

"How could I what?"

"You killed them," Laura accused. "You killed Jana. And Rosamunde. You knew that they were lovers with your husband. You knew that they were both pregnant with his children. And you killed them."

Elizabeth shook her head, weary, sad. "You jump to conclusions, Miss Faraday."

"How can I not? The pieces fit."

"I'm scared, Miss Faraday. It wasn't me. And I know I'm next. Can't you see the patterns? Rosamunde lost the child. So did Jana. It died a week after birth. And me? I never had a chance."

"And you were bitter."

"No. I'm not a murderer, Miss Faraday. I hated my husband, perhaps. But I never would've killed him. Please, come in. Check the bedroom. Check the whole warren. Do you have a gun? I have a gun. I'm scared, Miss Faraday."

Pathetic. Elizabeth was pathetic. Everyone was pathetic except for Rosamunde. Laura didn't bother to respond, brushing past Elizabeth. The door closed behind her, and she could hear Elizabeth following her to the bedroom. Doors were closed behind them.

"Are you locking me in here? Are you going to kill me, too?"

"The farther we are from everyone else, the better. There are so many rooms in this warren… I hate it here. I never wanted to live in a warren, but Theodore, he wanted to. He wanted to, so much. And I loved him. Twenty years ago, I loved him. I loved him through his first affairs. And then I didn't. I fell out of love, Miss Faraday. I wanted to leave. But I'm not a murderer. Can you see that?"

Laura didn't respond, bursting into the bedroom. She fell to her knees beside the dresser and reached under it, pulling out the hairpiece. She turned to Elizabeth and brandished it. "It's not yours, is it?"

"No. I don't wear hairpieces."

"That means that there was another woman in here."

Elizabeth wavered. "No. He wouldn't have—he never—he respected me, even if he didn't love me! I told him, do what you want, but don't bring that into our house! Into our bed!"

"But it is another woman's. That's undeniable." Laura examined it. It was a rhinestone. Worthless. There were a few hairs still wrapped around it, silky, white. Completely unlike Rosamunde, who was brown all over, and unlike Jana's spots. "Admit it, Mrs. Bushman. He brought someone in here."

"Don't—call me—Mrs. Bushman!"

"You hated him. You killed him."

"No! No! I drove him to it, fine—but I didn't murder him! I just found him! It was a suicide!" There was another woman in this room. That meant that something had gone far—too far. He had let someone into his life. A relationship had progressed. Had a child been involved?

Laura yanked open the dresser and started going through the clothes. Underwear, folded shirts. Nothing. The next drawer. Nothing. The next—

Papers.

She pulled out a huge sheaf of them and started going through them. There were streams of numbers, but luckily, numbers she could understand.

"Your husband seems to have gambled away his fortune," Laura breathed.

She could hear Elizabeth sobbing behind her. "It doesn't surprise me."

Laura continued to go through the drawers, placing the financial papers on the ground. The next drawer had an envelope at the back of it, so close to the color of the wood that anyone with poorer eyes would have missed it. Laura plucked it out and opened it.

Dear Theodore,
Linus is dead. I suppose you will wonder how this came to be. It was not through negligence, but through cruel fate. You will no doubt be grief-stricken. Perhaps you are right and this would not have occurred if I had left him with you.
Whatever the reason, I want reparations. I did it. I had the child that you demanded, and I kept him a secret from your wife and from the world. You listened to me. You brought me into your home. Then you threw me out. You refused to leave your wife.
You refused to let me into your bed. When I grew angry, you took other lovers. You tried to have children with them.
One way or another, you will pay.
I want $500,000. Or I will take away your dream of a child. I will take away all of your dreams.

- E

"Oh," Laura said, a giggle escaping her.

"What's *oh?*"

"I think I found our murderer."

"Theodore wasn't murdered! I told you, I would've heard some-one—I just left for a few moments—"

"I think you were right, Elizabeth. It was just a suicide. But he was driven to it by E."

"And you think—"

"No, no. You couldn't have children with him. It's not you. Maybe whoever it was didn't intend for the suicide to occur—in fact, I'm almost sure that they didn't. They wanted money, after all. But your husband had none. And he had lost his child. And you walked out of the room. And therefore…"

"He hung himself."

"So. E. We know that it's one of his old lovers. Do you know which ones he had children with?"

"He never specified. They were all rabbits."

"The pattern to the murders. Was it love? Maybe, but I don't think that E was jealous of them. She just wanted the money. I doubt that she truly loved your husband. So maybe… maybe it was the people that knew she was Professor Bushman's lover. Jana said that all of you knew each other. Some sort of little club—" Laura giggled. Something was very wrong with her. Rosamunde was gone. "And that means that Rosamunde knew, too. And all of his other lovers. And you."

Down the hall, something clattered.

"Emily," Elizabeth said. "*E.*"

"Did Emily—"

Something thumped.

Elizabeth went completely still. Laura carefully padded to the door, pulling it open. She didn't have a weapon. Rosamunde hadn't had a weapon. But she needed to protect Elizabeth like she hadn't been able to protect Rosamunde.

Think, she told herself, *think*.

"Sit there," she directed Elizabeth quietly, pointing at a wooden chair. "Sit there and pretend to cry."

Elizabeth gave her a horrified look, an untrusting look, a distinctly offensive one, but at least didn't ask questions. She gave a sob that was definitely real and buried her face in her hands. Laura turned off the light and bent down between the dresser and the wall. The closet where Professor Bushman had been hanging was empty: devoid of clothing, of that single red shirt, of the body. No life. Cold eyes, cold hearts. No clothes. Nothing and no one.

The door was pushed open unceremoniously and Laura saw a pure-white rabbit that practically glowed in the darkness of the room.

"Mrs. Bushman," she said, raising her revolver.

Elizabeth looked up at the woman, and Laura felt a sense of pride at how strong she was despite the tears that matted her fur and the gun pointed at her face. "Emily Waters."

And then Laura leapt out of her hiding spot, tackling Emily Waters. She and Emily went flying towards the wall, her goat's bulk aiding her. Emily screamed in surprise, but then Laura heard a gunshot—

She didn't register the pain for a few moments. Then it was as if she had been hit by a galloping horse. And then the pain intensified in her leg. But it was only her leg. No more than that. She groped for the gun, and then the two of them had their hands on it. Another shot went off, landing in the ceiling and ruining the woodwork. Another. Another. Another. Another.

Laura kept her hands on the gun but abandoned the trigger and Emily roared with laughter, pulling the trigger even as Laura's hands covered the barrel. There was a click, but nothing came out.

"Six," Laura said, and shoved the gun down into Emily's face.

There was a cracking noise and Emily's eyes unfocused for a moment. Laura got a better grip on the gun and hit Emily with it again, and again, in the nose so that it bled, and then in the head so that Emily's eyes rolled backwards and then Laura rolled off of her and started staring at the ceiling—

"Did I kill her?" she heard herself ask. Well, no, she felt her lips move, and saw Elizabeth say something, but her ears were ringing.

This wasn't glamorous. Everything hurt. She felt as if she was dying. And why not die? Rosamunde was dead.

Laura didn't want this. She wanted to go back in time. She wanted to go home.

"You're brave," she heard Elizabeth say, and then everything went black.

***

When she awoke she was in the hospital.

She looked around for Rosamunde before remembering that Rosamunde was… gone.

Oh, Rose.

Elizabeth wasn't there, either, and for a moment Laura panicked, thrashing. Then she felt a talon on her shoulder and looked up at Hall's beak.

"She's fine," he gruffly said. "You… did well."

"I did well?"

He nodded.

"Must be hard for you to say that," Laura said without thinking. Her brain was very fuzzy.

"You're in *so much trouble.*"

"I guessed."

"You were right. But you are most likely going to be dismissed."

"Yes."

"No fight?"

"I'm tired, Mr. Hall."

"Aren't we all. You have good intuition, Faraday. No self-control. But good intuition."

"Thank… you…"

"You're in trouble," Hall repeated. "But I'll see if I can… keep you on my team."

"Ha," Laura said. "You like me after all."

"I don't like you," Hall said, but he smiled anyway, and Laura was drifting off.

Rosamunde was dead. More than dead; Laura had destroyed whatever they had.

She had solved her first case. It felt so wrong. She didn't like this, not at all. And Rosamunde was dead. There was no one to prove anything to. No one to celebrate with.

Hall rubbed her shoulder as she passed out again, and as she fell asleep, Laura decided that she would bring all sorts of flowers to the grave, along with whatever stories she had of a better tomorrow.

SWALLOWED BY THE SEA

Ocean Tigrox

"You've done enough, Bonnie!" Captain Blackclaw called out, jabbing his cutlass at the rabbit balanced on the plank of his ship. "Now off to the depths with ya!"

"The captain's gone crazy! First my brother, Winston, now this?" Bonnie called out. The reddish hare struggled against the rope that bound her wrists together. "You'll regret this! Listen to my words: a great curse will take hold o' this ship if you go through with this."

The captain scoffed. "My ship's already been cursed from taking on a maiden o' your character. Calling up storms with your whistling aboard? Haven't really been given a choice now, have I?" The sneer of the black cat captain cut deeper than his cutlass could have. Blackclaw waved his free paw toward the bow. "Would you rather we strip ya down and strap ya to the masthead to appease the seas? Because I've got to get to Devil's Isle and can't be delayed any further."

"Is that why you can't investigate Winston's mysterious disappearance? You're late for a date? You've gone insane, Blackclaw!" Bonnie whirled around nimbly with a hop. She flicked out her ears in anger. "This is only the beginning of your bad luck. From here forth you've incurred not just the wrath of the seas, but that of a woman scorned. I'll get my revenge, even after my last breath."

"Well let me help you get to that next step."

Blackclaw slashed at the rabbit's midsection, but Bonnie jumped out of the way. When the captain lunged towards her, she snarled and dove off the long plank into the water.

"A curse on your head!" she shouted before the depths of the waves swallowed her up.

Blackclaw turned away from the railing and faced his wide-eyed crew. "Let that be a lesson. Whistling aboard only stirs up storms. I'll not have any more delays. Now back to work! Unless you're looking to join her?"

As the murmuring crew dispersed, the bumpy-scaled quartermaster stepped up beside his captain. The crocodile waited until it was safe to talk before muttering, "You sure about this?"

"You remember the last crew member who questioned my orders, Scales?" Blackclaw gave a side eye glare at the crocodile.

"I mean letting Bonnie go this close to shore." The quartermaster flicked his snout past the starboard side at the small uninhabited island nearby. "Wouldn't want her making her way there."

"She'd have to find a way to get out of those ropes first. You ever heard of a great rabbit swimmer?" The captain waved a dismissive hand. "Did we secure any supplies from the island?"

"Chopped some wood and found some fresh water to help supplement our rations. A few limes to stave off the scurvy and some coconuts to chew on. Still, island's bare as a walrus."

"So should the rabbit magically hop from the bottom of the ocean to land, she ain't surviving much longer past that." Blackclaw turned and shouted out, "Ruth!"

A squawk behind them startled the crocodile as a tall gull flapped over, the spyglass hanging around her neck bouncing against her linen shirt. "Yes, Cap'n!"

"Have you figured out yet how far that storm blew us off course? We're lucky enough we didn't lose the treasure with our supplies, but we need to get back on track."

Ruth's tail feathers splayed. "Well…" The navigator gull tensed up before answering. "Seems like that storm sent us off to the east. I have the logs to confirm longitude at sunset, but until the stars start shining, I'm unable to plot a full course."

Blackclaw displayed one of his fangs. "Fine, but get me those coordinates. We can't sit around like barnacles, so set sail west for now. Stay up in the lookout with Noir to keep watch for anything in our way," he ordered, strolling below deck before anyone could retort.

Scales took over, bellowing orders. "Alright you louts! You heard the cap'n. Stop lollygagging. Pull up anchor, trim the sails and let's be off!"

***

Below deck was loud with chatter and movement as the crew dashed to their positions to prepare to set sail once again. The clanking of anchor chains being lifting echoed throughout the gangway in tandem with clicking of claws against the hardwood decks. Despite the noise, Blackclaw's ears turned when he picked out one sound faintly hidden beneath it all.

He whirled around. "Whistling?" His ears perked and swivelled as he tried to confirm what he had heard, let alone where it might be coming from.

But the sound was already gone, leaving the captain to sneer and dismiss it. "Better not be any whistling onboard here. That damn lass whistled up that last storm. Bad enough she was a red-head. Always the troublemakers. Should have put her in her place earlier."

Grumbling to himself, the cat slunk away to his quarters. Upon reaching them, though, he found the door to his cabin ajar. The cat's ears flicked up and his tail stood on end. "What in blazes?" He shoved the door open and found the cabin a mess. The windows were wide open, curtains flapping in the salty breeze. Papers and maps blew about the room. Drawers had been pulled from his desk, their contents thrown to the floor.

"No, no, no," Blackclaw muttered to himself, fumbling under his shirt for his necklace. He pulled out the silver chain from around his neck, gripped the attached iron key between his fingers and scanned the bookshelf. The top shelf was thankfully undisturbed. After moving some of the books aside, he removed a small wooden chest that had been hiding behind them.

He placed the chest on his desk and slid the small iron key into the lock. The jewel inside the chest reflected the sunlight behind him back into his gaze. The treasure of Digoba had taken weeks of searching, paying off informants, and following leads, but finally the giant ruby eye was within the cat's paws. The lost treasure of fables was worth more than most could even imagine. Even now, the shimmer of the red rock mesmerized Blackclaw. Shifting the gem from side to side seemed to cause the boat to rock in sync. The captain shook his head and placed the ruby back in its hiding spot.

The largest buyer was leaving Devil's Isle before week's end. Time was the enemy of his fortune. Blackclaw would not let anyone stand in his way. Now that the gem was safe, he scanned the room, looking to see if the intruder left any clues.

A soggy mess of a pile in a dark corner of his cabin caught his eye. On closer inspection, it seemed to be a lump of seaweed and snail shells. Muttering, the cat kicked it, uncovering a black and yellow peel. His nose scrunched as he picked up the banana peel and hissed. He threw the bad luck omen out the window and latched it shut.

Blackclaw stormed out of his cabin, rushing topside. "Scales!"

The floorboards creaked from the weight of the waddling crocodile, who met him halfway to the upper decks. "Yes, Cap'n? Something wrong?"

"I oughtta toss you overboard right now." Blackclaw stared him down, baring his fangs.

The croc's eyes glazed over. "Cap— but— wh—?" he sputtered in confusion.

"Someone was in my cabin, rummaging about. First Bonnie, now someone else? Do you have a hold on this crew or not? I've come too far to get this treasure just to have it snatched away from someone working aboard my own ship!"

Scales blinked and tried to say something, but Blackclaw roared over him. "You're lucky I found a clue. Whoever it was had to be one of the crew you took onshore to that tiny isle. I found an accursed fruit peel in my cabin."

Scales shook his head. "There must be a misunderstandin', Cap'n. Are you saying someone brought bana—"

Blackclaw cut him off, slapping Scales' snout. "Don't even mutter that cursed rotten fruit's name. I don't need more bad luck after that woman whistled up our last storm. That damn fruit is just a welcome mat for the plague. Just find me whoever brought it aboard, and we find the traitor on board who's trying to steal our treasure."

"Well, uh," Scales stammered, trying to think. "A few of the powder monkeys were helping out climbing the palms for coconuts and limes."

"Of course." Blackclaw was already rushing to the gun deck. "Blasted buggers love the fruit, would have been easy to slip in through the window too."

"Cap, wait!" The baseboards heaved from the crocodile's weight as Scales chased after the cat.

Stomping to the gun deck, Blackclaw found the powder monkeys chittering to themselves as they went about wiping down the cannons.

"Okay you lil' buggers. Who did it?" Blackclaw's sword was already drawn, ready for blood.

The young capuchins froze, eyes wide, at the terrifying, threatening black cat overshadowing them. One trembled so much he dropped the cannonball he was carrying, the thud drawing the captain's complete attention.

"What do you know?" The captain loomed over the small monkey and snatched him up by the scruff of his neck. "What secrets are you hiding? You think you can run around this ship like it's your own personal frigate taking what you like? You'll be stealing from the bottom of the sea!"

The young capuchin trembled and curled up in the cat's grasp.

"Cap'n, please!" Scales shuffled up next to the cat, his hands up in defense. "You know these youngins can barely speak. They'd never go against your will. Just look at how they're quaking in their boots."

"Fine." Blackclaw snarled and plopped the young monkey down. "But if I find out any of you were in on this, your fate'll be worse than just a toss overboard."

Scales pulled the captain back out of the room for the powder monkey's safety. "We can ask if Cookie knows anything. If the thief brought more of that fruit onboard, maybe they'd have tried to slip it in with the other food."

"It'll be alligator stew if he let that happen." The captain's claws raked against the deck as he turned his rage to the galley.

Cookie paused from gutting fish to give the captain and quartermaster a dull stare when they both entered the kitchen. That was all the time he had before Blackclaw slammed his fists on the table.

"Who was it?" the cat demanded, glaring down at the alligator.

Cookie glanced from Scales to Blackclaw and back before tilting his head slightly to the side.

The crocodile sighed and filled in the blanks. "Someone's up to something funny. Cap'n found some bananas on board. Anyone bring anything like that by the galley?"

The cook stared off in thought while scraping some guts into a bucket beside the table. After a moment, he returned his gaze to the crocodile and silently shook his head no.

Blackclaw cried out in frustration, kicking over the bucket of fresh fish entrails before storming out.

Scales caught up to him, skulking just out of the cat's view. "How 'bout you go rest in your cabin, Cap'n?" he suggested. "I'll question the rest of the men who went ashore and see what I can dig up. If someone's hiding something on board, they can't hide it from me."

Blackclaw slammed a paw into the side of the ship, digging in his claws. As thoughts of who could be after him flooded his mind, a murky tentacle flicked out from a hole in a deckboard. He jumped, but it was no longer there. Taking a deep breath of salty air, the captain sighed. "Fine, just find them. And when you do, bring them straight to me."

***

A burst of wind whistled through the open cabin window, bolting Blackclaw awake in a sweat. Swearing he had locked the latch, the cat shut the window. The sun hung low on the horizon, leaning in to kiss the sea, and blanketing the cabin in a radiating glow. A plate of coconut chunks and citrus slices left on the captain's desk caught the cat's eye. Scales must have told Cookie to leave something for him. Deciding against returning to his nap, Blackclaw picked up a slice of lime, chewing the fruit to the rind.

He noticed his cabin had also been cleaned up. Blackclaw didn't recall doing anything of the sort—just collapsing in bed upon returning to the cabin. Regardless, he would have a word with Scales about allowing people into his private cabin. The less people with access to the gem, the better.

The cat captain eyed the shelf, chest still sitting atop it. A quick check and the giant ruby within glimmered back a hello. It was still safe, thank the seas. Now back to business.

He replaced the chest with a sea chart, rolling it out across the desk. "We were on our way back from Antigua when that storm blew us out east. We're heading west now so we'll probably just end up in Tortuga soon." The cat's tail twitched back and forth as he looked at the locations on the map. "Best to confirm with the bird."

He grabbed his overcoat and burst out of his cabin. "Ruth!" Blackclaw called out as he strolled to the upper deck.

He heard a distant, startled squawk. Ruth climbed down the mast and ran up, flapping and panting. "Yes, Cap'n?"

"Give me good news, bird," Blackclaw said, keeping a keen eye across the sea at the gigantic red ball dipping lower into the water. "It looks like the sea is back on our side."

Ruth wrung the telescope in her talons. "The stars have just started to come out, but it looks we were knocked off course a little more than anticipated. Luckily, if we cut in west even further, it shouldn't be far to the next port where we can grab a few more supplies before heading back to Devil's Isle."

"Excellent, so we're not far off from Tortuga then?" The captain flashed his first grin all day.

Ruth dipped her beak and looked away. "Not Tortuga. We're further north than that, which might explain why we haven't seen any other ships out here. We're most likely only a day's voyage to Nassau. We could port there easily." The gull gave a hopeful flap of her wings. "Once the sun's fully down, I'll know for sure!"

"What?" snarled Blackclaw.

Ruth nearly choked on the sea breeze. "I, uh, said we should be able to sail to Na—"

"No!"

"I'm sorry?" The seagull's webbed foot stepped back.

"Not Nassau! We stop at Tortuga as planned! You better not be leading us astray, bird."

"Uh, well," Ruth stumbled on her words, confused. "I can double check the map, but if my coordinates are correct, we wouldn't make Devil's Isle in time if we swung back around to Tortuga."

Before Blackclaw could argue, a shout from the stern interrupted them. "Sharks lurking!"

A swabbie stood staring over the edge of the ship. Leaning over, Blackclaw saw what had caught the lad's attention: a frenzy of vertical grey fins trailing behind the rudder.

Another sign today. This one, though, not of bad luck, but of death. Blackclaw chewed his lip. "…Fine."

He turned back to the gull. "Set a course to Nassau." He waved her off with a coal paw. "And send Scales up. I'll make sure he agrees with the plan."

"Y-yessir." Ruth squawked and rushed below deck to the charts.

Blackclaw leaned on the ship's railing, staring off at the blood-red sun sinking deeper into the sea. The black cat began swaying back and forth with the boat as the sun grew larger and larger, consuming the sky. His ears twitched as he once again heard faint whistling.

"Okay, who's doing that?" The cat whirled around. "Apparently Bonnie wasn't enough of an example."

The crew looked around, confused at the captain's question.

"Something wrong with the lot of you?" Blackclaw's eyes snapped between the crew members, his tail lashing wildly. Then his head began to pound. He glanced at the horizon in time to see the sun turning black and blotting out the sky. No stars appeared—instead the deck disappeared from beneath him and he fell back into the inky depths of the sea. He gasped for air but there was none, the water surrounding him, pulling him deeper. The pressure increased, crushing him, until a clawed hand clamped down on his shoulder and whirled him around.

"Cap'n?" The quartermaster crocodile looked his captain over. "Are you feeling okay?"

Blackclaw shook his head. He was back on board. "Uh, yes? What is it?"

Scales looked him over before continuing, "Well, Ruth said you wanted to see me. Something 'bout changing our course?"

"Ah, right." The cat shook out some fur. "Feathers there was saying we've skipped past Tortuga; she's charting a course to Nassau instead. I don't like it, but we have little choice if we want to get to the Digoba buyer in time."

"I understand," Scales said. "Not happy myself that we're returning to Nassau so soon. Losing Winston was hard, 'specially what with just throwing his sister overboard. Would rather we didn't have to revisit that port."

"Well, we won't be staying for long. Choose your offshore party now and take account of what supplies we need. We're only docking long enough to take on new supplies, then shoving off."

"But the crew, they'll want shore time." The crocodile's tail swayed as he tried to bargain. "And after today's… events."

Blackclaw sneered, his claws extending. "Don't let anyone off this boat who needn't leave. That's an order."

The large crocodile shrunk down. "Of course, sir. The crew'll understand."

"In the meantime, have you found out anything about our interloper?"

"Nothing yet. The rest of the men who went ashore all had alibis for the day."

"Well, do your job and get to the bottom of this," Blackclaw hissed. "Once we dock in Nassau, they may take the opportunity to grab the gem and dash. I won't let anyone get the better of me."

"Of course, just…" Scales paused, leaning in to whisper. "Are you feeling alright? I know we're on a tight deadline right now, but it seems like something else is going on."

"Like what?" Blackclaw's eyes formed slits, staring deep into his quartermaster's soul.

Scales stood silent for a moment. "Nothing, Cap'n. I'll prepare for our docking tomorrow. Take care." The crocodile left and wandered off below deck.

Blackclaw kicked a steel bucket near the stern. His nose wrinkled and his stomach churned at the fish guts that spilled out. "Something stinks around here, that's for sure."

***

Blackclaw gripped the banister and gritted his teeth as a wave crashed against the hull of the ship, spraying sea water over him. In the night sky, the sea of stars swirled, matching the twisting of the knots in his stomach. He swallowed the gorge rising in this throat. Cookie's evening meal wasn't sitting quite right. "Keep 'er steady, helmsman."

"Aye, Cap'n," replied the tiger. "This wind'll blow us straight to Nassau in no time, but she'll be a bit rough. Not like you to lose your sea legs, though."

The black cat's ears flattened. "Mind your own business." Taking a large breath of sea air, the captain padded below deck.

His eyes adjusted slowly to the empty corridors, lit only by a few scattered lanterns. Blackclaw winced and steadied himself against the wall. As the ship creaked and bent in the waves, the cat's ears twitched toward another sound hidden beneath it all.

"Whistling again?" he questioned, eyes darting around but finding nothing.

The shrill tune, in strange harmony with the crashing waves outside, only grew louder as he pursued it further down the corridor. Tracing the sound, he followed it straight to his cabin, the door once again ajar.

"Who would dare—"

The captain's thoughts were cut off when he stepped into a warm, wet oozing puddle running out from under his cabin door. Pushing the door elicited a ghastly creak as it opened, and more warm liquid rushed over his feet when he stepped into the room.

The first thing that hit Blackclaw was the stench. The wretched scent of rot and decay surged into the cat's nose, nearly doubling him over. The captain swung a free paw in front of his face to try and wave the miasma away, but something wrapped around his arm. With a cry, he tugged back, pulling at what felt like wet hands gripping his limb.

The door slammed shut behind him.

"Who's there?" Blackclaw screamed into the darkness. He swatted around at whatever held him, only to have his other arm also become entangled. "Don't think I'll let you out of here alive!" he bellowed, thrashing around.

A burbling voice answered him, "Then it's a good thing you already killed me, Captain Blackclaw."

Blackclaw's ears twitched. "That voice."

A flicker and flash blinded the cat as rows of lanterns ignited and lit up his cabin. Seaweed and wet ropes hung intertwined through the rafters, dripping a soggy mess of algae and sea water over the entirety of the room. Amongst the new drapery, a crude noose hung low, directly in front of the captain, inches away from his wrinkling nose.

"What is all this?" Blackclaw tugged at the seaweed-woven ropes. "Who let you in here?"

"I don't need your permission to go anywhere anymore!" the voice screeched so loud the windows blew open. The curtains flew in every direction as wind gusts screamed through the room, spitting sea water on anything that wasn't already damp.

Blackclaw let out a roar and wrestled one of his arms free. "Enough!" he yelled, unsheathing his cutlass and slashing the ropes to free his other limb. "Show yourself!" Reaching up, the black cat grasped the noose in front of him and yanked it down.

The coils of seaweed and rope receded and stretched as though he had activated a giant machine of fibers and algae. The rafters creaked as the bonds wrapped around them tightened and flexed. The wind at the back of the cabin picked up, violently slamming the window panes back and forth. The lanterns flickered until they could no longer stand up against the gale, fading out into smoke. Above it all, the whistling returned, its volume increasing until it became a shrill screech that transformed into cackling laughter. A dark mess of a figure swooped in through the window, suspended above the ground by the same cords and seaweed that enveloped the cabin, dripping a new fresh, disgusting mess of sea water, fish guts and sea scum upon the cabin floor.

Two glowing red eyes and a sickly yellow twisted grin materialized in the darkness. "Happy to see me again, Cap'n?"

Blackclaw squinted, his eyes adjusting to the change in light. The eyes and teeth slowly formed into a rotting, waterlogged, russet head with long ears tied back by a ripped blue bandana. A ruffled blouse and leather vest now stained with blood and algae covered a tattered and beaten chest. The black cat shook his head. "Bonnie?"

The geist of his previous boatswain tilted her head, showing off a wicked smile. "I warned you there'd be a curse on your head for what you did. Now face my revenge!" A flash illuminated the room again as all the lanterns ignited. The rabbit raised a cutlass above her head and swooped down at the pirate captain.

Blackclaw rolled to the side to dodge the attack, and Bonnie's cutlass swung down to take a chunk out of his desk instead. As the ghost swooped around for another slice, the cat sidestepped away and raised his sword to attack back, only to find his arm entangled once again. He tugged against the enchanted ropes, and the rabbit cackled, circling back around.

Readying her blade, Bonnie called out, "I told you your secret was safe with me. Yet you still found an excuse to toss me overboard."

Blackclaw extended his claws and slashed at the ropes, freeing his arm in time to parry Bonnie's attack. More strands of seaweed and rope lashed out at him, but the captain slashed them back. "How long would you even keep silent? Already the crew seems suspicious!" He swung at the flying sailor only to have his attack deflected, slashing his bookshelf instead, sending covers and pages flying.

"They're suspicious because of you. Look how far you've deteriorated." Bonnie sent more wet tentacles of rope after the captain before spinning around with another whirlwind of attacks. "You've caused your own downfall. Yet still you continue to blame others."

"I do what's best for my ship! No lowly boatswain will change my mind!" Blackclaw dug his claws into the soggy floorboards and catapulted into the air.

The ghost parried, but the captain's cutlass still claimed a small tear through her soggy blouse. Blackclaw pushed harder, jumping off one of the walls to pounce again, knocking one of the lanterns to the floor in the process.

The rabbit snarled, blocking the cat's strikes and shifting from side to side. "You're the anchor dragging this ship down to the depths. The crew needs to jump ship if they want to save their hides. That's still more of a choice than you bothered to give my brother."

A barnacle-encrusted rope curled around the captain's ankle and yanked him to the floor. He rolled to the side, narrowly missing the rabbit's blade carving out a large slash in the floor boards.

"Your brother had a choice, but in the end, he chose poorly," Blackclaw retorted, slashing the rope holding him down and bouncing back up.

A banging from the cabin door echoed over the fight as a voice from beyond the room called out, "Cap'n? Everything alright in there?"

Blackclaw glanced toward the interruption, giving Bonnie an opening. The spirit dove in, cutlass full of fury. The cat's whiskers twitched, leaning back as the tip of the cutlass grazed his cheek. He let out a roar of rage.

"Cap'n! Let me in!" The pounding on the door turned into heavy thuds as the crewmember tried to ram their way in.

"Your crew may have saved you this time, but you'll never do the same for them!" Bonnie hissed. She swooped backwards, falling out through the window.

Blackclaw ran to the window as all the rope and seaweed followed its mistress out of the room and into the inky blackness of the sea.

The door burst open and Scales stumbled into the cabin to find his captain leaning out of the cabin, searching every wave and splash with his eyes. "Cap'n?" the crocodile asked, glancing around at the mess of a cabin.

Water was everywhere, dripping from the shelves and the now soaked bedroll. Papers and maps littered the floor in soggy shreds. Scales stepped over to the overturned lantern and stomped out the flame before it had a chance to burn through the floorboards.

"Everything alright?" he asked again, slowly approaching the black cat still glued to the windowsill. He reached out and placed his hand on the captain's shoulder.

The cat whirled around, cutlass at the crocodile's neck. "Did you see her?" Blackclaw demanded.

The captain's eyes twitched crazily. His paws held the tip of the sword perfectly in place. A chill breeze blew through the cabin as Scales stood frozen, palms open in the air. Blackclaw's shoulders rose and fell with each deep breath. Nothing moved save for the curtains blowing in the wind and the occasional ocean spray.

Scales replied softly and slowly, staring at the blade pointed at him. "See who?"

Blackclaw blinked and gradually lowered his sword. "Apologies, Scales. I'm a bit on edge."

Scales gulped and took a slow step back. "Would you, uh, like to tell me what that was?" The crocodile scanned the destruction of the private quarters. "I heard yelling and noises, so I came running."

The cat spent another moment staring out at the sea before closing the windows. "A vengeful spirit of our late boatswain decided to visit." Blackclaw paused to take another deep breath. "Thankfully, you seem to have scared her off just in time. Thank you, Scales."

The crocodile blinked, once again looking his captain and the cabin over again. "Are you feeling all right? If Winston were still—"

"No! He can't—" Black stopped himself and rubbed his face. "I'm fine. We'll keep the window locked tonight. Just… go get me a spare bedroll." The cat motioned to his soggy, slashed up bed.

"Of course. There should be one in the hold or you can have mine." Scales nodded. "I'll find some new bedding for you in Nassau."

The black cat's tail twitched. His claws extended, but he took another deep breath and retracted them. "And send a swabbie to mop up this mess." He waved a paw to dismiss the crocodile.

Once Scales closed the door behind him, Blackclaw checked the small chest still thankfully safe on his shelf. A quick turn of the key and the ruby was back in his paws. "Just a little bit longer," he whispered to it.

***

It wasn't until late in the afternoon that Noir's call from the Crow's Nest marked the sight of Nassau's port. At the announcement, Blackclaw's door whipped open for the first time that day. Since the previous night's events, the captain had remained holed up in his private cabin, even refusing Cookie's breakfast when it came knocking on his door.

His tail lashed as made his way top deck. They might need to dock for supplies, but they could not afford to waste any time. No more delays.

"Scales!" the captain bellowed as the helmsman brought the ship near the pier.

The quartermaster hurried over, his claws clattering on the boards anxiously, as if carefully picking each step. "Yes, Cap'n?"

Blackclaw stared at the pier as ropes were thrown overboard to pull the ship in closer. "Everything ready to go ashore?"

The crocodile reached into his vest pocket, pulling out a crumpled list. "I've marked up a list of supplies, pulled the crew aside to join me, and made sure we have enough to pay for it. Assuming me mate Theo's not too busy for a rush order, we should be back at sea before sunset."

Blackclaw gave Scales a sidelong glance. "You're just grabbing essentials, right? Nothing that can't wait until Devil's Isle?"

Scales gripped his list tighter. "'Course, Cap'n."

"Just make sure you're back on the double. We hoist sail as soon as we have all the supplies. Anyone not on board is left behind." Blackclaw stared down his quartermaster. "Is that understood?"

"Aye, Cap'n." Scales raised a claw and paused. After a moment of thought he leaned in to whisper, "You should know, people have been talking about last night."

The crew grew noisier now with the boat tied to the dock and the gangplank being affixed to the side.

The cat's whiskers flicked. "They should know what happens to loose lips. Keep them in line." Before Scales could retort, Blackclaw gave him another yellow-eyed stare. "Get on with your duty, sailor." The cat motioned the crocodile away with a flick of his tail and yelled out, "Ruth!"

Scales sighed and walked away, barking orders to nearby crew members to follow him. Blackclaw watched him like a jungle cat stalking prey. As Scales stepped onto the gangplank, the cat noticed tentacles of seaweed creeping up from under the shadows to curl around the crocodile's ankle. The cat's ears twitched, but before he could cry out, a loud squawk interrupted him.

"Cap'n!" Ruth stood up straight at attention.

Blackclaw glanced at his navigator and then back at Scales. The crocodile continued to the dock, no seaweed or tentacles to be found. Blackclaw tried to groom his hackles back down and turned to the gull. "Ah… there you are, yes. What's the weather like for tonight?"

"All clear," Ruth said.

"Have you started plotting the course to Devil's Isle? I want to pull anchor as soon as we're done here."

Ruth nodded and smiled. "Already made the plans, but I'll double-check my notes now to make sure we're ready to go."

"See that you do," mumbled the captain. As the seagull dashed off, his attention moved back to the gangplank, searching for anything out of the ordinary but finding nothing. Shaking his head, he moved away from the railing to inspect the ship in Scales' absence.

***

By the time the sun dipped low in the sky, new lacquer was needed to seal over the claw marks in the deck from Blackclaw's pacing. His ears twitched at the return of the offshore party. Dashing to the railing, he saw the crew lowering the gangplank.

As a heron crewmember hoisted a sack on each shoulder and

yelled out, "You killed our doctor, didn't you?"

No answer came from the cat as he took a step back, his own legs beginning to wobble. His limbs were sapped of strength. His fingers failed to hold on to his cutlass, tumbling to the deck with a clatter.

Scales spat on the deck. "These curses you've been seeing. These monsters and attacks." The crocodile stretched out a single claw. "You've been hallucinating them the entire time. It's the yellow fever, isn't it?"

The cat looked around; the sea monsters were creeping closer. They were stealing his essence, weakening him. He coughed and wiped the blood from his muzzle. Blackclaw reached down to pick up his sword. "Stay with me, Scales. We can defeat these wretched lost souls. There's still time to get to Devil's Isle. Everything will be okay once we're there."

"We're not going with you." The crocodile kicked the cat back down. "We've been riding a bloody plague ship this entire time, with its captain leading us all to hell. Instead of saving the crew, you'd risk all our lives for a glittering jewel."

Scales clawed apart Blackclaw's shirt, grabbing the key hidden beneath. With a heave, he snapped the silver chain holding it around the cat's neck.

"No, please," Blackclaw coughed, trying to claw back at his quartermaster, but only able to weakly paw back. The black sludge pooled around him, turning to tar that held him to the deck.

"Now shove off, you traitorous cat." Clutching his chest with one hand and the key in the other, Scales kicked Blackclaw over the edge of the ship, sending him into the water.

Blackclaw tried to swim, watching the light above the waves begin to fade. Inky, dark tendrils of seaweed curled around his limbs, pulling him further into the depths. Sputtering and gasping for breath, he looked up, only to see Winston's rotting face smiling back at him. Waving from above, the rabbit's corpse followed him below. Down and down until the light no longer could reach them.

THE UNLUCKY

Sera Kane

TWILIGHT SONG BURROW

"Kennedy."

The sound of his name caught his attention, and he twisted one tall, black ear towards it. The rabbit could barely hear the soft padding of his friend's feet, a sound audible merely because the cat was currently walking about in his human guise.

Despite their long friendship, Kennedy's heart sped up at Samael's approach. Human or cat form, Samael moved like a predator. He slunk and slid noiselessly through the dark passages. And he took a distinct amusement in scaring the little kits. As if the entire warren wasn't already on edge having a cat living with them!

Said cat came alongside him, watching as Kennedy cautiously continued his wiring run near the ceiling. "Dolores is asking for you again."

"All right." The black rabbit kept his eyes on his work. Samael chuckled beside him, and Kennedy purposefully ignored him. He knew many made fun of his focus, but that skill was why he excelled at nearly everything he set his mind to. Suddenly, dark-skinned hands came up beside his paws, closing the tubing around the wires with ease. A reluctant smile tugged at Kennedy's muzzle. "Damn thumbs."

"Damn them, indeed," Samael agreed, but his tone was laughing. "Especially since they are making your job so much easier! If only you bunnies were as talented and powerful as us cats."

"Ah, but then we'd have to be just as arrogant, and after Creation filled us with such cleverness and bravery there just wasn't any room left for such a sad trait."

Samael snorted, moving down the hall to the next section of tubing. "Just due," the cat said. "For the brilliance that all cats have."

Kennedy went up on his toes, ears pressing against the ceiling as he began to thread the wires into place. He was over six feet tall, not including his ears, which gave him nearly another foot. Despite his lack of thumbs, his paws were dexterous, which allowed him to do all sorts of intricate tasks. Such as wielding weapons, a skill only the Luckkeepers were obliged to learn.

Pounding feet echoed through the burrow, alerting the two friends. Kennedy's nose twitched back and forth, scenting the movement of the air. "Tristan," he informed Samael. He bent down to close his tools. Samael fastened the wire to the tubing to prevent a running hazard. When Tristan rounded the last turn, Kennedy was ready.

"You may as well come," Kennedy said to the cat. "I'd appreciate the help."

"Kennedy!" Tristan's voice was near panic, the white rabbit dancing on his feet.

"I will never understand you bunnies and your superstitions," Samael said, but he was already transforming. On four feet in his natural form, he looked like a larger than usual short-haired black cat. His brilliant green eyes twinkled, and he darted down the hallway.

Tristan, already on edge, leapt upwards, his head colliding with the ceiling. He keened in fear and Kennedy winced. He quickly placed a calming hand on the quivering shoulder. "It's all right, Tristan. Samael will soak up some of the bad luck, too."

Recalled to why he'd rushed to the black rabbit, Tristan grabbed ahold of Kennedy's paw. "It's started! Kennedy! She's giving birth right NOW."

"Then we'd better run."

Samael yowled in agreement, disappearing around the corner. Kennedy followed him, and Tristan came pounding after. This, Kennedy thought with a wild grin, was one thing he loved: coming to the aid of his colony mates.

It took them only a few minutes to race through the maze of the warren to the birthing den. Dolores lay on her side amidst the sweet grasses Tristan collected for her, splotched brown and white ears flattened. She tilted her head at the intrusion, spotting Kennedy first and then her mate. She gave a small smile that wavered when she caught Samael's scent. "Tristan…"

He took one paw and stroked it gently. "Kennedy brought him."

Kennedy leaned in, touching noses with her. "It's all right, Dolores. He's a Luckkeeper of his kind. Your kits are safe."

Reassured, she nodded, eyes closing. Her breath hiffed swiftly as she endured the pain. Samael stood behind the doe, human again as he watched with vague interest. Kennedy gently touched Dolores' head before standing beside the cat.

"So, what exactly am I doing here?" Samael asked with an amused undertone.

"We will be picking up each kit after it's born to absorb its bad luck."

Samael lifted one black eyebrow. "Uh… huh."

Kennedy smiled. "It works, believe me."

"Well, you are the expert on bunnies," Samael said. "Cats are not nearly so difficult."

"Cats are equally good and evil," Kennedy pointed out. "And you *can* be because you become mostly solitary upon puberty. Rabbits live together, so we must be more on the good side than the evil."

"Bad luck is not inherently evil," Samael scoffed with a dark scowl. "Black cats are *not* servants of the Void simply because bad luck rides our backs."

The vehemence in Samael's voice startled Kennedy. "I hadn't heard of that one."

Samael shrugged, green eyes skating off to one side. "You know how it is. Someone decides that this or that thing is definitely bad or good luck, or just worth a handful of gold pieces. Next thing you know, humans are selling cat livers and rabbit feet on the black market."

Kennedy made a shushing motion with one paw, glancing significantly at the breeding pair. Samael grimaced in apology. The other rabbits, fortunately, were not paying them any attention.

"And so it was," Tristan crooned softly, "that the Void, called the Eater, the Devouring Cold, did fall by his own dark blade, and a new era was born. Yet even then, Creation's compassion went unto her brother, and she took into her hand both the Black Blade, His Ill

Luck, and Her Tears, known as Her Heart's Cry, the Pendant of Life, and cast them into the far reaches that never again should they war."

Samael snorted. "You bunnies and your stories."

"It's helping Dolores," Kennedy said with a smile. "Just listen."

By the time Tristan reached the prophesy of Creation's next triumph over her brother, the babies were born. Kennedy picked up the first kit, a brown male. He closed his eyes and pressed the tiny, furless forehead to his nose. He breathed in the baby scent, opening himself up to the full potential of this new life. He waited for the rush of energy, a filling of his senses that would then settle into him. With this baby, however, there was hardly anything. Kennedy frowned, pulling back the kit. It yawned at him, and Kennedy gently laid the baby down at his mother's side. Samael held a female kit with a bemused expression, glancing at Kennedy.

"I don't think it works for me." He passed over the baby to Kennedy's gentle paws.

Breathing deep, the black rabbit brought her tiny forehead to his nose. Again, he felt a tiny stir, like a distant breeze, yet there was nothing to take. Worried now, Kennedy put her down and turned to Samael, who had the third kit.

The black cat smiled down on the equally dark-furred baby. "She looks like you, Kennedy."

Kennedy froze and Tristan bit off a curse. The white rabbit looked worriedly down at his mate. She lifted one ear slightly. "What?" Dolores asked in a tight voice. "What's wrong?"

Samael raised his eyebrows. "Yeah. What's wrong?"

Kennedy shook his head, forcing a pain-filled smile as he reached for the kit. "Thank you," he said gravely. Here was all the missing luck. He could feel it roiling around inside of her, kept separate from his own by her natural shields.

Kennedy brought her within view of her mother. Dolores gasped, eyes wide, as she focused on Kennedy. "I'm so sorry," she said hesitantly. "I had no idea. I just thought it was a good pregnancy."

Kennedy gave her a small, lop-sided smile. "May I present to you the next Luckkeeper, an honor upon you and your bloodline for years to come." He hadn't been expecting this. He wasn't prepared! He had no name picked for this kit, who needed all the protection he could give her. His mind raced, covering his hesitation with a thoughtful expression. He hoped it did more for the worried parents than it did for him.

"Sidero," he said decisively. That was the name his father had chosen in case Kennedy was doe instead of buck. "She wears her name as a shield and a badge. To her will all the evil be drawn, and she will smite it down with cleverness, courage, and the colony's good will."

"It's a wonderful name," Dolores said, relieved.

Tristan nodded with a little smile of his own as he accepted his youngest daughter from Kennedy. "She'll be our nymph to protect the colony." He looked proudly at Kennedy, but then his smile faltered. "But…"

Kennedy shook his head, forcing a smile. "This is a time for joyous celebration. It's rare for two of us to be in a warren at the same time."

"Yes, for good reason," Dolores murmured, looking worriedly at her babies. "No offense, Kennedy, but could you—?"

"Of course." He smiled at her, taking a step back to encompass the family with his dark gaze. He took a deep breath, memorizing the scene. His eyes fell to Sidero. The ritual words locked in his throat. He could not give her the same words his father had passed on for him. Kennedy improvised. "To my successor, I bequeath what I am and have as a member of Twilight Song. Our luck, your guide, Sidero."

Guilt demanded he do more, but his heart could not bear it. Kennedy ducked out of the den.

Samael frowned at the pair who refused his gaze. He took after his friend. Kennedy was moving at swift clip, and Samael loped to catch up. "Kennedy, wait. Where are you going?"

"I have to leave the warren," Kennedy said tightly.

"Right now? It's the middle of the day."

When Kennedy ignored him, Samael narrowed his eyes in irritation. "What was that about? They were frantic for you, then suddenly they want you gone? I thought you were the most important rabbit here."

"The Luckkeeper is important, yes, but does are more important," Kennedy corrected him. The colony still slept, a bittersweet revelation. It would save them from seeing him go, yet he wished to say good-bye.

Suddenly he halted. He looked at Samael's hand holding his arm, then into his friend's eyes. "You have to let go, Samael. It's time."

Samael threw up his hands. "*Cats* are supposed to be inscrutable. Not bunnies! Tell me what's going on."

Kennedy glanced around them. "Once we get out of here. I promise."

Samael nodded, albeit unhappily, hesitating as Kennedy kept going. "What about your things? And mine?"

"I have nothing here anymore," Kennedy said. "But please gather your things quickly. I need to get as far away as possible."

Dreamscape, Personal

The blow knocked him right off his feet. The huntsman rolled to his right side. His back turned towards her. The kick slammed into his kidneys and he fell onto his face.

"Why are you (*mine*), Huntsman Jor?" The silky voice was a trap. Was it an honest question? The lead to another strike? Was she forgiving him? No way to tell but survive.

"To serve you, Mistress." Jor forced the painful words through his lips. He pushed upwards. His head hung as he fought back the nausea of pain. He deserved this.

Her foot connected with the back of his skull and his face slammed into the ground. Her boot landed hard, grinding him into the dull, grey sand. "Wrong." Her words hissed towards him, stinging him with freezing intent. "You are mine because you are a useless piece of flesh. I have given you powers because your life is worth nothing. Tell me!"

His cheeks scraped against the stones as his lips moved. "I am nothing."

"Yes. (*No.*)" She leaned on him again before stepping back. "Kneel, trash, and tell me what (*who*) you are."

Jor slid his hands under him. He kneeled before her, staring steadfastly at her golden leather boots. He remembered the fawn he'd brought back for her. He'd never seen a deer glitter like metal before. He had a scar along his ribs from the stag he'd stolen the baby from.

No, this wasn't right. His mistress's boots were made of metal, not leather. And his scar was from a blade, black and cold.

"I am," he said, beginning to shiver, "your Huntsman. You took me from nothing because I am nothing. I am your servant because I have no other worth but to serve you."

No! The exclamation warmed him, the little voice desirable to his ear. He knew that voice, one that saved him.

"Look at me."

Instantly he turned his face up to her. Her perfect features were always a shock. Her skin was alabaster, eyes glowing blue and gold, the colors swirling with her agitation. Even as he watched, however, the colors settled, gold at the top of each iris, sea blue on the bottom. Her pale pink lips curved upwards, her face surrounded by golden locks the exact shade of a perfect morning sun. "Yes," she crooned, stepping closer to run a hand over his red hair. "You are the human trash (*man*) I have chosen. With your dead soul hair and your imperfect gaze. (*You*) are (*my*) Huntsman. (*I have given you the strength of my kind, the cunning of the foxkin, the agility of the mongoose, the speed of star light. Love—)*" Her fingers tightened in his hair, pulling right across the top of his scalp. The blue and gold of her eyes began to spin, like a hurricane threatening to batter what remained. They flickered, black and red. "You will (*do*) not fail me, Huntsman Jor." Her voice was sweet despite the storm. "You will find my talisman. Do you understand?"

The last wasn't a question. It was a demand. "Yes, Mistress."

She flung him away from her and he flew almost halfway across the courtyard before hitting the ground and skidding another few feet. "Go, little nothing. (*Hear my voice. Jor, listen for me.*) And bring back to me the Black Luck."

FREELANDS

Samael caught up with Kennedy at the edge of Twilight Song Colony's lands. Kennedy stared out into the wilds. Through their years of friendship—as well as the fact that rabbits had trouble controlling their ears—Samael could tell Kennedy felt morose. He hitched his bag securely over his shoulder and came up beside his friend. "So."

Kennedy didn't turn toward him, merely started walking. His stride hesitated as they drew to the boundary, but his chin went up and he resolutely continued forward. Samael felt the boundary as an unpleasant ruffling of fur. Kennedy's crossing should have been difficult, the magic of the lands and his colony keeping him tied to them.

Yet the rabbit passed through without a flinch. Samael frowned, contemplating the unexpected occurrence.

"I will tell you a story," Kennedy abruptly said. When nothing further was forthcoming, Samael felt compelled to prompt.

"A story sounds like a great idea, if it involves an explanation."

The rabbit's forehead furrowed, dark brown eyes closing briefly in pain. "Once upon a time, not too many years past, the rabbits were at war. Hare versus hare, doe to doe, buck against buck. Too much land had been overtaken by the Void, and the colonies fought to take land from others. At that time, there remained but two black rabbits alive: Desmond of Flickering Streams and Abaddon of—"

"Twilight Song," Samael said. "Your father."

Kennedy nodded. "And Abaddon of Twilight Song. Now, it was known in those times that the lands of Flickering Streams and Twilight Song were not only neighbors, not only friends, but also the most prosperous and stable in the world. In greed, they were called hoarders. In jealousy, they were called evil. In hatred, three colonies banded together to overtake these promised lands."

"Night Joy, Lark Dawn, and Horizon Lay," Samael said.

"Yes. Three times they attacked the warrens of Flickering Streams and Twilight Song. Three times they were repelled. Then a devilish idea came to the attackers. They doused two of their warriors in the blood of the slain, cut them to grave injury, and sent them in to Flickering Streams lands. Compassionate, Flickering Streams took in the injured does. When they begged for a Luckkeeper—as their own had been killed early in the wars—to save them from the backlash of their clans' choices, Desmond went to them, despite his friend Abaddon's advice to stay away.

"And so it came to pass that even as Desmond's mate Mallory began to birth, Desmond was slaughtered by the traitors. Night Joy, Lark Dawn, and Horizon Lay flowed into the warren like oil, killing every pregnant doe and every kit they could find."

Samael stared at Kennedy, aghast yet unsurprised. War was terrible, often evil. He shook his head in sorrow for the wasted lives. Nevertheless, this explained nothing. In fact, Samael realized, it raised more questions. Rabbits were community-minded. "Why would they kill the pregnant does?"

Kennedy glanced at his friend, approval in his eyes as he nodded.

"Abaddon knew then what was to come."

"Kennedy, you didn't answer my question."

Kennedy's smile was sad. "I am." He turned down a small path and Samael followed him into a deep grove of trees. "At that time, Abaddon's mate was heavily pregnant. She, too, understood what the betrayal of Desmond meant. And so Brona went into hiding outside of the warren, making sure to leave signs of where she had gone so that she could be tracked."

A feeling of foreboding filled Samael's chest. "Kennedy, just explain. No more stories."

The rabbit shook his head, continuing onwards. "Abaddon gave unto his mate the name to give his offspring, and the words to speak over his lucky kit. Then he left her." Kennedy took a breath, sighing like a dying wind. "Their enemies came, to strike a deciding blow upon their enemy by killing his mate and unborn kits. But Abaddon was waiting there and fought off the attackers.

"They came again the next day.

"And again the next day.

"And again the next day.

"At twilight, Abaddon's mate went into labor. The hour had arrived, and their enemies came in force. Tired and injured, Abaddon struggled to protect his Brona and his kits. Brona had three kits, then four, and, then, a fifth, a kit black as night. And as Brona proclaimed his name, speaking over him the words given to her by her mate, at that time, Abaddon was felled by his enemies."

Kennedy stopped in front of a small burrow entrance, staring at it silently. Samael stared as well, knowing that this was where Kennedy's father died at the exact moment of his friend's birth.

"'This is my kit, my blood,'" Kennedy intoned in a slow, sepulcher tone. "'Unto him, my luck, the luck of our colony. So shall he be known, Kennedy, the Black Luck, to carry on my burden from this moment hence. Kennedy, take your heritage and be our shield. So spake Abaddon, upon his kit.'"

Samael inspected Kennedy's face out of the corner of his eye. The sorrow there made his chest ache. Finally, he asked softly, "Why did they kill the pregnant does?"

"At the birth of a new Luckkeeper, the old will die. And at the death of a Luckkeeper, a new one will be born."

"They killed the pregnant does to keep Flickering Streams from having a new Luckkeeper?" Samael couldn't keep the incredulity out of his voice.

"Did you know," Kennedy said suddenly. "The elders say the Void first came when two black rabbits lived within the same colony?"

Samael blinked. "What?"

"The old Luckkeeper was meant to leave the colony, many signs had been noted. Yet at her son's birth, she refused to go. She stayed, and their colony was ripped apart."

"That's ridiculous," Samael scoffed. Kennedy's expression was so serious, however, Samael nearly doubted his own words. "There's no proof. Is there?"

"There are the stories from the elders," Kennedy answered with a shrug. "The lore of the rabbits. Whether or not you believe is irrelevant. The rabbits believe and so…" He trailed off to let Samael finish.

The cat sighed himself. "So they believe, so the world is." Cats knew that better than anyone. Their world had long ago been swallowed by the Void, leaving them permanent refugees on Earth. He faced his friend. "You think you're destined to die."

"I *am* destined to die," Kennedy corrected him.

"Technically we're *all* destined to die," Samael countered sharply. "That doesn't mean it's happening right now."

"And it doesn't mean that it's not happening soon." Kennedy's shoulders slumped. "I expected many more years," he confessed. "I thought I would find my mate, that I would hold my own kits." He plopped down next to the stone marker and gently placed his paw atop it. "This is where my father fell. He died so I could live."

"He died because your colony was beset by enemies," Samael countered. He sat beside his friend. "I didn't realize rabbits were so fatalistic."

Kennedy didn't smile as the cat had hoped. "Perhaps it's all saved for the Luckkeepers."

"Look," Samael said, changing tactics. "You just said the Void was caused by two black rabbits."

Kennedy nodded.

"And the only reason was because the older one wouldn't leave. Right?"

Kennedy narrowed his eyes, then shook his head in disagreement.

"I understand what you're trying to say, Samael, and I appreciate it, but there were no signs that I was supposed to leave."

"And just what would those signs look like?" Samael pressed. "Lights across the skies? You're always indoors. A message from God? How do you know you didn't get one by the birth of another black bunny?"

"Don't mock my faith," Kennedy said sharply, ears sweeping up and forward in a flash of anger.

"Don't give up!"

They glared at each other for a long, tense moment, and then Kennedy snorted. "I'm not planning to just lie down and die. I'm going to fight."

"Well, you certainly had me fooled," Samael said grumpily. "What's your plan then?"

Kennedy sighed, shifting to lean back against the grave marker. "I have no idea. I never dreamed I'd ever leave the colony."

"Uh-huh," Samael said in disbelief. "I certainly don't remember a certain rabbit wishing he could see the markets in Zanzar or walk among the humans unseen."

The insides of Kennedy's ears went dark pink in embarrassment. He gently kicked at his friend. "I was twelve."

"You're still twelve inside." Samael swatted at the foot. "Why didn't you pack a bag?"

Kennedy sobered again. "Upon the death of the old Luckkeeper, everything belongs to the new."

"Yeah, but you're not dead, genius."

Kennedy chuckled softly. "Physically, no." His gaze went distant, looking back towards the warren. "To them I am."

Samael watched his friend for another moment. "Your culture sucks."

Affronted, Kennedy focused on Samael. "It does not!"

"You're dead to them because a baby was born. That is definitely a definition of sucking."

Kennedy frowned at him, and Samael smirked, pleased to see the spirit back in the rabbit's eyes. Good. "Well, now I have the chance to show you *my* world."

He was surprised to see Kennedy's brown eyes widen in horror, but when pain exploded from his back to his chest it all made perfect sense.

Calida Fornax, Second Bazaar

…and so it was that that feline smirk was the last clear memory I retained. The projectile came through his chest, streaming red with S—'s life blood. The cross bolt—something I would not be conscious of identifying until hours later—slammed into my hip. Later I would discover it had literally ripped my muscle from the bone, splitting it as one might a filet.

Jor sneered at the newspaper. The rabbit wrote as if Fate had directed the bolt. It had been skill and experience, nothing more. He skimmed past the exaggerated tale, looking for more clues.

As I said before, I left my home with nothing at all, no armor, no weapons. Yet when the monster charged me, I held a black-red blade in my hand. I answered his attack with an undulating battle cry, the voices of my ancestors joining in unison with my own.

Ooo-dalalooooo!

That damned cry, piercingly high-pitched, still rang in Jor's ears. He forced it from his mind, instead focusing on the fact that the rabbit had been surprised to have a sword in its paw. Rabbits were not fae; they had no true innate magic, other than their strange luck. The rabbit could not have summoned a sword from nothing. And only two Beings were able to endow that trait into an object. As his suspicion formed, his glower intensified.

It wasn't a large creature, but it was armored in gold and blue. I had the sense of a humanoid shape, and yet wings. It moved with speed and skill, for I was hard-pressed to hold my own. I knew these woods, however, and my instincts guided me as I wove and ducked, parrying and striking.

The battle had been swift, the injured rabbit far cleverer than Jor expected. The problem was solved by his mistress's axe. A Huntsman's weapon, the magical blade fit his needs at any moment. At that point, he'd needed to be able to cut a tree in half. So, he had.

The branches trapped the rabbit. Jor's victory was assured. Or so he thought. The creature kicked him with its good leg, slamming him into another tree. He'd gotten a concussion and three cracked ribs from that blow. Jor touched his side gently.

His mistress had tried to heal him. The magic backfired, throwing him into flashbacks of cold. The freezing cold of devouring darkness. And silence. A hungry silence that ate out his eardrums. Silence as he screamed through the King's games.

Jor was only human then. He failed the missions he was sent on—catch a fox, find the magic pebble. The King abhorred failure, loved to punish.

The loss of the fox's tail was when the King had slashed open Jor's ribs with a blade colder than ice. The magic pebble had been hidden within a white stag. Jor had been unable to make himself kill the sentient creature. So the King chose to 'heal' him.

When his mistress finally managed to pull him out of the healing trance, Jor had screamed for ten minutes. His right eye had begun to tic and, two months since his encounter with the Black Rabbit, still had not stopped. More than a little distressed for her Huntsman, his mistress had frantically sought to fix the damage. But the magic-friendly channels that ran through all creatures had been twisted. Jor shrugged off the knowledge and the possibility for magic healing. His mistress had saved him from the King many times over. She had spirited him from the Void, then had given him time and space to heal on his own. She'd granted him powers, and then created his weapon. And she'd given him a real purpose: true hunts.

In this particular battle, even with his injuries and slow healing, Jor had certainly come out luckier. After all, he had the rabbit's foot to prove it.

Bracing myself, I raised my sword high. The blade gleamed there, flashing in a shaft of afternoon light that broke through the canopy. I could not hesitate; time and strength were both against me. I brought the blood and shadow sword down, slicing through branch and leaf to strike my own leg.

The pain was immeasurable. The first blow broke the hock and cleaved nearly halfway through the joint. I went dizzy with the shock. The creature dragged forward another step. I lifted my sword again. For a mere heartbeat, my will wavered, my arm trembling. Yet death came towards me and I had promised S—: I would not just lay down and die.

My instincts sent me to ground, and I found the back entrance into my mother's old den, the place where I was born and, I feared, would die.

Brave, yes. And stupid. Jor hadn't needed to follow the rabbit. To his mistress he had brought the supposed prize: the left hind foot of a black rabbit, harvested by a red-headed cross-eyed orphan in a place of life and death. It should have been overflowing with luck.

It wasn't. Jor ground his teeth together, hindsight painfully clear. "Where is this published?" he demanded of the kiosk owner.

"F-fourth Bazaar," the imp stammered out.

His sneer grew wider, right eye twitching madly. He would not disappoint his mistress again.

Return next week for the next installment of Lost Luck: A Harrowing Tale of Survival.

Calida Fornax, Sixth Bazaar, Calico Manor

"Have you reached my glorious return yet?"

Kennedy looked up from the manuscript spread across the desk. His mind, scattered, settled firmly on his friend. Concern and curiosity bubbled up as it did every time he looked at Samael.

The black cat had changed. Not in any marked way, but Kennedy could see it. In his human guise, Samael now had faint wrinkles at the corners of his eyes and a dusting of white along his temples. It wasn't until the rabbit saw those changes that Kennedy realized he'd never before seen any indication of aging.

Of course, when he asked, Samael smiled inscrutably and slyly suggested that Kennedy wasn't as observant as he thought he was. Yet there was no denying the differences.

Samael smiled at him now. "Kennedy," he said. "Don't worry about it."

Kennedy shook his head, clearing it. "Yes, your glorious return has happened." He tried for an ironic twist to the words, yet all he managed was fearful relief. He cleared his throat, looking down at the pages. "I'm not sure what to do for the ending, however."

Samael cocked a hip and leaned against the windowsill. "What do you have so far?"

"It's through our journey to Calida Fornax," Kennedy said, handing the pages to Samael. Samael smirked as he began reading, but soon his dark brow furrowed. Samael frowned deeply.

"Isis's tail, Kennedy, what is this?"

Defensively, Kennedy asked, "What?"

"Are you trying to scare your readers away?" Samael stared at him, utterly aghast.

"Is it bad as all that?"

"*Yes.* If my tail was out, it'd be floofed quadruple its usual size!" Samael shook a handful of pages in one hand as he began to read from the other. "'None can say what lurked behind us in those dark, dilapidated woods, half-eaten by the Void. Should we stumble too closely to the ravaged edge, we, too, would become nothing but frozen shadows of the Void. We dared fate to turn us into those lifeless husks, even as we dared our attacker to find us again. We were weak, bleeding targets waiting to be torn to shreds by whatever predator might happen by.'"

"Oh." Kennedy didn't know what to say. He was writing a true account of what happened, obscuring only such details that revealed secrets. "I may take it to the publisher and let them decide—what?" He found Samael inspecting him seriously.

"Was it really that bad?" Samael asked softly. "I only remember the pain."

Kennedy looked away, unwilling to let Samael see the memories reflected in his eyes. "It's over," he said instead. "We're safe. That's what matters."

He felt Samael's gaze for several long heartbeats. Then the cat sighed deeply. "What did you write about the crossing?"

Despite Samael's even tone, Kennedy knew it was a charged question. The gate they'd taken was known exclusively to cats. Obviously, they wouldn't want knowledge of it to get out, and not merely because they liked secrets. Cats, Kennedy had learned, were being hunted. Whether the reason was a secret or the cats were actually blasé about being targets, he couldn't discover. Either way, the rabbit wasn't going to repay them by spreading information about the gate.

"I said the crossing occurred at a place of possibilities that I could not truly comprehend, especially not in the state I was in." He picked up a page, scanning his neat, cursive handwriting for the passage. "I wrote that you called for aid in the manner of your kind just as darkness took me."

Samael pursed his lips, drumming dark fingers against his elbow. "I'm not sure about the calling for help," Samael said, reluctantly. "It's not an unknown ability, but it's not one we tend to flaunt."

Kennedy could understand the hesitation. He inspected his words, feeling for truth without revelations. "What if I say…" He mentally turned over the phrasing. "I heard you calling for aid just as the darkness took me? It's clear there is technology here that I never heard of before, and I never specified what you brought to the warren."

Samael pursed his lips, yet nodded. "Do that for now. I will check with Madame."

Kennedy marked it, then put down his pen with a sigh. "I need to take this in tomorrow. And I still don't know where to go from here. It's not as though our lives have ended."

"That sentence has a 'but' attached to it," Samael said.

Kennedy chuckled, looking up again. "But. It feels as though there's more to write."

"Of course there is. As you said, our lives haven't ended. Now, to your foot, bunny. The therapist is here for us."

The cat reached out a hand and Kennedy took it, allowing his friend to pull him out of the chair and hand him crutches. He worried about this session, yet he went willingly with Samael. Likely sensing his distress, Samael kept their talk light.

"There's a new theory about taking back Void worlds. It involves throwing the remainder of your race upon the mercy of Creation."

"Well," Kennedy replied with an amused smile. "If anything was going to work, that would be it."

"Oh, don't be a ridiculous rabbit," Samael scoffed. The air caught in his throat, however, and the cat gasped suddenly, one hand pressing against his chest. Kennedy reached out for him, but Samael gave him a half smile and waved off the offer of assistance. "I'm fine," he said in a raspy voice. "Just don't make me laugh."

"That was all on you." Kennedy watched his friend worriedly.

"As I was saying," Samael said, ignoring the concern, "Creation has no use for a bunch of fanatics. Her hands are tied—"

"Debatable." Kennedy's voice was more scornful than he intended, and he quickly grinned reassuringly at Samael.

"I'm not going to argue about this again."

Kennedy shrugged. "She's a goddess. Nothing can contain her power."

"Except her own Word." Samael's eyes flashed. "Her name describes her nature. If she didn't contain her power, the worlds would be constantly overrun with new races."

"No proof," Kennedy said, stopping to rest. Using crutches was exhausting. Besides, Samael's dark skin had taken on an ashy quality. They were quite the pair, he wryly thought. But he was glad to see the cat's animation, even though he didn't want to overexcite his friend.

"Look around you!" Samael gestured broadly with his arms, then quickly tucked them back in towards his chest.

"I see world after world eaten by the Void. And a goddess who could snap her fingers and recreate them, but who chooses to do nothing."

"She has to work within the bounds of her Word," Samael insisted. "Look, the Gods' Agreement was that they would both put limits on themselves, right?"

"The Gods' Agreement was that Creation would limit the Void's power."

"And her own. She understands balance, Kennedy. That's why she limits herself to working within those willing to carry her power and follow her will. *We* have to choose to be used or she won't do anything."

"Won't," Kennedy shot back. "So children die and worlds are devoured."

"Can't then," Samael answered. "Don't you understand? It's because she loves and respects her creations so much that she must allow us to decide. Even if that means we damn ourselves."

Kennedy shook his head as they continued their slow journey. Despite the volatility of their conversation, the ritual of walk and discussion was soothing.

As they entered the ballroom, their therapist turned with a gentle smile. His bright blue eyes were crossed, yet it had no effect on his ability to see. "There they are. Samael, start your stretches. Kennedy, come over here."

Samael patted Kennedy on the shoulder. "This is a good step for you." His grin widened, and he waited expectantly.

Abruptly, Kennedy got the pun, and he huffed out a breath equally amused and irritated. "Go do your stretches, cat. It'll soon be your turn for torture." Samael laughed and went to his mats.

Kennedy approached the therapist slowly, perking his ears. The man was lean, with silver and brown hair. It was not, Kennedy had learned, a dye job, but the cat's natural hair color. Despite the silver, however, Lesovik was younger than Kennedy. And, despite his age, Les was incredibly good at his job.

"Go ahead and sit down," Lesovik said. "I've got a leg for you."

Kennedy did as he was bidden, watching with some trepidation as Lesovik opened a case and unwrapped a large, prosthetic leg. "Our company has never made this style so large before, but the smaller ones all work beautifully."

Kennedy nodded obediently, though his eyes held a great deal of distrust. "I'm really not sure if this is the right choice for me," he said, repeating an ongoing concern. "It's not natural."

"According to the humans, neither are we," Les told him cheerfully. "Unwrap your leg. It's time."

Despite his worries about having a false limb—would it stay on and how heavy would it be—Les made short work of his fears. In hardly any time, the leg was on and the therapist finished giving pointers on how to use it.

"All right. Now you go to the newest torture device: parallel bars." Les smiled at him. "Dun, dun, dduuunnn." Samael cackled a few yards away.

With the therapist's help, Kennedy made it to the bars and learned how to put weight on his new leg. After ten grueling minutes, Les brought a chair for Kennedy to rest on. "Don't worry, you're not done yet!"

Thankfully, the therapist then went to hassle Samael. Kennedy watched the pair, only idly listening as Les told Samael to take in a deep breath, hold it… breathe out in a hard cough.

"Need me to hack up a hairball, too?" Samael asked with a small wheeze.

Kennedy smiled, but soon enough his gaze went to the prosthetic. He carefully lifted the leg, surprised that it didn't feel entirely alien. It had enough heft that he could feel it, yet wasn't so heavy he felt as if he was raising a brick wall. He wondered if his reaction was normal.

"Well, Samael, you chose to spend only one life on this incident, so now you get to strengthen this heart."

Les's words shocked Kennedy out of his reverie. Startled, he met Samael's waiting gaze. After a moment, however, the cat half-smiled at him and gave a Gallic shrug.

"I only have so many to spare," Samael said cheerfully. "Now go torture my friend so I can relearn how to breathe."

Kennedy narrowed his eyes at Samael, letting the cat know that this little betrayal was not going to be forgotten. Samael simply grinned as Les chivvied Kennedy to the bars to further torment the rabbit with walking.

By the time Kennedy and Samael headed back to their suite of rooms, they were too tired to speak. Kennedy questioned whether he should say anything at all about what he'd overheard. Another cat secret, and a much bigger one than the location of a gate. Samael opened the door for them, shooing Kennedy in first.

"I think I'm going to take a nap," Samael said, green eyes uncertainly scanning Kennedy's expression.

That look decided Kennedy. If Samael wanted him to know, Samael would tell him. "That's a great idea," he said. "I think I will, too."

Surprise then gratitude flowed over the cat's features. "All right. See you for dinner."

Kennedy nodded and headed for his room.

"Kennedy."

The rabbit found Samael staring at him. "Thank you."

Kennedy smiled and tilted his head, winking at his friend. "Always."

CALIDA FORNAX, SIXTH BAZAAR, CALICO MANOR

"What else have you let slip, Samael?" Disapproval lay heavily in Madame's voice. "How many more secrets have you shared?"

Samael shrugged, staring out the window of Madame's luxurious salon. The kittens were visible on the lawn, playing Stalk, Catch, Kill. Half were in human guise, half in their natural state. That was his favorite game in his first two lives, he mused. He'd been quite the bloodthirsty beastie, constantly in trouble, especially as a second life who should have had better control. In his youth, kittens almost always remained in their natural form, a fact that likely had prevented Samael from inadvertently killing someone. A small smile quirked his lips. No reason to trick oneself: the kill was still his favorite part.

This was partially based on his inborn abilities. And that taking life had never bothered him. In fact, he enjoyed it. Samael gloried in the power held within his claws. He loved controlling fate. And that, of course, was the main reason he enjoyed the kill. Samael wanted control.

"No defense?"

"You've already made up your mind," Samael said breezily. "What's the point of beating that dead horse?"

"Hhhrrmmmm. Then I suppose you will accept your punishment without a scratch or a bite, will you not?"

A grin flashed across Samael's face. "I have five lives to spare." His tone was negligent, implying his contentment in doing whatever he wanted regardless of threatened consequences.

"And *I* have seven." Madame's voice was suddenly a growl, too deep for her currently human throat.

The level of aggression surprised him. Madame sat tall in her chair, stiff and challenging. Her young, twenty-something face was set in hard, unforgiving lines. Her upper lip twitched as he watched, almost showing teeth. Her eyes, brilliant gleaming amber, were wide circles. In startling contrast, her pupils were the merest pinpricks of black. Samael felt his eyes responding with equal wideness. The lights seemed to grow brighter, a sign his pupils had blown out rather than constricted.

Nonchalantly, Samael sauntered—at a respectful distance, his body angled slightly towards her—past the cobalt chaise upon which she sat. He kept one ear cocked in her direction as he took his time choosing a seat. The golden recliner? It was too throne-like. Perhaps the blue and white chevron ottoman. No, too subservient. There was always the dove grey loveseat. Neutral color.

The rustle of silk tensed his shoulders. He tilted his head slightly, still looking towards the loveseat. At the same time, his attention was focused on the queen. She hadn't moved, only shifted. Her stare remained fixed, laser-like, upon him. He almost resented her youthful appearance, something she maintained easily even with naturally silvery grey hair.

After another show of deliberation, Samael gracefully settled on the loveseat. He sprawled across the suede surface, taking up every iota of space with both his body and his aura. There was room for two and he wasn't going to share.

Her stare eased, and Samael looked at her with pointedly hooded eyes before deliberately returning his gaze to the window. From this vantage, he could watch her as well as the kittens. He saw her squeeze her eyes at him and, like that, the tension dissipated.

"You are a disrespectful wretch, Samael," Madame said, lying back on the chaise. She was like the moon on a dark night: a pale, small form on saturated blue. She held not only the secrets of her own history, but those of their entire clowder. "Yet I find myself forgiving you time and time again."

"I am rarely wrong," Samael said haughtily.

She shook her head. "No, that certainly is not true. It must be your arrogance. And ability to come out of every situation covered in glory."

Samael sent her an oblique look. "What's this about, Madame?"

Madame smiled, matching his arrogance with her own. "I have a situation that you are required for, you and your unlucky luck."

Samael sat up, his fur bristling. "Neither I nor Kennedy are fit enough to go anywhere."

"Not according to your physical therapist. Who," Madame said archly, "admitted already to giving away the secret of our lives. Really, Samael, you need only have said."

Samael merely shrugged. Madame stared at him, eyes hooded. "Come walk with me, pet."

Samael trailed after the woman into an enclosed garden. "To you, Samael, born of death and war, I give a secret. Into your keeping, to be shared with only one other. Samael of death and war, do you accept my secret?"

"Madame," Samael protested. He paced beside her in agitation. Like all cats, he loved secrets. But this, a ritual secret? No, he *didn't* want that. Those trees were tall, and the forest went deep. The only way to find the path would be to accept this secret. And the secret the first led to. And the next one. Until he, too, was a part of the unfathomable forest, living high in the branches of mystery. "Damn it," he muttered. "Madame, queen of clowder and kind, keeper of my history, I do accept this secret into my keeping, to be shared with one other of my choice."

Madame's eyes squeezed at his wording, but she nodded as though this was expected. "Manchester colony was destroyed three days ago."

"*What?*"

Madame stopped when he did, facing him. "We had three survivors. Now there are two, soon to be none."

"Manchester holds our history. That's where the killers train," Samael argued, as though disbelief could change reality. "Manchester is full of both the lethal and insane. It can't be destroyed."

"The Void."

Samael's eyes tightly closed, and he shook his head again. He had friends at Manchester. Some crazy, yes, but all of them strong. Very strong. "What happened?"

"It is unclear how," Madame said. "But there is no question that the Void itself was there. We believe it learned of Creation's Tear."

"Shit," Samael whispered. "That will do it."

"That did it," Madame said, watching his face. "It was a colony of three hundred and twenty-four. And now we have only five reliable cats with any of their knowledge."

Samael stepped away from her. "Oh, no. I'm not a teacher."

"You are what you must be," Madame hissed at him. "You are a *cat*. We are what we are, and we do what we must to survive. You also jump to conclusions constantly." She straightened, smoothing her hair automatically. "You are not one of those five. Note I said that we have five *reliable* cats remaining.

"No, Samael, I require your skills for something else." Madame sounded weary. "You are charming often, social when you feel like it, but, to your tail, you are a killer." She reached up to catch hold of his chin, tilting his head down to look in his eyes. "I have a mission for you."

Calida Fornax, Fourth Bazaar

Screams hit the street as soon as the body did. Huntsman Jor followed it through the window. He crossed his arms over his chest, head ducked. His tic beat wildly, in time with his heart. His cloak flared out to each side. It flapped, like a swan's wings, slowing his fall. The second story was just high enough to gain painful speed and just low enough that his mistress's gift would not slow him enough. Jor hit the ground hard. His momentum played itself out through a long tumble. He rolled several yards, stopped by crashing into a newspaper kiosk.

The owner was gone. Jor was grateful, grabbing at the kiosk as an anchor. Behind him, the dogs easily leapt to the street. He used the word 'dog' loosely. They had six legs, three tails, and no eyes. Their coats were an oily white, dirty and clean at the same time. Looking at them made him cold.

Three creatures hit the ground in a wave of pressure, yet no noise. The closer the creatures came, the more sound disappeared. Silence, once his ally, had become a warning. His tracking was impaired.

The newsman's desk, where Jor had expected to get information, became a pile of dull grey sand at a single bite from one of the beasts. The elf who knew the address he was looking for lay in the street. Jor hoped he lived. Elves looked fragile, but they tended to be hardy. Regardless, Jor couldn't do anything for him. Well, except one thing: kill.

The Huntsman pulled the axe from his belt. The gold and blue weapon fit easily in one hand. His mistress's emblem glinted on the shaft. To their many successful hunts, he would add another. He spoke the activation word, his lips moving. Silence.

The axe didn't change.

The first creature leapt at him. Jor readjusted his grip and swung. The blade ripped through the beast's face. It dissolved around the weapon, falling like wet sand. Jor frowned, ignoring the movement as the second dog charged him. The final one began to circle around towards the prone elven man.

Jor needed him alive. He threw the axe. It felt true. He couldn't watch, however, as he braced for the attack. He lifted his left arm like a shield, the beast's mouth closing on the golden armor. The armor sparked and lit up like a rocket. The dog tossed up its head, shaking it hard. It had no teeth, but its lips themselves were jagged and sharp. At least, they had been. Jor watched them liquefying. The particles coming off were tiny prisms, a darkness that reflected the light. Cold seeped into his bones. A familiar, devouring cold. His right eye twitched madly.

Terror. Absolute terror. He knew this. He cursed, backing up. It wasn't just the mouth dissolving now. Whatever it was that reacted to Jor's armor continued to eat the dog. The beast's face was a gaping mess now, holes blooming. Holes which opened into nothing.

Further startled, Jor punched the thing in the neck. A leg came swiping at him, claws tearing at his shin guards. The creature jerked again, weaving away from the huntsman. Jor let it go, looking towards the editor. His axe lay in a pile of dust, less than a yard from the fallen elf.

The huntsman collected his weapon. He rolled the elf over, reaching for the man's neck. After a moment he found a pulse. Jor breathed out in relief. Relief that doubled when he realized he could hear his sigh. Good. Now to get out of here and find the rabbit.

As he scooped up the editor he saw the silvery sand begin to tremble. The piles began to flow towards each other. With another silent curse, Jor fled. This wasn't the hunt he'd been called to; a greater one awaited him.

But it was maddening to leave behind such predators.

Calida Fornax, Fourth Bazaar, Ruins of Manchester Cove

Kennedy stared at what used to be a building, lips set in a tight line. He cautiously bent over, running his paw through the strange, grey sand that covered everything. He straightened and wiped his paw absently.

A black cat trotted up to him. In the next moment, Samael stood human before him. The cat took a key out of his mouth. "I found it." He tilted his head in the direction he'd come from, but pointed off to their right. "There's a path there we can get through."

"Lead on, cat-tain." The quip did not earn him a smile, nor any reaction at all. The rabbit frowned as he followed through the debris. Les had said that Kennedy was ready to graduate from prosthetic school, but Kennedy kept a sheath strapped to his back for his cane, which he currently held in paw.

Kennedy hadn't known why they were going. Samael had requested Kennedy's presence and then… nothing. No jokes, no teasing, no smiles. The destruction, Kennedy realized, was the answer.

As they crept through the maze of ruin, Kennedy couldn't even recognize the items they passed. He guessed most of the debris had been furniture. He was afraid of what the rest might have been.

Samael pushed forward, face grim, even when he glanced back to check on Kennedy's progress. Finally, they reached what must have once been an inner sanctum. Samael stopped in front of a partially dissolved wall. The cat's fingers drummed against his leg.

Kennedy gave in to his worry. "Samael."

The cat stilled. Kennedy shuffled closer. "Talk to me."

"I didn't want to pull you into this." Samael stared resolutely at their grey surroundings. "You weren't supposed to get conscripted into our war."

Kennedy shrugged despite his surprise. "What happened?"

"Madame."

"Ah."

Samael sighed and faced the rabbit full-on. "Why were you not killed as a kit?"

Kennedy cocked his head to the side. "Why? Well, I suppose because... because..." His frown returned. "I suppose because my father defeated our enemies."

Samael nodded, yet his face was grave. "That's, well—that's what we wanted you to think. But you know Horizon Lay merged with your colony."

Kennedy shifted his weight from his foot to his prosthetic. He glanced around then sank to the ground. Samael watched him and then abruptly followed suit. The cat sat close, his knee resting against Kennedy's thigh. "We—the cats—know all about the Void. It's not that we created it, but..." Samael trailed off for a moment. "We are intimately tied to it. Through our arrogance and vanity, it was able to grow. And through those things, it ate our world."

Kennedy's ears twisted briefly as he sought to process this information. "I'm sorry, Samael. I don't understand at all."

For the first time in hours, the cat's lips quirked in a small smile. "That's to be expected from a dumb bunny, right?"

"Haha," Kennedy said dryly, though he was greatly relieved by the quip. "Get on with the story, hairball."

"Aren't you the hare ball?"

Kennedy groaned, amused. "I get it, I get it. Explain about the cats and my father."

Samael sobered again. "Look, I was there at the warren. I wasn't at your mom's den. I want you to know that now."

"All right?"

Samael took a deep breath and blew it out. "The cats let your father die."

"What!"

"Just wait a minute, Kennedy, let me explain."

Black ears erect, Kennedy's paw tightened painfully on his cane. Anger made his words harsh. "Oh, you're going to explain, Samael. Tell me now!"

Samael shifted to face him straight on, intent and serious. "The *Void* came to the rabbit world. I don't know why it went there. What I do know, what the cats know, is the Void somehow learned or figured out or, I don't know, something, that it could use the rabbits' magic against them."

Kennedy felt nauseated. "Our luck."

Samael nodded gravely. "The *Void* ate the Luckkeepers of Night Joy, Lark Dawn, and Horizon Lay. After it did, it used that as a key to devour those warrens and their lands. When it did that, it infected the rabbits themselves, driving them to madness. That's when the war started. And every time the Void found a Luckkeeper, it ate them."

"Oh, Goddess."

"But Abaddon was far wilier than the others, and he was able to not only hold off the Void's minions—voidlings—he was able to keep them away from the warren itself."

"So he was a hero. A hero the cats let die." Bitterness rang in the air, the first brick in a wall that could be built between them.

Samael stared helplessly at Kennedy. "I wasn't at the den, Kennedy, I swear."

The black rabbit sighed and deliberately set his cane down. Their friendship meant more to him than the deep surge of emotion. "I know you weren't, Samael, and I'm not blaming at you. I am *incredibly* angry right now. But I'm not angry with you."

"Okay." Samael ran a hand over his tight curls. "Okay. Good. Thank you."

"Now tell me why."

"They were afraid he'd been infected. He was such a brilliant strategist, and an amazing fighter. They didn't want to take the chance that he would be eaten. They let him be removed from the playing field."

Kennedy nodded, staring sightlessly past his friend. He found the idea laughable that his father could be turned by the Void. Abaddon was larger than life, the hero, the savior. The father he had never met. A hero stranger. It was painful to hear, frustrating, and, in the end, the information made no difference.

"Okay," Kennedy finally said. "Tell me about your war."

Samael's eyes shone suspiciously, but he started talking. "Just as the Void uses the Rabbit's luck against them, it uses our lives against us. Voidlings can eat our lives and send that power back to the Void. We, well… we didn't believe we could be beaten." Samael smiled bitterly. "Right up until the Void ate our queen and used her lives to eat our whole world."

When Kennedy didn't interject, Samael continued. "When we got to earth, we were livid, spitting mad. And seeking anyone or anything that could help us get revenge. I wasn't even born at that time, but we all carry that seed of rage, that possibility of evil you like to pull my tail about.

"As we sought an answer, we brought that evil to worlds where no evil had previously existed. And the Void could get a foothold in." Samael looked out across the dunes of sand and ruination surrounding them. "We don't actually know how many worlds were eaten because of our search, though I wonder if it's just that we're unwilling to look that closely at the secret store to learn. In the end, we were taken by Creation.

"She was astounded by our nature, always on the edge of good or evil. Though she said we were full of most possibilities. In the end, she listened to our plea and struck a bargain with us. The cats would keep her talisman, her Tear, until such time that we could strike our blow against the Void. She would put within her pendant some of her power, that it would be a mortal blow. Until that time, the cats were to hunt for signs of the Void, seeking a way to fight it."

Samael sighed and looked back to his friend. "The Void has long sought Creation's Tear. If it manages to take the pendant, it could be capable of removing the limits Creation put on its power."

"We're here to retrieve some sort of religious artifact that will draw the Void?"

"It's not a religious artifact," Samael said stubbornly. "It's a spiritually linked talisman that happens to be deeply sought by the Void."

Kennedy raised his brows at the man. Samael huffed, eyes narrowing to glare at the rabbit. "So," Kennedy repeated, "we're here to retrieve some sort of religious artifact that will draw the Void."

"Fine!" Samael threw himself to his feet and stalked towards the wall. "We're here for some sort of religious artifact." He kicked at it and it crumbled further. The cat dug into the wall, grumping the entire time. "I've told you some of catkind's greatest secrets, about the war, and incredible power, and all you can do is make fun. Oh, yes, that's great." From the wall, Samael jerked an object the size of a bread loaf. He faced Kennedy, holding the wooden chest in both hands.

"Get your tail out of its twist, Samael," Kennedy said in a mild tone. "Why are we getting this artifact now?"

"Because we have to call the Void. So we can kill it."

"Every time I think you're done with your jokes—"

"It's not a joke, Kennedy." Samael's expression was grave. "The cats lost so much here." He gestured with one hand. "This was our history. Our library, the sole information bank of everything we knew about how to fight the Void. And now it's gone. My friends." The words croaked out. "They are all dead. You and me? We have some uncanny luck, my friend. And that's what we're going to need." Samael abruptly shook his head. "No, I can't ask you to sacrifice yourself for a cause that isn't yours."

"Of course you can," Kennedy said, wryly smiling. "Because we're friends."

"This isn't your fight."

Anger helped Kennedy surge to his foot. "The Void is the reason half of my world is missing. The Void is the reason my father died before I could meet him. Don't tell me what is or is not mine!"

Samael's shoulders slumped. "Kennedy, I'm probably going to die here."

"I should have died two and a half months ago, Samael. My account has come due."

"How touching."

The cat and the rabbit whirled as the golden monster came floating down from the sky. It wasn't wings at all, Kennedy saw, but a cloak. He felt strangely disappointed.

"Cat, I'm here for the rabbit, though I'm guessing you're going to get in my way again."

"*This* is what killed me?" Samael screeched. "This… this measly *human*?"

"That's a human?" Kennedy asked in surprise. "But the metal

shell?"

"Armor, you dumb rabbit! He's a human in armor!"

"Stay out of it, cat. I just want to know where the Black Luck is."

Kennedy shook his head, confused, fearful, and swiftly growing angry. "Black luck? Is that some sort of species slur?"

"It's a different talisman," Samael said, moving closer to his friend. He set the chest down by Kennedy's foot. He smiled, the look dark, as he slipped something into Kennedy's pocket. "I wonder if I can help him find it." Samael dove at the human.

Fear flashed in Kennedy's chest. "Samael! The axe!"

"*Tallihandres!*" As the human unsheathed his hand axe in one smooth motion, it grew and grew, until the short swing became the full length of the war axe.

"Isis's tits!" Samael somehow managed to duck under the blade. He rolled again, scrambling further away. "He's a huntsman!" Abruptly, he looked proud. "I survived a huntsman!"

"Not for long," the huntsman said, swinging the axe again.

Samael retreated further. "Kennedy! Get that to Madame!"

"I'm not leaving you here!" Especially not with the man who had killed Samael once before.

"It's not leaving without giving me the Luck." The huntsman rushed Samael again. He was fast, almost as fast as the cat. Samael barely ducked the axe in time.

Kennedy lifted his cane. He hopped on the tips of his feet, settling into the sensation of his flesh and blood toes and the metal tip of his artificial leg. Then he, too, leapt into the fray.

Kennedy's first swing bounced off the huntsman's bright armor. The rabbit was distracted briefly by a dark mark, shaped like a bite, marring the otherwise mirrored finish. The shaft of the axe slammed into his stomach and he dropped from the pain.

"Kennedy!"

The axe came flying around again, and Kennedy kicked awkwardly to get enough leverage to save his right leg from the same fate as his left. Hissing and yowling proved Samael had renewed his attack, and the rabbit forced his feet under his body. He remained crouched, watching as Samael landed blow after blow on the huntsman's armor. They didn't faze the human at all.

"Ooo-dalalooooo!" Kennedy shoved strongly with his hindquarters and barreled into the huntsman. Samael jumped out of the way with a curse, scrabbling to keep his feet. Shoved up into the huntsman's space, Kennedy grabbed the shaft of the great axe. He gave a small, powerful hop, jerking the weapon upwards. Bracing himself on it, he kicked with both of his feet. The attack staggered the huntsman, breaking his hold on the axe.

"Ooo—laloo!" When the huntsman lost his grip, Kennedy's body dropped like a stone. He couldn't get his legs beneath him fast enough to keep from falling. He twisted immediately, getting his feet in position. The huntsman slammed into him, following with a punch to the face.

Samael grabbed the axe and tried to drag it away. But the weapon was heavy, magical, and at least half of the 6' rabbit lay atop it. Another blow knocked Kennedy's head the other direction. His eyes threatened to roll back, as he clawed at the huntsman's chest. The armor prevented any damage. A strong hand wrapped around the base of his ear, twisting it cruelly.

Kennedy cried out in pain and swung the sword in his paw. The black and red blade bit into the armor, and now the huntsman cursed and retreated. Kennedy blinked stupidly at the weapon. "Where have you been?" he asked the sword, as though it might answer.

"You have the Black Luck?" Samael's voice cut through his confusion.

Kennedy glared at his friend. "I thought you said Black Luck was an artifact."

"Swords can be artifacts—"

"Give me that sword!"

"Run, you stupid rabbit!"

The huntsman rushed Kennedy, and the rabbit responded by rising to his full height. He settled into a ready position, daring the huntsman to come at him. Instead, the huntsman slammed into Samael, freeing his axe. He swung it around with alarming speed.

Samael twisted impossibly. The blade did not cut him in two, but it still sliced through the cat's upper arm. Samael's mouth opened in a yowl, the sound not nearly as loud and shrill as Kennedy expected. He started his own rush at the huntsman, only to stop, surprised, as the human reared upright and whirled, turning his back on them.

Ignoring his confusion, Kennedy ran to his friend's aid. He ripped away a strip of shirt and tried to ask, "How bad is it?" No word passed his lips. He stared at Samael's flash of panic, yet forced his paws to move, binding the wound. The cat shoved at his shoulder until Kennedy turned to see what was going on.

The huntsman sliced through two of the strangest creatures Kennedy had ever seen, two monsters that instantly set every hair on Kennedy's body upright. Samael pulled his ear, yelling something.

Despite exaggerated lip motions, Samael's mouth moved too swiftly for Kennedy to understand. The cat patted Kennedy's pockets, finally reaching in and pulling out the key. He jabbed it in the direction of the chest and then imperatively shoved the key into Kennedy's paw.

The chest. Kennedy pushed the key into his pocket and sprang to his feet. As he brandished his sword, however, three more of the creatures took shape from the grey sand that filled the ruins. For a second, Kennedy stepped back, then he twitched his nose in determination. He charged, slashing with the sword. Where the Black Luck touched, the creatures shriveled inward, like burning sheets of paper. A glance towards the huntsman showed that the axe turned the creatures back into sand. Voidlings! They were voidlings.

Is this sword the only thing to damage them permanently? One weapon in a field of endless sand. Those bad odds didn't stop him from fighting his way to where they had left the chest. Except where it once had been was yet another pile of sand.

He turned to warn Samael. His friend was in cat form, bolting after a voidling. It held what appeared to be a glowing blue light. The great axe flashed by Kennedy's head and the rabbit shouted silently, jerking away from the weapon. The huntsman, however, simply continued past, chopping at a voidling.

Recalled to the task at paw, Kennedy whirled, flourishing the sword. He jerked when something bumped into his back, his ears turning automatically. With no sound to clue him in, Kennedy glanced swiftly over his shoulder to discover the huntsman was there, defending his back. *The enemy of my enemy*, Kennedy thought, settling in to do justice.

CALIDA FORNAX, FOURTH BAZAAR, RUINS OF MANCHESTER COVE

Samael had felt the instant the chest had opened. The artifact could not be allowed to fall into the Void's control. Black paws raced after the voidling. He wasn't sure where it was headed, but Samael needed the pendant to be near Kennedy, who was apparently far more unlucky luck than he'd ever expected.

If only he'd realized that the phantom sword Kennedy had written about for his newspaper readers was an actual sword! Clever cat? What a joke!

There! The voidling ran straight ahead, to the entryway of the old dormitories. The oldest ones were built more like bomb shelters than living quarters: one way in, one way out. Sure enough, the voidling reappeared, head turning back and forth as it sought the exit. With a hiss, Samael batted at the voidling's head and mouth. He used lightning fast strikes, inflicting damage and pulling away before he could be infected by the Void.

Finally, the creature dropped the pendant and Samael rewarded it with two more good buffets across the sensory sockets before grabbing the pendant and bolting. All he had to do was cut through the old refectory, and then he could leap the disintegrated walls back into the sanctum. In cat form, he could make his way around obstacles that Kennedy's prosthetic limb couldn't handle.

An unexpected collision sent his body flying into the wall. He clenched his teeth. Pain flashed in his mouth. He was certain he'd chipped a tooth. He took off again, a voidling right on his trail.

He held his tail up high, out of the way. He wasn't surprised, however, when a burning cold snapped the tip. He twisted onto his back, all claws extended, and ripped into the voidling's head until it released him. On his feet, he ran as the last quarter of his beautiful tail turned to sand.

"Samael!" Kennedy's voice was all panic. The entire world snapped into hyper focus. Nothing else mattered but reaching his friend.

The ruins flashed past him until he dropped behind a wall, panting. All he could see was the Void, a large, man-like form, lifting Kennedy by the ears. The rabbit struggled, kicking. Yet despite the length of his legs, despite the fact that he physically should be able to reach, he could not. Every swing of his legs stopped well short of the Void's form. At his feet, the Black Luck lay. Behind him, the huntsman's still body.

"*I do not understand,*" the Void spoke from an endlessly far distance. His voice was a nightmare's chill, a loss of hope. *"How did my Luck come to be here? You are a Rabbit. Rabbits belong on their warren world. Tell me, Rabbit, how did you find my Luck?"*

Kennedy gurgled, paws scrambling at the dirty-clean hand holding him. Samael fought the urge to run in and scratch the Void's skin off. Knowing the monster did not have actual skin almost helped. More than that, however, was the knowledge that doing so would only kill Kennedy faster. He had to get the Black Luck. And hope for the best.

He slunk forward, slowly, slowly, trying desperately to turn a deaf ear to the horrible sounds being wrenched from his friend. The implacable questions continued, even though the rabbit couldn't answer them.

Samael moved unseen, flat against the grey ground, his black fur camouflaged by the void sand covering him. He was five feet away. Two. Eight inches. Six.

"Cat, I see you."

Instincts and desperation kicked in. Samael shifted, throwing a hand out to grab onto the sword as the Void shoved him away. Bright, sharp pain sliced through his palm. He was like a leaf in a hurricane. The sword skittered a short distance with him, but he could not hold onto it, not by the blade.

Samael's head cracked against the remains of a wall. His body slumped to the ground. Liquid tickled from his nose, and all he tasted was blood and dust. Blood and dust. Memory overlaid the present. The Void wasn't just interrogating a dying rabbit, he was methodically ripping the flesh off Samael's father. The Void wanted to know how skin worked. The dead huntsman was joined by Samael's mother, her head caved in, her body being devoured by voidlings. All around was death. All around was decay. And it was the end.

Blood ran from his ears, making the world stuffy and dull. Or perhaps the voidlings had returned. All he had was his failure. Kennedy's legs kicked once. Not a conscious response. Samael recognized the nature of the movement. The nervous system, losing the last bits of its stored energy. One more, smaller jerk, and the rabbit's legs hung as dead weight. Samael felt the anger distantly. Anger and sorrow and grief and despair. But they all existed separate from his body. Over there, perhaps, where the huntsman's hand was closing over the hilt of the Black Luck.

The huntsman was dead, wasn't he? Samael wanted to frown, but that required so much effort. Wandering thoughts distracted him, but he needed to understand why the huntsman and the sword were so important.

Oh, but the sword wasn't enough. If it was, then Kennedy would not be dead weight right now. Samael let his chin fall. The blue amulet glowed dully at him, waiting for something important. The sword would probably like the pendant. They should go together. Quickly, before the huntsman's corpse did something stupid.

Samael's hand was covered in the weight of the world. It took forever to lift. But it was good that he did so. The blue pendant was at eye level now. He didn't know what material the pendant was made of, but the shape gave the impression of wings. They filled him with peace. Or perhaps, he thought sardonically, that was him dying.

Which also wasn't right, he realized from that great distance away. Cats didn't die all at once. They died life by life.

The blue flashed in his eyes, nearly blinding him. It gave him strength. The sword wanted the pendant. Yes. He walked the chain up his fingers until he held the pendant itself in his hand. He smiled a little, feeling life and power filling his hand, his arm. He drew it back and laughed as he threw the pendant with every last bit of his being. He saw it sailing through the air, hit the ground. It bounced up, hit the ground, and skittered across to where the huntsman stood.

Samael's head fell to the side and there was nothing left to see. Nothing left at all.

CALIDA FORNAX, FOURTH BAZAAR, RUINS OF MANCHESTER COVE

Everything had gone wrong fast. He'd found the Black Luck. It was nearly in his grasp. Then sound vanished. A sea of those damn sand creatures. The Rabbit had managed not just to stop but kill the irritating beasts. That was good. They would kill the beasts. He would get the Black Luck. His mistress would be pleased.

Then *It* had appeared. And Jor knew that his mistress would never be pleased with him again. Because the Void King made certain nothing existed anymore.

Jor was not surprised to find himself squashed like a bug. The Void

King recognized the armor of his greatest enemy, Creation. Her signature covered every inch of the metal, after all. He also wasn't surprised the Void King had struck to kill him. The King would never forgive Jor's betrayal.

What did surprise Jor was that he was not dead. What surprised him even more was the soft voice in the hidden depths of his mind.

I chose you, Huntsman Jor. Why did I choose you?

Because I am flawed. Because I am nothing.

Jor. That wasn't my voice. Why do you listen only to the voice of insanity? Why do you let his seed remain in your soul? Why do you hurt yourself in my name?

No, no. It wasn't crazy. It was true. He destroyed everything and everyone. He deserved the beatings. He deserved the punishments. He deserved every scar carved into his skin.

My poor huntsman. You still have not found the absolution you seek. Will you let me grant it now?

He didn't deserve forgiveness. He didn't deserve freedom. But he was so tired. Everything was so painful. Each day was another day of hell. Could he really choose a different path?

Her voice was quiet, but he could feel her waiting, his mistress. The one who had chosen him. Finally, Jor chose himself, too.

Yes. Yes, please free him. He wanted to be free.

Huntsman Jor of Barenbreck, I forgive you for your sins. I love you, just as you are. Now take up your sword, my chosen one. Righteousness is your shield, and justice your cause.

Fill me, mistress. Let me be your servant in every way.

Huntsman Jor's body filled with light, effervescent light. And warmth, finally, warmth and light to drive away the devouring cold. He breathed in, tasted joy and peace. Radiant joy that flowed through and from him. Abundant peace as he saw the familiar symbol of Creation. He took up her pendant in one hand, and the Void King's sword in the other.

From his mouth, her voice rang forth. "*Brother mine, I greet you in peace. Lay down your burdens and join me once more in balance.*"

The Void King jerked towards her voice. Animosity filled the air, battering at the peace billowing around Jor like a cloud.

"*My sister. You are imprisoned.*"

"*Love and creation cannot be imprisoned, brother. I accepted your terms of our bargain. I present to you my servants. Rise up, Kennedy of Twilight Song, guardian who sacrifices all for the good of others."*

The black rabbit rose, wounds closed, brown eyes filled with kindness.

"Rise up, Samael, birthed of death and decay, redeemed by the responsibility he holds for the sins of his kin."

The black cat shivered, going natural form for a moment before standing tall and proud in human guise.

"And here, my chosen one, my redeemed one, Huntsman Jor, once of the Void Court, and now a disciple of Creation."

Jor tilted his head back, staring coolly at the creature who had once been his liege.

"No," the Void said, leaning in close to stare at the human. *"You are my slave, you have carried my seed from world to world! Take up the sword, slave, and drive her from your heart!"*

Jor lifted the sword above his head. He turned the blade that the Void King could see his reflection. And then he pressed the Creation pendant into the base of the blade.

"NO!"

The blade shot gold and blue, the light of the change searing the air itself. The light grew brighter and brighter, surrounding Creation's servants and filling them with the light. It bubbled outwards, kissing voidlings and burning them away. The void sand glittered like diamonds and then faded into the very light they were reflecting. And the Void King cringed away from the light, turning his head away that he might yet deny her glory.

He shrunk in on himself. Further and further, diminishing in every moment he refused her call. The world became light, a beacon for every other world in the universe.

And when the light settled into the very ground, there remained but three figures: a rabbit, a cat, and a human.

Twilight Song Burrow

"Sidero!"

The young rabbit's bright blue eyes remained glued to the page in her paws. Her voice rang true and clear to all the kits surrounding her, their eyes just as avid.

—his claws were lightning flashes, ripping through the voidling's flesh. Huntsman J— swept in, catching the sealskin before it could touch the ground. I knew there wasn't much time before the selkie expired, should he continue to be separated from his skin. Yet only J— would be fast enough to get it to him in time.

"Oodalaloo!" I cried.

"Oodalaloo!" All of the kits howled in response.

"Ooodalaloo!" Sidero read again, crowing out the call like victory, pumping the air with one paw.

"Oodalaloo!" cried the kits again.

"SIDERO!"

Shocked, Sidero quickly shoved the newspaper behind her body just in time. Dolores stared down at her youngest with a fierce frown. "Just what is it you are doing now?" Exasperation and affection warred in her mother's voice.

"We are practicing war cries," Sidero answered quickly. She sent her brothers a dark, warning look before smiling up at their mom again with cheeky innocence.

"No more of that then!" Dolores answered, with a shake of her head. "The elders are having a meeting and we can hear you clear across the warren!"

"Sorry, mother."

"Sorry," the other kits all added in obediently. Sidero nodded at them approvingly.

Dolores shook her head, but she was distracted by a distant call, her brown ear twisting back towards the hallway. "All right then. Quietly from now on, my loves."

"Yes, ma'am!" chorused behind her as she swiftly hopped away.

Sidero hurried to the doorway and watched her mom leave.

"Sidero, Sidero! What happens next?" the littlest of the kits asked, a young doe.

"Well, let me just find my place." Sidero quickly flattened out the paper and traced the words with her paw.

"Oodalaloo—"

"Ooda—" The kits began again, but Sidero swiftly shushed them.

"No, shhh! Or someone will come and take the story away!"

Instantly, the sound was zipped up, with the kits giggling and nudging each other. When Sidero continued to read, however, they all grew silent again.

The red and black blade came to my paw called by our need and joined will, and I all but flew to the creature. Snickety-snap! With one swift flick of my wrist, the voidling's head became a blackened, curling mess that dissolved in the wind of my movement.

J— already knew what to do. He leapt into the air, his goddess cloak flared like wings and he disappeared off into the dark, leaving S— and I to finish the altercation. As I have mentioned before, the voidlings absorb all sound, so S— and I had to rely on our knowledge of each other as another wave appeared on the horizon. Yet, outnumbered though we were, we both knew just how vital our work was.

Despite his wound, S— moved like a demon, a black shadow trained by Creation's own Huntsman. He slit hamstrings, gave concussions, and caused havoc. And I did my own small part as well; every voidling S— incapacitated, I decapitated, until not even a single grain of sand remained.

As we paused to take a breath, however, we heard the most terrible cry. I looked into S—'s bright green eyes, and he looked into mine, for we knew that voice. J— needed us!

As I took my next step, however, my prosthetic leg snapped in half. With a cry, I tumbled off the side of the cliff.

A chorus of horrified cries accompanied Sidero's reading, and she rushed on for their sakes as well as her own.

I grabbed frantically for anything to help stop my momentum as my body rolled and bounced from rock to rock. Finally, I was able to latch onto a small boulder not much bigger than myself. By then I had fallen nearly 120 yards. S— was faced with the most awful of decisions: to whom did he go first? I was closer, yes, but J— sounded as though he was in deathly danger.

I looked up at my dearest friend and knew what he was going to do. I smiled at him, shaking my head no, then, before he could come after me, I let go.

"No!" The first kit's cry of distress was soon taken up by others when Sidero began folding up the paper.

"But we don't know what happens next!"

"Is he okay?"

"Sidero, don't stop there!"

"There's no more," Sidero told them, folding back the page to point to the final line. "See? 'Return for next week's installment of *The Unlucky*'. We have to wait until next week."

Disappointed, the kits soon moved off to play or chat or nap, according to their nature. Sidero took the paper with her over to her desk area and she stared at the words of the article. Within her chest, her heart pounded, and not just from the adrenaline of the story. No, the words called to something deep within herself. She lifted a paw to press against her chest.

She slipped it open and carefully dug through the purposefully placed layers to reach her greatest treasure, the one she found within the old Luckkeeper's quarters. From a shining, golden chain hung a bright, gleaming teardrop pendant. Something about the blue stone spoke peace to her, and Sidero lay one paw over it now, soaking in the stillness it granted her.

Not yet, the little voice seemed to tell her. *Not yet, but soon.*

Soon. Sidero smiled and carefully covered the pendant again. Soon.

An Orange by Any Other Name

Watts Martin

Cracker Key, my home, may be the biggest lie in the Gulf of Mexico: just two words, and neither one's true. First, it was founded by and mostly populated by Northerners, either seasonal visitors or retirees. I might be the only genuine Florida native who ever lived here. Second, it's not a damn key. See, a key forms on top of a coral reef. This is basically a sandbar anchored by condos.

It's still beautiful, though, especially if you find the secret areas without the crowds. If you get to McGee Circle—it's not easy—and go down a one-lane dirt road that starts at the BIRD SANCTUARY NO HUNTING sign, you'll dead-end at a driftwood-colored shack with a tin roof, right on the ocean. It's a hundred dollar hut with a million dollar view.

The kitchen window gave me a clear view over the sea grapes of a red two-door coupe bumping its way to a stop beside my big avocado-colored Buick. The vixen who peeled herself out of it tried just two mincing, awkward steps on the sand before taking off her high heeled sandals, tossing them back in her car and going bare-pawed. Point for common sense.

She walked up onto the porch, lifting her hand toward the door to knock, then stopping. She pulled it back, fussed nervously with her tail, then went through the same motions again. And again. My patience ran out on the third run-through. I marched to the door and swung it open. "Can I help you?"

"Oh!" She jumped back. "I… um, I'm not sure I'm at the right house. I'm looking for Mr. Fixer?"

It's not hard for a young vixen to make herself pretty, but this one didn't have to put in much effort. Swimsuit model curves, sunset fur capped with strawberry blonde hair, emerald eyes even I could get lost in for a second. "Fixer. It's a nickname, not a last name, and congratulations. You found me." I held the screen door open.

"Oh." She stared down at me, and I could see her daydream of a handsome knight errant deflate like a punctured tetherball. A chubby squirrel woman in her late forties rarely met anyone's ideal of a romance hero.

We stayed frozen that way for a good four seconds until I sighed. "You coming in or not?"

Swallowing, she nodded once, flashing a sheepish smile and stepping past me.

I let the screen door slam shut, and walked into the kitchen. "Can I get you anything? I have…" I looked in the refrigerator. "Water, orange juice, and iced tea. And bourbon. And bourbon with orange juice or iced tea."

"Iced tea, please. Thank you." She'd stopped in the center of the sitting room, looking around at my bric-a-brac: bookshelves, motel-quality paintings I should be doing a better job of keeping out of the sunlight, sad plants I should be doing a better job of keeping in the sunlight.

I scooped ice into two big Tervis tumblers and filled them up with sweet sun tea, then motioned the vixen to follow me over to the couch. I handed her a glass when she sat down.

"How much do you know about Orange Blossom Estates?"

"Let me see." I sipped my tea, thinking. It rang a dim bell, at least. "That's what some real estate baron from Ohio plans to call a thousand acres of orange groves and cabbage palms after he replaces them all with tract homes, right?" It was close to twenty miles inland. The name followed our grand Floridian tradition of naming new subdivisions after whatever you'd bulldozed to build them.

"Barton Development, yes. That's what they plan. But they can't do it unless the biggest grove owner, Roy Albrott, sells. That's over three hundred acres. Twenty-six thousand trees. Without that land, the project can't happen."

I'd heard of Albrott Citrus, too; anyone who looked at what they were throwing into their supermarket carts would have. The Albrotts were a true old Florida family, with all the good and bad that implied. "And you're looking for a way to encourage Roy to sell, I'm guessing."

"No, you misunderstand. He wants to sell. *We* want to sell. I'm Albrott's daughter."

That brought me up short. I didn't have much love for house farms, so I'd already started searching for semi-polite words to decline the job. "Aren't the Albrotts rabbits?"

"I'm adopted. And he's the only Albrott left, after his wife and son died last year." The vixen sighed, leaning toward me. "We refused their first offer. We expected they'd just come back with a better one. Instead, they've sabotaged the deal. We came back from an out-of-town trip to find the land had been flooded with... I don't know what, but it's unspeakable. And the very next day Barton had inspectors out to declare the groves contaminated. They're offering us a *fraction* of their first offer now."

"So you think they've deliberately sabotaged the deal."

"There's no other explanation. But the police are barely treating it like a crime. You know the local politicians here—they've never heard of a development project they're not fully behind. Albrott might be a big name in citrus, but citrus is nothing next to real estate."

"Got it." She was right, and that was a problem. Sunshine State politicos would have Albrott's back in any other battle, but not this one. And frankly, as little love as I had for developers, old Florida money tended to bring a whole lot of baggage. "But tell me why your father wanted to sell in the first place. He's been in the business for nearly as long as God's been making oranges."

"Some days he wants to sell, some days he doesn't, Miss Fixer." She sighed. "He's been... declining, ever since my mother and brother died two years ago. He can't take care of the land on his own, and I don't want to take over the business myself. I've been managing his affairs for him, trying to wind down operations, but he deserves a fair price."

"True enough."

"If you can find proof of what they've done, I can take it to the family lawyers. They're building a case against Barton as it is, but I want a smoking gun."

I pursed my lips, staring into my own tea. I should have taken myself up on the bourbon. "All right. I'll dig around and see what I can see, Miss…?"

"Laura Albrott."

"No promises, Laura. I might not find anything you want to hear. And I'll need money up front before I start."

She nodded, reaching for her purse. "All right." She started to pull out a slim checkbook.

I held up a hand. "Sorry. It's a cash business."

Laura paused, ears lowering. "I don't carry much cash on me, Miss Fixer."

"I understand. You know where to find me when you get it." I smiled. "More tea?"

***

I still had a few friends in high places and more than a few in low ones, but people always underestimated the value of friends in medium places. They had just enough pull to get me access I shouldn't have, and just enough resentment to give it to me. For instance, letting me into files at the county records office. I was chatting in the break room with the chain-smoking clerk who'd brought me the folders I wanted to see. "So your inspector went out there because Barton called your department out?"

"Yep." The rat snorted, lighting a new cigarette off the smoldering stub of the last one. "Larry was ranting about the smell for a *week*. Said it was like somebody'd drilled for oil and struck a shit geyser."

She wasn't speaking metaphorically. A good chunk of Albrott's land had flooded with partially treated sewage—worse than if it'd been raw. It wasn't just shit, it was shit steeping in muriatic acid. "Any theories as to how a working citrus grove suddenly became a wastewater marsh?"

"Don't need a theory." She shrugged. "Unless there's a sewer plant out there nobody told us about, somebody drove it there in tanker trunks and dumped it."

"Huh. And you said the Albrotts called about this, too."

"I said the daughter called. By 'called' I mean screamed like a banshee with a butt plug. Threatenin' to sue us, Barton, you name it."

I pushed the folders back to her and rested my chin on my hands. "I can see why she'd be mad about your report. But you think Larry's a straight shooter, huh?"

She snorted again. "Oh, that fucker'd sell his first-born for a strip steak and a fifth of bourbon. But unless he's in it with the daughter, this is real. You haven't been out there to check it out yourself?"

I shook my head. "Nope."

That earned me a grin, and a puff of a smoke ring. "Well, that's your next stop, sugar. If it's what he says, it ain't gonna be subtle."

***

I didn't get any closer to the ruins of the grove than the gravel road going past them. I didn't have to. I'd been half-expecting a poop lake from the flood waters, but it was worse than that. The wastewater had concentrated in the lowest part of the grove, turning into poop quicksand: deep, noxious muck swamping neat rows of now-wilting orange trees. And good God, the smell would knock a buzzard off a gut wagon.

So this confirmed what Inspector Larry had said, and what Laura had said. But that raised one big question: Good Lord, *why*? If Barton Development wanted to pressure Roy Albrott into selling, they could have pulled strings at a half-dozen county departments. Threatened him through his daughter, if they wanted to get dirtier. Hell, they could have just started building around his land, leaving themselves as the only practical buyer when he kicked the bucket. It sure wouldn't be the first time somebody'd built a Florida subdivision right around a stubborn land owner.

I was starting to come up with a crazy theory, but I'd need to do some digging. Fortunately, I wouldn't have to dig in actual shit. I'd just have to talk to companies that *moved* shit.

First, though, I needed to find someone in a medium place at the Probate Court.

***

The only people I knew at the courthouse were on the criminal side, in all senses of the phrase. I needed the civil court, but I guessed they'd know the right legal incantations for me to get at the records I wanted to check, and I was right.

Sure enough, Roy Albrott had been declared mentally incompetent five months ago. It looked like all the t's had been crossed and the i's dotted; the "family lawyers" I was supposed to be gathering evidence for knew their stuff. But I recognized the name of the doctor who'd done the evaluation, and he was no psychologist. There's a certain kind of doctor people in my profession called when they needed to fix specific problems, especially for my former, less savory clientele. Wounds and illnesses you didn't want reported. Prescription drugs you might not have a strictly medical need for. And sworn medical statements for legal documents.

He'd set up office in a light industrial district rather than the medical district near the hospital; the waiting room had all the charm of a muffler shop. Three pawn shop salvage couches surrounded a sagging coffee table bearing one *National Geographic* and three *Highlights for Children,* all from about seven years ago.

The receptionist looked up when I entered. "Do you have an appointment?" The mink made a show of scanning her datebook.

"Sure don't. Could you let Doc Silverman know that Fixer wants to talk to him? I only need a few minutes."

"If you don't have—"

"I only need a few minutes." I smiled, folding my arms in an *I'm going to stare at you until you go get him* pose. She returned the stare dolefully for a good five seconds before giving up, rolling her chair back and getting to her paws with a melodramatic sigh.

About ten seconds after she vanished, Silverman came out. The rabbit seemed less surprised to see me than wary. "Well. Miss Fixer." He chewed on his lower lip, then motioned me back toward his office.

"It's been at least four years, hasn't it?" He closed the door behind him. "I thought you'd stopped moving in the circles we used to be in."

"I have." I took a seat, leaning back. "Have you?"

"Oh, mostly. Although I've found once you're favored by certain kinds, the requests from them never stop." He narrowed his eyes at me.

"Don't I know it. Tell me about Roy Albrott."

His brows lifted. "What about him?"

"You think he's incompetent?"

His nose twitched, and he looked away. "I signed the papers."

"Not what I asked."

He stroked his chin, not turning back toward me. At length he sighed. "Based on what his daughter told me, the case is perfectly sound."

I drummed my fingers on my knee. "You didn't examine him yourself, did you?"

"Based on what his daughter told me," he repeated, "the case is perfectly. Sound."

"Got it." I grunted, standing up again.

He looked at me sidelong. "What's your interest in this?"

"Doc, your single saving grace has always been your disinterest in asking your patients questions." I patted his shoulder. "If you don't screw that up, I won't, either."

He swallowed, nodding almost imperceptibly.

***

It was the next afternoon when I headed back out to Albrott's land. I was pretty sure I'd put it all together, but I wouldn't know the why until—if—I could talk to the man himself.

I drove past the dying grove and down a second gravel road, lined with pineapple palms, toward the Albrott "estate." I couldn't help but put the word in air quotes when I thought it; I'd been to mansions before, and this wasn't one. It was *nice,* sure, but down-to-earth, a long, low ranch home, maybe two thousand square feet tops. It didn't even have a full garage, just a disconnected two-space carport. The high-end homes in the future Orange Blossom Estates would be far more ostentatious, and far more cookie-cutter. I liked the house's look: classic 1940s Florida style, with an open design to take advantage of natural breeze. It'd likely stay tolerable, if not cool, even without air conditioning, although I could see a couple window units.

A vintage olive green Ford pickup truck took up one of the carport spaces; the other one held Laura's sporty coupe. My tail drooped. Well, that made this more complicated. The court documents I'd seen didn't show this as her address; I supposed I could try and come back later. But I couldn't drag this out too much longer. And it might be in my best interest to get money from her now.

I parked my Buick in the circular driveway, opened the door, and staggered straightaway from the odor. The house backed right up to the lowest part of the grove, which meant right up to the waste swamp. The muck had even seeped around the house's sides. Covering my nose, I walked up to the front door, ringing the bell.

As I expected, Laura answered. Her eyes widened when she saw me, and she stepped outside, closing the door behind her. "Miss Fixer."

"Hi, Miss Albrott. Can I come in?"

Her ears lowered. "Can we talk outside? I'd rather not disturb Father."

"Well, for one, your advance only covered one day, not the four I've been working, so I'd like to get payment for the other three. Two, it's hot out here, and it *really* stinks, and it looks like your lovely home has lovely air conditioning. And three, I need to ask your father a question or two before I finish up."

"Finish up?" Her ears lifted. "You've found something?"

I nodded. "I have."

It still took her a couple seconds of deliberation before she nodded back, opening the door again. "Let me get my handbag. I'll pay you in the foyer, and see if my father's in any shape for receiving visitors today."

"Sounds good."

The foyer—and what I could see of the house behind it—carried through the Old Florida feel: hardwood floors, plain but high-quality wooden furniture, a vibe that was less coastal beach town than range-riding cowboy. Some Albrotts had undoubtedly been cattlemen; beef had always been one of the state's biggest businesses. A faded photograph of the family—three rabbits and a younger vixen—sat in a small brass picture frame on a marble-top console table.

She returned with a fistful of cash and a dour expression, which didn't lessen when I accepted the money and put it in my own pocket. "My father is... he's not in the best mental state right now. Could we just talk alone in the sitting room about what you've been able to find?"

"It'd be best if I could talk with him. I understand I might have to work to get an answer or two, but it'd tie up a few loose ends."

Laura looked like someone had just shoved a lemon into her muzzle, and she focused a dissecting gaze on me for a few seconds. I hoped I'd judged her correctly as the kind of woman who didn't carry a gun. "Fine," she finally said. "Let's head to the sunroom."

We walked through the nicely-appointed sitting room, then stepped down onto a tile floor into the huge sunroom—what I'd usually heard called a "Florida room." Multiple sets of floor-to-ceiling sliding glass doors formed each of the four walls. I guessed the two to either side opened onto bedroom wings, currently hidden by curtains on the other side of the glass. The outside set of doors had sliding screen counterparts, but they remained closed today. As hot as it was, the smell would be worse: the toxic sludge was at the glass's edge. The air conditioning barely reached here, though, and the lazily-spinning ceiling fan didn't help much.

Cushioned rattan couches, upholstered in floral prints, made up most of the room's seating. One piece, though, was a huge, round papasan chair. In that chair sprawled a fat, elderly rabbit. Stretch shorts didn't stretch enough not to look too small for him. A stained, sun-faded red T-shirt rode up on his stomach, exposing greying, patchy fur. He had a tumbler glass by him full of ice and, guessing from the smell, blended Scotch of the quality you find in plastic bottles.

Laura leaned down over him. "Roy? There's someone here to see you."

He didn't look at her, or at me, as I sat down. His cloudy blue eyes remained unfocused.

"Roy?" She touched his shoulder.

The rabbit grunted, pushing her hand away, then picked up his Scotch.

"Roy." She sounded reproachful. "Can you answer just a few questions? Miss… ah… Miss Fixer wants to talk about Barton Estates."

"Poop," Roy said clearly, and took a big guzzle.

Her ears colored, and she looked between her father and me.

"Poop all over!" he continued, waving his free hand in the air. "Fuckwads."

"Yes." She nodded. "Miss Fixer is trying to find proof of what they did, so we can sue the, ah, fuckwads for what they've done to your land."

His gaze flicked to me for just a moment before he fell back to looking vacant. "Poop." He shook his head. "Poop poop poop." He cradled the Scotch in both hands like a teddy bear, dribbling it onto his shirt.

Laura's ears folded back. "I don't think we're going to get anywhere today. I'm sorry. We can go back to the sitting room, like I'd first suggested, and talk there."

I sighed. Maybe I should leave well enough alone, just tell her what I found wouldn't support her lawsuit, leave the ball in her court. But I'd never been satisfied with four-fifths of an answer. "Could I speak to him alone for a couple minutes?"

She straightened up, ears lowering. "You can see he's not having a good day."

"It's important."

Laura's expression grew frostier. "Miss Fixer, I said—"

I steepled my hands, leaning forward and meeting Roy's eyes. "Three Bridges Septic Tank Service."

He set his jaw.

"What?" Laura stared at me, then at him, then back at me. "Are those the people Barton hired to destroy our grove?"

"How you wanna do this, Roy?" I straightened up and crossed my arms.

He slowly set down his Scotch, then leaned back in his chair, staring at the ceiling. "Shit," he said. I'm pretty sure he didn't mean his grove this time.

I turned to Laura. "They weren't hired. They did it as a favor to a long-time friend." I looked back to Roy and tilted my head. "And I have to imagine that friend must still be awfully persuasive, given how insane it must have sounded. Dumping hundreds of thousands of gallons of half-treated sewage on his own grove? I can't even imagine how they pulled it off."

Roy didn't say anything. But he grinned. Then started laughing.

Laura, though, gasped. "You… you think Roy…? No. No. Roy, tell her no." She swallowed, voice rising. "Dad, *tell her no.*"

He turned toward her, gaze as sharp as it must have been when he made cutthroat distribution deals fifty years ago. "Shut up, you goddamn bitch."

Her eyes widened to twice normal size.

"Oh, drop it." He stabbed his finger in the air. "I could have sold the damn grove for nearly a million dollars, if *you* hadn't conspired with my own damn lawyers."

"It's easily worth twice that! Or would have been until you dumped shit and acid all over it! Why would you *do* that?" She waved her hands. "I knew you were going crazy, but I had no idea!"

"You killed them," Roy growled. "Sidney and Roy Junior. I don't know how you did it. But you killed them."

"For God's sake, it was a car accident!" Laura threw her hands up in the air, and bared her teeth at her father. "I am so tired of you hating me! This is why you were declared incompetent, you know that?" She glared at me. "You see it, don't you?"

"I do. But I also see that you got a doctor who didn't bother to examine Roy before the declaration, and you gotta know that's not a good look." I sighed. "He wanted the first offer, didn't he? *You* turned it down. Because you want *all* of a bigger share."

"And I can't cut the bitch out of my will because she's my legal guardian. You thought you'd thought of everything, didn't you?" Roy grinned, in about as diabolical a way as a bunny could. "But I don't care if I don't get a goddamn dime as long as *you* don't get a goddamn dime. Nobody screws an Albrott, you pointy-eared bitch. And you're no Albrott."

Laura balled her hands into fists. "You crazy fucking bastard!"

"Never trust foxes. Even your own adopted daughter." Roy spat on the floor.

Laura shrieked in rage, running out of the room.

Roy looked back at me with a sneer. "Doesn't matter if you tell anyone. The land's still all but worthless now."

I shrugged. "That's not my business. I was hired to see if I could get proof that Barton poisoned your land, and it turns out they didn't." I rose to my feet.

He grunted, picking up his Scotch again.

"You have any proof Laura killed your son and your wife?"

"If I could prove it, we wouldn't be here now, would be?" He snorted. "Maybe I shoulda been the one to hire you."

"Maybe so."

I'd almost gotten out of the Florida room when Laura reappeared, brandishing a snub-nosed revolver. So much for my good judgement. She wasn't targeting me, though. She marched right past me toward the papasan chair.

I spun around. "Laura, *no.*"

She stopped, pivoting on a heel to point the gun at me. Her hands shook, but the gleam in her eyes had gotten as crazy as she'd accused Roy of being.

I raised my hands. "Look, either you get a few bucks for your sewage farm out there, or you get a moment of angry satisfaction at the cost of committing a capital crime you will *not* get away with."

She shook her head fractionally. "There's only one witness."

"So *two* capital crimes you won't get away with?" I lowered my hands enough to spread them in appeal. "Come on. You know damn well you'll be suspect number one."

Laura lowered her eyes slowly, followed by the gun. She took a deep breath. I figured I might be able to talk her out of doing anything suicidally stupid, but before I got a word out, Roy started laughing. Raucously.

And that was it. With a snarl, Laura lifted her father out of the chair, hauling him toward the sliding glass doors to the outside, unlatching them, shoving them open. The heat—and stench—crashed in like a wave. I winced, staggering back involuntarily.

"Only if they find the body," she hissed. She dragged Roy outside, straight into the acid muck. And kept going.

He bellowed, starting to kick. As old as he might be, he could still kick like, well, a rabbit. She staggered, losing her balance, then pulled him down with her, claws and teeth out.

"Good Lord, you two!" I made my way to—but not past—the glass door. "Have you lost your minds?"

The question, though, had become rhetorical. Laura had gone well past listening—and as she rolled over, holding Roy under the sludge, he wasn't in any position to listen. He thrashed furiously, spraying a plume of toxic waste up over her. She coughed and spat and snarled. In a very short time, though, the splashing settled down.

The vixen straightened, muck up past her knees, and howled, looking positively feral. She tried to wipe the muck off her face, with limited success, and took a single step forward. I don't know if she'd just spent all her strength, or she tripped, or Roy managed to get a hand around her ankle, but her eyes grew wide and she toppled fully over. As she started to sink, she flailed frantically—just about the last thing she should have done. Which made it just about the last thing she did.

"Good Lord," I repeated, this time just a whisper.

***

With the disappearance of both land owners, the former Albrott Groves was simply condemned. Instead of paying the thousand per acre Laura would have wanted, they got it for about a buck an acre. That didn't count the remediation work, though; that put the whole development close to a year behind schedule. Granted, becoming a crime scene for a while didn't improve the timeline.

When they were discovered, the bodies were such a mess nobody could prove there'd been foul play. The working theory was that poor mentally unstable Roy had taken a stroll into the toxic waste dump, his noble daughter had gone in to save him, and they'd both drowned horribly. At least that last part was true.

To satisfy my own curiosity, I briefly looked into the car accident that had claimed Roy's wife and son. Single-car accident; they'd smashed into the underside of an overpass. The ruling was his son had taken a curve too fast and lost control. If Laura had had anything to do with it, she hadn't left a shred of evidence.

I visited the model home office for Orange Blossom Estates a few days ago, not too long after it opened to the public. All two-story stucco homes, all a shade too large for the undersized lots they're on, all with central air, all with identical kidney-shaped swimming pools in screen rooms. No Florida rooms, or anything else Floridian at all—the bland styling could blend in anywhere in the country. I guess that's the point, isn't it?

The sewage stench is long gone. Of course, so is anything resembling an orange blossom.

The Road to Macluske

Nathan Ravenwood

It was on a winding road, fog flowing over the packed asphalt like wisps of those long dead, that the Survivor met the rabbit.

At first glance, the rabbit was just like most of the others that the Survivor had encountered. His green and black flannel was worn, a litany of day to day survival told in stains and patchwork repairs. He wore jeans of a similar condition, one leg torn open to expose a lean knee, scraped and scabbing over. His fur was mottled brown and gray, his big ears turned towards the low rumble of the Survivor's motorcycle.

From a distance, the Survivor could make out a white lump of something on the rabbit's neck, tucked where his head met his shoulder. As he drew closer, however, he realized it was a hasty bandage job, and underneath that, dark red stained the rabbit's collar. The Survivor knew immediately what had happened.

"Hello!" the rabbit called, standing up atop the rock where he sat. He waved. "You there! Otter! Hello!"

The Survivor stopped his battered motorcycle, planting one booted foot on the road to steady himself. Twenty feet separated them. His careful eyes looked the rabbit over. Both his paws were visible, no obvious signs of weapons. He didn't look like a fighter, perhaps an academic in his past life. He wondered what the rabbit saw in him. Did he notice the two rings on the thin chain around his neck? The riding jacket that was a little too big for him? Or the leanness to his frame, hardened by three years on the road fleeing Them wherever they could?

"Hello there!" the rabbit called over the sound of the idling engine. "Could I ask a favor?"

The Survivor's eyes scanned the trees, above the wild, unchecked growth along the sides of the highway, looking for any sign of an ambush. These days it was easy for people with dark fur to daub themselves with plant dye and blend into any environment. Out of reflex, he ran through the litany of his armaments—one long rifle in the leather holster on the side of his bike, a pistol on his person, a shiv in his back pocket.

"Please," the rabbit said. "I'm all alone. I've *been* all alone for days now."

The Survivor didn't move any closer to him. "How long?" he asked, pointing to the bandage on the rabbit's neck.

"Recently," the rabbit said. "Ran afoul of a group of Them up by the river in the early morning." He laughed, the kind of borderline hysterical giggle made by someone who knows they made a horrible mistake. "I'm not much of a fighter. Let them get too close."

The Survivor lowered his muzzle a little, his dark eyes boring into the rabbit's. "How long *exactly?*"

The rabbit rubbed his whiskers. The motion seemed so banal, a holdover from a more mundane time. "About three hours, give or take."

Which meant he had about thirty-three hours left to live. "What do you want?" the Survivor asked.

The rabbit slid off the rock, landing unsteadily on the grass. "Transportation. I came from Macluske, a small town a few hours up the road." He pointed north, the same direction that the Survivor's bike was pointed. "My group has holed up there for a few weeks." He swallowed, the wad of bandages bobbing slightly. "My husband is there. I want to see him one last time before, well, you know."

A gentle breeze blew across the road, carrying a few leaves that gamboled in the current before being carried away down into the ditch where the once-maintained undergrowth now grew wild and free. The Survivor watched them for a moment before looking back to the rabbit. His body language was open, completely non-hostile. But the Survivor had been fooled before. "Is it along the highway?"

he asked.

The rabbit nodded. "Yes. Runs right through it."

The Survivor knew he couldn't afford the distraction. That he should just gun the engine and drive away, leaving the rabbit to his fate. For a moment, rage prickled his fur. Who was this sorry soul? Why did he deserve to get closure when so many hadn't?

His paws curled around the bike throttle, one twist away from gunning the engine and leaving. But he remained where he was. *It's the same direction,* he thought. *No diversions, no straying from the path. You'll get to where you're going all the same. All you have to do is drop him off in the town with his group and leave.*

He'd *want you to show him kindness.*

The Survivor gestured behind him, at the empty space on the bike seat where another body could fit. "Get on."

The rabbit heaved a heavy sigh, then hurried over, moving quickly so his bare footpaws didn't linger on the warm asphalt. "Thank you, kind stranger," he said, throwing his leg over the seat with all the balance and poise of someone who had never ridden a motorcycle in their entire life. "My name is Brian. What's yours?"

A quick twist of the throttle set the bike in motion. "Don't have one," he said as they drove away.

"Nonsense," the rabbit said, sounding taken aback. "Everyone has a name."

The Survivor didn't offer a response as he drove. He'd given up his name, stopped thinking about himself as an otter, as a person, as a living being, but rather a nobody. Names made things personal. All of Them had once had names, and if you thought about that, you didn't last very long. Every survivor lived with that weight.

For a long time, there was only the roar of the motorcycle carrying them forward through the winding mountain road. Every so often, they would pass a relic of a time years gone—a car, abandoned by the side of the road, nature slowly creeping up its sides to reclaim what civilization had taken from the ground to build it. They weren't as numerous on the state roads and two-lane highways as they were around the deserted metropolises, but even here, people had tried to flee. Further down was a burned-out vehicle, the equipment in the back too damaged to be of any use. Plus, it looked heavy, and there was only so much the motorcycle could carry, so the Survivor didn't slow down.

They were around, too. The Survivor only caught passing glimpses—here a rotting limb wrapped around a tree like a vine, there further on an indistinct mound of fur and decay on the ground. He was grateful that the noise of the bike engine drowned out the sounds they made, and that the bike's speed meant he didn't have to suffer an onslaught of bitter, eye-watering putrefaction.

He could feel the motion of the rabbit looking at Them as they passed by, brief glimpses of his fate. "How many of them are in these woods?" the rabbit asked, having to raise his voice to be heard over the bike engine.

"Don't know," the Survivor responded. "Probably more than you might think. More opportunities for food out here."

"Eugh," the rabbit said.

They emerged from the tree line onto a long stretch of open road, winged by gently sloping plains. In the distance, purple clouds heavy with rain drenched the soil below, the downpour appearing as a soft gray haze to the two travelers. "That's right over where Macluske is," the rabbit said, pointing into the background behind a abandoned farmhouse. A bolt of lightning struck the ground in the distance, the peal of thunder reaching them a moment later. "I hope they're staying dry."

The Survivor noticed one of Them standing upright on a hill some distance from the road, too far to be a threat. "Why were you out there all alone?" he asked.

"Initially, I wasn't," the rabbit said. "There was a group of us, out hunting and foraging for food. A storm came out of nowhere, and in the middle of it some of Them showed up. It was dark, and we got separated into two smaller groups. Peter, my husband, and a red panda named Kiyo were with me, but none of us had a map. We wound up going in the wrong direction and got lost in the woods. Night fell, and we were attacked in the dark by some nomadic thugs, and all got split up on our lonesome. I wandered alone for a day, and this morning, well..." His paw went to the bandages.

The Survivor took a deep breath, willing his paws to loosen their iron grip on the handlebars. Memories of gunfire, flashes in the darkness, and an awful, terrible pain dispersed like smoke in his mind. "Unfortunate," he managed. He had to admit that if he'd survived on his own for a day, perhaps the rabbit wasn't completely useless.

"Yes," the rabbit said. "It is." A long time passed before he spoke again. "What about you, stranger?"

"Hm?"

"Why are you all alone on a motorcycle heading north?"

"I'm looking for someone."

"A friend? Family? Spouse?"

Slowly, the Wanderer shook his head. "No. Someone else."

"Who…" The rabbit trailed off as he made a hissing sound. Soft leporine fur bumped the Survivor's shoulder, and he reacted on instinct. His foot stamped on the brake and he elbowed the rabbit as he threw himself off the bike. In a flash his pistol was in his paw with the safety off.

"Wait wait wait!" the rabbit said, holding his paws up.

The Survivor's every instinct screamed at him to shoot. The rabbit was bitten. He was one of Them, or he would be eventually. What was the point of dragging things on? One twitch, one sound, one bullet. He'd be doing the doomed creature a favor.

A long moment passed as they each remained still. In the distance, the storm rolled closer. Over the sound of wind buffeted forth by the oncoming front, a soft rustle could be heard. The Survivor tracked his aim to the right, the muzzle pointed away from the rabbit's face, and pulled the trigger.

One of Them who had slowly risen from the roadside ditch, rustling the reeds with its motion, gurgled and fell back into the depression, never to rise again. The safety went on and the gun went away.

"I'm sorry," the rabbit said. His face was beginning to swell where the Survivor's elbow had cracked into his cheek. "My wound flared up."

The Survivor went to the duffel strapped down on the bike's rear fender. He rummaged inside for a moment before pulling out a small bag and setting it on top of the bike. "There's painkillers in there," he said, turning and walking a few paces away from the bike to steady his nerves. He laced his webbed fingers atop his head, closing his eyes.

A voice whispered in his memory. *Inhale. Count to four. Exhale.*

"Thank you," the rabbit said.

The Survivor opened his eyes and stared out over the plains. A few more of Them had risen up in the distance, roused by the gunshot. But they were a space away, and by the time they'd limped their way over, the Survivor and the rabbit would be gone.

"Why do you have a cigar and a lighter in here?" the rabbit asked. He tilted the bag, showing off the plastic-wrapped length of paper and tobacco from the south.

Thunder clapped in the distance. "I'm saving it."

"For what occasion?"

The Survivor turned and moved back to the bike. The rabbit downed three painkillers dry, zipped up the little bag, and put it back. "I was never a smoker," the Survivor said. "But my husband was."

The rabbit blinked in that moment of connection that queer people could make regardless of age, species, or degrees of which they were doomed.

The Survivor straddled the bike seat. "And when I find the man who killed him, I'm going to smoke that cigar nice and slow as I inflict the worst pain that I possibly can on him."

The rabbit nodded. "I understand."

They remained stationary for a time. "What are you going to do when you find your people?" the Survivor asked.

"I simply want to say goodbye," the rabbit said. "Many of them I've known since everything fell apart. It will be rough, but they're a good group. Peter, though…"

He said nothing more, and a few heartbeats later, the Survivor heard the rabbit sobbing quietly. He stared ahead at the road, then kicked the bike into life and drove onward.

Over the next few hours the rabbit's condition worsened, as did the storm growing closer and closer. The wind picked up until it was flattening small bushes and wild wheat, the plants bending against the weather.

"We're going to have to find someplace to wait for the storm to pass!" the Survivor yelled over the wind and the bike.

"What kind of place?" the rabbit asked, punctuating the question with a heavy cough.

The Survivor scanned the horizon, then pointed. "Someplace like that!"

Ahead was a middle of nowhere intersection of two state high-ways: the north-south one they were on and one going east-west. On one corner was the husk of a gas station, the skeleton of the building blackened and twisted, an upended tanker truck butting up against the ruin, surrounded by other, smaller vehicles packed into a grid-lock so tight that it was a challenge to even get the bike through. The Survivor looked inside the vehicles as he rolled by. Most of them were empty, but a few contained bodies. The travelers tried to not look at those too long.

On the other corner was an auto shop at the end of a short gravel drive. It was a small, squat building made entirely from concrete. A single pane of one of the front windows was broken, but the rest of the front facade was in one piece. The actual garage was shuttered, secured at the bottom by a heavy lock. Spray-painted along the side wall were the words "LOOTERS FUCK OFF" in big black letters.

The pair drove up to the heavy shutter, and the Survivor dismount-ed, grabbing the rifle out of the holster on the side of the motorcycle. "How are we going to get inside?" the rabbit yelled over the wind.

By way of answer the Survivor aimed the rifle down at the lock and waited. Lightning flashed in the distance, and a moment later the thunder came. In time with the noise, the Survivor pulled the trig-ger, masking the noise of the gunshot. It took two more thunderclaps before the lock was damaged enough for him to reach down and get a grip to rip the lock free. He minded the damaged edge as he lifted the door up. The long-unused track and ball bearings squealed in protest. "Bring the bike in!" he called.

The rabbit pushed the motorcycle inside the garage just as the rain came pouring down. The Survivor let the door drop, and shook water off his arm. "Just in time," he said.

"Good thinking with timing the gunshots," the rabbit said.

"Wish I hadn't had to use that many rounds." The Survivor rum-maged in his duffel bag and pulled out a box of .30-06 rifle cartridg-es. He shook it by his ear. "Only two left."

"When we get to Macluske I'll see if my group has any to spare," the rabbit said. "Those are… big bullets, right?"

The Survivor raised an eyebrow. "You don't know much about guns, do you?"

The rabbit's ears drooped. "Not really, no. I learned how to shoot to survive, but I know next to nothing about ammunition. I've always relied on others to load the guns for me." Disdain rose like bile in the Survivor's throat, but he suppressed it and grabbed a flashlight out of the duffle bag. He drew his pistol and moved to the door that led from the garage to the rest of the auto shop. It was closed, but not locked, and squeaked as he opened it. His light beam cut a swathe through the gloom as he checked every corner of the auto shop for anyone—or any of Them—that might be lurking. Much to his relief, he and the rabbit were the only two there.

The Survivor walked behind the shop counter. The dusty register drawer was cracked slightly, and he opened it. Inside was a pill bottle full of paperclips and a few faded receipts dated years ago. He knelt down and opened the cabinets underneath the counter. A strange smell hit his nose, and it took him a moment to spot the long-neglected box of pastries shoved into a hidden nook inside the cabinet. As delicious as he remembered them being, the Survivor didn't want to risk food poisoning for a brief sugar rush.

Inside the cabinet was a trash can, and the Survivor upended it onto the floor, sifting gently through the contents. His paw brushed aside a faded newspaper flyer for a lumber liquidation business and a pamphlet about the warning signs of rabies. A crumpled piece of paper tumbled free, and he grabbed it.

Spreading it out on the counter revealed a letter with a photograph crumpled within. The photo showed a vixen standing atop a mountain with her arm thrown over the shoulders of a pretty doe, both of them sweaty and smiling. Wedding bands glinted on their fingers, and the Survivor became acutely aware of the pair of rings hanging from his neck.

The letter was handwritten in dark purple pen. *Missing you much, Pops! Ophelia and I will be back from the honeymoon soon! Love you!* It was signed Grace, with the tail of the last letter becoming a heart.

"Find anything?"

The Survivor looked up at the rabbit as he walked into the main room of the shop. He shook his head. "Nothing useful. Unless you want to take a chance on the snack cakes under the counter, see if that myth about them never expiring is true."

The rabbit actually laughed. "I'll pass, thanks. I'd rather not get food poisoning on top of what I already have." He walked over to the counter. "Is that a letter?" He took the photo and the letter from the Survivor and looked them over. His ears drooped. "This is dated a week before the outbreak."

"I'm surprised you remember the exact date."

"Well, I don't know when it *started* started, but I remember the day I first heard about it on the news," the rabbit said. "To me, that's when it started." He looked down at the photo for a long time. "Poor things. I hope they survived together."

The Survivor almost said, "most don't," but had the tact to keep his muzzle shut. The rabbit didn't need that, not now. He reached out and took the photo back from the rabbit, setting it back on the counter.

Both travelers walked back into the garage. "I don't have much that you might be able to eat," the Survivor said as he dug out the food from his duffel. He laid out a package of fish jerky scavenged from the back of a supermarket, along with some apples that he had harvested from a tree in front of an abandoned orchard. He picked the least suspect-looking apple and tossed it to the rabbit.

"I wasn't expecting the luxury of a last meal anyway," the rabbit said, waving the paw that held the fruit. "Thank you." He took a big bite, his buck teeth slicing through the apple's flesh like it was nothing. For a brief moment, the Survivor imagined the rabbit as one of Them, those big teeth chomping down on flesh of a different kind. His paw strayed towards his gun before snapping back to his side.

The rain intensified as they ate, streaking across the windows, the wind whistling in through the one missing pane in the other room. Each of them were absorbed in their own thoughts, and the Survivor felt his eyelids grow heavy as he leaned against one of the wall of the garage.

He dozed off at some point, and awoke as something metal clattered against the floor. Quick as the lightning splitting the sky outside he had his gun in hand and was on his feet.

"Don't worry," the rabbit said. "It's just me." The contents of a toolbox were strewn across the floor, the rabbit's paws rifling through them. "I was just looking for a rag of some kind."

The Survivor made a soft noise as he saw the beginnings of the froth at the corners of the rabbit's mouth. He'd slept through the night. The rabbit was within the twenty-four hour time limit now.

"Oh, God."

"Yes," the rabbit said, his voice bitter. "You're telling me." He coughed heavily. "Ah, there we go." He pulled out a reasonably clean rag out of the corner compartment of the toolbox, using it to wipe away the white. He sagged against the wall.

The Survivor watched the rabbit, listening to the sound of his breathing. The noise was like someone forcing air through a dish sponge: wet, ragged, and laboured. Within the next twelve hours, the rabbit's entire body would begin to shut down, and he'd be in agonizing pain for the short rest of his life. Then, afterward…

"If you don't mind me asking," the rabbit said, sitting up a little and working the rag with his fingers. "What happened to your husband?"

Groaning, someone snarling, flashes in the darkness of the forest. "The two of us were driving late at night," the Survivor said. "It was risky, but we needed to find someplace to hole up. All of a sudden, someone started shooting in the woods, and then there were others that shot back. We tried to hide and avoid them, let them kill each other, but then one of them stumbled into our hiding spot. Before either of us could react he shot…"

The Survivor stopped himself before he could say 'my husband.' Jayce didn't deserve that. "He shot Jayce and ran. I don't know if he was the one who started the shooting or the one who was being shot at, and I don't care. I'm going to find him. And he's going to pay."

The rabbit nodded. "Do you remember what he looked like?"

"He was—"

Something heavy smacked against the metal outside. The Survivor surged to his feet, his gun ready again. "What was that?" the rabbit hissed.

The smack came again. "They're in here, I told ya!" a reedy voice called out. "Saw 'em pull in yesterday afternoon!"

"Well, open up the damn door!" a heavier voice said. "Look, they've already blown it open, come on."

The Survivor grabbed the rifle out of the bike holster and held out the pistol to the rabbit. "Take it, come on!" he hissed. Using his left paw to keep the cloth over his mouth, the rabbit took the pistol with his right. The pair of them scurried into the other room of the auto shop just as a big hand curled around the underside of the garage door and lifted. They ducked behind the counter as the door raised, the metal track squealing in protest as it had the day before.

"Come out, come out!" the reedy voice called. "No need to play games with us, boys, we know you're in here. The bike's a big fuckin' clue, heehee!"

"My friend is right," the heavier voice called. The Survivor heard the clop of hooves against the garage floor. "Come on out. It's just the rabbit we want."

The Survivor and the rabbit looked at one another, both of them puzzled.

The hooves clopped closer, into the room where they were hiding. "His friends did a nice little number on our group, and we're here to collect," the heavier voice rumbled. "Red panda slipped away from us, but we'll get to them in a bit."

The Survivor peeked out from behind the low counter. The heavier voice belonged to a horse—big, if a little malnourished, the scars from several stab wounds crossing his beefy arms. His companion with the reedy voice was a ferret, the left side of his neck furless, red, and patchy with a rash. Both held baseball bats—the horse's had a big rust-colored stain near the top. They were slowly walking among the shelves, tapping the aluminum weapons against the sheet metal.

"Just give us the rabbit and you can go, otter," the ferret called. "We know he got chomped on. What's the use in trying to keep him alive when he's boned anyway?"

For a moment, the Survivor considered it. He could pass the rabbit off to the scavengers, take his bike, and keep heading north to find the man who killed Jayce. It would be so easy, and it didn't have to affect him. The rabbit would just be one of the many who died every day, as the world continued to turn, They continued to feed, and everything came unraveled.

His paw gripped the stock of the rifle so hard he thought the wood might crack. There was no guarantee they wouldn't just kill him too. Social norms had gone out the window when the outbreak had engulfed the country. And he had to survive to find Jayce's killer.

The Survivor turned to the rabbit, pointed to him, then pointed down. *Stay here.* He tapped his chest, then motioned around the counter. *I'll go around them.* The rabbit nodded furiously.

Careful of his steps, the Survivor moved out from behind the counter. He stepped in time with the big horse, masking his pawsteps with the clicks of hooves against tile. The horse's steps gave his position away easily, and it was trivial to anticipate his path and move into a position behind him.

At least until he rounded a corner and came muzzle to muzzle with a crouched ferret. "Hiya!" the mustelid chirped, his eyes radiating a mad cheerfulness.

The Survivor got the rifle up just in time to keep the metal baseball bat from cracking him in the head. He drove his knee into the ferret's midriff, then made to bludgeon him with the stock of the hunting rifle. He missed, and the rifle butt hit a shelf with a bang.

Hooves clacked on tile as the horse darted behind the Survivor, menacing him with his own bat. "Big mistake."

A bullet zipped past the end of his muzzle and shattered a pane of glass in the window by his head. The horse whinnied in shock and clapped a hand to his mouth, his head snapping towards the counter. The rabbit stood tall with the gun aimed in the general direction of the horse, though his paws were shaking. "Dammit," he muttered, then collapsed into a paroxysm of coughing.

"There you are!" the horse roared, changing targets and stomping towards the counter.

"Hang on!" the Survivor yelled. He ducked the ferret's next wild swing, then clubbed him in the stomach with the butt of the rifle. The ferret doubled over. The Survivor shoved him to the floor. He levelled the rifle at the horse, but the moment his finger squeezed the trigger, the ferret's bat smashed into his ankle. The round went wide, punching a quarter-sized hole in the wall near the rabbit. Pain shot up the Survivor's leg and he staggered.

"Just hold still, bunny," the horse said as he walked around the counter, swinging the bat as if he were stepping up to the plate. "Gonna swat your head into Macluske like a friggin' baseball before we take out all your friends."

"Don't you dare!" the rabbit yelled. He lunged at the horse, batting at him with the butt end of the pistol instead of shooting it. Was it desperation, or did he just not think to do it?

The Survivor hopped back to avoid another swing of the ferret's bat. The bat smashed into a shelf and bent it into a wide V shape. His webbed paw closed around the shiv in the back pocket of his jeans and he stabbed forward with it, aiming for the ferret's throat. The ferret twisted to the side, the business end of the makeshift blade digging into the meat of his shoulder. He nailed the Survivor in the stomach with the bat, doubling him over.

"All this effort for one of Them!" the ferret seethed, raising the bat to bring it down on the Survivor's skull.

A pained whinny made the ferret hesitate as both he and the Survivor looked over at the horse. "God dammit!" he roared, swatting at the rabbit. It took the Survivor a moment to realize that the rabbit's big buck teeth were lodged in the meat of the horse's bicep, and he wasn't letting go no matter how hard the horse hit him with the bat.

"Fuck, he turned!" the ferret yelled.

As he whirled around to go to the horse's aid, the Survivor grabbed his ankles and pulled, tripping the mustelid so that he fell flat on his muzzle. The otter scrambled forward, grabbed the ferret by the back of the head and drove his face into the tile floor. With the ferret out cold, he went for the discarded rifle.

The Survivor got to his feet just as the horse threw the rabbit off him. "You piece of shit!" he roared, blood streaming from his meaty bicep. His frantic eyes looked for the Survivor. "You! You keeping him around is the reason for this!"

The rifle cracked, the sound incredibly loud in the cramped space, setting the Survivor's ears ringing. The horse staggered, then slumped against the wall, spattering the grimy tile with blood from the wound in his head. The Survivor hurried to the counter and peeked over, making sure the big equine was down for the count.

Metal shifted to his left, and he swung the rifle around. The rabbit picked himself up with far more care than They did. They just kept flying at you in a rage until you put them down. "Is… he dead?"

They didn't speak, either. The Survivor lowered the rifle. "Yeah. Gutsy move, biting him."

"It was all I could think of in the moment. What about his friend?"

They moved to the fallen ferret. The otter rolled the mustelid over, and he let out a groan through a broken nose as he did. "You fuckin' prick," he spat. "Why'd you have to kill Relly, eh? The fuckin' rabbit's gonna turn, you asshole!"

"Doesn't matter," the otter said, planting a foot on the ferret's chest. "You attacked us."

"His fuckin' group attacked *us!*" the ferret protested. "In the woods three nights ago!"

"That's a lie," the rabbit hissed, leaning on a shelf for support. "We would never!"

"Bullshit," the ferret said. "Everyone does it, don't lie. You just don't want to admit to it because you think you're just so much fuckin' better than everyone else." He grinned, showing a muzzle full of crooked and broken teeth. "Well it don't matter anymore. Nothing matters anymore. Especially for you. How much time you got left, rabbit?"

The rabbit looked out the window. "The rain's letting up." He winced and pressed a hand to his side. "It's only another little while to Macluske. Please, stranger. I want as much time with my people as I can."

Outside, the rain had tapered into an almost non-existent drizzle. Cool air blew gently through the broken window pane, rolling over the debris and carnage in the auto shop. "What about him?" the Survivor said.

"I don't care," the rabbit said, and it was the first time the Survivor had heard anything approaching hostility in his voice.

"Don't be a bitch," the ferret said. "You know what you gotta do. Otherwise I'm just gonna keep coming, after both of you now, especially you, otter."

The Survivor looked down his muzzle at the ferret. "Just one question. Is there a black-furred wolf in your raiding band?"

"What kinda dumbass question is that?" the ferret said. "No, we ain't got no black wolf."

The Survivor nodded. "Good." He yanked the shiv out of the ferret's shoulder, making the mustelid screech in pain. "That means *this* isn't about to go in your throat." He looked up at the rabbit. "Pistol, please."

"What are you—" was all the ferret got out before the Survivor cracked him across the jaw with the butt of the pistol, leaving the ferret moaning on the floor.

"Let's go," the Survivor said.

The pair gathered their meager belongings and lifted the garage door. Mid-morning sunlight shone into the small space. The Survivor began to wheel his bike outside, then stopped. "Give me a second," he said to the rabbit.

He hurried back inside the auto shop and went to the counter, ignoring the corpse of the horse. The Survivor grabbed the letter and the photograph, folded them neatly, and shoved them into the pocket of his riding jacket.

When he returned outside, the rabbit was staring off into the distance, his face grim. The Survivor followed his gaze. A pair of Them slowly shambled towards the auto garage, drawn by the sounds of the fight. He and the rabbit shared a long stare. Then they straddled the bike and drove off.

"So what did you do before all this?" the Survivor asked as they passed a "Macluske, ten miles" sign.

"I was a doctor," the rabbit said. He was leaning back slightly, the passing air making his long ears trail back behind his head like streamers. "Lived in Oleander when everything started falling apart. Peter and I have been together for almost fifteen years." He sighed. "When you put it like that it sounds like everything's been just fine. Even though the last three years we've been on the run."

The Survivor nodded. "Where to?"

"We've tracked east across the country for three years, but we started trekking north about three months ago. Apparently the infection didn't spread as much up there, something to do with the cold killing the virus. There's safe zones, food, shelter, actual survivors."

"I thought those were just rumors."

The rabbit shrugged one shoulder. "They could very well be. But we didn't have any other destination in mind, really. Could be worth a shot, if that's what you're looking for."

"After I find the man who killed Jayce, I just might."

"What did you and he do?"

"He was a psychiatrist, specialized in treating anxiety in young adults." It still felt weird to talk about Jayce in the past tense, and feel the tightness of emotion around his throat, but the Survivor pushed onward. "I was a high school music teacher."

"How did you two meet?"

The rubber of the handlebars felt comforting against his fingers as the Survivor rubbed it. "Mutual friend. We bonded over motorcycles. Everything else just kind of followed, no real 'love at first sight' with us. You?"

"Same, but change motorcycles for wine." The rabbit leaned against the Survivor's back. "Best trip we ever took was overseas to Bellavia to sample vineyards. I don't think we spent a moment of that week sober. But God, it was a good time. I wonder what's happened to those fields…" He trailed off.

Another sign whipped by soon after—Macluske, seven miles. "It's funny, really," the rabbit said. "I barely slept last night. On some animal level, I know that every moment brings me closer to my last. And while yesterday that was terrifying, now it simply is."

"Isn't that true of everyone?" the Survivor asked. "Even those of us that aren't infected."

"That is true," the rabbit admitted. "But the *knowing* part is the worst for me. I dealt with cancer patients before all this, so I know what it looks like from the outside in to know your end is coming."

"That's every day now, though," the Survivor said. "Could be Them. Could be thugs like that horse and the ferret. Hell, I could hit a pothole and that'd be the end of me."

The rabbit's arms wrapped around the Survivor's waist, an intimate gesture. "I think you handle yourself fine. And I think you will find what you seek."

Silence grew between them as they whipped past the next two road signs. In the distance, growing closer by the minute, was a vista of small buildings, a podunk town in the middle of nowhere. As they passed a tacky wooden sign with "Welcome to Macluske!" written in large red block letters, the rabbit finally spoke. "You could have left me in the auto shop," he said. "Or on the rock where we first me. Or on the road after I spooked you. Why didn't you?"

The Survivor slowed the bike down as they entered the small town, the engine echoing off the buildings with the finality of a funeral dirge. They coasted to a stop underneath the town's one stoplight, its lenses unlit. The otter steadied the motorcycle and looked up and out beyond the town, towards the small mountain rising in the north.

"I didn't get closure," he said. "I ran after the wolf that shot my husband, and by the time I got back to him, Jayce was already gone. I never got to say goodbye." The Survivor's paw closed around his necklace, the two rings there icy against his webbing. "So many people don't get any closure these days. I guess I just wanted *someone* to have some." He looked up the road. "Or, you know, maybe it was just that your destination happened to be along my path. Either way works."

A paw patted him on the shoulder. "Your kindness means everything to me, stranger," the rabbit said. He slowly got off the bike and ran a paw over his head, his ears springing back up with a surprising amount of vigor. "I wish you the best of luck in your travels."

The Survivor leaned over the handlebars, looking down the road leading out of Macluske. "Simon."

"Hm?"

"My name is Simon."

Brian the rabbit smiled, an expression that seemed so out of place for him. "You're a good person, Simon."

Simon nodded. "I hope your last hours are… what you need them to be."

"Just the chance, I think, is enough." Brian swallowed, wiped a paw across his eyes, then turned away from him. "Farewell."

He took a shaky step away from Simon, towards a nearby building. Simon picked out a few faces hidden tactfully in the shadows of the building's base. Then Brian's stride became strong as he walked towards the building. A few people came out to meet him—a bear, a mare, a red panda. Though Simon couldn't hear their words, when Brian peeled off the bandage on his neck, their expressions said all they needed.

A moment later, a new figure emerged from the building. A massive black wolf rushed forth from the shadows, making a beeline for Brian. He wrapped him in a hug, and Simon could see him sobbing deeply. They pulled apart for a moment, foreheads pressed together, and spoke. Brian pointed towards Simon sitting on the bike, and the wolf looked over at him.

Their eyes met. And what followed was a moment of terrible recognition, one that flashed through their minds as one, there and gone like the flash of lightning that had illuminated those eyes three nights ago. Simon's mouth dropped open slightly, a terrible heat burning in his gut. He closed his eyes, his heart thundering in his ears. He hadn't reloaded the pistol since the auto shop. It had three bullets in it. Easily enough to take his revenge. His paw jerked towards the gun in his belt.

Inhale. Count to four. Not three, hon, four! Four. Exhale. There you go.

Simon opened his eyes. The black wolf was hugging Brian, but his gaze was fixed on Simon. The eyes were the same, but where then they had been full of anger and panic, now they held only a hollow emptiness, fathomless in depth. It was an expression that said both, "Thank you," and, "How could you do this to me?" at the same time.

Simon kicked his motorcycle into life, not willing to face those eyes any longer. He drove away, away from the rabbit and his wolf. He almost gunned it down the road, but then saw a turnoff. He took it, the road angling up onto a small promontory that overlooked the town.

A long time ago, even before everything had fallen apart, this place had been a drive-in movie theater. The bluffs allowed Simon to look out over Macluske, this small town in the middle of nowhere. He drove to the very edge of the cliff, then shut off the bike engine. He reached behind him into the duffel bag and withdrew the cigar and the lighter. The plastic wrapping parted under his claws, and he let the breeze carry it away. Two flicks of the lighter produced a flame.

He remained up there for a long time. How Jayce had ever enjoyed these things was a mystery to him, but he persisted. In the distance, over the plains through which he and Brian had driven, another storm began to gather, clouds coalescing into a thunderhead that began to crackle with power. It flowed over the rolling hills, traveling to the west. It likely wouldn't impede his travels. The sun began to set, bathing Macluske in a beautiful orange light that made it look picturesque, like nothing had ever happened, They were a myth, and his husband wasn't dead.

As the cigar burned down to a stub, and the last of the ashes drifted away from his muzzle, a single, loud gunshot rang out from the center of town, scaring a few birds in a nearby tree into the air. A moment later came the mournful howl of a black wolf.

There had been no point in exacting his revenge with violence. There was nothing that Simon could do to him now that would hurt him more than what he had to be feeling right now. His self-righteousness had deserted him, leaving him hollow and empty. It seemed paradoxical—in his efforts to show some kindness, any kindness, all he had done was cause more pain. He himself had done nothing to Brian, sure, but was it really better that Brian's wolf had closure? Had Simon deprived him of the small light of hope of not knowing Brian's fate, allowing him to believe the rabbit might still be alive? Had he really done the right thing?

Simon bowed his head into his paws, breathing deep to steady himself. What would he do now? What *could* he do now?

As he bent over, the letter and the photograph fluttered out of the inside pocket of Jayce's riding jacket and landed on the dirt below. Simon reached down and took hold of them, staring at the photo of the vixen and the doe for a time as the breeze threatened to tear it from his fingers.

It wasn't much. But it was some direction, at least. Better that than wandering aimlessly until the rabid dead ran him down.

Simon dropped the remains of the cigar onto the ground and ground it out under his heel. Then he straddled his motorcycle, throttled the engine, and drove back to the highway. He turned right and followed the road north away from Macluske.

THE SNACK RABBIT

Lloyd Yaeger

The rabbit was dead through most of the surgery. Which felt weird, if he was being honest, like sinking into an ocean, thick with sleep and memory. But then he heard the word "Clear!" and woke up gasping, lying on a metal table, wearing nothing more than a cloth gown, electrodes stuck to shaved patches on his chest.

The surgeon, a hyena, was staring down at him from under her mask. "Oh good. You're awake," she said. "You were gone a minute ago."

He blinked in the lamplight. A tray on a swing arm next to him held several scalpels, clamps, and syringes. An EKG and an IV drip stood close by. And yet there were also signs that this was not what he would consider a reputable medical establishment. It was cramped and dingy, and the air weighed down on him.

"What did you just say?" asked the rabbit.

"Please do not move," said the hyena. "This is very delicate. To repeat, you were dead. Now you're not. Everything making sense?"

"None of that makes sense!" There was a cloth stretched over part of his forehead. Behind it, his open skull exposed part of his brain. A surgical droid was manipulating the metal and plastic components that he knew were lodged in his head, even if he couldn't feel them. He tried to lift his paw, but he could barely move. On top of that, his wrists were tied to the table with elastic bands. His heartbeat pounded, knocking around against his ribs. The EKG squawked rapidly.

"Please relax. I need you paying attention. Let's test something. Do you remember your name?"

He closed his eyes and thought about it. "Orio..."

"That's funny. Because you look like one, right?"

Of course she would ask that. His whole life, he'd dealt with the consequences of his distinctive fur, with its off-white coat and puddles and speckles of grey and black. But the resemblance between his name and his fur was a coincidence. He learned this when he received his first ID, where, due to what he assumed was a clerical error, the final letter of his given name, "Orion," had been left off. When he checked the paperwork himself, it was plain as day. He was Orio. While it embarrassed him, the truth was that he had grown attached to it over the years. At gay bars, the name had been an excellent conversation starter, and it always led to a cute and well-rehearsed pick-up line. So it stuck.

"Sure... like the cookie."

"What else?"

"I'm a debugger... I work for NosCo."

"Tell me about that," she said. "What was it like?"

"Numbing. Like bleeding all the time and never knowing where it hurts."

"You mean you remember that too? Interesting..."

"Can I ask a question now?"

"Wait let me guess. You want to know why I'm inserting these nanodrives into the artificial homeostatic structure where your brain stem and cerebellum used to be? Is that it?"

"Yeah... so why are you... that?" He tried to focus on his breathing. He was overwhelmed with information, but he could process none of it. The hyena's conversation was the only thing keeping the ensuing panic attack at bay.

"You died of a brain aneurysm. And now that you're dead, your body has been donated to science (Hello I'm doctor Kiva nice to meet you by the way) and it just so happens that science has decided to revive you as a vessel for this valuable piece of... whatever this is." The droid placed several tiny spheres into concave slots, and something inside his head made a high-pitched whirring and clicking noise. He tasted rubber.

"You mean you don't know what you're putting inside me?"

"You're adorable," she said. "Listen. I know this is hard to believe here, but I'm *just* the surgeon. I don't design this. It comes black-boxed. You, frosted fur, are what we in the biz refer to as a corpse.

Technically and officially deceased, but still walking around. They buy the parts. I install them. For a nominal fee, that is. Your particular buyer is very… private."

"Are you even licensed?"

"Well, in the most technical possible sense… no. But that's a whole paperwork thing. Who has time for that? Not doctor Kiva. Now tell me. What day of the week is it?"

He said twelve, and after that, everything melted into a blur. He only had a vague recollection of Kiva installing the display panel, or grafting the metal plate onto the back of his head and neck, or inserting the tiny screws to close it up. When he woke up again, she was sitting next to him, twirling a scalpel between her fingers, staring at it with intimate focus.

"We're finished," said the doctor.

Just then, there was the sound of a metal hatch scraping against an old hinge, groaning open and then slamming closed again. Two figures were descending a ladder. They approached the table.

"Oh excellent. You're back," said Kiva. "Did he confirm the wire transfer?"

One of the figures came closer, a stocky lynx with ears that curled at the tips. Thick tufts of fur emerged from the gaps in her body armor, all taupe and tow, with stony patches here and there. She looked down at the rabbit. Her left eye was fitted with a small device that looked like a spider was roosting over her pupil, grasping her eye with its legs.

"We have some bad news," said the lynx.

"What news is that, Phoebe?"

"You won't be getting paid," she said. Now the second figure came close. Orio recognized him immediately. The tall Labrador—no, it couldn't be. But he looked just like him. The same fur more silver than sandy, always shimmering when he came under the bright lights. It reminded Orio of fiber optics.

"Tenebre… is that you?" He couldn't say his husband's name without feeling the blood rush to his face. But it's impossible, he told himself. Tenebre had died over a year ago.

And anyway, the lab didn't so much as glance at him. They both came close to the hyena, looming over her. Kiva looked askance at the lynx.

"And why is that?"

"He's dead," said the lab. "Someone got to him. We found the wolf lying in a pool of his own blood."

The hyena's jaw hung open for a moment. "He's dead? Shit. Double shit. First you two, now this."

"Someone is after us," said the lab.

"We'll have to find another market…"

"Actually," said the lynx, raising her paw, "about that…" Narrow claws extended from her fingers. They were tiny scythes, curved over, white and iridescent.

"Your claws… Those look like diamonds. They're… beautiful, Phoebe." The hyena stared into them, but then her eyes melted from hypnotism to disappointment. "So you had someone else put them in. Do I mean nothing to you?"

"You bet I did," said the lynx. "And I'd do it again. It was that good."

Kiva rushed in with the scalpel. But the lynx ducked under it and swung her paw like an axe, catching the hyena on the side of her head. The blow took her down to the floor. She whined as the blood ran from her now torn ear.

"Did you think we wouldn't figure it out?" asked the lab. "We're all linked. Us and the other corpses you've created. Tell us about the system."

"I have nothing to tell," said Kiva, clutching her ear. "I only do installations. It's not my fault some of the buyers end up dead. What was I supposed to do with you two? Scrap you?"

"How many of us are there? Don't make me kill you, Kiva."

"Eighteen… plus the rabbit."

"We're taking him," said the lab.

Orio's ears twitched. The anesthetic must have been wearing off. He wiggled his toes and found that, with enough effort, he could make a fist with his paw.

The lab came up close. He loosened the straps and then wrapped his arms around the rabbit. Orio sniffed at his fur. The scent was earthy and familiar. He bathed in it. Yes, it had to be him. But Tenebre still wouldn't acknowledge him.

"Look at me. It's you, isn't it? Why won't you answer me?" he asked.

The lab's tight grip made him wince. He reached for the syringe on the tray, but he could barely make his muscles tense up. Still, he kept trying. He managed to grab hold of one of the needles just as the lab slung him over his shoulder. Without looking where he was stabbing, Orio jammed the needle down into the lab's side.

"Don't move," said the rabbit. "Or I'll inject."

The lynx pivoted, her claws extended. "Need help?"

"No. Hold on," said the lab. He lowered his voice to a growl and spoke directly into the rabbit's ear. "Listen to me. I know who you think I am, and you're wrong. My name is Tenebre. I have never met you before. I won't hurt you. But I don't have to save you either. If you want to stay here, that's your choice. But I am not your enemy."

The rabbit's paw locked up. Even if he were at his full strength, he was hardly in a position to make any demands. It didn't make sense. Nothing did. The lab wasn't his husband, but he sure smelled like him. And right now, that meant Orio trusted him more than Kiva.

"Okay." He pulled the needle out of Tenebre's side and dropped it on the floor.

The lab slung Orio over his shoulder and carried him up the ladder, through the hatch, and onto the deck. They were on a ship, floating far away from any visible land. The moon was bright behind the clouds.

"You're making a mistake!" said Kiva.

"By not killing you? Probably." Phoebe sniffed, keeping her claws extended and her head half-turned toward the Hyena.

"By taking the rabbit," said the doctor. "This one is… different. His hardware isn't the same as yours."

"What's the model?"

"I don't know. It's custom. But he remembers everything. The gear is on his brainstem. It's keeping him alive."

They came up to a platform at the stern, where two aerocycles were tied down beneath a canvas sheet. When Tenebre had gotten them untied and revved up, he lifted Orio onto the seat and told him to hold on. Then they rose up off the ship's deck and flew back to the port.

***

Under the night watch of the Dalkin skyline, they sped through midtown, dodging traffic and buildings. So that's where he'd been taken:

the invisible city, scrubbed from every map, and like him, assumed to be deceased. It wasn't surprising that Kiva was conducting her shadowy business here, of all places. There were the itinerant drinkers, and the addicts passed out on benches. They passed by the clubs, the boozy holo-ads, the used part dealers. The rabbit clung to the lab's jacket, barely able to keep himself awake. Tenebre had said there was someplace to go, and he had that familiar look in his eye that made Orio trust him.

A series of abandoned hangars rested in a field on the outskirts of the city. They were once part of a spaceport, monuments to a time when Dalkin was recognized by NosCo as a legitimate branch. Tenebre lowered the bike onto the uneven dirt outside one of the wide buildings. The hangars reminded Orio of coffee cans buried sideways in the dirt. A large chain was wrapped around the latch of the door, secured by a wide padlock. Tenebre unraveled it, seeming to know it would break apart and fall to the ground, and it did.

"I cut this a few months ago. I keep it here for show." He dragged the gate open.

The lynx hoisted Orio off the bike. "Can you walk?" she asked.

"Not really." He was sitting on the ground. Phoebe got down and lifted him onto her shoulders. She carried him in like a backpack.

The inside was pitch black except for dusty moon rays that shone through the row of thin windows near the ceiling. The darkness made the building seem even vaster. Tenebre cracked a few lumen rods and threw them on the ground, filling the room with a dull blue glow. The three stood in the middle of a concrete floor, dirty and busted up in places. A few rusty catwalks and girders formed a canopy. At the far end of the room was the leftover half of a decommissioned shuttle, partly converted to scrap, its hull flayed and charred in places. It rested somewhere between ship and wreckage.

"So what now?" asked Phoebe.

"I want to know what that Kiva put inside us," said Tenebre. "I'll find out, whatever it takes."

"She said there were others…"

They hunched down in a corner of the hull of the ship, and kept going on like that, talking about corpses and hardware and secrets. Sighing, the lab lit a cigarette and then cracked a few more lumens in a pile between them, along with a heat stick. But Orio couldn't stop staring at him. This Tenebre was just like his husband, restored like a back-up from his memory. Well, not exactly. He was older now, and sadder-looking.

"Don't sleep just yet, okay?" he said.

"Okay…"

"What's your name?" When the rabbit told him, the lynx snickered to herself. The lab only nodded. "Look," he continued, "I know what this looks like, but there's something you have to understand."

"What's that?"

"I'm not the same guy as your husband. The stuff they installed in us—me and Phoebe I mean—it's different than yours. We don't have any memory of the people we were when we were alive."

"I see…" said the rabbit. "So you don't remember me? Not at all?"

"It's like this: I know about you. I've heard of you. You're in a file somewhere inside me. I know you the way I know stuff I read a long time ago. But I've never met you."

"So why should I trust you then?"

In response, the lab shrugged. Orio let his head fall into the crook of his arm, his ears spilling over. He hated the lab for telling him the truth. More than that, he hated Kiva for bringing him back to life only so he could grieve again.

"Hey, don't get down," said the lynx. "It's hard. The first night's always fucked up. I'd offer you a drink, but it's not usually good after this kinda thing…"

"He liked rye," he said. Then he looked at Tenebre. "It was your favorite."

"I hate rye," he said.

Those were the last words that floated through Orio's mind before he drifted into the longest sleep he'd ever experienced. All through the night, the morning, and the next evening, they couldn't wake him.

When he did open his eyes, he was hungry. It felt like a lifetime since he last ate. "There's gas station snacks," said Tenebre. "I'm going out for supplies later. Till then, this is all we have."

Orio annihilated a bag of wasabi peas. They were, at that moment, the best thing he had ever tasted.

Meanwhile, Tenebre kept itching at a small opening on the back of his skull. The port was round, and not much wider than a nickel.

Its edges were raised, folding over into the collapsed center, which tapered, like a funnel, to a much smaller metal ring surrounding a thin shaft that led even deeper, like a mine dug into a snowy mountain.

He caught Orio staring at it. "We woke up with these. I don't recognize the hardware."

"Let me see," said Orio. He peered closer. "It's NosCo tech. I used to work for them. You'd need a rig, first of all. We don't even have that. And the components... They're not anything standard."

"But you know what we'd need?"

"I'll get you a list..."

The next night, the lab took the bike out, saying he'd be back in a few days with as much food and tech as he could gather. Orio didn't need to ask how he planned to acquire it. He and the lynx spent most of their hours quietly. Every so often, she would type out something on her holopad, nod, and then close her eyes.

After a while, she nudged him. "You worked for NosCo? Well so did I. Tenebre too. I was a programmer. The lab was an engineer."

"I thought you didn't have any memory of that," said Orio.

"We know things," said Phoebe. "We just don't know what it was like. There are no feelings attached to them."

"Your intra-ocular is strange," said Orio. He was referring to the dark lens on her pupil, with its thin plastic tendrils that wrapped around the sclera. "I've never seen one like that. Did you have that when you were alive?"

"I use it to message Tenebre. Kiva installed it."

"Just because you asked for it?"

"Pfft," said the lynx. "She just likes sticking gizmos in people. It's her fetish or something."

Orio nodded. "Did it... hurt?"

"It doesn't feel good," said Phoebe. "It needs direct access to the retina. But the pain only lasts a moment. Sort of like getting your ear pierced. Or in this case, your eye."

"If I got one," said Orio, "would I be able to communicate with you two?"

"We'd need some more parts, but yeah..."

The rabbit wanted to be inside the lab's head. He wanted to reach in there and dig through the grey matter until he found the memories that would remind Tenebre of the half-decade they shared—the lonely days, the long nights spent resting in each other's arms.

"Can he get one for me?"

Did Phoebe mean to look so suspicious of him? She narrowed her eyes, and then gave a long, silent yawn. Her holopad appeared, and she began typing, the sigils glowing violet under her quick and delicate keystrokes. Her fangs poked over her broad smile.

The next evening, the lab returned with two crates, in which he had packed a cheap-looking rig, three display terminals, several cans of preserved meat, bottled water, dried fruit, blankets, and some clothes for the rabbit. He had an IO applicator too. It looked like a nail gun with a concave nozzle at the top.

"Keep your left eye open and your right squeezed shut."

Orio leaned back against a girder. They didn't have a speculum, so Tenebre held Orio's eye open while Phoebe scanned it. She pressed a few buttons on the side of the gun and then fitted the IO onto the nozzle. Then she poured vodka on it.

"You're gonna need to hold real still," she said, placing concave surface of the applicator over his pupil. "I just have to calibrate it."

It closed over his open eye. He could see nothing besides the few spots of lingering afterimage. A ruby-colored dot blinked in the darkness. It moved around in a circle, then centered in his field of vision.

He fidgeted. "Is it supposed to do that?"

"Relax, Cookies," she said. "Stare at the dot."

Then she pulled the trigger, and everything went even darker than before. There was a sharp, stabbing pain. Something broke through the cornea. He wanted to yell, but it happened too quickly. For a moment, it felt like his eye had exploded from the inside. Then, an instant later, the pain faded away.

Tenebre let go and Orio squeezed his eyelids shut. He felt something that wasn't there before. When he opened them again, everything bloomed back into view, as bright and clear as it had been before, maybe even brighter. The sunrise was filtering through the windows in the upper rafters of the hangar, sending shafts of peachy light down onto the concrete.

"Ah… Am I bleeding?" he asked.

"A little," said the lynx. "We'll need to wash it out a few times a day for the next few weeks. Go easy, though. We have limited water."

Orio's head was spinning. Or was it the room? Tenebre was telling him to breathe in a hollow voice. The lynx was typing something on her holopad. Suddenly, in the left-hand corner of Orio's field of vision, a message popped into existence.

PHOEBE: Are you getting this, Cookies?

PHOEBE: Blink if you can see this.

And he blinked.

***

The months began to pass in a steady rhythm. Tenebre would ride away every week to gather supplies, while Orio and Phoebe did research, working their way as deep as they could through NosCo's numerous and sophisticated security systems. They learned little, except that a number of other employees had also died under similarly mysterious circumstances.

Orio didn't like being around a stranger who looked like his husband. There was the lab he married, and the lab he knew now, and as hard as he tried, he could never figure out how to separate the two. He thought all the time about leaving. But just like Tenebre, he wanted to dig up the secrets between his ears. That and the image of his husband were enough to keep him around.

They managed to jerry-rig a prototype converter that would, if the design worked, allow them access; at least, to Tenebre and Phoebe. After all, they were the ones with ports in their skulls. Orio was different. A metal flap on the back of his neck opened up to reveal nothing more than a plastic panel with several LED lights, one of which always glowed a dull green.

One night, they tried to connect the port directly to their rig. Orio fed the spindly wires into the thin opening at the base of the funnel in Tenebre's skull, where flesh ended and metal began. Once the wires were correctly positioned, that is to say, properly held down with duct tape, the rabbit loaded the script he had composed to copy down and transmit whatever was inside him.

"Are you ready?"

"Yes," said Tenebre.

No sooner had Orio switched the converter on than the screens went black, and the rig crashed. For a moment, there was text on the screen. But it disappeared before Orio could read it.

"Shit," said Tenebre. "That hurt… How's the rig?"

"It's bricked," said Phoebe.

"Maybe it's too much data," said Orio.

"I bet it's a security measure," said Phoebe. "If we could find an old NosCo rig with facsimile credentials…"

"I'll do my best," said the lab.

He left the next night. In the meantime, he and Phoebe modified the code, building in new workarounds. It took two days for the lab to return. When he did, he had a large plastic crate strapped to the bike. Inside was an unassuming black box, the size of a small modem. It was heavy. Orio had trouble lifting it.

"It's a system," said Tenebre. "She'll be able to handle whatever's in there."

"She?" asked Phoebe, arms folded.

"Or he… I mean I suppose it depends on what we call… it."

"Dolores," said Orio. "She's Dolores."

"Why Dolores?" asked Phoebe. "Are we naming her after my grandma? How about Agnes? Why not Gerty, while we're at it?"

"It just… seems right."

And Dolores, just like Orio's artificially sweetened moniker, stuck. She was a jail-broken NosCo series two, Dolphin model. Beyond the inch-thick walls that protected layer after layer of nanoglass, Dolores had internal cooling, emergency power, and—Tenebre could hardly avoid sounding like a sales clerk—could even survive a two-story drop. Supposedly, anyway.

"Where'd you get her?"

"I went back to the dead buyer's apartment. The place was trashed. The body was gone too. But this wasn't."

After he brought the bike back inside the hangar, he leaned on it for a moment. His tongue hung from his mouth in a pant.

"You okay, sunshine?" asked Phoebe.

"I'm tired. I grimace when I wake up. And when I flex my knees, the tendons make the same sound as when you tear apart beef jerky."

"You look like you're twice your age," said the lynx.

He looked at Orio. "What do you think? Do I look old?" His expression made the rabbit think about sex. One night, a month or so ago, emboldened by boredom and box wine, he and Tenebre had kissed for a minute in the dark. To Orio, it was both familiar and forced. Tenebre shrugged it off afterward.

"No," said Orio, his ears standing on end. He felt ashamed for a moment, though of what, he wasn't sure.

They spent a few hours getting Dolores up and running, after which she became a centerpiece to the room. They arranged their three display modules around the outside so that they formed an even triangle. Tenebre said, "Let's boot her up," and after a few tugs at the generator, they managed to get an even flow into the power supply. The deck ascended quickly to a steady hum, and then the three display terminals lit up all at once.

"Let's try again," said the lab, tail whipping like a live wire.

Once Orio had fed the cables into Phoebe and Tenebre's ports, he switched on the rig and loaded the script. Then he flipped the converter again.

"I feel it," said Phoebe, staring up at the roof of the hangar. "It's weird. Like getting a tattoo inside your brain, if that makes any sense. It's irritating, like an itch I can't scratch."

"Hey! It's working!" For the first time since he died, Orio was excited about something. Text was printing on their display modules, the screens filling with what seemed like random and illegible characters.

"Okay, well it's obviously encrypted," said the rabbit.

"Well sure," said Phoebe. "Why wouldn't it be?"

"I just had this weird fantasy we'd learn something today. I wonder how many dirty words I can spell in any direction…"

"I have a theory," said Tenebre.

"What is it?" asked Orio.

"You're gonna hate me," he said.

"Go on…"

"Think of a cookie."

"Okay, I hate you. I hate you so much right now."

"Bear with me. You know what I mean. It's just text. You put it somewhere temporarily so that it can be retrieved later. That's like our chips. Phoebe's and mine. They're just holding something, recording it as it comes. The question is what, and where is it originating?"

The transcription took six hours, and in the meantime they fell quickly from anticipation to boredom. When they weren't staring silently at the beams above them, they laughed and drank and speculated about what was in their heads.

"I bet it's a bunch of bank account numbers," said Phoebe. "Huge sums, growing for years. We're walking, talking shell corporations."

The question had gripped Orio with dread. "It's something dangerous. It wouldn't be locked down so tight if it weren't threatening."

"A weapon?" asked Tenebre.

"Or a way of accessing one," said the rabbit. "Well, what do you think it is?"

The lab shook his head and drained his cup. "Forget it. I don't have the energy to sit here wondering about it."

Phoebe laughed at the lab's attempt at depth. "Give him more wine. He might philosophize for us." But the rabbit could see in his face that Tenebre had done nothing but wonder about it since the day they escaped from Kiva.

***

They made it their goal to develop a program that could learn the encryption method, building software to analyze patterns in the raw data. One night, while they dragged themselves through the caffeinated tedium of their work, an alert appeared in the rabbit's IO. It was nearly midnight, and he was feeling it. His vision went blurry whenever he blinked. The message was from Tenebre. Phoebe was there too. So why couldn't he just say it?

TENEBRE: We are in danger. Don't talk about this out loud. Message me.

Orio scratched his neck, sighing at the annoyance of re-syncing his deck with his IO. After thirty long seconds, the purple glow of a second work-surface faded into existence. Still working the bottom layer, he switched his left paw to the upper pad and began typing.

ORIO: Why? What's wrong?

TENEBRE: There's another body in the room. Above us. I picked up some movement just now.

PHOEBE: How the hell did they get in?

TENEBRE: I don't know. She had some kind of cloaking device on.

ORIO: Did you guys hear that?

"I'm gonna get some coffee," said Phoebe. She stood up. The bands of light that were her keyboard traveled with her as she made the trek to the coffee pot, and she kept typing all the while. Orio couldn't shake the feeling that, any moment, something horrible would happen, and he'd have to watch his friend fall over dead.

TENEBRE: What are you doing!?

PHOEBE: Did you not hear me? COFFEE.

TENEBRE: Do you see anybody?

PHOEBE: I haven't looked. Whoever is up there probably doesn't want us to know they're here.

TENEBRE: Steal a glance on your way back.

She sat down again, typing with one paw and holding her mug with the other.

PHOEBE: It's hard to make out, but there's definitely movement up there.

ORIO: One of us should make contact.

PHOEBE: One of us should.

TENEBRE: You're saying it should be me.

PHOEBE: Fine. I'll do it.

TENEBRE: no DONT!!!!!

"Hello up there," the lynx yelled. She kept staring at her display. "We know you're here."

Nothing. The silence was not unusual, since, for the last several hours, all three of them had been mostly wordless, typing into the night. Yet there was something about it that bothered Orio, since he was by now used to a near-constant stream of noise from every corner of his world.

But then there was the sound of breathing, high above them, a long, deep exhale full of annoyance. "Fuck it," said a throaty voice. A woman's, but not one he recognized.

"Do you want to come down?"

"Nope," said the voice. "I'd much rather work from up here."

"What line of work are you in, mystery person?" asked the rabbit.

"Hunting," she said. "We detected access. Where is Orion?"

He regretted speaking. The question prompted a wave of typing from his two friends. Both of them had apparently felt it necessary to remind him, as if somehow he were truly that oblivious, not to reveal himself. The rabbit would have been irritated if he weren't so afraid.

"My facial recognition can't place any of you," continued the voice. "It's telling me your files have been corrupted. I see that you've decided to make this hard for me."

"So which one of us are you after?" asked Orio, his voice cracking.

"The sooner you tell me, the easier this gets."

"What happens to Orion if we tell you?" asked Phoebe.

"Swift death," said the voice.

"Why not just kill all three of us?" asked Tenebre.

"Oh, believe me, I want to," she said. "But it's not that simple. Only Orion. I need the other two corpses alive. Unscathed is preferable, but not required."

ORIO: She needs corpses alive? That doesn't make any sense.

TENEBRE: It doesn't matter. We need to throw the scent off. Don't use your names. Refer by species. Call me lab. Orio will be rabbit. Phoebe is lynx.

ORIO: Lab isn't a species.

PHOEBE: Neither is lynx.

TENEBRE: Just do it.

"Alright," said Tenebre. "Which one of us do you think is Orion?"

"I'm pretty sure it's the rabbit," said the assassin. "He sort of looks like an Orion to me."

"I find that offensive," said the rabbit, though he wasn't sure why. For a moment, he appreciated being called something other than food. Only now, more than anything else, he wished for another name.

"So you can see my dilemma," said the assassin. There was a laugh from above. It was a smoker's laugh, throaty, full of the confidence that Orio imagined predators must feel when their much smaller prey decides to fight back. It bothered him that she seemed think they all found this as entertaining as she did.

"Suppose we choose not to?" said Tenebre.

"Up to you. I can wait. Mind if I light a cigarette?"

"Sure," said Tenebre. "Get comfortable."

Orio heard a ruffling noise. Then there was the swift scrape of a cheap lighter and a flare up above. Orio took advantage of the moment, craning his neck in the flickering glow. A figure hung, by her tail, upside down from a catwalk. Only it wasn't an ordinary tail. It was mechanical and segmented, covered in metal plates, layered one over the other. She was a marsupial, at least by the look of her long snout and fleshy paws. Her fur was matted and poorly groomed. A long rifle rested in her paw. And in both her eyes, there were IO lenses, just like the ones he and the others had. Her whole body seemed momentarily bathed in fire. Then, just as quickly, the flame went out, and she sank back into shadow, leaving only a dull dot of ember and a trail of smoke. Orio began typing.

ORIO: She's an opossum.

PHOEBE: I'm detecting several foreign scanners attempting to read Dolores. They're being kept out, at least for now. But whoever it is, she wants what we have.

ORIO: She's armed with an automatic. Looks like she's made some kind of modification to her tail. Added graspers so she can hang like that for extended periods. There might be other tech too.

"You know," said the possum, pausing for a long exhale. "This will all be easier if you just give me who I want. Which, again, I'm pretty sure is the rabbit."

"Not happening," said Phoebe. "Move past that."

"Kay. Why don't I shoot you all in the feet so you can't escape, then break all your fingers, one by one, until you tell me what I already know?"

"That's one option," said the lab. "But it's risky. We could run. You could miss. The wrong person could end up dead."

PHOEBE: What if we just stood up and left?

TENEBRE: I'm trying to get a read. She could be bluffing.

ORIO: But what does she want?

TENEBRE: Worry about that later.

The assassin kept talking. "You think you're being clever. But the thing about me is that I have good timing. I'm as patient or impatient as I need to be to get the job done. What's your plan? Try to leave? You have one point of egress. I could pop off your kneecaps before you make it halfway."

"How much longer are you willing to wait for the name?"

"I've got two cigarettes left."

TENEBRE: We might have to fight. What's the plan?

PHOEBE: No weapons…

ORIO: Let me think.

PHOEBE: She said something about facial recognition. She must have a display of some kind. Maybe it's ocular.

ORIO: Dolores is detecting a device that I don't recognize. It must be her IO. Whatever it is, there's only one layer of encryption. We could get through it in fifteen minutes.

PHOEBE: We have to stall.

TENEBRE: Start that process, rabbit.

ORIO: Started. It's working now. I'll broadcast something bright and distracting at full-screen. It'll blind her, and she won't be able to close it.

"What kind of name is Orion, anyway?" said the possum. The comment made Orio's neck twinge. "What are you, an operating system?"

Orio was about to blurt out something, when suddenly Tenebre asked, "why don't you grace us with your name then?"

Another long breath dragged smoke through the room. "Thyra." She said it abruptly, like a bullet shot through a silencer.

They spent the next ten minutes like that, typing and listening while the possum worked through the last of her cigarettes. Orio asked Tenebre what they should do if she started shooting. Tenebre wrote back saying they should run, distract, and try to buy time. But time was running short.

"Okay, pups and kits. I'm bored and all out of smokes. Give me Orion or I start hurting people."

TENEBRE: How close are we?

ORIO: 5 minutes at most. But we need to get her on the ground.

There was a flash, and a piercing bang. Thinking he'd been hit, Orio jumped out of his seat a little. He felt all over his body only to realize he was unscathed. The shot had gone straight through the display module of his deck. A single bullet hole punctured the screen, which flickered briefly before going dark. A few sparks popped up. Phoebe hissed, ears folded.

"I didn't miss. It's a warning."

"What do you want to do?" asked Phoebe. Tenebre's expression was one of complete loss. Orio closed his eyes and counted for five long seconds as the wave of panic passed over and through him. When he opened his eyes again, he had an idea. His holopad was still connected, and it had built-in hotkeys. Since the system was still functioning, he should be able to switch to an auxiliary display using his paw. Touching his thumb to his two index fingers, he swiped through the air. All the windows from his monitor slid neatly into his IO, crowding his view.

They were still infiltrating. But they were running out of time. He wanted Tenebre and Phoebe to escape. He didn't want to lose the lab again. So he stood up and stared up at the assassin hanging from the beam, her tail coiled, legs dangling.

"Rabbit, what are you doing?" asked Phoebe.

"It's me," said Orio. "I'm the one you want."

"Of course it was you. I could have figured that out. Thanks for wasting my time," said the possum.

"Don't act too shocked."

"I'm not. Like I said. You look like an Orion."

"It's Orio."

"What?"

"You meant to say: I look like an Orio. That's my name. Get it?" When he explained it, she laughed again, but unlike before, there was something uncalculated about it, as if she were surprised to have found genuine humor in the situation.

"You must be joking. Like the cookie?"

The rabbit sighed. "Like the cookie…"

"Okay then, popular snack rabbit. You want a one-two-three? It's a professional courtesy."

"Why do you want him dead?" interrupted Tenebre. "Tell us." Orio nodded. They exchanged glances that told Orio they understood one another. The rabbit kept making little circles with his paw as if to say, "Keep stalling."

"You already know the answer. Don't you want to know what's hidden in those skulls of yours?"

"More than anything," said Tenebre.

She took aim. Orio felt another rush. It told him to run. He dove forward, arms outstretched. There was a brief moment of floating in uncertainty, between the sound of the gun and the impact of the ground. He braced for the hot burst of pain, but it never came. Thyra had missed.

"I—can't see!" she yelled. "What is this? Make it go away!" She fired a few rounds into the concrete, inches away from Orio's paw.

"We're in!" shouted the rabbit. "She's blind!"

"Scatter!" yelled Tenebre.

The rabbit scrambled along the ground, then pulled himself back up on his feet and ran. A few feet to the right was the flayed hull of the shuttle. He decided to hide behind it.

The possum tried to pull herself up onto the catwalk. She curled up toward the railing. But just as she managed to grab hold of it, the whole structure shifted and groaned. Something snapped. Then the scaffold slipped, its rusty beams shrieking and scraping each other as it fell. Thyra dropped straight down, flipping over in the air to land on her feet just as the beams crashed down behind her. She fired off more rounds, and then spun around on her heels.

Phoebe was down on all fours, poised. She leapt across the room, claws out, making a noise somewhere between a roar and a shriek. Her pounce landed her squarely on the possum's back, pulling her to the floor. The rifle slid across the floor. The lynx dug her teeth into Thyra's neck, while the assassin raved and thrashed beneath her.

Baring his teeth, the lab sprinted at the grappling animals. His ears were hiked up, and rage burned in his eyes. The rifle lay close by. He made a dash for it. But Thyra managed to push the lynx off of her and spun around. Her tail lashed through the air, catching the lab in his side and knocking him to the ground.

She picked up the rifle. Then there was a fast and angry fusillade of bullets fired off in different directions.

"Rabbit! Where are you? Come out, and I promise to kill you slowly…"

Orio smelled something. Was it gasoline? An instant later, from the tip of the possum's tail, a long rope of flame unspooled. She circled and swept her tail through the air, flames dancing around her. Phoebe dodged and wove her way around the whips of fire. She pounced on Thyra again. Grappling, they fell together into the rig, toppling the workstations, taking Dolores down with them. An alert flashed across Orio's IO, written in urgent red capitals: CONNECTION INTERRUPTED. One of the displays caught fire. Orio bit his paw to stop him from yelling. In one instant, all their work had gone up in smoke. The familiar sparks of panic electrified him inside.

"No…" groaned the lab.

Phoebe tried to pin Thyra down, but the possum rolled with her, pinning her in turn. She wrapped her paws like a vice around

Phoebe's throat. The lynx breathed in desperate gasps. If she was trying to scream, no sound was coming out. The rabbit wanted to rush in to help Phoebe, but Tenebre stood between them. He pushed the rabbit back behind him.

"You've got one more to get through!"

Thyra left Phoebe limp on the ground. She turned and stared across the barrel of her rifle at Tenebre. "You're a lot tougher when you're fighting a blind opponent…"

"You said you need me alive, right? Well, I need the rabbit," said the lab. "You can see my dilemma."

"I don't want to hurt you," said Thyra. There was something desperate in the way she said this. "But you're… You're putting yourself… between me and the lock."

"Why do you want him dead?"

"Don't play dumb. You were there when the rabbit was activated, weren't you? Don't tell me you didn't feel something. We're all one system. You, me, the lynx. All eighteen of us.

"It was you. The dead buyers. Leaving Dolores for us to find. You've been waiting for this."

"Your bodies were shipping containers for your brains. You weren't sent here to Dalkin to be revived. You were brought here to be packed, transported, and harvested."

"Where were the buyers sending us?"

Thyra laughed like she couldn't hold it back. "Don't tell me you didn't think about it. It's NosCo. It always was. And do you know what they wanted us for? Go on, ask."

Tenebre growled, crouching low. "Tell me."

"That's just it," said Thyra. "You have to kill the rabbit."

The lab charged headlong at the assassin. The shot, when it rang, made everything stop for a moment. There was blood seeping into the lab's shirt. He stumbled, lingered, and collapsed. Orio's paws locked up. Something unreachable began to burn and twitch in his eyes, beneath the plastic. His legs felt like a tower of Popsicle sticks, barely able to support his weight.

The possum was walking toward him, slowly, almost casually. Her expression, the way her teeth protruded from her wide unsmiling mouth, the way her eyes seemed like two inlaid arrowheads pointing at each other, reminded him of Kiva, looking down at him through her mask.

"Time to burn," she said.

"Tell me what happens afterward," said the rabbit. "After you un-do the lock."

"Lock? Don't flatter yourself," she said. "You're more like a wax seal. All I need to do, snack-rabbit, is break you open."

She raised her rifle. Orio ducked and rolled as she fired, leaping away from the shots. But she kept up the volley, patiently, one bullet at a time, until finally she caught the rabbit in his foot paw, and he fell screaming to the ground.

There was a moment of hesitation, a second that drifted and lengthened, made stranger by the shading of death in the light of burning electronics. She had one eye closed and the other covered up by her scope. But there was someone else too. Behind her. The lynx stood, a silhouette with diamond claws poised against the possum's neck.

"I don't understand," said Thyra. "Don't you want to know?"

At the first sign of movement, Orio flinched. But there wasn't any gunshot. Only the sound of Thyra collapsing, and then her screams as Phoebe began mauling her.

Orio ran to Tenebre's body. The tiny shimmer of his fur told Orio he was breathing. He groaned as the rabbit rolled him onto his back. The bullet had pierced him through the shoulder, just above his collarbone.

"The rabbit..." he said. "What happens to the rabbit?" He was losing blood, and delirious. Orio pressed his paw against the wound to stop the flow.

Thyra lay a few feet away, motionless as Phoebe slashed at her face and neck, each attack whetted with greater and greater fury. The lynx annihilated the possum, stroke by stroke. Even if she wanted to play dead, it would only get her there faster. Finally, Phoebe stood, panting. The fur on her paws was matted and glistening. "You have to kill him," said the possum. She was coughing up blood. "You have to kill Orion..."

***

They flew away on the bike. The rabbit could still see the hangar behind them, miles away, a tiny orange dot and a trail of smoke in the dark. Tenebre clung to him, asleep but stable. Orio held him propped against his side, nuzzling into his neck fur so he could feel the lab's pulse.

"We have to lay low. We'll borrow the Aria. I'll apologize to Kiva later," she said. So they rode to the harbor, back to the boat where he had first awakened. Orio knew it would only be a matter of time before there were others who came for him. So they weighed anchor, setting off into the open ocean.

"What happens when I die again?" asked Orio. They were on the deck of the ship, surrounded by the sound of choppy waters. Orio was stitching up Tenebre's shoulder. "She said I'm like a wax seal..."

"It doesn't matter," said Phoebe. "She's road kill now." She lay on her back on the deck, staring up at the sky. A few minutes later, she told them she was tired and that she was going to go to bed, then stabbed herself with a shot of endorphins and went into the cabin, the door squealing shut behind her.

Orio stayed on the ship's deck and preoccupied himself with tending to the lab and his injury. The bullet had, luckily, gone straight through. Tenebre was awake now, but still quiet. He stretched himself out on the stack of plastic crates and kept his eyes closed most of the time, wincing occasionally as the rabbit applied the isopropyl-soaked rag to his shoulder and then wrapped it in gauze. They both swallowed some painkillers and stayed on deck for a while, staring at the sky and the constellations.

What he did have to say, after a little while, made Orio uncomfortable. He asked the rabbit what he thought he should do. The sun was just starting to come up now, and the seagulls were complaining in the distance.

"About the wound? Ice it, rest it. Keep it clean, I guess."

"You know what I mean," said Tenebre. "What should we do about you?"

But in fact, he didn't know what the lab meant at all. There was something threatening in the question. "I don't know. What do you suppose 'we' should do about me?"

"Do you... want me to remove the system? From you?" His voice was flat and his expression unmoving.

"I don't know," said Orio. "Like you said. It's dangerous."

"I could do it. If it meant making sure nobody would come after you."

"That wouldn't matter much if you killed me under the knife."

Tenebre pulled himself to his feet. His knees made a popping sound, and his breathing became heavy. He looked at Orio with a scowl that reminded him of Thyra, a look of calculation and intent.

"We need to, Orio. I need to. They'll keep chasing us as long as it's intact. If we remove it and destroy it…"

"You don't know what will happen." The rabbit backed away and Tenebre followed.

"It doesn't matter, Orio…"

"Don't I matter to you? I want you to say it. You don't know what will happen. Say it."

The lab's eyes narrowed. He reached out and wrapped his paw around the rabbit's arm, gripping him tight and lifting him so his foot paws slid out from underneath him.

"You're hurting me…"

"You think I don't know? I've done everything for you. I saved your life. And now you're talking to me like… like I'm some kind of idiot."

"Let go of me!" The rabbit tried to tug his arm away from the lab, but kept getting pulled back. Tenebre had an unnatural strength that Orio had never known in his husband. Because Tenebre was gentle, not like this. "I don't know you! I never knew you! You're not—"

"Put him down." Phoebe stood in the doorway to the cabin. She must have heard the noise. Her claws were extended, pale in the morning light.

"We're so close, Phoebe… We know what we need to do now."

"Don't care. Not having this conversation." She approached, one paw half-raised to strike. "I said put the rabbit down. You're not thinking."

"I'm thinking more clearly than ever. Don't you care, Phoebe? Doesn't anyone care?"

The rage that had been welling up inside the rabbit was taking shape. When he looked at Tenebre, all he could see was the possum, the way she stared at him with the rifle in her paws.

"Listen to me, rabbit. All you have to do is trust me. That's gotten you this far, hasn't it? You know I won't hurt you… You'd believe your husband, wouldn't you?"

That did it. Screaming, Orio launched himself into the lab and bit down into his arm. They fell together on the ship's deck. The lab reached out and grabbed the rabbit's neck and tried to push him off. But Orio held tight. He dug his claws into Tenebre's shoulder and tore at the bandages. The lab howled in pain, writhing and kicking his legs beneath him.

"That's enough," said Phoebe. She grabbed Orio by his ears and pulled him away. He was still swinging. "I said that's enough!"

Her claws pierced him. They felt like little pins digging into his skin, and for a moment Orio felt as if Phoebe wanted to cut him open too. He squeezed his eyes shut but the tears came anyway. They were warm against his whiskers.

It took a minute or two for Tenebre to pull himself upright. His silver fur was streaked with red. "I want to protect you. But you won't let me. I'm not your enemy. I'm not." Then he turned around and walked over to where the bike was tied down, and started undoing the hooks and cinches.

"Where are you going?" asked Phoebe.

But he didn't say anything. He simply got on the bike, started the motor, and rose up from the deck of the ship. Then he turned around and rode away, back toward the city.

"He's really gone…"

"He'll come back."

"No. He won't. I didn't want to believe it. I spent two years saying it wasn't true. That one day, I'd come home from work, and he'd just… be there. We'd have dinner, watch TV, and fall asleep, and everything would be normal again."

"Hell, Cookies… You're the only one who's ever really come back. Have you thought of that?"

He had to admit he hadn't.

***

The lab returned two days later, hauling a familiar modem-sized package wrapped in tarp. He stumbled off, bedraggled and bleary-eyed, his legs barely able to hold up the rest of him. Orio helped prop him up when he stumbled near the cabin. Phoebe lingered in the distance. She muttered something under her breath, and then asked if he was hurt.

"Just tired mostly," he said. "Joints ache."

"You're an aging infant," said Phoebe. "There's water in the cooler." Orio went and got him one. They watched while he drank down the whole bottle in one long chain of gulps.

"I thought you were gone forever," said the rabbit.

"Me too," he said. And then he set something on the counter. It was a glass tablet, dusty and cracked in one corner. "Dolores was there. She was still running. Can you believe it? The whole time. Even after all that, she could still function. The housing was only a little melted on the outside. That rig has officially taken a bullet and survived a fire."

"And?" asked Orio.

"The decryption program we wrote," said Tenebre. "It worked... sort of. It was able to get through a few thousand characters worth of information."

"You mean we got around me?" The rabbit's ears were tilted slightly askew, like a pair of windshield wipers.

Tenebre pressed a button on the tablet, and a text file appeared on Orio's IO: a plain white screen and a string of characters, arranged line by line, with no punctuation. It reminded him of a log, the kind used when a programmer is testing a prototype. When he read the file, the rabbit felt an eerie sense of familiarity and guilt.

> the rabbit is the key need to know but voice sounds like honey and Orion(FALSE) I dont understand why ive never met him Orion(FALSE) and why sometimes i want to like rye Orion(FALSE) i could do it while hes asleep it would only take a moment Orion(FALSE) what are you thinking whats wrong with you Orion(FALSE) i should just leave before i hurt anyone

They went on like that, rambling half-ideas arranged in strains of anguished prose. Orio felt that he was somewhere he didn't belong reading something that ought to get him in trouble.

"Is this... inner monologue?" asked Phoebe.

"It's mine," said Tenebre. "From the night Thyra appeared."

"So..." said Phoebe. "They store our thoughts."

"Some of them, anyway," said Tenebre. "The conscious ones. The ones that have words."

"What is this Orion function?" asked the rabbit.

"It's checking for you..." said Tenebre. "It's trying to see whether or not it can transmit something. As long as you're alive, everything stays encrypted and private. But once the lock is undone..." He turned to Orio, and his face made that guilty expression that his husband was so good at.

Orio's ears stood up. He was afraid of the lab, and he would feel that way for years. He gripped the countertop. He wanted to snap Tenebre in two so he could put him back together again. But that wouldn't bring his husband back.

"I'm sorry, Orio."

"Sorry? That's what you have to say for fantasizing about my death? For trying to cut me open?" he said. His voice always cracked when he tried to sound angry.

"I was wrong... I was wrong about everything."

The rabbit closed his eyes. He couldn't stop thinking about thinking. He imagined his thoughts being written down somewhere, set down as a record. He was angry with Tenebre, but also at himself. The strange guilt he felt came from the words in the file, from knowing that they were never meant to be seen.

"You're not the person I thought you were," said Orio. "I've accepted that. It doesn't mean I hate you. Or that I'll ever forget what you did."

"What about Thyra?" asked Phoebe.

"She was a corpse like us... Maybe she knew. She said NosCo was harvesting your brains... I'd guess this technology was meant to enable some kind of—"

"Telepathy," said Phoebe. "Or telecognition. Thought-sharing."

"A hive mind," said Tenebre. "Linked minds capable of lateral thinking and high-level decision-making processes."

"Doesn't that mean that there are lots of people who are going to want me dead?" said Orio.

"I bet they do," said Phoebe. "Which means we'll have to return to NosCo. They're the ones who built the system."

They looked at Orio with angular, closed-off faces. He could see sparks in both their eyes that kept growing. They wanted to chase this. Was that what he wanted?

"Will you come with us?" asked Tenebre.

Orio was uncertain, which was the worst way for him to feel. It was a dull torture that made his ears stand on end, a place between hearing danger and not knowing when or how it would come, or whether he'd survive it. Letting go was also a kind of clinging. He kept coming up against waves and currents beating against every attempt to move on, to get on, with living, dying, whatever it was. All he knew was that at least he had company.

"I will," said Orio.

"I'll set sail," said Tenebre.

"It's weird," said Phoebe. "You're like some kind of glue. I feel stuck somehow."

"What if I die before you two? For whatever reason… What happens then?"

"Relax, Cookies. You're not dead yet."

Two Blocks Apart and the Universe in Between

Taylor Harbin

Badger Bremen sat at a table outside the A-Z Cafe, exactly as I remembered him: pudgy with a gray-on-black striped fur coat. Didn't see how he could stand it. Only an idiot—idiot *human*—would've dressed like that in L.A. In April. But that's beside the point. He was a badger, *and* one of the most prestigious producers in Hollywood. You see, boys and girls, in those days the Uplifted (Uppers, if you like) had not been around very long. Scientists were at a loss to explain how it was happening, and it happened so fast that people barely had time to adjust before the Supreme Court made its decision in *The Mindful v. United States*. If someone could pass the Dolman Criteria, regardless of species, then they were declared sentient and given full legal rights. This badger seemed to be adjusting fine. He put his fork down when I came over.

"Mr. Bremen, sir?"

He looked up. "Ah, Wilkes. Good to see you, kid. Sit down, sit down. Glad you made it." He whistled. A waiter appeared from inside holding a breakfast platter: eggs, bacon, tomatoes, and a yogurt parfait.

I swallowed. Yvon, my agent, told me not to bring it up, but the words came in a dribble. "Sir, I know it was three months ago, and it probably doesn't mean anything now, but I wanted to say how sorry

I am for what I did. Believe me I—"

"Stop, stop," Bremen said. "Worst thank-you I've ever heard in my life."

"But—"

Bremen was about to take a drink. The cup stopped short of his lips. A tiny knot formed on his brow. "Animal. You made a joke and called me a crazy animal. Last time I checked that's still accurate, Uplifted or not. Eat."

"Well, I'm sorry."

Bremen set the cup down with a *thunk*. "Say ten Hail Marys and three Our Fathers." He raised a paw and made the sign of the cross with exaggerated seriousness. "I absolve you of all your sins. Now, if you're finished, maybe we can get down to business? Eat! And start with the bacon. Don't tell me you're one of these nice humans who've forgotten how to be predators."

I grabbed a piece with my fingers and took a bite. It was probably lab-grown meat, not… made the old-fashioned way. Bremen smiled and nodded with approval, then took his delayed drink. He went into a leather shoulder bag and pulled out an old book with a tattered dust jacket.

"Have you read this?"

I saw the title: *Two Blocks Apart and the Universe In Between* by Addison Cordwainer.

"No, but Yvon mentioned something about it when she called this morning. They think this is the first novel written by an Uplifted."

"Yeah," Bremen said. "Pretty good, and nobody will touch it despite renewed interest in Upper art." His gaze drifted into the street where people of all stripes and spots walked, a scene that would have been unimaginable a century ago. "I got the rights from the publisher for a song, but friends keep telling me to leave it alone; says it brings up painful memories of Integration. They don't understand"—he sipped his drink—"that it's our shared past. The waters are being muddied. Did you hear about that idiot who thinks humans ought to pay reparations to pigs, chickens, and cows to make up for the 'genocide'? There was an op-ed in *Cosmopolitan* last week saying it ought to be illegal to use Uppers in advertising because it reinforced species stereotypes. Ridiculous! You'd think after making a quantum leap in evolution they'd put their enlarged brains to good use. What do you say?"

He turned his beady eyes on me.

"There were animal rights groups before the Uplifted appeared," I said.

Bremen shook his head. "I know, and I still don't get it. You've been at the top of the food chain for thirty million years. Why stop now?" He waved a paw. "Anyway, I think we could have a great movie and I want you to write it. I'll sign you for the treatment now. If I like it, then we'll do the screenplay. If I don't like it, you get paid. If I like it and the studio gives us the green light, you get paid *more*. Of course, Yvon can look the contract over. Check for pitfalls."

I shifted in my seat. Producers rarely solicit writers, but here he was talking like we'd worked together for years.

"Why me, of all people?"

"*Children of Thomas.*"

"That old thing? I'm surprised you've heard of it."

"I was at the Rosewoods' charity dinner when it premiered. The Thomas Fire hurt people of all kinds, and you captured that. Great script. Nominated for an award, as I recall."

I scraped out a tiny helping of yogurt with my spoon. "No. Dan Juniper got nominated for directing and Klive Fargo for the narration."

"That's a shame," Bremen said. "Still a great documentary, and I still think you're the right guy. You've done well enough on these small gigs, but how'd you like to really sink your teeth into something? Could be your big break."

I'd never met a badger who was more persuasive.

***

I wrote the treatment in three weeks while trying to dig up whatever I could on Addison Cordwainer. Very mysterious. Nobody knew his/her exact species. The only interview on record was for *Scribner's Magazine*, which referred to Cordwainer as a primate. I made detailed notes as I went along. Mr. Bremen let me borrow his copy, a book so old I thought it was going to crumble in my hands. It was never reprinted, despite positive reviews at the time of release and considered a classic by some. And Bremen was right. It was surprisingly good.

Two Blocks Apart was published in 1931. Set in the fictional city of Animopolis, it tells the parallel lives of a human and a rabbit: Bob Peters and Quickie. They live on the edge of their respective neighborhoods, a distance of two blocks from each another. Peters is an English teacher at the local high school who dreams of a university career. Quickie is a foot messenger at a telegram company, barely making ends meet. The novel opens with Quickie getting fired because he's now the oldest runner on the payroll and his times have been getting slower. Although horrified, Quickie takes his lumps and spends the day walking his familiar routes, noticing things he hadn't before. Meanwhile, Peters is fired from his job because the school is making budget cuts. The incoming P.E. teacher will replace him, teaching both subjects. Both characters meet at the same bar late in the day. During this scene we get a good look at their psychology. Quickie goes on about what he's discovered on his walk and thanks Peters for giving his son, Barney, an education, which he believes will lead to a better future. Peters hardly acknowledges the compliment as he drinks himself into a stupor.

The climactic scene in the novel happens the following day. After collecting his last paycheck and turning in his uniform, Quickie decides to buy a soda for Barney. He arrives at the school to find it surrounded by police and firemen. Turns out Peters didn't have a good last day. Not only was he fired and forced to give his replacement a tour of the campus, but he lost his job to a guy named Gym. Peters stabs him to death with a ballpoint pen, writes J-I-M on his forehead in his own blood, then takes Barney and some other kids hostage before barricading himself inside a classroom. After several hours, negotiations break down and the police storm the building. An officer, using a scoped .30-06, shoots Peters in the leg. Before he can bleed out, the enraged and insane man grabs Barney, and by the time the other officers finally break the door down, he's mauled the little rabbit to death. The last chapter shows Quickie sharing the soda with the rest of his family before going to visit Mrs. Peters in the hospital, who has suffered a mental breakdown in light of her husband's crime.

It read like *Breakfast of Champions* meets *Winter of Our Discontent*. Despite shifting points-of-view and frequent internal monologues, it was a good story.

Bremen liked the treatment and signed me for the screenplay. Yvon was able to wrap my other commitments up so I could work without interruptions. Took me about four months to finish the draft, and that was in between giving interviews for *Hollywood Times*, Movieguide, and the like, meeting with the studio execs, and trying to find anything else on Cordwainer. The great thing about being a screenwriter is that you just write. Very rarely will you have a hand in production. I've sold over a hundred scripts and only gone on set a few times. Making film is a cumbersome process with lots of moving pieces. More people on set means more people can get in the way, more things can go wrong. Might be a letdown if your idea of writing in Hollywood is hobnobbing with actors or watching climactic moments from behind the camera, like Humphrey Bogart telling Ingrid Bergman to get on the plane. Sometimes you meet people, but I prefer the other side of that coin: *not* worrying about budget, location scouting, casting, props, schedules, makeup, lighting, or publicity. Sometimes a writer will be invited to give his opinion if a director has a problem.

And it wasn't long before we had problems.

***

Esther Mason Forge. Can't say that without your jaw clenching up on the last syllable. She was a powerhouse, revered for films like *Vanished in the Crowd*, *Bleeding Heads*, and *Strike of a Broken Clock*. A visionary to some, a Komodo dragon to everyone else. She called me at home to discuss the project since we hadn't been able to meet. There was a distinct, underlying hiss behind every word.

"I'll get to the point. We're going to shoot out of sequence. Scouting tried to get us into an old neighborhood, but now that the elections are over the new guy wants to start on his development projects right away. They revoked our permits."

"Uh huh," I said. No biggie. Most films are shot out of order. "So where does that leave us?"

"The school siege," Forge said. "Got a derelict place on the cheap. We're blocking everything out tomorrow. Masterson Central. Be there at seven." She hung up before I could ask any more questions.

Blocking is the part where actors walk through the motions as they read lines. It helps the camera crew figure out the best shooting angle, but it's *before* the lighting people do their work. Thankfully, Masterson Central wasn't far from my apartment, so there I was the next morning with a box of donuts and tray of coffee, the universal friendship offering. Masterson was an old K-12 school on the southwest side of town left to rot when the districts reorganized. I knew what to expect, yet it was still impressive to see how the place had been transformed. There were old-timey police cars, fire trucks, onlookers, and a small group of folks we credited as "Grammar Nazis." These characters come to picket *in favor* of Peters because they agree that Gym is a stupid name (and yes, that's from the book). A security guard collected his peace tokens, then took me inside.

The crew was about fifty-fifty humans/Uplifted. There were advantages to this. When your sound engineer is a fox, you can rest easy knowing there won't be so much as a unwanted pin drop on the master tapes. And why invest in a camera boom when a giraffe is just as good? I spotted Forge at the far end of the cafeteria, chatting and pointing to the south hallway. They were blocking the part of the rampage where Bob Peters runs out of the principal's office after killing Gym and yells, "School's out!" to the bewildered kids. It was April, but she was dressed in a long-sleeve shirt and sweat pants (with a generous opening for her tail), jacket, and rubber guards on her claws. She was still talking and only gave me a sideways glance.

"...and since this guy doesn't have a plan, get jittery. Look indecisive."

I hung back and waited. Last thing you want to do is jump in feet first and start making suggestions. I usually carry a notebook and write as the director works things out; helps me stay in tune with their thought process, so if they want my opinion, I can at least give one based on what I see and mesh that with their vision. For some reason, I didn't bring it that day, and I immediately regretted it. Figured someone as accomplished as Esther Mason Forge wouldn't need my help with anything except editing the shooting script. But... at the same time I was tempted to be bold, project a confidence I didn't have, thinking about what Bremen had said: this could be my big break. Forge was talking to Sam Corinth, who played Bob Peters. He was from Kentucky with only a faint trace of an accent, and like any good actor, he could turn it off at will. At the time, he was still considered a new face in Hollywood, but with notable roles in several indie films, people were beginning to notice. Next to him were two other humans: Quinn Flyer, the assistant director, and Mitty Conner, the script supervisor. I looked around, but didn't see Bab Fisher, who played Quickie. Probably wasn't on set. If this really was the first scene they were shooting, then he wouldn't be needed until—

"Hi!"

I started and looked down. A rabbit sat at my feet, rocking back and forth on his haunches, clutching a stuffed dinosaur.

"Oh. Hey," I said. "Are you one of the extras?"

"I'm Benjamun."

Of course you are, I thought, shifting my weight. "Nice to meet you, *Benjamun*. I'm Wilkes."

I reached down to shake his little paw, but he drew back.

"You shot Lincoln."

My voice cracked as I burst out laughing, which drew some awkward looks.

"I promise you I didn't."

"You sure? You look like a guy from the old days."

"Oh, the beard? Yeah. Thought I'd try a new look."

"Lemme touch it," Benjamin said.

"My beard?"

"Yeah. Please?"

I got down on one knee, feeling more than a little ridiculous, careful not to spill my drink. Once his paws made contact he was kneading my face with delight, giggling.

"It's poofy! Never knew humans could grow fur."

"Guess I'm just one of the lucky ones," I said. "So, do you know somebody who works here?"

Benjamin pointed to one of the camera crew: a rabbit with his ball cap on backwards. "That's my dad," he said. "He's never brought me to his work before, so I begged him to take me just this once. He said ok but only if I was a good boy and didn't get into trouble. Everyone at school is always asking me what it's like to be on a movie set and now I can finally tell them." He sighed. "It's not as exciting as I hoped."

I shrugged. "Well, we're just getting started. I'm sure something will happen."

"Haven't gotten any autographs."

"You can have mine," I said. "I wrote this movie."

"But you're not in the movie at all."

Ouch.

Flyer spoke up from across the room. "Ok, everybody. Listen up! Closed set. Rehearsal time. Everyone else out."

"I'll see you later," I said to Benjamin, and stood.

Forge came over. I could tell she was stressed by the way her tongue flicked in quick jabs.

"We've got a problem. How fast can—" She looked down at Benjamin. "Who are you?"

Before he could say anything, his father came over.

"Son, what did I tell you? Don't bother anyone and don't touch anything. I'm sorry, Ms. Forge. He was supposed to be with his mother this weekend, but she's off in Paris with her new... and I couldn't get a babysitter before we started shooting, and Mr. Flyer—"

"Fine, William," Forge said, waving a paw. "Just get him off the set so we can rehearse."

Benjamin hung his head. "I just wanted an autograph. This guy wrote the movie, Dad."

"Why don't I look after him?" I said. "Benjamin, once Ms. Forge is done talking to me I'll get you your very own copy of the script's title page, and then you can have everyone else sign it."

His ears straightened. "Really?"

I put a finger over his lips. "But you have to be good while I talk to the director, ok? She has an important job."

Benjamin mimicked my finger-over-the-lips gesture and smiled. William gave me a nod and went back to work.

"Fine, fine," Forge said again. She grabbed my arm and pulled me towards the exit and into the parking lot, Benjamin hopping along. "How soon can you change the script?"

"Depends. What's the problem?"

Forge whipped out her cell phone—protected by a steel case—-and pulled up an article from *The L.A. Times*. "Bremen sent this while we were setting up. Did you know that whole Bob Peters incident was based on a real crime?"

"Yes," I said. "I found one or two articles that mentioned it."

"Turns out one of the victim's next-of-kin is still alive," Forge said.

"I'll text the link. Says they hated Cordwainer for putting it in the book and now they're threatening to sue the studio if we don't change it. Bremen's got his paws to the fire."

I scrolled through the piece. "'Great emotional stress'? Says here the person is ninety years old. The book came out in 1931. They couldn't possibly remember anything."

"Even so, they've whipped up a storm. People are threatening boycotts."

I looked up and caught some sun in the face. "Well, what do they want us to do? It's essential to the story of Peters' mental deterioration: a so-called intelligent creature losing control and acting on primal urges. I mean, it's not like we're filming *Caligula*."

Forge shrugged. "I don't know what to say, except fix it."

***

Film crews usually work twelve to fourteen hours a day. I had my laptop, but I didn't get much done. I was too focused on watching Benjamin. About the script, to this day I can't understand what the problem was. I'd seen old Nat Geo documentaries that were bloodier. Nobody from Ed Gein's family ever sued for the films he inspired. But they say movies are made by committee, so I kept tweaking the script (whenever I wasn't worried about Benjamin bouncing off the walls) while Forge did the rampage. We wrapped around six-thirty. Forge came out of the building at a quick, shuffling pace, her clawed feet clicking on the pavement, tail swishing.

"Did you drive yourself?"

"No," I said. "Cab."

"Then come with me."

"Where?"

"Dinner," she said. "I'm hungry and we've got to get this script nailed down."

She grabbed my arm and dragged me to her car, and it hurt in spite of the rubber guards. As we sped through town, streetlights glinted on the places where her *un*protected claws had cut into the dashboard and steering wheel cover. She even turned the heater on! Add to that her overpowering musk and we had ourselves a rolling greenhouse. When we stopped and got out, it was all I could do not to suck air in deep, comical gasps. She made for the door and I followed at a distance, wary of the tail; another weapon in her impressive arsenal. There was a sign on the door: a paw print encased in a heart. *We serve all kinds here.* One of the human waitresses spotted Forge, waved, and seated us at the table she'd just cleaned.

"Long time no see, Esther."

"Hi, Susan. The usual, please."

"And I'll have—"

But she was already gone. Another server came by with two glasses of water (no ice for Forge). The cold liquid tickled my stomach as I sipped, trying not to think about my hunger. It was a decent place, and as my gaze swept from one end of the room to the other I caught Forge staring at me. Her eyes were like a solar eclipse: perfect black spheres wreathed in fiery rings, and set against deep burgundy.

"You going to send those changes now?" she said.

We synced phones and for the next few minutes I listened to the dull tap of her padded claw against the screen as she read. Susan came back with two sirloins: tartare for her and well-done for me. She just kept scrolling. I found that I was too scared to eat, scared of breaking her concentration, and rapt by the sight of this ancient creature thinking so intently. She nodded and put the phone down, then stabbed the steak with her fork, ripped off a chunk, and swallowed it whole.

"Aren't you going to eat?" she said.

I came back. "Uh, yeah, yeah. So, what'd you think?"

She took the rest of the steak in one bite. "The changes are good. Not showing the murder is just as effective. We'll see what Bremen says."

"I still don't get it. He's fought studios before and won. Other directors have done much worse. Spielberg killed a kid in *Jaws* and it became a classic."

"Yeah, and he hasn't killed a kid since." Forge emptied her glass in a single gulp. "Speaking of which, if we get any more unexpected visitors, security will handle them. If you're going to work on my set, I can't have you getting distracted."

"Oh, you mean Benjamin? Sorry. I was only trying to be nice."

"*Nice* isn't something I need from you right now. And another thing: don't bring snacks if you can't be bothered to get something for everyone," she said.

"What are you talking about? I brought plenty of donuts and coffee. You could have had as much as you—"

Forge jabbed a finger at me. "*Coffee*. And half the crew is Uplifted. Did anyone ever tell you that caffeine is toxic to most animals? And there were hardly enough donuts to go around. If you want to make a nice gesture, talk to one of the assistants. They know who can eat what and where to get the right stuff."

Remember when I made a joke about Bremen and regretted it? I should have learned.

"The great Esther Mason Forge. Director. Mother to her crew."

A hairline crack appeared in the side of her glass. It stopped my heart.

"And just what did you expect me to be? Disinterested? Uncaring?" Her eyes narrowed. "Cold-blooded?"

I swallowed in a dry throat. "No, that's—I didn't think—"

"My first boyfriend wouldn't let me kiss him because he thought I was venomous. People cross the street to avoid me. Do you know how hard it is for reptiles to get decent roles? We're not cute and fuzzy. You won't see *us* on milk cartons or cereal boxes. We're still the beasts of your nightmares. Even some of my own crew get nervous around me. Did you see how William trembled? Did you think I wouldn't notice you giving me such a wide berth when we came in here?"

I grasped for words. "I was only trying to be polite."

"You're *afraid*. I can smell it. Whether it's me or something else, I don't care. But you need to know this: I don't have any use for vacillating people who can't handle a bit of discomfort," she said, standing. "Bremen picked you. I won't add to his problems by complaining. But you need to get your act together, unless you think we'd be better off working at a distance. Your choice."

Then she left. Just walked right out of the joint, muttering something about an errand.

Susan came round a minute later. With the check.

***

The next day I considered staying home, but then I remembered my promise to Benjamin. When I arrived on set, the crew was standing around in the cafeteria. Quinn Flyer was skittering about giving orders, but nobody was really working. When he saw me, he walked right over and shoved a piece of paper into my hand.

"She's in the classroom, third door on the left. Do something."

It was a copy of *Hollywood Hijinks*, a gossip column. The headline read, "Broken Hearts Amid Controversial Film Adaptation of Cordwainer Book." There was a photo, centered, of Forge walking out of the restaurant. I'm in the background, looking after her. One of the camera guys nudged his buddy and snickered. It's funny *now*. Sure wasn't funny right then, not after losing sleep wondering if I'd just blown my reputation and my career. Third door on the left. The room where Peters is shot and killed by the police. I already had an apology worked out. At the same time, I was worried. Surely I hadn't made her *that* angry. What else could have happened? I found her slumped over a chair by the window, basking in the morning sun, head buried in her paws. When I cleared my throat she snapped upright, her eyes boring into me.

"I hope you've come prepared," she said.

"Yes. Let me start by apologizing. I didn't mean to be so careless. It was rude and—"

"Not that, you idiot," she said. "The script. Bremen had another fight with the studio. The changes we made weren't good enough. They want the whole death scene taken out."

"But *why*?" I said. "It's pivotal to the story, part of the theme."

"I know, and you know," Forge said. "That's not the only problem. The schmuck who owns this place has been dealing behind our back. Sold it to a development firm and they're coming to finalize the agreement tomorrow. We have to finish shooting *today*, but we can't because the rabbits are sick. Flu! Flu in April!"

"What, *all of them*? Bab Fisher? Kyle Jones?"

Forge nodded. "And a lot of the extras too. I swear this is the last time I allow communal lodging. One got the sniffles, and now they're all down. We can do without the extras. Got plenty of other kids. But Jones is a major supporting role. He plays Barney, for crying out loud."

"Call the understudy," I said.

"We don't have one. Once word got out we were doing Cordwainer's book, a bunch of parents decided to boycott the auditions. Kyle was our best chance. Couldn't find anyone talented enough to be his understudy." She gave a hissing sigh. "The studio is circling the wagons. The lawsuit threat was bad enough, but now we're behind schedule and we'll go over budget if we don't get with it. If this movie flops, they'll blame me and that'll be that. I'll never work again."

I felt something just then: a spark of recognition. Beneath the green skin, pungent musk, sharp teeth, and long claws, there was an artist trying to share something with the world. I sat in the desk opposite her.

"My parents don't think writing is a respectable job. We almost lost everything back in '08 and they wanted me to get a career that would pay. Safe. They raised me for a *safe* world. Elbows off the table. Say please, thank you. I was thrilled when Bremen picked me. Couldn't wait to get started. But now I'm here and it's all different. Not as strong as I thought. And when I feel the pinch, when I get stressed, I switch to safe mode. You asked what I'm afraid of? Failure. Going back home and admitting they were right all along, and spending the rest of my life just like them."

Forge was looking at me thoughtfully now, head resting on one arm. "It never gets easy," she said. "You want something from life? You have to take it and dare everyone to stop you. Ask any of those people outside. They'll tell you I'm cool, calculating, unshakable. Usually it works. But some days life hits so hard you stagger and fall. I think this might be one of them."

"Maybe not," I said. "If the studio wants to play hardball, let's play hardball. You're a *dragon* for Pete's sake! Don't you have a threat display, something that says *back off before I rip your face open*? I didn't spend five months of my life writing this thing just so some corporate suit could tell me how to make art. We're the ones doing all the hard work!" I kicked a chair over (ok, *tipped* would be more accurate) and huffed. "I say we shoot the rotten scene how *we* want it and dare them—no, *make them* make us take it out!"

Forge cocked an eyebrow at me.

Then she laughed so hard she almost fell out of her seat.

"You are the least threatening thing I've ever seen. You'd make a terrible dragon." She clapped her paw on my arm. "But I get what you're saying. And I like it." She jumped up knocked half a row of chairs over with a single flick of her tail, then gave a loud hiss. "That's how it's done. QUINN!"

Flyer appeared in doorway. "M—ma'am?"

"Get everyone ready. We shoot in five minutes."

"Without Jones?"

Forge looked to me.

"Yes. I have an idea," I said.

***

"You're crazy."

"Not so loud." I glanced over my shoulder. Benjamin was waiting for us by the cafeteria door. "He's about the same age as Jones and he's healthy."

"But can he act?"

"We're about to find out."

She flicked her tongue once, then walked to where the little rabbit sat.

"Hi there, Benjamin."

"Hi there, director lady."

"Benjamin, we've got a problem and I think only a big boy like you can help us. One of our actors is very sick and he'll be in bed for another two weeks. Problem is we just can't wait that long for him to get better. A big boy rabbit had to be in this scene and you're the only one around. So, do you want to be in the movie?"

"Yes yes yes yes," Benjamin said, hopping up and down in place. "What do you want me to do? Jump out of an airplane? Karate? Give a speech?" He slicked back his ears and looked at his stuffed dinosaur. "'To be or not to be, I don't know the answer to that question but it must be important and here I am speeching about it.'"

Forge's tail twitched as she suppressed a laugh, but kept her game face on.

"No, not that. I need you to be scared."

***

I re-wrote the scene to make it easy on him. He didn't have any lines. We started with Peters right after he kills Gym. He grabs Benjamin in the cafeteria before barricading himself inside the classroom. The whole time we were rolling, I was nervous. A million thoughts flooded my mind.

Then, the climax.

To prevent any mishaps, we told Benjamin over and over again that he wasn't *really* going to die, that he was just pretending. Didn't seem to bother him. So, I said a prayer as the crew prepped, orders going back and forth between Quinn Flyer and the rest.

"Places everyone."

"Quiet on set. Roll sound."

"Sound speed."

"Roll camera."

"Speed."

"Marker. Cue background."

Forge and I locked eyes for an instant.

"And—action!"

In the script, Peters realizes the magnitude of what he's done. He's been given one hour to release some of the hostages as an act of good faith. He's starting to believe what the negotiator is saying, that he'll get off easy if he surrenders. The police captain on scene has a different idea. When Peters stands up to speak through the open window, a sniper takes him in the leg. To the character of Peters, this symbolizes another betrayal, another time in which the world has swindled him, another broken promise. In a fit of rage, he decides that the best thing to do is to take something from the world, out of spite. He can hear the police moving closer. Time is short. If he wants payback, he's got to act fast. The nearest victim is Barney. Sam Corinth was supposed to pull himself along the wall, limping on the bad leg, fall down near Benjamin, grab him, then kill him, the whole time muttering incoherent gibberish.

I didn't tell Benjamin any of this.

All he knew is that he was supposed to look scared and follow Mr. Corinth around. The other parts weren't in his copy of the script. When Corinth's squib burst just above the kneecap, I saw a spark in the rabbit's eyes, and as Corinth came at him they grew wide with pure terror. He tried to back away, tripped over a chair leg, then scooted on his tail till he hit the wall, whimpering. Corinth grabbed him by the scruff of his neck, the moment of death where the camera was supposed to cut away.

And Benjamin screamed.

Folks, let me tell you something. There is no sound on the face of the Earth more horrible, more blood-curdling, than a baby rabbit in distress. A shockwave tore through the room that made the hairs on my neck prickle. Corinth froze, stock-still. Nobody said cut. The man, this trained actor, pulled away as if he had really murdered the boy. He looked around the room with a stupefied gaze, then broke down and started crying in big, heaving sobs. In the confusion and awe of the moment, nobody told the background to stop. The police were coming down the hall. Soon they were banging on the classroom door.

"I'm sorry!" Corinth said, still in character. "I didn't mean any of it!"

I wish I could say what happened next was my idea. Wish to the stars above I had thought of it because it was magic. The police were supposed to try the doorknob, say a few lines amongst themselves, and then hit it three times with a sledgehammer before it gave way. Corinth was in the fetal position when the first blow fell.

One.

Benjamin started at the noise, then looked back at Corinth.

Two.

He hopped over to him and put a little paw on his shoulder.

"Hey. Mister. Don't cry. I'm all right. See?"

Corinth looked up. Eyes red, face streaked with tears, and snot coming out his nose. "Yes, I see. You're a good boy, aren't you?"

He reached out to pet the rabbit on the head.

Three.

The police burst in and fire their guns. Corinth's other squibs went off. He shook once or twice and went down. The cops pulled Benjamin away, one officer went to the window to signal the rescue had succeeded. That was the last line to be spoken in that scene. Then, silence. The actors stood around, looking at each other. They were still police officers and terrified students. And as the moments passed each face showed a fatigue, a creeping exhaustion. I glanced at the crew and they had the same look: totally absorbed. Forge finally spoke, in a soft whisper.

"Cut."

***

"Again!" Benjamin said. "I want to see it again!"

"No, son," William said. "Come on. You've seen it a dozen times. Let the people work."

Quinn Flyer smiled and led him away from the station where the dailies were being viewed. I was checking email on my phone when I felt something bump against my leg and squeeze.

"Thank you," Benjamin said. "Thank you thank you thank you! I can't believe I'm going to be in a real movie. Wait till Mom hears about this! She'll be so proud. Do you think we'll get to walk the red carpet, Dad?"

William had a far-off look in his eye but came around. "I don't know, Benjamin. I guess that's up to someone else."

I knelt. "Hey. Remember that promise?" I handed him a piece of paper in a plastic sleeve, the title page of the new script, with my name scrawled across the top. "Here."

Benjamin started bouncing like a jackhammer. "Yay! Oh, thank you so much. I'm going to get everyone to sign it right now. Hey you! Giraffe! C'mere!"

He was off like a rocket. William offered his paw.

"I can't thank you enough, pal. He still hasn't gotten over the divorce. Haven't seen him this happy in ages, even on his birthday. Can I buy you a drink?"

I shook his paw. "No need. Can't promise that he'll actually be in the movie, but I'm glad he had fun."

"Well, thanks."

I found Forge outside, wrapping up a phone call.

"Problem?"

"Nope," I said. "Sure am beat. What's next?"

"Got an old warehouse lined up for the next sequence. Should make a good telegraph office."

There was a pause.

"Think they'll go for it?" I said.

"Sure hope so."

Venus appeared. A few minutes later, the rest of the stars felt brave and came out to join her.

"Probably won't be seeing much of you after this. Still got a whole movie to make," I said.

"But there are plenty of loose ends. With Jones still sick and Benjamin in the mix, we have to figure out casting."

"We could always write him in as a secondary character, or a sibling. Give me a day or two. I'll figure it out."

She faced me. "It'd be easier if you came with us." Her expression was set, yet pleading.

I flushed. "You want me on set?"

"This is a tough business, Wilkes," she said. "And you've got a lot to learn. But you *are* talented, the way you improvised that scene. And when—"

"Sounds like you've got a lot on your mind. Want to hash it out over dinner?"

Forge gave me a look. "After what happened last time? I left you stranded in the middle of L.A. with the bill for two steak dinners."

"You can make it up to me," I said. "Just don't knock the table over."

She grinned. "You're one to talk."

I offered my arm.

THE CARROT IS MIGHTIER THAN THE SWORD

Nidhi Singh

A great rustling swept over the treeless tracts as droves of furry hares, kestrel-eyed and keen, lanky-legged and tough, fanned out to munch on sedge and dwarf shrub. They rested and foraged in turns, leaping and lolloping across the heather and the bent, as the cold wind, bemoaning the winter just departed, passed with a sigh over the yellowing grasses and fire thorns crouching low. Some, in spring frenzy, chased one another, sparring with their paws. Leverets, with long ears and black markings, rubbed their eyes; sleeking their furs with well-licked paws, they raced the sun with eyes cocked to the sky, where peewits, with their slow wings squeaking, and golden plovers, with reedy whistles piping, circled.

By the pool with grey reeds at its rim, King Carrotta, warm as an oven loaf in his brilliant white coat, surveyed the soggy realm with satisfaction; twirling his whiskers, he drew a straw to suck from a pitcher plant. As he hummed and slurped in tandem with the concerts of nature, another sound that didn't quite agree with the general sunshine rang in: the slow weeps of a creature, proud, ashamed of his pain.

King Carrotta, with many a winter past him, knew well to mind his own business; the craft of surviving in the bitter, wild white was a tricky one. So he chucked the straw and bounded away in large merry leaps, and found spike rush to whiten his teeth upon. But the cries, like misty wreaths fluttering, wheeling about over the moss and heath, followed him, and he could no longer shut his ears to them. Unhappily he tossed over his shoulder a juicy blue-black bearberry, and contrary to his good sense, bounded across the bog to see what ailed this poor soul.

There, near a frozen tarn, at the mouth of the barren cavern, lay a giant fire-breathing dinosaur, writhing and worrying, grieving and growling, raging and raving, howling and heating, and turning and twisting, around and around, with endless rebound. He could barely spit fire, and smoke wisped out his damp nostrils. He had an arrow ripped through his wing, which he beat weakly. Drenched in tears of shame, but not of his own making, his eyes, big, black, fearful, and staggering, implored for help.

"Whatever happened to you, silly bird?" asked the King, staying a safe distance behind an alder brush—just in case. "Who are you?"

"Doesn't anyone even know? I am Terex—the fire breather—arch of the alpine forest!" Scooping air into his lungs, he exhaled with force—a tiny cloud of vapor popped out of his face, lingering briefly in the bracing cold, before vanishing. The arch-firebomber hung his head in shame.

"What in blazes!" Carrotta scurried a little closer. "What brings you so far up north?"

"I used to feast upon veggie Sauropods that mow the earth like cows. Not long ago, some crazy Nenets, not content with hunting Caribous, shot me down with an arrow when I was only minding my own business—flying low, hugging the treetops, looking for some warm, succulent meat to dig my teeth into. Why, I wasn't even firing up when these looting, lust-dieted, lowlifes shot me down just for sport—for I have armor on my back, club on my tail, fire in my entrails and dung in my horns—what use are these in any hearth? I flew as far and away as I could, my wing bleeding, till I could no more, and crawled into this hollow to die."

"Why the howling, the tossing and turning then, mate? Spring doesn't last here forever—you're disturbing the peace. Do what you have to, and keep it low, okay?" The King crouched on his powerful hind legs and made to spring off.

"Hey, wait… err… umm… I could do with a little…" mumbled Terex, his dark face blanched with pain and blood loss, all of his six monstrous eyes downcast in humiliation.

"Oh, so the mighty Tyrannosaurus needs help from a humble bonnybunny then?"

"Must you… really speak aloud…" the dinosaur darted glances left and right.

"Right-ho then—keep tight." The Bonnybunny hopped close to the mauled wing and hummed and hawed. "Nothing the sharp cogs of a drove will not set right. Wait here for me," said he, and leaped across the marsh to marshal his marshals.

Soon, a vast oinking and honking advanced over the mellowing permafrost, and in no time the Bigwigs, the Cottontails, the Flopsies, and the Pookas had chewed through the hardwood shaft and elk sinew of the arrow and pulled it out.

Dr. Jack Quack, the local on-call GP, boiled some carrots in a geyser and rubbed the mashed taproot on the wound. "You'll be good to go in no time," he said, stepping back to admire his handiwork.

"What's that?" the monster wailed, all his six eyebrows shooting up, when the does brought before him a sumptuous spread of liverworts, carrots, lichens, and caribou mosses. "Where is the meat?"

"Eat your veggies; it's low fat and won't clog your arteries," the doctor firmly declared. "The carrots might even help you see in the dark."

"Only wabbits eat carrots," the proud predator moaned.

"Watching too much television, has our sickly boy been? It's not your Bugs Bunny show Mr. Raptor—eat 'em."

And so the raptor soon recovered; a dark flush once again suffused his handsome fiendish looks, and he was able to flap his wings without wincing. When he could take short flights over the bog and take his pickings from the Caribou and Musk Ox, the lapins knew it was time to let the visitor head back to his forests down south. The brief spring was already waning and the coldhearted dusk was beginning to close in like a slow trap of ice.

So one morning, by the long creek, on mist-blurred grass, Carrotta shook his visitor's claw and bid him adieu. "Can't say I'm sorry to see you go, though—you know, with bunnies—they get a little hot under the collar with all those blazes and flames. They got better tricks to keep the old gal hot. "He winked as the raptor flapped his mighty wings, and soared away in a wake of soot and ash.

***

As early as the next winter, on a dark frozen night, Terex was back in the rabbit kingdom. This time, he had company—more winged, taloned, horned and fire spitting beasts following him—each more desperate than the other. Word skids fast on the frozen swampland, and the hares were on the ready with a reception.

"What brings you back?" King Carrotta slammed a parsnip-tipped spear against his iron breastplate and signaled the uninvited guests, creatures that left a bloody and blazing brume in their wake, to halt at the gates of his realm.

"A massive rock has hit the earth. Almost the entire population of our non-avians has been wiped out. I liked what I saw here the last time. We come in peace, brother—to take over new territories and advance our race. We were friends once; remember me—you hosted me last spring as well?" Terex flapped his wings, large as the sails of a galleon, and hovered over the king and his assembled guard, his nostrils seething and smoking.

"You come in peace, yet you slash and burn our lands?"

"That's what fire breathing dinosaurs do, brother—breathe fire."

"Well, it doesn't suit us. It thaws the permafrost, and burns the food on the table, not to mention the greenhouse gases that discharge because of all the warming. I ask that you spend the night here and return to your Taiga in the morning. When you were sick, we took you in, and now that you've returned to your previous fiery splendor, we don't want your dark blood-gouts of flame and phlegm scaring the kits."

"I mean no harm to the cupcakes—see, we don't eat no wabbits. Who wants to be coughing up fur for days afterwards?"

"We are no cupcakes or bunnies to you Mister Terminator—we are Hares." Carrotta drew up to his full fuzzy height and raised his lance aloft.

"So are you going to stop us with a handful of pink carrots and doll faces," asked a smirking dragon minion. Sweeping his spiked tail, he sent the hare's entire front line scrambling into disarray.

Worthy King Carrotta, having proved himself in many a battle with marauding weasels, ripping white foxes, and squawking harlequin ducks, on seeing his battle formation in a state of near-rout at the very first feint enemy maneuver, turned to his soldiers, and lifting his big voice, shouted, "Hooold! Rrready for battle!"

On cue, his guard brought up its banners, and sounded the giant bugle. In a flash, as the dinosaurs blinked, an army of a hundred thousand assembled in battle formation on the vast fields of tufted saxifrages and foliose lichens. The front lines were made of several thirty-two-hare-deep phalanxes that locked their shields together and thrust their spears; behind them were yeoman archers and stalwart redcoats at the ready; on the flanks, infantrybucks with shakos raised on muskets; lastly, chariots of toboggans pulled by grays and piloted by martial lemmings brought up the fighting rear.

Well-armed with both bucklers and steel, the gathered army felled the affront of the air, as a growing tempest vexed the skies. "Dex Aie!" "Out out!" War cries pierced the air; impatient steeds of war stamped their angry hooves on the trembling land; and such a blasting and noise with their horns and drums, and flapping of pennons and screeching of copper-coat cottontails, and stomping of hobnailed boots, they made that it seemed all the great devils of hell had descended there.

"Forward!" commanded their leader, and the army began to march in step, slowly gathering pace and momentum. "Halt!" the King shouted, as his frontlines advanced within thrust and parry range of the enemy. The lines turned a quarter right, and muskets were brought to the ready.

The ardor of the monsters seemed to abate a bit; the sounds weighed heavily on their spirits, and they became chary of being put furiously to the slaughter. A knave and a cad quivering in the rear did make a lame attempt at spitting a flame, but such an accurate volley of carrot-tipped arrows descended that it seemed thunderbolts were falling from the heavens.

Clutching a bleeding eye, seeing his rank and file descending into disorderly rout already, Terex, the arch-talon of the woods, made a wise decision to stay alive for battle on another day. "O mighty King," he said, "you're taking this a tad too seriously. We are inclined to accept your generous offer of staying the night and returning peaceful and vacant possession of your lands at the first break of light.

Peace, brother!" Spreading his giant armor-plated flanks, he slowly took a step back.

"Return then, beyond frozen lakes yonder, and do not bother to say goodbye in the morn," King Carrotta raised a paw, and pointed their way out. The visitors flapped their leathery wings and meekly retreated to lick their wounds and count their losses.

***

In the hare's camp the elders gathered in council, some heady with victory of the day, some drunk on carrot wine, most waiting for a sign from their meditating King to disperse to their warm warrens and waiting does—for spring was waning, spent, and the desire rousing, unspent.

"Hark ye all," spoke the monarch at long last, after much reflection. "I don't expect the raptors to leave us so easily in peace. Master Hedwit, the wise owl, brings word that the Pangaea is indeed breaking up, and a massive rock has crashed into our world, snuffing out entire species. These are dark times indeed, when we must keep the faith. Let us do our bit to preserve this biome, home to our ancestors, and legacy to our children. We must rally the white bear and the gray fox—even the flapping swamp geese, and the hardline hawk to save this planet, and if..."

"What if, if," asked of him Roger R. Rector, head priest and chief savant.

"If only man was on our side—rapacious, ravenous, ruthless, ruinous man. Or if he became the enemy of our enemy, the battle would be easily won."

"Look around you sire, we are a million strong, and growing; what devil may not we easily vanquish?" asked General March.

"True—our strength is in numbers—but as the first beams of sunlight glance across the fenlands, he will return, in greater numbers, better organized. Today we took him by surprise, tomorrow, we need another trick up our sleeve," said the wily Hare Monarch.

"What do you suggest we do?" asked his general.

"I want you to take four divisions of our finest infantry, battle-scarred and war-worthy, and steal the carrots from man's farms."

"Carrots, me lord? Only bugs bunnies eat them on television," reminded the sage.

"It's not for eating, O wise one. We have enough food—for now. When the village finds its carrots plucked, vamoosed from its fields, barren, like the pleasures the rake seeks, it will fetch its hounds, and after us. At that moment, I expect to be joined in battle with the raptors unrepentant, and once man arrives on the bent, his badgers and fleabags on the scent, his kettledrums and whistles in a torment, and his temper and thrill on ascent, we shall beat a hasty, well organized retreat, and let one felon deal with another, to their heart's malcontent."

"A wonderful idea, me Regent!"

"To the village then, my Braves; hasten, before the night's dark veil lifts on our fortunes and intent."

***

On the morrow, as Carrotta had predicted, the Godzillas returned, perched on the willow, ready to heap burning coals upon their heads. His armies too, out in full heraldry and badges, shouldering muskets and pikes, had assembled ready for the sparring. Pavisiers and cross-bowers oiled their weapons and cracked their knuckles, and gunners winched down catapult beams, carrying bushels loaded with carrots, slate, and magma. The cavalry commanders, wearing orange surcoats and blue helmets with coronets, their mounts in caparisons decorated with the national vegetable, the carrot, hoisted the colors. The Tribunes, ever and anon, blew their olifants to summon retribution; and solemn the misery pipes wailed. The hares took defenses behind a long line of iron ties joining blocks of stones together, and once the paeans had been sung, the frontlines began to march unwaveringly into combat. The monsters hissed and seethed, and battle was joined.

Flying arrows carpeted the sky; the silver sun blacked out completely; mounts leaped and scurried, and flames in the winds of death shivered incessantly. The armies marched, the fires blazed; the armies fell, the lusters died. Again the glows returned, the lands burned, and down the red-hot valleys the armies marching went. Embers blinked and lives crumbled in hell's furnaces; bodies shone and dusked in fitful glows; red tongues darted and snaked in the smoky air, fields and hills lay black—one could taste the burning grass. Next season's bud was roasted, her larvae toasted, the lichen cooked brown, soot on its stem, writhing half-dead.

In the pandemonium the leftmost flank began to sound their bugle, and Carrotta knew, the enemy of his enemy had arrived. Upon his order to the guards, a trusty messenger streaked through the battle order, barking his king's command to the captains and commanders. The rearguard turned about, hoisted its colors, and began to march in orderly retreat. Slowly, the flanks opened up, letting hollering man and feisty dog into the heart of battle, till only the frontlines in contact remained to face certain death.

Along with them, many a man, taken aback with the violence and mayhem, perished, but not before many an enemy had been shot to the blazing ground. Valiant Carrotta, himself wounded badly, made away with most of his army, while the monsters lost most of theirs.

The men would return, he knew, with many more, for retribution, and that would be the end of the invaders. Many lives had to be lost, but land would be restored to its pristine glory.

***

In the Hare's camp the war council, joined by the bear, the gray, the goose, the owl, and the weasel, and many more, had gathered again, huddled in dialogue. The silent King lay in agony, his end near.

"What is to be done next, King dear?" asked General March.

"You did well today, my general. I leave a proud man." He beckoned the general with a painful paw, bandaged in moss and carrot mash. The general walked over to his bed and held his hand to his wrenching heart; tears welled up in every eye.

"I leave this kingdom in your able charge, General March; lead our brethren, every living soul that walks the earth, or swims in its waters, or flies in its skies, every blade of grass and leaf and fruit that sustains life, unto everlasting peace; this I command, nay implore you, will be your holy grail, the reason for you to prevail."

"No, my king, come morning, and you will be upon your paws, proud and doughty, showing us the way," the General cried.

"Promise me this," the King clasped his General's hand, and implored him with dimming eyes, "promise me now!"

"I promise, my Lord."

***

The curtains of the royal tent flapped and a messenger stepped in. "Hail the king! My Lord, a most unlikely visitor has appeared at the gates—we have him detained at the tower. He asks your audience."

"And who might this intruder be—an informant... a spy... a laggard... an envoy—who dares to vex when we are in council?" asked the head priest.

"It is he—T-T-Terex—in p-person!" The messenger bowed.

"It's a trick!"

"Knavery!"

"A double-dealing treachery!" The assembly roared. "Dispatch him at the gates—finish the lying villain."

"Wait," the King rasped. "Take me to him." he waved aside the protests and howls and bade his guards carry his palanquin to the tower.

Terex, his feet chained to a turret, sat crestfallen on the ground, his shoulders hunched, his wide plume spiritless and flagged.

"How do you want me to treat you?" asked Carrotta.

"The way one king treats another," said Terex.

"Free him at once," Carrotta commanded. "What is it—what trickery assails your manner now?" he asked when the raptor had risen on his feet.

"I know I'm not worthy of your trust, mighty Hare, but like you, I was only saving my kind. Alas, that strange insertion of man and his wily ways into the fracas did us in. As I look back, I see friend and foe, family and fellowship, perished. I repent mocking you—what valor, what sacrifice, what discipline your ranks showed today—I salute you and this land. I am at a crossroads, my troops have no more stomach for battle, I know man will return tomorrow and annihilate us with his devices— Tell me, O king, what must I do," he wailed, his giant frame wracked with sobs.

"Return to your forest, raptor, save the last living of your kind. Shrink, sprout wings, change into a bird, or something, adapt, learn patience, and you will be fine."

The raptor nodded, he knew change was upon them and they had to learn. "Hail! Take care, good friend," he said, and fluttered away.

"What should we do now, my lord?" asked General March.

"Return to the old ways. What man or hound could ever catch a fast hare?" He winked. "Man has a short memory—he will never have any dearth of hunt and sport as long as this land lives. Till then, good runnings, my friend."

His general nodded in agreement, and gazed up at the skies, the freezing stars had begun to twinkle again, as the smoke and haze of battle started to clear. It was quite some time before he realized his king's hand had gone cold and lifeless in his grasp.

DEATH ON THE TILE

Kyell Gold

The rabbit's white-furred face broke into a wave of relief as she took in the three people standing on the threshold of the modest Tudor building. "Oh, Ellie," she half-sobbed, throwing herself past the uniformed wolf onto the slight weasel in the shabby traveling-coat. "I'm so glad you came."

Ellie hugged Abby tightly back while Sergeant Cooke coughed into his paw and the portly fox in the navy peacoat behind him shifted his doctor's black bag from one paw to the other. "Oh, it's been horrible," the rabbit went on. "No-one knows what to do and that constable insists it's only a heart attack but I know there's something peculiar going on. She doesn't have any perfume like that, only I'm not clever enough but you are."

"I know, Ab." Ellie smiled and patted the rabbit's shoulder, disengaging gently from the hug. She wanted to hold Abby forever, to take her up to her room and kiss that beautiful smile and stroke those ears, but even though it had been a couple weeks, public decorum won out. It always did. "Look, I've brought Sergeant Cooke and Dr. Rousse."

"I'm not a doctor," the fox said mildly, "despite the bag. I'm a medical examiner, and I'm here on my day off, and Sergeant Cooke there owes me a steak dinner if this turns out to be nothing, miss, so I do hope that your instincts are misplaced."

"They're not," Ellie said before Abby could defend herself. "If she says something's wrong, I believe her."

"And I believe Miss Stone," Sergeant Cooke said. "But Miss Rose, please do announce us to the proprietor. My ears are sadly unprotected from the winter chill."

As they trooped inside, Ellie's uneasiness returned. Abby had been scattered like this on the telephone, but so insistent that Ellie had agreed to bring Sergeant Cooke. Abby wouldn't be that upset unless something was really wrong. She hadn't counted on Sergeant Cooke also pulling Dr. Rousse away from his day off, and even though the fox had retained a sense of humor about it all, she worried now about wasting both of their time.

But she couldn't tell Abby that. So as the others moved ahead, Ellie hung back a step, and said softly to Abby, "You're greeting guests at the door now?"

"That was—it was Camilla's job and—and Mrs. Dower thought it best that another rabbit continue to do the job until she can hire a replacement, and anyway the only other servant in the house is Mister Lancaster and he's the cook and nobody would want to be greeted by him at the door, he'd frighten away half the guests. Hold on one moment." Abby ran ahead of the weasel to stop the wolf and fox in the parlor, a tasteful room with royal blue wallpaper and white trim and an extensive mat on which all four of them wiped their feet. "Wait here, I'll just go tell Mrs. Dower that you've arrived. I think she's still in with the constable."

Surrounded by watercolor paintings of cottages in the summer that bore no resemblance to the snow-dusted landscape they'd driven through, plus one posting that read: "Dower Hotel: Rules of the Establishment," Ellie turned back to Sergeant Cooke as the wolf removed his overcoat. "Thank you again for coming," she said.

"Do hope your Abby's right," Cooke said, and then caught himself. "I mean—of course I don't wish there to be a murder. It's just that Rousse there has expensive tastes in steak, and I live on a sergeant's salary."

The fox smiled a long smile. "Nothing in the bet says you have to join me for the steak, Cooke."

"I'm determined to get some pleasure out of it, at least."

"More than the pleasure of a colleague enjoying a fine Ritz-Carlton dinner?"

Cooke groaned.

***

Mrs. Dower, tall for a dormouse and skinny as an underfed weasel, entered the parlour with a bustle of energy and determined good spirits. "Sergeant, is it? And Doctor?"

"I'm the medical examiner," Dr. Rousse said.

"Oh, I beg your pardon, the girl said your name was Dr. Rousse."

"I'm a forensic pathologist," the fox said. "I find that if I tell people I'm a doctor, they ask me to diagnose their coughs or aches or swellings and then I have to tell them that I'm no use until they're dead, and then there are upset feelings all around."

"Understood." Mrs. Dower leaned in conspiratorially. "I shall introduce you simply as the medical examiner, then. I certainly appreciate that you and the sergeant have come all this way in this frightful cold. I fear it will all be a waste of your time, though I do admit there's something odd about it. Young ladies don't simply drop dead of heart attacks in my experience."

"It can happen, Ma'am," Dr. Rousse said. "But it's rather rare. If I may—where was the young lady found?"

"In the servants' bath. We've left her there for the moment on the advice of Constable Polter, though it's a trifle inconvenient. Abby's having to use Mr. Dower's and my bath for the moment." She made as if to leave the room, the fox trailing behind her.

"Ah, Mrs. Dower?" Sergeant Cooke spoke up. "If I might interview the guests?"

The dormouse turned. "Of course, of course. We've only three staying with us. I'll have Abby inform them of your request."

"I'd prefer to inform them myself. Which room would be most convenient for us to use?" the wolf asked.

"Oh, let me see." Mrs. Dower peered through the parlour door. "Why not the sitting-room? It's normally used for afternoon tea, so we won't be needing it for several hours, and if you're still using it then, we can of course serve tea in the, ah, in the dining room." Her muzzle crinkled at the thought of this breach of protocol, but she gave a quick nod. "Yes, the dining room will do. Oh, Abby, would you show Sergeant Cooke to the sitting-room, please."

"Yes'm," the rabbit said. "Ma'am, Mr. Damonica is in the hallway insisting to Constable Polter that he be allowed to leave and I think Constable Polter is about to allow him to go."

"Blast." Sergeant Cooke turned to Ellie. "Go wait in the sitting room, please. Mrs. Dower, if you'd be so kind as to take the M.E. to the body? I'm so sorry to impose on you. I believe I can hear the row in the hallway well enough to find my way to the constable's relief."

"Not at all, not at all." Mrs. Dower's eyes alit on Ellie, who had been making herself very unobtrusive up to them. "And who is this?"

"Miss Stone is my assistant." Sergeant Cooke rested a paw on Ellie's shoulder. "My very capable assistant."

This fit into Mrs. Dower's world. She gave an approving nod and hurried away with the fox in tow. Sergeant Cooke smiled apologetically and removed his paw from Ellie's shoulder, then walked quickly toward the faint sound of a raised voice.

Abby led Ellie to a pleasant sitting room with several small tables set with lace and a china cabinet to one side. She closed the door behind them and then embraced Ellie with a warm kiss.

"Mmm." The weasel kissed her back, holding her tightly. "I'm sorry your friend died. You're being very strong."

"I'm sorry too." Abby pressed her head against Ellie's. "But I want it to come out right, and I know I'm not clever enough to see it through on my own."

"You're clever enough to recognize that something's wrong," Ellie said. "And that's something."

Abby smiled. "I love you."

"Love you too."

The rabbit's long white ears flicked. "That sergeant likes you."

"Cooke? No, he's just…" Ellie paused. "We're friends, that's all."

"Don't worry, El, I'm not jealous. I know you're not encouraging him and he can't know about us. I think it's sweet."

"I'm not encouraging him."

Abby nodded and brushed Ellie's cheek with a paw. "I know." Her smile grew a touch sad. "We can maybe be old spinsters, but sometimes it might look odd if we don't at least acknowledge a fellow's affections. I know where your heart is, no matter what."

"There's nothing between Cooke and me, old soul." Abby was distracting herself from her friend's death, Ellie thought, and maybe that's all that was. But she wasn't wrong.

The rabbit's long white ears perked. "Someone's coming."

They separated, paws lingering on each other for a moment, but by the time Sergeant Cooke came through the door, followed by a rotund red squirrel whose constable's uniform looked in danger of bursting several buttons, Ellie had cleared off one of the tables and set it up with two chairs on one side and one on the other.

"...asked everyone where they were last night, but I haven't spoken to them much at all, sir, to be honest. Ah..." The squirrel eyed Ellie. "I'm still not quite sure I understand how you've come to be here, sir."

Cooke walked over to stand beside Ellie and put a paw on the back of one of the chairs. To Ellie, it was clear that he was formulating an acceptable answer. "Slow day up at the station. They asked me to accompany the M.E. over to investigate," he said.

"But I've not filed a request for the M.E. There was just the call to attend to here and I hadn't confirmed—"

"Yes, that's what I meant. Ah, thank you, Miss Stone." He smiled and sat in the chair she pulled out for him.

"Sir," Ellie said quickly, as the constable seemed about to renew his objections, "Abby has been here with the guests for several days. It might be worth asking her impressions of them."

Both the wolf and squirrel turned their attention on Abby, who clasped her paws together and stared down at them. "Oh, I don't know," she said. "Mr. Damonica's only been here two days. Though he has been here before, I believe."

Ellie laid a paw on her arm. "It's okay, Ab. Just tell the sergeant anything you can think of about the guests."

"Well… oh, thank you." The sergeant had gestured toward the seat across from him, and Abby sat down. The constable moved toward the seat next to Cooke, but the wolf waved him back to the table and gestured Ellie forward.

With a little nervousness, the weasel took the chair next to him and perked her ears. Abby smiled at her and went on. "Mr. and Mrs. Macintosh are regulars here. They come every winter from what I understand it. Camilla knew them quite well."

"Those are the red deer?"

"Yes." Abby nodded. "Mr. Macintosh is a sweet old fellow. He's partly blind, I think, at least, he gets around by his sense of smell mostly. He was an MP, now he's retired, and he works with an orphanage— no, two orphanages—down in the city. He and his wife go on long walks and he brings back aromatic plants, mostly fir branches. He used to ask Camilla to put them in water for him."

There was something about the way Abby said that last part that Ellie filed away to ask her about later. Sergeant Cooke made some notes and then said, "And his wife?"

"I don't know that she likes it here much. She always finds something to complain about in the way we do up the rooms. Mrs. Dower told me not to worry about the complaints, that that was just how Mrs. Macintosh is. And Ca…" She swallowed and then forged on. "Camilla said last night she sent back her soup to be warmed three times. Mister Lancaster asked if she'd like him to bring the fire out to the dining room." Abby stifled a giggle.

"Camilla served the food?"

"Oh, yes. There was only her and me, and a badger who comes in to do the gardening, but of course he doesn't come during the winter. Unless it snows quite a bit, then he clears the drive. I do the bedrooms and help in the kitchen sometimes, but I only help serve when the hotel is full."

The wolf scribbled a few more notes and then said, "And Mr. Damonica?"

"He's a vice-president somewhere in the Midlands, I think. Something to do with coal, I believe. He's frightfully important. He says he likes Dower Hotel because it's near the city but also peaceful enough that he can relax. He spends most of his mornings reading the paper and then makes phone calls from his room in the afternoon once it's made up."

Cooke set down his pen and met Abby's eyes. "There wasn't any trouble because he's a hare and you and Camilla are—were—rabbits?"

"I thought there might be as well," Abby said. "I asked whether I should avoid him. But Mrs. Dower says he's Kanatian, you know, came to this country on a boat ten years ago, and he doesn't hold to our customs so much. It was odd for us serving him, but…" She hesitated.

"Go on?"

Abby looked at Ellie, her eyes wide. The weasel nodded reassuringly. "If there's anything, Abby, go ahead. It won't get back to Mrs. Dower."

"It's just—I think he might have been getting familiar with Camilla. Not that it went farther than that, but—but yesterday he put his paw on my arm in that way, and when I turned he took it off straight away and said he was sorry."

"When he saw it was you and not Camilla?" Sergeant Cooke asked.

"Yes. And Camilla quite looked forward to seeing him, not like—" Again she broke off, but at Ellie's nod, she went on. "Well, not like Mister Macintosh, to be honest."

"Mister Macintosh also acted 'familiar' with her?" Sergeant Cooke scribbled another note as Abby nodded.

The constable leaned forward. "Ah, sir, nothing odd about that, certainly. Fellow stays in a boarding house, the service is quite attractive, he expresses his appreciation."

Ellie didn't say anything, but Sergeant Cooke turned to her and gave her the slightest hint of a smile, before responding very seriously, "That's as may be, Constable, but some appreciation might be more welcome than others."

"I suppose." The squirrel sounded as though he did not really understand what difference that made.

"All right, thank you, Miss Rose," Sergeant Cooke said. "Constable, please show Miss Rose out and bring in whichever of the three guests wishes to be interviewed first."

When Abby had left, trailing the constable, Cooke turned to Ellie. "What do you make of it?"

The weasel shook her head. "I suppose if there were an obvious motive, everyone would know of it. But we don't even know if it was murder yet."

"It was." The M.E. stood at the sitting-room door, inside-out gloves in his paws. "Alas for my pocketbook, but score one for your friend, Miss Stone. Hydrogen cyanide."

"That's a poison of some kind," the sergeant said as Ellie felt a wave of relief, followed quickly by sadness that Abby's friend had been killed, and guilt over her relief, and then pride at how strong Abby was.

"You might know it as prussic acid." The fox came in and settled himself into the chair the constable had just vacated.

Ellie sat up straighter, the name overwhelming her confusing tangle of emotions. "Yes, of course! Oh, dear."

Cooke half-turned. "Your police stories?"

She nodded. "It was rather quick, then, at least."

"Yes." Dr. Rousse shook his head. "She wouldn't have suffered much. And it resembles a heart attack, at least to the lay person, so I can't fault the constable overmuch. He's not trained to recognize a bitter almond smell nor to know what it might mean." He did not tout his superior sense of smell, though he did scratch at his long nose.

"Definitely not." Sergeant Cooke stared down at his pad. "I suppose we can't exclude the proprietors as suspects."

"The thing is," Ellie said, focusing on the crime, "I know what prussic acid *is*. But the people in my stories just have it. I've no idea how one would actually go about *getting* any. I don't suppose you can walk into the chemist and ask for it."

"I'd think not." Dr. Rousse smiled. "It's manufactured industrially, so one would likely be able to get some through industrial channels."

"If, for example," Sergeant Cooke said, "one were highly placed in a coal company?"

"Or," Ellie added, "a retired Member of Parliament with business connections."

"Or, for that matter, his wife," the fox concluded. "Or a hotel proprietor who's had any number of guests come through."

The wolf sighed. "Back where we started, I suppose."

"The thing is the motive," Ellie said. "I can't see that anyone in particular benefits from Camilla's death."

Constable Polter knocked on the door, then cracked it open. "Sir," he said, "I have Mrs. Macintosh for you."

The red deer filled the doorway, sweeping into the room in a blue chiffon dress with white paisley prints, a flowery bonnet atop her head. "More police!" she exclaimed in a light brogue. "I'm not afraid to tell you that during Seamus's time in Parliament, we learned much about the police and their allocation of funds. Sending such a contingent to question us about a young rabbit suffering a tragic heart attack? Are there no criminals to catch?"

She sat heavily opposite the sergeant and stared at him. He cleared his throat. "As it happens, Ma'am, Dr. Rousse here has just come from confirming that Miss… that the young rabbit was poisoned. So it seems there is a criminal to catch, and he is in this hotel." He paused. "Or she."

Mrs. Macintosh snorted through her long nose. "I hope you're not implying that I might have had anything to do with it. Certainly

I shouldn't mind if she came down with a stomach flu, or perhaps a touch of mange." She said those things with more relish, Ellie thought, than was appropriate for a discussion about a person who'd just died. "But I would never poison her. Imagine! Ha! Ha!" Her laughter boomed throughout the room.

Sergeant Cooke cleared his throat, the flicking of his tail showing Ellie that he felt the same as she did about Mrs. Macintosh's outburst. "It's my job to imagine all possibilities," he said. "So if you please, Mrs. Macintosh, could you tell me about your interactions with the deceased?"

She stared at him and then laughed again, shortly. "Ha! I suppose you're not interested in what she served me at tea. You want to hear about her and Seamus."

Ellie sat up straighter. Cooke kept his expression neutral. "If you like. Or we could have Mr. Macintosh tell us about that."

"Oh, heaven knows what he'll tell you. One moment he swears 'ne'er my ship shall leave your graceful shore' and the next he's bragging about some poor girl he's stolen a kiss from. Have you ever had fleas, Sergeant?"

"Er. As a cub, once."

Ellie, too, nodded, but Mrs. Macintosh paid no attention to her. "Then you know how they're nearly unbearable when they're biting. But when they're not… you can either ignore it and be happy, or you can think about it and imagine yourself into a frenzy of scratching." The red deer met the wolf's eyes with a level stare. "I have decided that my own happiness is paramount."

"Very, er, wise." Sergeant Cooke wrote a quick note. "But to be clear, are you saying your husband wasn't having an affair, or that it didn't bother you?"

She levered her body forward, leaning in to look at him. "I'm saying, Sergeant, that I have no idea whether he was or not. Yes, of course I noticed things, but Seamus has always been one to express his affection openly. Over the years, affairs have undoubtedly happened. But as you can see, we are still together. Our marriage is stronger than his weakness."

"I see." Sergeant Cooke did not note anything on his pad. "Can you perhaps account for your movements last night?"

"Of course." She settled back in the chair. "We all had supper here as usual. That maid was present, serving. Seamus and I retired to our room to listen to the news of the day on the wireless. We listened for about an hour, discussed that Kilkenny fellow who made a speech about the labour crisis, and then retired to our beds."

"You were together the whole time?"

"We each used the lavatory at one point." She gave a small smile. "We do that separately."

"Of course, but that would not have taken you outside your rooms?"

"The guests share two common lavatories between the six rooms," Mrs. Macintosh informed him. "As it was only us and Mr. Damonica here, we arranged with him to each take one as a semi-private lavatory. Ours is the one at the end of the hall closer to our room; his closer to his room."

"So you both left your rooms at some point."

"Nature being the mistress she is, yes."

"All right. Thank you. I think that's all for now."

As Mrs. Macintosh rose, Ellie leaned over to whisper to him, "Oughtn't we to fetch the husband before releasing her?"

"Ah, yes. Ellie—Miss Stone, would you see Mrs. Macintosh out and bring her husband in?"

"One moment, please." Dr. Rousse stood and approached Cooke and Ellie. He leaned in to whisper as well. "Miss Stone made me think: where did the cyanide come from? It might be worth searching the trash if it hasn't been picked up."

"Oh, yes," Ellie said.

Cooke pressed his paw to the bridge of his muzzle. "Doctor, could you please find the constable and instruct him to see to that? Make certain he uses gloves." He waved toward the ones the fox had left on the table. "Give him some if he hasn't any."

***

Mrs. Macintosh objected to being escorted. "I can find my own way," she said.

"I'm just going along to fetch your husband for the sergeant, ma'am," Ellie said.

"Hmph." The red deer strode quickly on her long legs so that Ellie had to hurry to keep up. She glanced to either side to see if she could spot Abby, but even in the small downstairs of the hotel, she didn't see many other people.

Mrs. Macintosh took the stairs with determination, as though late for an appointment. Ellie scurried up behind and caught her at the door to her room. "Seamus!" she boomed. "The policeman would like a word with you."

Her husband pushed himself up out of his chair, next to their large bed, and placed his newspaper on the sideboard next to two sherry glasses. "Of course, of course." His deep voice, with a sharper burr than his wife's, resonated in Ellie's chest, making her shiver. He must have been a very effective public speaker. "Downstairs in the tea-room?"

"Yes." Mrs. Macintosh crossed to the desk, littered with paper and a few pens. "I'm going to write back to Honoria and tell her we can bring the marmalade. I'll go to Fortnum tomorrow." She glanced back at Ellie. "Or whenever this business is done."

"So this…" Mr. Macintosh's nose lifted to the air. "This delightful young weasel shall see me downstairs?"

"Yes, sir," Ellie said.

"You can find your own way, Seamus."

But once they were outside the room, Mr. Macintosh put a broad hand out. "I could find my way," he said, "but I have such a fear of falling. May I please hold your arm?"

"Of course," Ellie said.

His hand reached for her and touched her breast at first, then found her arm. "Thank you, my dear," he murmured. She would've thought that this was an accident, but on the way through the parlour, he stumbled against her and his fingers pressed against her rear. Sweet old fellow indeed, Ellie thought.

Dr. Rousse hadn't yet returned. Sergeant Cooke looked up from perusing his notes as Ellie guided Mr. Macintosh to the chair. "Officer," the red deer rumbled. "It's my pleasure to assist you."

"Sergeant Cooke," the wolf said by way of introducing himself. "Please have a seat, sir. This won't take long. I'd like to hear about your relationship with Camilla and your activities last night."

"Ah, yes, of course. Such a tragedy. Such a lovely young lady. Of course I knew her rather well; we stay here for months at a time. She has worked here for two years, as I recall. Quite promising. I offered to help her with a position at one of my charities, but she liked the life here. Has a young chap courting her in the village, though they had a terrible row yesterday."

"A row?" The sergeant looked up. "About what?"

"I'm not precisely certain. I know her voice, and he was yelling at her outside the window. I could hear her better than him—higher register, you know, sharper tones—and she was telling him not to be jealous, I believe."

"Did he think she was carrying on with…" The wolf stopped. "Mr. Damonica?"

"Oh, I suppose, or one of the guests who was here last week. There was a young fellow, a badger, named Trent or some such."

"Did you often observe Camilla carrying on with other guests?"

The red deer shifted in his seat. "Ah. You know, one doesn't like to speculate on such things. She's an attractive young rabbit and may do as she pleases." He caught himself. "She was, rather."

"And last night, your movements? After the attractive young rabbit served you dinner." From the emphasis Cooke placed on the words "attractive" and "young," Ellie presumed he was making the same connections she was about Mr. Macintosh's relationship with Camilla, and itched to be able to ask Abby about it.

"Oh, Diana and I retired to our room and we remained there for the rest of the night."

"Were either of you out of the other's sight?"

"To use the necessary. No longer than that." Mr. Macintosh inclined his head. "I say, Sergeant, this seems rather like an intensive line of inquiry surrounding a heart attack. May I presume that the presence of a fox at the hotel suggests that foul play is suspected?"

"Indeed." Sergeant Cooke rested his paws on the table. "It is the belief of the M.E. that Miss Camilla was poisoned."

"Poisoned?" Mr. Macintosh sat up in his chair. "Good gracious. With what?"

Cooke looked at Ellie for a moment, not so much asking her whether he should tell the deer as working it out in his head and sharing that decision with her. "We're going to keep that to ourselves for the moment, sir," he said. "I'm sure you understand."

"Of course, of course. Ongoing enquiry, all that." He took in a breath and let it out slowly. "Poisoned! I say, you don't expect the boyfriend had anything to do with it?"

"We're currently examining all the possible angles." The wolf tapped his pad with one claw. "Have you heard anything else that might be relevant or might provide a motive?"

"Goodness, no. Everyone loved Camilla. She had a lovely warm personality and such a friendly manner. Never quarreled with a guest."

"What about with the staff?"

"Oh…" He paused. "Mrs. Dower did have to remind her of her duties on occasion, but I'd hardly call that quarreling. If they did have more heated words, I'd never have seen it. Mrs. Dower runs a tight ship and keeps the guests insulated from all that."

"Of course," Cooke replied. "What about Mr. Damonica?"

"The hare? He put on airs around her from what I saw. She wasn't falling for it, I thought, but was always polite to him. Never gave him any reason to want to harm her. Of course, one never knows what goes on behind closed doors."

"Of course not." The sergeant nodded his head. "What did you think of him?"

"Damonica? Tried to chat me up first thing, was excited when he found I'd been in government." The deer's laugh was a hoarse huff. "Found out all my friends were dead or retired and lost interest right quick. Knew plenty like him in my time, though. He wanted us to be impressed with this deal he was doing, but you know, in my experience, these deals are often more impressive before they happen than after."

"How do you mean?" The sergeant's interest was not, Ellie thought, entirely pertinent to the case, but she too wanted to hear the answer.

"Oh, well." The deer waved an arm. "You bring together an 'historic' meeting and people are going to address some question, but everyone is mostly interested in keeping things the way they are, so if anything happens it's no more than a formality. I don't know the particulars of his meeting, but I'd be very surprised if it changes the future of Anglic coal."

"I see. Thank you." Sergeant Cooke leaned back in his chair. "If you think of anything else, do let us know."

"Certainly." The red deer rose. "Could the young weasel walk me back to my room?"

Sergeant Cooke nodded to Ellie, who rose. "I'd be delighted to," she said.

"And could you show Mr. Damonica in when you've settled Mr. Macintosh?" the wolf asked.

***

The red deer touched her breast again while taking her arm, but Ellie managed to keep his attentions otherwise away from her while escorting him up to his room, where she left him to the care of his wife. Rather than look for Mr. Damonica right away, though, she found the servants' stairs and hurried up to look for Abby.

The white rabbit wasn't in her room, but next door, Dr. Rousse's bright red tail waved through the door to the bathroom. Ellie padded along the carpet to get a look inside and caught her breath.

The M.E. knelt on the bright white tile next to a female rabbit, just as attractive as Mr. Macintosh had said (though not more attractive than Abby, Ellie said to herself). Her eyes stared up at the ceiling and her ears lay askew on the floor. At Ellie's gasp, the fox turned and looked up at her. "Ah, Miss Stone. I'm just attempting to ascertain the time of death. Please do remain outside the room for the moment." He bent back to the rabbit, touching her gently on the arm and leg and then sniffing near her mouth.

Ellie had seen only two dead people up close, both in the span of two days several months before. It seemed unfair that Abby, who'd been working with her at the time, would have to experience two murders in six months. She'd discovered one of the bodies at that previous position (Ellie had discovered the first), and she had likely been the one to discover Camilla's body as well. How horrible it must have been.

Still, there was no blood, and if Ellie ignored the smell that had begun to collect around the body, she could believe almost that the rabbit had simply fallen. But the eyes continued to stare, and the body remained motionless, and the smell couldn't be ignored.

Ellie scanned the room, looking for clues, anything out of place. On the small nightstand near the sink stood a toothpaste-stained drinking glass and two toothbrushes near it, both wide-bristled brushes made for rabbits. Beside those stood another glass, this one a snifter that Ellie guessed to be from the hotel's store for guests only.

Dr. Rousse stood. "It's more or less twelve hours, I would say. The smell and rigor mortis appear consistent with that timeframe." He appraised her. "Not many people outside of my line of work or a war who've seen three dead bodies."

"No," Ellie said. "Unlucky, I suppose."

"Cooke thinks highly of you." The fox scanned the bathroom, from the sink and nightstand to the toilet and the claw-footed bathtub. "What do you notice in here?"

Ellie hadn't expected to be put on the spot. "It all looks quite normal. But prussic acid acts quickly, so I would guess it had been added to her glass." She pointed. "And that's not a glass that should be in a bathroom."

"Good eye." The fox stepped over Camilla's body and leaned over the glass, putting his nose inside it without touching it. "There's a hint of some sort of alcohol in it, but it's been rinsed out, I should say."

"Mrs. Dower wouldn't approve of the help drinking on her premises."

Dr. Rousse nodded. "I'm of a similar mind. So someone gave Camilla a drink and she brought it in here so she could wash the glass out."

"And brush her teeth afterwards."

"No doubt." The fox stared down at the glass and then returned to his small bag, from which he drew a white cloth like a large napkin. Without touching the glass, he wrapped it in the napkin and deposited it in his bag. "I don't suppose there will be any oils but the rabbit's on it, but we should bring it in anyway."

"Camilla seems like the sort who would have been very open to sneaking a drink, especially if it was one given to her by one of the attentive male guests." Ellie leaned against the outside of the doorway. "I'd like to hear what Abby thinks of her, but from listening to Mr. and Mrs. Macintosh, I believe Camilla appreciated a bit of flirting and probably flirted back."

"And perhaps allowed things to move beyond flirting?" Dr. Rousse closed up his bag.

"Abby said no, but…" Ellie considered. "I'll have to ask in private.

That's a large leap. Mr. Macintosh did say she was having a row with her boyfriend, so it would be good to be sure."

"We'll look into the boyfriend, of course."

Ellie nodded. "But I shouldn't think it was him."

The fox raised an eyebrow. "He would be most likely to be jealous."

"Yes, but…" The weasel hesitated. "If he wanted to give her liquor, wouldn't it be more usual for him to have it with her? And besides, this wasn't a crime of passion. This was planned in advance." She rubbed her whiskers. "I rather think it will be important to learn more about Camilla as well as the other guests."

Dr. Rousse smiled. "I can see why Sergeant Cooke thinks highly of you."

Ellie's ears flushed and lay back. "Oh! I'm supposed to be fetching Mr. Damonica for him."

"I'll come with you." Dr. Rousse picked up his bag.

***

The snowshoe hare sat in the parlor reading a newspaper and stood the moment Dr. Rousse entered the room. "This is quite intolerable," he said. "I've an appointment in Londinium that is exceedingly important. I'll have you know that I've a reputation for being prompt. When I met with Lord Chancerton, he remarked on it. 'Damonica,' he said, 'I appreciate a fellow who arrives punctually. It shows a respect for the time of others.' I won't have you forcing me to be late."

"I'm merely the medical examiner," Dr. Rousse said equably. "Like you, I am here at the pleasure of the sergeant. I imagine that once you've interviewed with him—"

"I have been waiting to interview with him," Mr. Damonica said tightly. He pulled on the lapels of his charcoal-grey jacket. "Nobody has yet given me a satisfactory answer as to why I must speak to the police at all, much less why I must wait to do so. I've asked the constable and been told that I'll get my explanation in due time. Sir, I consider it well past due time."

"Unfortunately, sir, in the course of a criminal enquiry, the determination of due time rests with the investigating officer."

The hare's eyes bugged out and his ears lay back. "A—a criminal enquiry? But surely—Miss Teller suffered a heart attack?"

"Brought about by poison. In my professional medical opinion." Dr. Rousse seemed very satisfied with the effect of his news on Mr. Damonica.

"But that's—that's preposterous. Who would want to poison her?"

"Indeed. If you'll follow me."

The hare continued to talk as they entered the sitting-room, Ellie trailing behind him and the fox. "I've played golf on many occasions with the Chief of Police up in Milshire. Do you know him? Captain Trevalyan, a fine wolf. He sometimes discusses cases with me, you know, nothing he oughtn't, but we talk about the whys and where-fores. He says I've got a keen insight."

Sergeant Cooke's ears perked as Mr. Damonica sat down across from him, uninvited. "So as I say, I've a little experience in criminal matters," the hare went on. "And if I can be of any assistance, well, you've only to ask. Only I really must be on the two o'clock train to Londinium at the very latest."

"I'm not familiar with Captain Trevalyan," Cooke said evenly. His eyes flicked over to Ellie, who gave him a minute shrug and settled herself at Dr. Rousse's table. She wasn't sure what the bombastic hare would make of her joining Cooke behind his. "But please tell me anything you can about your relationship with Camilla."

"Oh, well, there's not much to tell. I've stayed here once or twice before, prior to meetings. I recommended Mrs. Dower's place to Terence Dallmer—he's the playwright up in Yove, you know, quite well regarded."

"I'm sure he is."

"But at any rate, Miss Teller served meals and made up the rooms. I think there was another girl who also did the rooms, but there's a new one now. I'm not sure of her name. At any rate, Miss Teller's see-ing a young fellow from down the road. I believe they had a quarrel outside yesterday, and I can't swear to this, but I believe he said 'you'll regret it' or something to that effect. I say." He sat up and leaned for-ward. "You don't suppose..."

"We'll be talking to the boyfriend, of course," Sergeant Cooke said. "And can you account for your whereabouts last night?"

The hare settled back. "Oh, well, I dined with the Macintoshes, and after they went up to bed, I spoke to Mrs. Dower. Her husband is away recovering his health in the south, and I recommended a doctor I had occasion to visit in Milshire. Londinium doctors have all the reputation, you know, but that comes with a price." Dr. Rousse favored Ellie with a sardonic smile at that remark as Mr. Damonica went on. "Dr. George has had three publications in the Lancet and was voted one of Anglia's top young physicians two years ago. He's quite busy, but I offered that as a close personal friend, I could secure Mr. Dower an appointment."

"And after?"

The hare seemed disappointed in Sergeant Cooke's impervious demeanor; at least, his ears sagged and his shoulders slumped. "I retired to my room. I didn't see Miss Teller at all."

"Can anyone else verify that you were in your room all night?"

"I don't suppose so," the hare snapped. "We're not in the habit of checking on each other's whereabouts at odd hours of the night, are we?"

"Of course not, sir." Sergeant Cooke made a note. "Thank you for your time."

Mr. Damonica stood. "May I be permitted to leave for Londinium now?"

The wolf's ears flattened. "I'm afraid I must request that you remain on the premises until I've reached a conclusion in my investigation."

For a moment, the hare stared down at him. "Very well. Very well, you leave me no choice." He strode stiffly out of the room.

Sergeant Cooke shook his head and turned to Dr. Rousse and Ellie. "I didn't think I had," he said. "But it was polite of him confirm it."

"I suppose it's too much to ask that he be the poisoner," Dr. Rousse said. "It's never the unpleasant ones, is it?"

"They were all three unpleasant in their own way," Ellie said. "The problem is that I can't see any motive for any of them. None of them knew Camilla beyond her station as a servant. Mr. Macintosh and Mr. Damonica might have been carrying on with her—perhaps that's what her fellow was jealous of—but I don't know that that could lead to poisoning."

"I don't see it either." Sergeant Cooke sighed. "Any word from the constable?"

Neither Dr. Rousse nor Ellie had heard. "Might we speak to Abby again?" Ellie asked.

"Of course, and Mrs. Dower as well."

"Yes." Ellie paused. "Something's off. I think it's something to do with Mr. Damonica, but I can't quite locate it."

"They're all a bit off, but that's what happens with upper middle classes." Sergeant Cooke drummed his claws on the pad. "Bit of entitlement and next thing you know they think they've a right to poison someone."

"Depends what kind of MP Macintosh was." The fox folded his arms on the table. "Some of them are quite respectable."

"I rather see Mrs. Macintosh as a Lady Macbeth," Ellie said. "I wouldn't be surprised if she'd directed her husband's career."

"Yes." Sergeant Cooke tapped his pad with his pen. "And did you hear the analogy she used? Like her husband's girls were 'fleas'? You can only ignore fleas for so long, and then what do you do with them?"

"Poison them." Dr. Rousse nodded. "I suppose we must wait for the constable and check the glass for skin oils."

"May I go fetch Abby?" Ellie asked.

"Please." Sergeant Cooke gestured, but before Ellie had even completely stood up, Mrs. Dower came into the room wringing her paws, her thin tail twitching.

"Sergeant," she said. "There's an official on the phone from Her Majesty's government wishes to speak to you. That is, to the person in charge of the investigation here."

Cooke and Dr. Rousse both looked as bewildered as Ellie was. "All right," Cooke said, rising. "Thank you, Mrs. Dower."

Dr. Rousse smoothed his whiskers back as the wolf followed the dormouse out of the room. "Why don't you go find your friend, Miss Stone?"

***

She found Abby holding a tray in the kitchen and waiting on the cook, a giant panther of some sort who was stirring a pot on the hob. "They're waiting for the soup," Abby said as Ellie entered the room.

"Well, it is not ready." The panther had a Slavic accent that Ellie couldn't quite place. "I will not send out bad soup." He held his nose over the pot, then dipped a spoon into it and tasted it. Without a word, but with an expression and drive that Ellie recognized instantly, he reached out to a plate and cut another square of butter to drop in.

"Cheddar onion?" she asked.

"Yes." The panther turned and fixed her with a look. "Who are you? Why are you in my kitchen?"

"Ellie's a friend of mine," Abby said. "She's a cook, a really good one."

The panther dropped his spoon with a clatter and turned to Ellie, paws on his hips. "So. You come to take over from Darius?" He gestured around. "This tiny kingdom, even this is no longer to be mine?"

"No," Ellie protested.

"If Miz Dower does not trust me, she may tell me to my face, not send in little weasel to run between my feet. Darius will not be toppled!"

"I'm not here to cook," Ellie said. "I'm helping the sergeant investigate Miss Teller—Camilla's death."

The panther's ears came back up. "Ah! So sad, that little one." He placed a paw over his heart. "The heart, it should not fail in one so young. But perhaps it was broken."

"She and her boyfriend had a row," Abby said. "Darius and I thought she was very sad over it."

"The broken heart can be worst illness of all." Darius returned to his soup, taking another taste. "Ah. Ready now. Miss Rose, you may serve this soup."

"After that, Abby," Ellie said, "could you please come to the sitting-room?"

"Oh, just please wait for me, Ellie? It won't take me but a moment to serve."

So Ellie went to the parlour, where Sergeant Cooke was just hanging up the phone, ears flat. "Ah, Miss Stone," he said, and his ears came up halfway. "We've been given a time limit."

"Oh, dear."

"That was the Assistant to the Undersecretary of Trade or some such. It seems our Mr. Damonica is meeting with trade representatives of Moravensko. Not on his own, one would presume, but he is important enough that an Undersecretary of Trade has taken a personal interest in him."

"Hardly surprising," Ellie said, and then stopped and lowered her voice. "But it is surprising that he didn't tell us that."

"Oh, these state affairs are hardly public." Cooke matched her tone. "But they did just tell me without any caution."

"And Damonica is hardly the kind of person to hold back his association with a famous person." Ellie cut her words short as Cooke raised a paw, and turned to see the hare himself coming out of the dining room, wearing a self-satisfied smirk.

"Well, Sergeant?"

"I've been instructed," the wolf said stiffly, "to see to it that you are on the two p.m. train to Londinium. Which means we will leave here at half-past one, in one hour. So you might as well finish your luncheon."

"I will." The hare smiled and returned to the dining room.

"But why," Cooke asked, "would he not want us to know about the meeting? And what has Camilla Teller to do with the Moravensko trade delegation?"

"Maybe nothing," Ellie said. "He's hiding something, but not necessarily murder. Maybe Abby can help."

***

They brought the rabbit into the sitting-room after luncheon service. "Anything you can remember, Ab," Ellie said. "About Camilla or anything that happened last night."

"The row with her boyfriend, for instance."

"Oh. She told me that he was jealous," Abby said. "But I don't know why he would be. Cam did flirt with the gentlemen, took gifts sometimes, but she never went into their rooms alone. But El, listen. I was going up to announce that luncheon would be served and I heard the Macintoshes arguing. She said, 'I can't believe you'd think that,' and he said, 'You've done worse,' and she said, 'Well, you haven't a reputation to protect now.' Do you think he thinks she did it?"

"You didn't hear any more?" Sergeant Cooke asked, ears perked.

"Oh, no," Abby said. "It's not proper to eavesdrop."

It was moments like these that made Ellie love Abby, because of course Ellie would have stayed and listened to as much as she could, but Abby was more concerned with being a good person.

"Quite right," the wolf said with a hint of a smile at Ellie. "Do you know what Camilla did last night?"

"She served dinner while I turned down the rooms, and then I helped with the washing up after Mr. Lancaster left."

"Mister Lancaster doesn't live in the hotel?"

"Oh, no, he lives down the road. I'm certain he left last night at the usual time."

"He didn't give Camilla anything to drink?"

Abby shook her head. "Not that she mentioned to me."

"Did anyone?"

"I didn't notice. There was a smell of liquor about in the hallway last night, but it was very faint."

Sergeant Cooke leaned forward. "What kind of liquor?"

"Oh, I'm so sorry, I don't know. I can't tell them apart." Abby looked at Ellie. "El would be much better at that."

"But it was liquor."

"Yes." Abby's nose twitched, making Ellie want to kiss it. "It had that sharp sting. And I know someone met her on the stair, because I heard murmurs. But I was sleepy and Camilla often stayed out past the time I went to sleep."

Cooke's ears perked again. "Perhaps spending time with the guests?"

"Oh…" The rabbit shook her head. "She would've told me. I think. No, she had more evening duties than I did and I must get up quite early to take deliveries and to tidy the common rooms."

"Ab, did any of the guests have liquor in their rooms?"

Abby paused. "The Macintoshes have sherry before bed. I clear their glasses during luncheon. I should be doing that now. I—I don't know about Mr. Damonica. I suppose he might. Oh! Mr. and Mrs. Dower have a liquor cabinet in their bedroom. It's locked."

"If…" Sergeant Cooke paused and gathered his words. "If one of the guests had given Camilla a taste of some expensive liquor, do you think she would've told you about it? Would that be the sort of thing she would like?"

"I expect she would like it," Abby said. "She would have told me, but only after, you see what I mean? She wouldn't likely share it unless it were a big bottle and she'd had all she wanted."

There hadn't been any after this time for Camilla, not that there'd been enough to share. Ellie pictured the rabbit taking a drink, grimacing at the strength of the alcohol and perhaps the underlying bitterness. Had she had time to begin feeling flushed, thinking perhaps it was the alcohol working? Drunk the rest quickly? Had she wanted to keep it for herself or was she worried that she would faint and the alcohol be found with her? Ellie couldn't remember how prussic acid worked from her stories; she knew only that it was fast and left the victim feeling they couldn't breathe. She'd had time to set the glass down, anyway.

"Had she mentioned anything like that in connection with one of the guests? Someone had promised her a taste of something?"

Abby shook her head. "I'm sorry, I don't think so."

"And you haven't seen any of the guests acting out of the ordinary?"

"Well… the Macintoshes have been here two months. I don't think they did anything last night they wouldn't ordinarily. And…" She put a finger to her chin and tilted her head, and again Ellie was seized with a powerful urge to kiss her. "I don't know Mr. Damonica, but everything seemed normal last night."

"Camilla wasn't excited about anything?"

"She was cross with her boyfriend, I think, but not terribly so. Just saying things like, 'Justin's so hot-tempered, but it'll be all right.' I mean… I think he was upset because perhaps there were stories that she was over-friendly to the male guests. But really, she loved him. Nothing she did meant that she didn't love him." Her eyes stayed on Ellie's.

"It's good that they talked about it, even if it was a row," Ellie said, and then worried that she'd said too much.

But Cooke didn't seem to have noticed anything in her tone. Desperation for some kind of clue came off him in waves. "Not looking forward to anything, was she?" he asked.

Abby shook her head. "No, I'm sorry."

"All right." Cooke gestured. "You may go."

When Abby had gone, Ellie and Cooke sat in silence, looking over at Dr. Rousse at his table. Cooke looked down at his pad and leafed through it. "I don't know what we've got," he said.

"We've got a murder," Rousse said. "I suppose I can't rule out that she drank the cyanide purposefully—"

"What?" Ellie asked. "You mean to end her own life? That seems very unlikely to me."

"And to me," the fox said, "but it remains a possibility, however remote. We should search her quarters and look into her correspondence. As Miss Stone said, one can't just walk down to the village and procure prussic acid."

"There's something." Cooke made a note. "We can call Midlands Coal and see if anyone's asked for samples of hydrogen cyanide from the factories."

"Processing, more likely," Dr. Rousse said. "But yes. Can we do that all in the next forty-five minutes, though?"

"Can't they put off his meeting?" Ellie asked.

"Evidently not." Cooke grimaced at his pad. "I asked. The assistant told me that the trade minister is terribly busy, and that if they put off the meeting, it might not happen again for months."

"A rare opportunity," Ellie said. Something nagged at her; trusting her intuition, she thought back over the day. Something Mr. Damonica had said?

The door to the sitting room opened to admit Constable Polter. The squirrel gave off an aroma of dirt and rotting vegetables, but he wore a huge smile as he held up a wax paper bag. "Found it, sir, I think. Here you go."

"To the M.E., please." Cooke held a paw to his nose.

Dr. Rousse looked no more pleased to be approached by the fragrant squirrel, but he took the bag. With a cloth over his paw, he extracted the contents and sniffed the glass bottle. "Mm, yes, that's what we're looking for," he said, and brought out a piece of tape from his bag to seal up the plastic.

"Constable." The wolf drew the constable's attention back. "This was in the trash from which room?"

"Well, ah." The squirrel shook his head. "The young rabbit told me the refuse from all the guest rooms was put together into one bin and held for a day. Mrs. Dower has had guests look for items they'd mistakenly discarded, or that the help cleaned up in error, so now she holds their refuse separate from the hotel refuse, which goes out every day."

Dr. Rousse held a cloth to his nose. "You smell like you went through both."

"I did, sir." The constable's ears folded back. "The young rabbit led me to the daily refuse first, and Mrs. Dower came by to take me to the correct bin after. That's what took so long."

"Any markings on the bottle?" Cooke asked.

"Nothing identifying." The fox held up the plastic bag. Ellie read "HCN" in scrawled marker on a white patch on the glass. "It's a common enough bottle from laboratories, though, so I presume we could call Midlands Coal's research laboratory and ask about it. I don't expect they get requests for hydrogen cyanide on a regular basis."

"If it was Damonica," Cooke added. "If it was one of the Macintoshes, it might've come from anywhere."

"And if it was Damonica," Ellie said, "I don't expect he would've asked for it himself."

"It doesn't matter if he did." Cooke pointed to the bottle. "If we can link that to Midlands Coal and here…"

"But what if someone else requested it for some other reason?" the M.E. responded. "It would be a great coincidence, but you can't hang a fellow without proof, and unless we have his skin oils on this bottle or on that poisoned glass—which I doubt—it's going to be devilishly difficult to tie him to the crime."

"Ellie." Cooke turned to her. "What do you think? That argument of the Macintoshes?"

She shook her head. "I rather think that clears both of them. If Mrs. Macintosh did it as a warning to her husband, it wouldn't be a very effective warning unless she told him. Or if it was a punishment. Whereas if he did it, for whatever reason, well… like Abby said, he's a sweet old fellow. He wouldn't go accusing his wife of it. He doesn't seem the type. He'd more likely say, 'let's just forget this unpleasantness' and would do his best to do just that himself."

"So you think it's Damonica."

She turned to the fox. "I do. You know, Abby may not be very observant, but she does feel things even if she doesn't quite understand why. She told me that Mrs. Macintosh was 'sour' and that Mr. Macintosh was 'sweet,' and that's a very simple way of looking at it, but it's not wrong, is it? Mr. Macintosh seems to be the type to put everything in the best light, even if there are unpleasant matters underneath, where Mrs. Macintosh brings those unpleasant matters out into the open to have them out. So I don't think it likely that Mrs. Macintosh would have poisoned Camilla. If she'd had enough of her husband carrying on with her, I feel she would've let him know, and likely he would've stopped. But she likely knows he flirts to make himself feel better, and he knows that she complains about it to make herself feel better."

"And what did Abby say about Damonica?" Cooke asked. "That he was puffed up?"

"No, she said he was important, if I recall. 'Frightfully important.' Which is of course exactly the impression he wishes to make on everyone. We all saw that."

Dr. Rousse nodded thoughtfully, while Cooke said drily, "I hadn't noticed."

"Which is why it's so curious that he wouldn't tell us he was meeting with a trade minister from another country," Ellie said. "An 'historic' occasion!"

"So." Cooke held up a finger. "Why would he not want us to know? Sworn to secrecy? No, because the undersecretary's assistant knew and told me without being asked. It does seem like there must be some connection between Camilla and that meeting. Perhaps she was threatening its success."

"He could simply be a psychopath," the fox suggested. "There was a case five or so years ago of a very mild-mannered deer who competed in bridge competitions, I believe it was, and he had to kill someone before each competition to steady his nerves."

"Maybe." Ellie shook her head. "It would fit, I suppose, but…"

"You never know with those types. They're excellent at blending in. Don't read the medical journals, you'll never trust anyone again." Dr. Rousse lay his ears back. "That said… I agree, I don't think it fits. It seems likely the killer wasn't present when she died, and hasn't even seen the body. Psychopaths need some kind of interaction. Usually prefer the direct methods." He mimed stabbing with a knife.

"Don't." Ellie shuddered.

Sergeant Cooke checked his pocket watch. "Ten minutes until we must let him go. I presume," he said to the constable, "that he's pacing the hallway."

The squirrel nodded. "Like a racer waiting for the starting gun."

"But," the M.E. went on, "I keep coming back to what you said, Miss Stone, about procuring the prussic acid. Damonica isn't a chemist. If he were going to kill someone, why go to all this trouble?"

"To hide that it was a murder," Sergeant Cooke said. "That almost worked."

Ellie stood up very suddenly. "That's it," she said. "That's why. Oh." She put a paw to her mouth. "Oh, it's horrible."

Dr. Rousse raised an eyebrow, but Sergeant Cooke smiled and clapped his paws together. "Just in the nick of time, Miss Stone. What is it?"

"It was the cook," Ellie said. "I knew something was nagging at me, and I've been going over what Mr. Damonica said, but it wasn't him at all. It was the cook."

The wolf's smile faded. "I thought the cook left the premises."

"He did." Ellie shook her head. "He's not involved, it was something he did. Something I've done. I'm sorry, I'll explain."

"Please," the fox said.

"The cook was making a cheddar onion soup for the luncheon. And he tasted it to make sure it was right before he let Abby serve it."

Cooke and Dr. Rousse exchanged looks, understanding dawning. The constable said, "So… Mr. Damonica tasted the cyanide?"

"No," Ellie said. "He had Camilla taste it. Unwitting, of course. But you're right." She turned to Dr. Rousse. "He had no experience. So he had to make sure it would work."

The fox picked up the wax paper bag with the glass bottle in it and turned it over. "The rabbit had to die first," he said. "He was plotting to kill that foreign trade minister, and they were only going to get one chance. That's why he didn't tell us, so that if we read about the minister dying the same way, we wouldn't make the connection."

All three of them, Cooke, Ellie, and Dr. Rousse, made the next logical leap at the same moment. Ellie ran to hold the door open as the wolf and fox hurried through to the hallway, the squirrel a few steps behind. Ellie didn't follow them; for one, she had no place to, and for another, she was trying very hard not to think about how easily the hare might have decided to poison Abby instead of the unlucky Camilla.

"Mr. Damonica," Sergeant Cooke said. "We're glad to let you go on your way, but we'll just need to search your possessions first."

Constable Polter scratched his ear. "What do they want to search his things for?" he asked Ellie.

"Listen here," Mr. Damonica said outside in the hallway, "you can't—I'm a private citizen."

"Because," Ellie explained to the constable as Sergeant Cooke explained that as the officer in charge of a crime scene, he was authorized to conduct any search he pleased, "if this murder was a test, if he's planning another one, then that means he must have another bottle of prussic acid on him." She pointed to the one that Dr. Rousse had left on the table. "If they find a match to that bottle, that's a very strong case against him."

"Ooh-ah," the squirrel said. He and Ellie stood in the doorway watching as the sergeant took a set of gloves from the M.E. and went through the clothes Mr. Damonica was wearing: his coat pockets, suit pockets, trouser pockets. Over the hare's objections that he was going to miss his train, Sergeant Cooke opened his bag and rummaged through it. A moment later his ears perked up and he pulled from the bag a glass bottle that even at this distance Ellie could see was a perfect match for the one behind her on the table.

"That's a sample of industrial chemical," Mr. Damonica blustered. "I need it for our meeting."

"I'm very sorry," Sergeant Cooke said, standing up straight. "Her Majesty's government will need it as evidence in your trial." He held out the bottle to Dr. Rousse, who took it in a handkerchief-covered paw.

The hare's ears folded back. "T-trial? You're joking, of course."

"You're under arrest for the murder of Camilla Teller." Sergeant Cooke produced a pair of cuffs from his belt, adjusted them to the size of the hare's wrists, and clicked them closed.

***

Ellie got to see Abby in private for a few short minutes while the arrest was being formalized, but Mrs. Dower had warned the rabbit that she was going to be very busy, being the only servant left. "So I must hurry back downstairs in a moment." Abby's paws clasped behind the small of Ellie's back, showing little inclination to leave.

"I'll see you in a week," Ellie reassured her, reaching up to stroke those long ears. "And two weeks after that as well."

"If things happen with the sergeant," Abby said, "it's fine, you know. And you don't even have to tell me. But I won't mind if you do."

"Nothing's going to happen." Ellie pressed her muzzle to the rabbit's and breathed in the scent. "I hate that we have to be apart now, but we're enduring it."

"Of course."

"And if something happens with the guests here…" Ellie hadn't really thought about it, but Abby's statement had brought those thoughts back. "That's okay too. You can tell me or not."

"I can't not tell you things. You know that."

"I know." Ellie kissed Abby again. They held each other for precious seconds, and then Ellie said, "You'd best go. Don't want you to get fired."

Abby held her for just a moment longer. "One day, El, it'll be us two old spinsters in a cottage together."

"Of course, old soul," Ellie said. "The sooner the better."

***

"I'm glad you're letting me take you to dinner." Sergeant Cooke smiled across the small candle-lit table at Ellie.

The frock Ellie had borrowed constricted her about the neck and waist and made crinkly noises when she moved too much, so she did her best to sit very still. "You were very insistent," she said.

"I'm getting a commendation for preventing an international incident." He looked quite handsome in a dapper blue evening jacket with matching bow tie. "I kept putting your name in the report and nobody wanted to see it, so this is the best I can do to thank you on behalf of your country and myself."

"I'm just pleased to have been of help," she said. "And I would like to know what he hoped to gain by poisoning that minister."

"Money, of course." The wolf grimaced. "That particular minister opposed the lowering of tariffs on coal, or some such. They were hoping that if he died, the more sympathetic members of the Moravenskan government would prevail. Their business would be worth millions of pounds."

"They? So it wasn't only Mr. Damonica?"

Cooke growled. "Of course it wasn't, but that's the line they're taking. Nobody can prove otherwise, and Damonica's now being convicted of murder, so anything he says is suspect. He doesn't have any incentive to give them up. Miss Teller's murder is a separate thing, and he won't get a reduced sentence for giving up a few conspiracy to commit murder charges. I believe he still hopes the company will take care of him if he ever gets out of prison."

"He shouldn't," Ellie said.

"No. I think he had read a few too many police novels himself. Not to take away anything from your contribution, but he was really rather clumsy. We only had to call three Midlands laboratories before we found the one that had created the prussic acid samples, and they described Damonica perfectly. Oh, and so did the owner down at the Three Coins in the village. He said some hare from the hotel had been around bragging about feeling up a rabbit at the Dowers' place. No doubt Damonica hoped to get her boyfriend to come yell at her, to throw suspicion off himself if foul play was suspected."

Ellie shook her head. "The criminals in the police novels are much better than him at it."

"Still, if it hadn't been for Miss Rose, he might have gotten away with it. And if it hadn't been for you, he might've carried out the rest of his plan before we stopped him. But enough about him." The wolf smiled at her. "Do you like this restaurant? I tried to pick something nice but comfortable."

She wouldn't have described The Gilded Peach as "comfortable," even if she'd been wearing something other than this borrowed dress. Elaborately carved, straight-backed wooden chairs kept her sitting right up to the table with the spotless cotton tablecloth and the candle burning in the short silver candleholder. Five utensils crowded around her plate; she thought she knew what most of them were from her time serving, but she was more used to placing them around a plate than using them. And all the waiters, white rats as spotless as the tablecloths, bustled about placing napkins on laps or removing and folding them, or else they were bringing drinks or taking orders and menus. Cooke had already told her twice to relax, and she was doing her best.

"I like it," she said. "I hope the food is as good as it smells."

"I'm told it is. Go ahead and order whatever you like. After all, Rousse is paying." The wolf took a breath. "The other way I can thank you," he said, "is by—well, I'd like your permission to call on you when I've got a case. I feel you've got quite a knack for seeing things that—it could be quite useful. Helpful, I mean."

"Oh, I…" Ellie's ears flushed and folded down. Abby's sweet smile came back to her and the rabbit's words. They could have their cottage together, but first, there would be a great deal more that might happen. And perhaps—perhaps Cooke's interest was purely professional, though her instincts told her that was unlikely.

She could very easily tell Cooke that she preferred not to be involved in cases, and if it were just a matter of seeing the wolf again, she would do that. She liked him quite a bit, actually, but it would be cruel to lead him on when she had no intention of letting their association go further than friendship. But there were the cases, and if there were truly a threat to her relationship with Abby, it wasn't any person but the lure of deciphering a puzzle, the righteous thrill of seeing a guilty person punished. Surely Abby would understand the need for Ellie to do good work, especially in the name of justice.

So she smiled at the wolf. "Yes, I suppose that would be all right."

Acknowledgements

Thanks to Mary E. Lowd and Ocean Tigrox for their invaluable advice in how to edit and put together an anthology.

Thanks to Tim Susman, Watts Martin, and David Cowan for help with reading and selecting stories (not their own, I promise).

Thanks to Teiran and Fuzz of FurPlanet for giving me the chance to put together this lovely little collection of tales of bunny murder.

Big, big thanks to Dark Natasha for her gorgeous work on the cover art. Find more of her work at darknatasha.com

And thanks, finally, to Haberdasher, crafters of the best cocktails in the world, who provided the confidence and inspiration, two drinks in, for me to say, "You know what would make an awesome writing prompt?"

About the Authors

Mog has been lurking around the fandom since the early 2000s. He started writing furry stuff just for fun in 2004. Since then, he's posted several free stories on SoFurry.com and his first printed stories released in 2016. In 2018, he won the Leo Literary Award for his poem *Top to Bottom*, which appeared in Sofawolf's *Heat 14*.

When not doing furry stuff, he's usually trying to figure out how to do more furry stuff. He loves to travel and see new places, and really enjoys furry conventions.

He's usually a friendly type of critter that enjoys hugs and loves talking to readers and fellow writers. Feel free to contact him and let him know what you think of his story, (or his terrible bio.)

Tym Greene is a writer and artist, particularly of anthro things, and aspires to work in concept art. In the meantime he fulfills his world-building desires with fiction. Apart from a few entry-level college courses, he's mostly self taught with regard to writing, and has to thank the pantheon of authors (both classic and otherwise), his editors, and his boyfriend for helping him to be the writer he is today.

http://www.furaffinity.net/user/tym/

David Green grew up playing in the Douglas fir forests of Oregon. He was fascinated enough by shapeshifters and animal people that he started writing stories about them, some of which were published in *Yarf!* and other fanzines. Now a technical writer in Silicon Valley, he still enjoys making stories about those animal people, with assistance from his cats Nia and Willow, who help with inspiration and other portions of the writing procdxz000000000

Franklin Leo is a writer and academic researcher living in sunny Southern California. Her fiction ranges between science-fiction and horror, while her academic work focuses on cultural studies, queer theory, and posthuman literature. She lives at home with her two cats and a consistent supply of raw fish.

Jellybean is sometimes a goat, sometimes a crow, but always in love with fiction. She is new to furry writing but hopes her English degree from Central Washington University will help her along. She spends her days searching for monsters in closets and thinking about dragons. You can follow her on Twitter at @Imagining_Ink.

Mary E. Lowd is a science-fiction and furry writer in Oregon. She's had more than one hundred short stories published, and her novels include the *Otters in Space* trilogy, *In a Dog's World*, and *The Snake's Song: A Labyrinth of Souls Novel*. Her fiction has won an Ursa Major Award and two Cóyotl Awards. She's also the editor for FurPlanet's anthology series *ROAR*. She lives in a crashed spaceship disguised as a house, hidden inside a fairy's rose garden. Learn more at www.marylowd.com.

Maya Levine was born and raised in Chicago, IL, and currently lives in Palo Alto, California. She has had work featured in Bluefire 2016, Bluefire 2017, Palo Alto Roots Magazine, and Enchanted Conversation. She enjoys hiking and studying history. She believes that success in writing comes from working at the craft, taking failure in stride, and being brave enough to ask for help.

Sera Kane is a 30-something lady, caretaker of one Spawn and three dogs, and married to a wonderful former sailor. Without all of these factors, her life would not be nearly as rich and beautiful. She's gotten to live many lovely places including Alaska and Japan, and most recently moved from California to Texas. Writing has been her passion her entire life, as word-smithing is a beautiful and creative art form. Her grandest wish is to write pieces that the reader can't stand to put down.

Sera believes everyone should be in therapy and wants to remind people that Hope dies last. There is always a chance for happiness and improvement with each breath you take. So keep breathing: our world is definitely better with you in it.

Watts Martin lives in Silicon Valley, and can frequently be found writing (and drinking) at microbreweries around Northern California. Watts's works include the Cóyotl-winning *Kismet* and

Indigo Rain, and short stories that have appeared in anthologies including *Inhuman Acts*, *The Furry Future*, and *ROAR*. Follow Watts at @chipotlecoyote on Twitter, or get more information—and read some free stories—at coyotetracks.org.

Nathan Ravenwood dabbles in many genres: sci-fi, fantasy, horror, romance, and combinations thereof, and also likes to write both erotic yarns and tales of anthropomorphic animals. He's been writing seriously since high school, where he fell in love with the furry community—while it's not the only fandom he writes for, it is an ever-present fixture in his life and a constant inspiration. His debut story "The Paledrake" was published in Uruk Press's *Sex and Sorcery 3*, followed several months later by his first novel *The Cordax Mondotta*. Since then, he's published three more novels with Uruk Press, with plans in the works for many more. You can find his ebooks on Amazon.

In his free time, Nathan enjoys video games, metal concerts, cooking, and geeking out over professional wrestling. He lives in Florida, which continues to provide him with inspiration in it's gorgeous natural beauty and eccentric people. His goal is to make each story and novel better than the last, and to one day own a great number of cats.

Lloyd Yaeger is a doctoral student and part-time teacher who swears he will finish his dissertation (eventually). He has been a furry fan since his teen years. Only recently has he found a cozy life with his partner in Los Angeles, California, where can be found gorging himself on queer pulp, espresso and cat videos. Lloyd enjoys writing character-centric stories, particularly in sci-fi or other speculative genres. In his spare time, he likes to cook and ride roller coasters, but not at the same time.

Taylor Harbin is a historian from Arkansas. His fiction has appeared in *Bards and Sages Quarterly* and Fred Patten's anthology *Dogs of War*. Easily distracted by the pleasures of the internet, he composes all of his work on a manual typewriter. He can be reached through his blog: www.gutsofimagination.blogspot.com

Nidhi Singh lives with her husband in the idyllic Yol Cantonment, an erstwhile POW Camp for German and Italian soldiers during the two World Wars.

Her short work has appeared internationally in *Phenomenal Literature, Pen and Kink Publishing, The Sunlight Press, Riggwelter, A Lonely Riot, Mirror Dance, Body Parts, Military Experience and the Arts, Grey Wolfe Publishing, Expanded Horizons, Vagabondage Press, Rigorous, TQR, Fantasia Divinity, Fiction on the Web, Storyteller, TWJ Magazine, Indie Authors Press, Flyleaf Journal, Liquid Imagination, Digital Fiction Publishing Co, LA Review of LA, Flame Tree Publishing, Firefly Magazine, Four Ties Lit Review, The Insignia Series, Inwood Indiana Press, Bards and Sages Publishing, So To Speak, Scarlet Leaf Review, Bewildering Stories, Down in the Dirt, Mulberry Fork Review, tNY.Press, Fabula Argentea, Aerogram, Asvamegha, Fiction Magazines, The Dirty Pool, Flash Fiction Press, Thurston Howl Publications* and elsewhere.

She has also authored several novels and translations of Sikh Holy Scriptures.

Kyell Gold has won twelve Ursa Major awards for his stories and novels, and his acclaimed novel *Out of Position* co-won the Rainbow Award for Best Gay Novel of 2009. His novel *Green Fairy* was nominated for inclusion in the ALA's "Over the Rainbow" list for 2012. He helped create RAWR, the first residential furry writing workshop, and has instructed at each of its sessions through 2018.

He lives in California, loves to travel and dine out with his partners, and can be seen at furry conventions around the world. More information about him and his books is available at www.kyellgold.com, and you can follow him on Twitter at @KyellGold.

About the Editor

Ryan Campbell has been involved in the furry fandom for 20 years as both a fan and a writer. He has contributed to *ROAR, X, New Fables*, and *Abandoned Places*, and is the author of *The Fire Bearers* trilogy: *God of Clay, Forest Gods*, and the in-progress conclusion, *God of Fire*. Other published books include *Koa of the Drowned Kingdom* and *Smiley and the Hero*.